MY LIFE'S AN OPEN BOOK
A STORY OF SEX, LOVE AND POETRY

by ALEX HAIRSTON

Published by Open Book Press
Open Book Press, P.O. Box 1138
Randallstown, Maryland 21133

Publisher's Note

FOR KIM, LUVU4LIF

4THE2WHOMADEME
MY PARENTS...LUVU2

ACKNOWLEDGEMENTS

I thank God for blessing me with my gift and for helping me realize my gift. For so long I knew I had a hidden talent. Nursing is cool, but writing is my first love. To my wife, Kim, words can't possibly express how much I love you. Thank you for all of the support, encouragement and most of all thanks for loving me the way you do. To my kids Terence, Terell and Alexis, thanks for being such wonderful kids and always remember to stay focused because anything is possible and nothing's impossible. I love y'all. To my parents, Alex and Marie, thanks for making me the person I am and for all the years of unconditional love. Thanks to my grandmothers, Betty and Chrissie, for helping to mold me. Special thanks to my sisters Erica a.k.a. Kel and Nokie for being sample readers. Kel congratulations to you and Phil on your baby girl, Jada. Don't forget to hit Jonathan for me (Smile). To my brothers Chaz and Darryl, love y'all. Thanks to my niece Plum for your encouragement and for telling all your friends about my book. To my nephew DJ, start writing 'cause I know you have a raw and original story to tell. To the rest of my family I love y'all. To the Hairston Clan, this is for the legacy. Thanks to all of my sample readers. Special thanks to my cousin Wendy for the positive feedback after reading my manuscript. Very special thanks to Marcella and Stacey for pumping my head and diggin' my poetry, love y'all. Francine a.k.a. Queen Imani, the world is officially yours. Takiyah, thanks for the encouragement and congrats on your new baby boy. Tracy, thanks for encouraging me to buy my laptop. Michele, thanks for lookin' out for a brotha.

To my readers, thanks for your support. I hope y'all love this book and the characters. You may not love Eric, but try to understand him. Check out my website www.alexhairston.com and please e-mail me with your comments I'd love to hear from you. I'll definitely send a response. Thanks again to everyone for spreading the word about my book. 17 7073 1 & 17 0334 1. PEACE.

PART: I

LIFE, LOVE AND SEDUCTION

ERIC'S INTRO

I've always viewed my life as an open book. Day by day blank pages become filled with my life story. I've often heard old people say we're just living out a script and God's the director. Maybe, they're right. This is my book, my life and I'm the author. I give God credit for everything I've done. My name is Eric Brown Jr., I'm a single thirty-year-old African American male. I'm a graduate of the University of Maryland School of Nursing. I'm currently working as a part-time trauma nurse at the University of Maryland Hospital. I live alone in a pretty luxurious condo in Baltimore County. I recently purchased a Lexus GS 430. I believe in living life to the fullest. Happiness means everything to me. I've been told I'm a very handsome guy. I'm a 5'11" 185 lbs. dark-skinned brother with a medium muscular build. I wish I was a few inches taller, but I can't complain because I was blessed when God put those extra inches somewhere else. I chose to work part-time because I'm involved in so many other things. My first love is writing poetry. Poetry is my life and my life is poetry. I'm a songwriter and I play a few instruments. I'm best at playing the piano and guitar. I'm also a writer for a local African American magazine. I'm happy with my life, but I really want to be famous one day. I want to be known for something great. Whichever of my talents help me to make it is fine.

My parents live about twenty minutes from me in Randallstown, Maryland, where I grew up. My Father, Eric Sr. is a 59-year-old trauma surgeon. Did I mention he's perfect? He's a perfect pain in my ass, but I love and admire him. I think he's been cheating on my mother for years. My mother and I have always heard stories about him with other women. I'm really happy that we could never prove anything. My mother, Margaret is a 63-year-old retired emergency room nurse. At one time, we all worked at the same hospital. She's the sweetest thing God ever made. I consider myself a perfect mixture of the two of them. My father thinks I'm too much like my mother. He resents the fact that I'm a nurse. He has never said it, but I know he thinks male nurses are queer. I think he's funny as hell. My mother just wants me to get married soon. She wants me to have a son to carry on the family name. Our name is Brown. I'm sure that name is going to be around forever. Marriage and children are wonderful, but not for me. I have too much going on in my life to settle down with a family. I just love being single. I don't have to answer to anyone and I can come and go as I please. If I stay out all night, nobody cares. Women have always been my strength and my weakness. I love all types of women. I truly lust after too many women to ever commit to one. I don't have a girlfriend. I only have "female friends." Somewhere in my life something went wrong. Since I can remember I've always been a student of love and an incredible sex fiend. I've been dating for some time now. I don't consider myself a playa because I like one woman at a time. But that hasn't always been true for me. I never look at relationships as a game because someone always ends up getting played. Sometimes in life the strangest things happen. There's only one special lady who has my heart. Candie has my heart under lock and key. The sun rises and sets in her ebony eyes. She's all I see. She's the air I breathe. She's my greatest inspiration. She's my best friend Troy's wife. Troy has no idea how I feel about his wife. The important thing is that I realize something's wrong. As a child my grandparents gave me the nickname Man because they said I was an old soul. I lost my virginity at sixteen and I think this is where things may have started going wrong. My life is filled with intimate stories and details that shaped me into the person I am today. My life is truly an open book.

NORTH CAROLINA: 1

One *hot* summer about fourteen years ago, I went to visit my family in North Carolina. Both sides of my family are from the same small town, just outside of Charlotte. My father used to tell me, "Boy, you better go down there and get yourself a girlfriend." I thought he was so stupid, because it seemed like I was related to everyone in town. It's weird, but I have Browns on both sides of my family. I would like to think it's because Brown is such a common last name. I know there's a good chance my parents are related, but I don't want to focus on that.

My parents and I arrived in North Carolina on a Friday morning for our 32nd annual family reunion. The reunion didn't officially begin until the next afternoon. We always had a pre-reunion meeting and a Friday night fish fry at my father's grandmother's house. My great-grandmother was our oldest living relative. She had even outlived her children. It was a blessing to have her around.

Cancer, heart disease and alcoholism had claimed the lives of my other grandparents. My family was and probably still is one of the largest and most prominent families in North Carolina. We can trace our family history back to the early 1800's. My father's great-

great-great grandfather, Jasper Brown was born in 1835. He was a slave of William Brown Sr. William inherited his plantation from his Uncle Samuel Willingham. Jasper Brown is credited for keeping our family together. Because of his hard work and dedication, William Brown promised to keep Jasper's family together. Although Jasper was a slave, I'm sure he was a proud man. He actually sacrificed himself through hard work for future generations. To this day we still honor Jasper at our annual family reunions.

The reunion began Saturday afternoon at a local park. This was probably our largest celebration ever. It was like an outdoor music festival. We featured local blues, jazz, rap, R&B and gospel acts. Some of the acts consisted of actual family members. Later that night, we had a more formal banquet and ceremony in a ballroom. That year we had a dedication ceremony for my great-grandmother in honor of her ninetieth birthday. My great-grandmother was like a living history book. She was in excellent physical and mental health. She was tiny in stature, but her voice was strong and clear. My parents knew that I had written a poem for my great-grandmother and they had me recite it in front of everyone. I was nervous because the room was filled with about fifteen hundred people claiming to be descendants of Jasper Brown. I thought no one would pay much attention to me, but the entire ballroom was quiet when I stepped up to the microphone.

I said, "Good evening, I'm the great grandson of Edith Brown. I'm going to recite a poem that I wrote for her entitled *Grandma's Poem.*"

You've always been there for me
Giving me love and affection
Guiding my life in the right direction
Hold me...mold me
Make me the man I need to be
The greater the influence

The greater the outcome
So much wisdom comes from within
Knowledge of the past and present
From slavery to freedom
My family history is no mystery
The knowledge you speak
Is the knowledge I seek

Senior citizen to others
Supreme citizen to me
The river of life flows through your veins
In the center your heart beats to the rhythm of life
You wake up with physical, mental and spiritual strength
Thirty two thousand, eight hundred fifty mornings
The sun has greeted you
Marching to your own beat
Ninety years under your feet

Nine decades of flavors marinade your mind
So much in front...so much behind
Strong memories of good and bad
Knowledge of old and new
Ups, downs, tragedies and fights
Still in search of civil rights

From a huge family tree
With deep southern roots
One of ten
Now the one and only
Time continues to move on
The river of life continues to flow
Where it stops only God knows

Everyone loved my poem. My great-grandmother stood up with

tears in her eyes and gave me a big hug. The next day the reunion ended after service at the family church. That was probably the best reunion we've ever had.

My parents were about to leave for a two-week trip to Hawaii. Back home some rumors about my dad cheating with some woman had surfaced. This was his way of smoothing things out with my mother. They had me stay with my father's brother, Uncle Charlie Brown. He was a divorced father of two. My Aunt Helen left him for a twenty-year-old Tom Cruise lookin' white guy from next-door. She packed up and moved the two of them to the next town. For years, this guy used to play with my cousins. No one knew it, but he played with my aunt too when my uncle wasn't around. All and all, Uncle Charlie took it well. He used to say, "At least she left me for a man."

Uncle Charlie was a truck driver who had his own trucking company. Before acquiring his trucking company, Uncle Charlie worked as a truck driver for another company. I thought it was strange that he owned the company and still drove a truck. I guess he continued to drive because he had a genuine desire and an undying passion for truck driving. Uncle Charlie hired other family members to help run the business. He planned a cross-country drive to California and his son, Charles and I were supposed to join him on this ultimate trucking adventure. Charles was my age, but we had nothing in common. I hated him and he hated me. On the other hand, his sister, Tammy was my favorite cousin. She was eighteen and absolutely beautiful. Sometimes I felt like she was the most interesting part of North Carolina. We used to spend hours talking about anything and everything. Our favorite topic was sex. I used to make up sexy stories just to keep her interest. I think she knew I was lying, but my stories turned her on a lot. Tammy introduced me to her friend Stacey and from that point, my life was never quite the same. Stacey was even more beautiful than Tammy. It was love at first site. Well, for me. When Stacey entered the room the look in my eyes said it all. This girl had me sprung, my nose was wide open. She smelled like a fresh country field of

15

wildflowers. A gentle summer breeze and her fragrance could make the strongest man weak.

There was one big problem, Stacey was eighteen and I was only sixteen. I found out that Stacey definitely wasn't related to me. She had just moved to North Carolina a year earlier from Jacksonville, Florida. That night I couldn't sleep because I was supposed to leave for California the next morning with my uncle and cousin. I played sick so I could stay behind with Tammy and Stacey. I was starting to feel sick for real because I really didn't want to ride all the way to California in a truck. I was dreaming of being with Stacey. Tammy knew what I was doing and she helped me convince her father to let me stay behind. My uncle fell for it. I just had to go to my great-grandmother's house and pretend for a few more hours. Later that afternoon, the girls came over to pick me up from my grandmother's house. Tammy drove a red Mustang convertible. I begged her to put the top up on that thing and turn on the AC. Slavery was over and we had a choice not to suffer in that southern heat. I felt like the sun had something against me because it was on my back all day. We were the only black people riding around in a damn convertible. The girls laughed and told me to get used to the southern heat.

Tammy told Stacey all about the sexy stories that I told her. At first I was a little mad at Tammy for doing that, but Stacey started showing me even more attention. Tammy did me a big favor by sharing those stories. The next thing I knew, I was telling Stacey the same stories, but making them even hotter. I felt myself falling even deeper for Stacey, but I wasn't sure if she even liked me.

SEXY LITTLE SECRET: 2

Tammy and Stacey were showing me a good time and that beat the hell out of a truck ride to Cali. The three of us went to the mall for lunch. I couldn't take my eyes off Stacey. I watched her as she ate bite by bite. She was the most beautiful girl I'd ever seen. Stacey and Tammy both looked like they could have passed for Sade's little sisters. I was stone cold in love with Sade. I thought she set the standard for beauty. Sade was the model I used to judge all women.

I was having the time of my life with those two. We went to the movies and arcade. I met more of Tammy's friends. They all seemed pretty cool, but no one compared to Stacey. She was planning to spend the night at my uncle's house. Later that night she gave me a cheap goodnight kiss on the cheek. I thought of her kiss on the cheek as an insult. It seemed like her way of saying, *Goodnight little boy.* I knew I didn't have a chance with her. Since she treated me like a little boy I planned to act like one. I came up with a crazy plan to hide in Tammy's closet while Stacey was in the shower. Tammy had a sliding closet door, which made it perfect for viewing. I heard the shower running and I made sure it was all clear. Nobody was home except Tammy, Stacey and me.

They weren't anywhere in sight, so I hid in the closet. Stacey stepped into the bedroom dripping wet. I was so nervous that I stopped breathing. I knew I was wrong, but she deserved this for that cheap-ass kiss on the cheek. It was almost as if she knew I was watching. Stacey turned her back and took off her plush hot pink towel. Her body was perfect. She had a sexy round ass and nice firm breasts with the prettiest little brown nipples. I wanted to kiss her all over. She bent over drying her legs. Stacey looked so good that she made me come in my pants. Before I knew it Tammy stepped in the room wearing the same kind of towel.

I thought, *Oh my God.*

My heart stopped beating. Tammy walked right up to Stacey and kissed her on the lips. This was the first time I had ever seen girls kiss. I had heard of lesbians, but I had never seen them in action. I was so nervous I thought I was going to die. This was too much for a sixteen-year-old boy to see, but I loved watching every minute. They were so into one another that they never noticed me. I think even if I had stepped out of the closet they would have kept going. They kissed like they were so in love. I watched the gentle touches and the deep slow kisses. When Tammy was missing I never imagined that she was in the shower with Stacey.

Tammy and Stacey finally fell asleep. I stayed in the closet until 2 or 3 a.m. It wasn't too hard sneaking out of Tammy's bedroom because they were sound asleep like newborn babies in their mother's arms. I went straight for the shower. I had masturbated earlier, but I just couldn't stop. The sight of Tammy and Stacey together had me worked up. They made me want to watch again. I wanted to let them know what I had seen, but I kept thinking they would hate me if they knew that I had been watching. I wanted them to let me join in or just let me sit in a corner and watch. To this day, I've only told my friend Lisa what I saw.

The next day I had a new empowered feeling. I was completely on a mission to make Stacey mine. When I saw Tammy and Stacey I had the biggest smile on my face. They couldn't figure out why I was so happy. I told Stacey I loved her and I wanted to make love

18

to her before the summer was over. She had the most intriguing look on her face that I've ever seen. She loved the fact that I was so forward. I told her I was focused and I knew exactly what I wanted. I pulled her closer trying to kiss her, but she told me to slow down. I thought back to the way she and Tammy looked kissing. I moved toward her slowly running my hand down her cheek and neck. When our lips touched I instantly felt her tongue penetrate my lips. I gently worked my tongue to her pleasure. I started kissing on her neck and feeling her breasts. We both were aroused.

Stacey abruptly stopped kissing and said, "Damn, that was good. Let's save some for later."

She really didn't want things to go too far with us. She didn't want to appear like a child molester.

"I know I'm young, but I can be your dirty little secret."

"You're kind of young, but there's nothing little about you. Instead of my dirty little secret, you can be my sexy little secret." Stacey had a way with words that made me feel good about myself.

This was a hot summer and it was about to get much hotter. Tammy and Stacey invited a bunch of their friends over for a pool party. I noticed Stacey giving me some sexy stares. I could read her mind. Her eyes told me how much she wanted me. At first, I thought she would be ashamed to be so forward with me in front of all her friends, but she didn't care. Anyway, her friends didn't have any idea how old I was. Stacey's stares confirmed that she was really into me. The strange thing was that I wasn't intimidated or nervous around her at all. She was comforting to me. The fact that she was older and experienced turned me on even more.

Stacey and I played around in the pool and I got so aroused that I couldn't get out of the water. It was getting late and it looked like everybody was trying to stick around for an all night party. This had kind of messed up our plans. Stacey asked me to sneak away with her so we could play in private. There were teenagers all over the house, so we ended up going to the only vacant room in the house, my uncle's bedroom. This made me a little nervous, but I had nothing to lose. Except my virginity. I jumped on the bed and started free-styling a poem called *My Rhythm*.

Check my rhythm
Check my flow
Check my rap
Check my rhyme

I vibe to your rhythm
I dig everything you're giving
I'm a slave...I'm a slave...I'm a slave to your rhythm
I wanna take away your blues
Jazz you up
Sax you down
Give you a classical love session
Boom your body with bass
Introduce you to my slow jam
Rock and roll your soul
Soothe you with some sexual healing

Dance to my rhythm
Feel my beat
Groove me...move me
Shake me...take me
I'm going off to your sexy symphony
Your rhythm's taking me somewhere I've never been before
Let my rhythm take you
And together we'll be soulmates vibing to internal rhythms

   Stacey moved closer to me in a smooth seductive way. I stood up
to undress and she grabbed me. We kissed. I undressed her with
one hand and felt her up and down with the other. I kissed her all
over. Before I knew it she had my pants down around my ankles
and she started performing oral sex on me. I had always wondered

how it would feel. I had tried simulating this during masturbation with soaps and lotions, but no soap or lotion could ever come close to the feeling. I never dreamed it could feel so good. Stacey was so focused on pleasing me and I didn't want to make her feel left out. I was young and inexperienced, but I wasn't the average virgin. I had seen some of my father's porno movies before and I learned a few tricks. I wanted to share the pleasure with Stacey, so I picked her up and laid her on the bed.

I looked right into her eyes and said, "It's my turn to please you now."

I caressed her breasts and ran my tongue around her perky little nipples. I made my way down her abdomen with my tongue, then I buried my face deep between her thighs. Stacey wrapped her legs around me pulling me in deeper. I could tell that she enjoyed what I was doing because I'd never heard her moan like that before. It was such a turn on for me to give her pleasure like that. Stacey had an unforgettable orgasm.

I climbed on top and slowly penetrated her wetness. Stacey's eyes rolled back in her head. She screamed with pleasure. I had to muffle her mouth with a pillow so no one would hear her moan. I got lost inside of her warm-wet-tight-little hiding place. My penis was still erect even after I reached my climax. I stayed hard almost all night. This was when I realized that I had a gift. We just kept going and going. We did almost every position I could remember from my father's porno movies. I was like a kid with a new toy.

The next morning, Stacey and I woke up in each other's arms. We showered together, then we headed down to the kitchen for breakfast. Tammy was in her bedroom still asleep. Stacey and I talked about everything we did the night before. We couldn't stop complimenting each other. I confessed to her that I was a virgin. She thought I was joking and refused to believe me.

She said, "You're the best I've ever had."

I just smiled and said, "Same here. I can't wait to do it again."

Tammy finally came down to the kitchen.

She asked, "What the hell happened to the two of you last night?

I couldn't find you two anywhere."

I came up with some weak excuse. "There were too many people around for us last night and we couldn't stand the noise."
Tammy automatically knew what the deal was. Stacey and I never confessed to anything, but Tammy did seem a little jealous. If she had a problem with what Stacey and I had done, she never mentioned it to me. We found out that Tammy wasn't exactly innocent. Some guy named Tim came down and joined us for breakfast. My mind was full of questions.

I thought, *What the hell have I gotten myself into?*

I started wondering about Tammy and Stacey's relationship. I was dying to ask someone what was going on, but I didn't. Stacey and I went into the living room to watch television.

Stacey said, "You look worried. Don't worry I'm on the pill."

"Yeah, that's what I was worried about, but I feel better knowing that."

I was really worried about what I meant to her. The second issue that bothered me was wondering what Tammy meant to her. Was I Stacey's boyfriend?

I asked, "What do I mean to you?"

"Whoa, check you out being all serious."

"I am serious. What do I mean to you?"

"You're a special friend."

"I wanna be more than a friend. I want a girlfriend."

I was as serious as a heart attack, putting myself on the line. Stacey was laid back. It was almost as if she had one hand in her pocket and joggling my emotions with the other.

In a nonchalant way she said, "Look, titles aren't important to me."

Stacey started going into all types of details, telling me about her old boyfriend from Florida named Chris. He was eighteen and about to start college. I thought it was strange that she never mentioned what college. She assured me that he was the past.

"You're bigger and much better than Chris in the bed."

"Are you serious?"

"Yeah, I swear."

That was all I needed to hear. I didn't even want to ask about Tammy anymore. Maybe that was just a one-time thing with Tammy. For all I knew girls everywhere could have been doing the same thing behind closed doors.

I gave Stacey a long passionate kiss. This was my way of saying, *I'm sorry for doubting you.*

Out of nowhere I said, "I love you."

Stacey looked surprised. "You're too young to be in love."

I didn't say a word. I just gave Stacey a peculiar stare. I never said that I was in love with her. I simply said I loved her. I was too young to be in love and she was too stupid to know the difference. It's funny how we get ourselves into crazy shit and how fast we regret it. I always liked beautiful and intelligent girls and Stacey only seemed to offer half of what I was looking for. She must have had some kind of spell on me because when she started taking off her clothes I forgot all my issues. She was the finest little thing I'd ever seen. We grabbed a blanket and started having sex behind the sofa. For the rest of that day we distanced ourselves from Tammy and Tim.

Stacey and I went to her house so she could pick up some extra clothes. We were in the house acting silly when I heard a male voice say, "You're finally home." It was her father. At first, I was scared because I didn't know if he heard the freaky stuff I said to his daughter. He just smiled, shook my hand and asked how I was doing. Her father told me that he had heard a lot about me and I looked confused. He asked me what college was I planning to attend in the fall.

I thought, *This guy has no fucking idea who I am.*

I didn't know what to say, so I lied. "I'm planning to attend the University of Maryland."

That was a good answer. The University of Maryland happened to be his alma mater and my favorite college. Stacey's mother entered the room smiling.

She said, "He is cute."

23

I smiled back and extended my hand for a handshake. Stacey's mother gave me a nice big hug and a kiss on the cheek. I was trying to get out of there as soon as possible. I didn't know it, but Stacey had told her parents that I was a big-time high school football player from Baltimore. I wondered why they were so nice and they never asked my name or anything else. They already felt like they knew me. I guess that made things easier for Stacey. She was pretty slick. She lied to make me seem older. Stacey was ashamed to let her parents know that she was dating a sixteen-year-old. She told her parents that she would be back the next evening. They were fine with her staying at Tammy's because they had no idea I was staying there too.

I was going to be seventeen in a few days and most people thought I was around eighteen-years-old. At this point, I felt like Stacey should have focused less on my age and more on the person I was. It seemed like she was really into me, so why did age matter? I was old enough to drive. I had my own car back home. My parents had bought me a black VW Jetta. Stacey had a VW Jetta too, but hers was red. She let me drive her car and I think this was her way of adding some balance to our relationship. Stacey thought we looked better in public when I drove her around. To be honest, I did feel like a kid when she drove me around.

I drove to Piggly Wiggly Supermarket to pick some snacks. Stacey had planned a romantic picnic in the park for us. She prepared a basket of strawberries, grapes, sparkling cider, garden salad, fine cheeses and crackers.

After lunch we ended up having sex in the back seat of her car. Stacey was really making a man out of me. The sex was so good that we just couldn't stop.

Summer was drawing to an end and my uncle and cousin would be back in less than a week. My parents were due back from Hawaii in a week. I felt like after all the things Stacey and I had done, I still didn't know her. I was really falling in love with her. It was the simple things I loved about her like her accent, her brown eyes, her long dark hair and her caramel skin tone. She was delicious. I've always loved soft beautiful skin. Stacey's legs were perfect, so shapely and silky smooth. She must have shaved them everyday because there was never a trace of hair. Her legs were as smooth as a baby's bottom. I was lost in her love and I never wanted to leave that place. For the next few days we made love everyday. I was starting to feel better and better about our relationship. Stacey was starting to share her dreams with me. She had been accepted to the University of North Carolina to study law. Stacey showed me some awards that she had received from the past school year. To my surprise, she was an honor student. Stacey was awarded a full academic scholarship to UNC. She wanted to get married at twenty-four and have three kids. She planned to stay in North Carolina with her husband and raise their kids. I was following every word and imagining myself as her husband.

On my birthday, Stacey surprised me and took me to her bedroom. Her parents went out for the evening with some old friends from Florida. Stacey figured they would be gone for hours. After all that time I had never been in her bedroom. We were always hanging out at my uncle's house. I liked Stacey's bedroom a lot and instantly felt comfortable. Her room had a strong feminine appeal. It was tastefully decorated in pink and white. She had a soft pink canopy bed that smelled exactly like her and I got turned on just lying there. I knew I was in for something special. There were candles all around the room. We actually made love by candlelight. This was our most romantic and intense lovemaking session. I stared deep into Stacey's eyes and asked if she loved me and a tear filled her eye.
She said, "I love you. I love you so much."
I held her so tight that it felt like our hearts beat to same rhythm for the first time. As I held Stacey, I whispered a poem in her ear.
From Stacey's bedroom, we noticed storm clouds moving in. The storm clouds were a welcome sight because we knew they would break the humidity in the air. It started to rain outside.
Stacey asked, "Have you ever made love in the rain before?"

I smiled and said, "Not yet. Making love in the rain has always been a fantasy of mine."

We went to her backyard under an awning and stood still watching the rain.

I said, "I really wanna get wet."

We stood in the middle of Stacey's backyard as if we were the only two people on earth. I couldn't help thinking about the fact that this all would be ending soon. I only had three more days until my parents returned. No matter how hard I tried I just couldn't hold back my tears. Stacey felt the same way and she broke down crying too.

I said, "I don't want this to end."

As I wiped the tears from Stacey's eyes she said, "Neither do I."

We stood there holding each other crying with the rain washing our tears away.

I thought, *Why does love have to hurt so bad?*

Uncle Charlie and Charles returned from their trip bragging about what a good time they had. If they only knew what an adventure I had. Tammy was so cool, she covered for me. She told Uncle Charlie that everything went well. For about a week, I probably spent about fifteen minutes with her. Tammy was truly my favorite cousin. She asked me how things were going with Stacey.

I smiled and said, "Your girl's in love."

Tammy laughed at me for being so silly. "Be careful."

"Everything's okay."

I knew that I was neglecting Tammy, but I had to go because she was cutting into my time with Stacey. I was supposed to stay a few nights with my great-grandmother, but I didn't. I did find some time to visit her, with Stacey right by my side. I couldn't get enough of her.

My parents arrived two days later. I had to pretend like I was glad to see them. We planned to leave for home the next morning. That night I invited Stacey to go out to dinner with me and my parents. We went to a local seafood restaurant. The menu featured

Maryland Crabs. These crabs didn't compare to the crabs back home.

I looked at Stacey and said, "You'll have to come to Maryland and get the real thing, *hot and steamy* just like you like it."

Stacey smiled because she knew my words always had a hidden message. My parents looked at each other as if they were thinking, *Who the hell is this boy?* I had to tone it down a lot and act like the little virgin they knew and loved.

Stacey looked beautiful sitting at the table. At seventeen, I was thinking of how proud I would be to have her as my wife. She seemed comfortable with my parents and I knew they were impressed with her. Stacey was so intelligent that she could relate to almost any topic they threw her way.

Stacey and I enjoyed dinner with my parents, but this was our last night together. All we did was sit in her car kissing and listening to music. That was fine with me because we couldn't possibly top the other night at her house. It was hard to believe that this was our last moment together. It was getting late and I had to get back to my great-grandmother's house to meet up with my parents. The good times were slowly ending. I had to be a kid again. My parents were probably at my great-grandmother's house watching the clock. They would have killed me if I stayed out all night. Stacey and I promised to keep in touch. I told her I would call and write her everyday. I'll never forget our last kiss because it seemed to have gone on for an hour. There we were about to cry again. I thanked her for all the love she gave me and for giving me the chance to share some wonderful experiences. Saying goodbye to Stacey was the hardest thing I ever had to do.

My father was ready to roll out bright and early the next morning. I begged him to let me stay another week. I knew that I had to leave and it was probably better that way, but how do you say goodbye to your first love? I had to start school the next week and my mother was excited about going school shopping. One good thing was that my parents agreed to spend more money on my school clothes.

The entire ride home my parents kept talking about school and planning for my future. My father kept talking about me following in his footsteps and becoming a doctor. I didn't want to hear that shit. All I could see was Stacey. I felt tears filling my eyes, so I laid down in the backseat of my father's Jaguar dreaming of all the things Stacey and I had done. I probably said three things to my parents before my mother mentioned Stacey's name. When she did, I lit up like a Christmas tree. My father asked if I had sex with Stacey. At first, I wasn't going to answer, but I didn't want him to think I was weak when it came to girls.

With little emotion I said, "Yeah, we had sex."

My father asked, "Did you like it?"

I thought, *What a dumb-ass question.*

"Yeah, I liked it, that's why I'm like this. I miss her like crazy."

My mother asked, "Are you in love with Stacey?"

"Yes, but can we stop with all the questions?"

My parents finally stopped talking. Suddenly, every song on the radio reminded me of Stacey. I couldn't eat the whole way home. I was lovesick.

As soon as we got home I ran to the phone to call Stacey. She was home and that was a good sign. Stacey's father answered the phone.

He said, "Stacey, I think it's that football player from Baltimore."

It was nice to hear Stacey's voice. I loved hearing her southern accent.

She said, "I miss you so much that I don't know what to do with myself. I must have cried half the day, but I don't want to be sad anymore."

"I feel the same way. I got so used to seeing you everyday that now nothing's the same since I left you. I know we talked about this before, but I want you to be my girlfriend. I promise to be faithful to you."

"I think I like that idea. No, I know I like the idea. It's been awhile since I've been somebody's girlfriend."

"Well, you're mine now and I love you."

"I love you too, Eric."

"I'm going to write you a letter tonight."

"I already mailed you one."

Even though Stacey and I were miles apart, she made me feel complete. She was giving me everything I needed. I loved the way she changed her outlook on our relationship. It meant a lot to me that Stacey agreed to hold the title of my girlfriend. We continued talking about how much we missed each other for over two hours. Neither of us wanted to hang up the phone, so after a few failed attempts we finally agreed to hang up at the same time.

As the days went by Stacey started missing my calls. I got mad, but at least she kept the letters coming. Writing her poetry was a nice outlet for me. I had to stop worrying about Stacey so much and refocus on my life at home because I was about to start my junior year of high school in a few days. Stacey was so heavy on my mind that I didn't even want to hang with my friends anymore.

The first day of school went pretty good. I was in the eleventh grade. This was the beginning of my second year of public school. It was a lot different than private school. My parents let me leave private school because at that time Randallstown High School had the best football team in the county. I wanted to play football that year, but I changed my mind and that didn't go over too well with my parents. Another reason they let me change schools was because my best friends went there. Troy and Keith had been my best friends since elementary school. They played football for Randallstown and pretty much made the team as good as it was. Instead of trying out for the football team, I went to North Carolina for the summer. Troy and Keith were a little pissed with me for not playing football until I told them all about my vacation. They thought my story was made up until I let them see pictures and read some of Stacey's letters. They almost died when they saw how beautiful she was. They wanted to know if she had any sisters.

About a week went by when we got a call from Uncle Charlie. My Aunt Helen was found dead in her house. She had died from a massive heart attack. I was sad to hear the news, but I wasn't completely devastated because the funeral was going to be in North

Carolina. This would give me another opportunity to spend time with Stacey. The next day my parents and I left to be with our family in North Carolina. We went straight to my uncle's house. I was surprised that no one really seemed so sad. Uncle Charlie was greeting everyone and holding regular conversations. Charles was a little different than the last time I saw him. He actually had something to say to me. I told him how sorry I was to hear about his mother. Tammy was the saddest. I gave her a hug and she said she would be fine. After about an hour I asked where was Stacey. Tammy said she hadn't talked to her all day, but Stacey was probably at home. I sensed that something was wrong.

I said, "Your mother's died and your best friend isn't here for you?"

Tammy looked at me with the saddest eyes.

She said, "He's here and I know she didn't tell you, but he goes to UNC." University of North Carolina hit me like a ton of bricks. I knew exactly what that meant. My body went into automatic shut down. I don't know where I got the strength to leave my uncle's house, but I had to see this for myself. I was on my way to Stacey's house. I saw her car and noticed an unfamiliar car in her driveway. Stacey had no idea that I was in town. It took everything inside me to knock on that door. This tall slim light skinned guy answered the door. I knew this was Chris. I knew he didn't know who I was. I asked to see Stacey and he called for her. She came to the door smiling until she saw my face. I don't think I've ever been more serious.

I said, "We need to talk."

I could feel my heart breaking as I spoke. I started rambling on and on nonstop like a fool.

"How could you do this to me? How could you throw our love away like it didn't mean anything? Why did you deceive me like this? Girl, I gave you my all and you just destroyed my life. I trusted you. I gave you my heart. I know you love me, so tell him to go home. You belong with me. I need you."

Stacey looked at me with tears in her eyes.

She said, "I love you, but I can't be with you. I have to be with Chris."

I was crying so hard that I felt myself shaking. I couldn't talk, so I just walked away with Stacey yelling, "Eric, I'm sorry", over and over.

Chris was a high school basketball player on his way to play for The University of North Carolina Tar heels. I had seen him on television, but I never realized that he was Chris Franklin. Stacey knew Chris was on vacation in Florida and I would be gone by the time he returned. She played me like a fool and I was a mess. I couldn't go back to my uncle's house like that.

As I walked down what seemed to be a dark endless road to nowhere, I noticed Tammy's car pull up next to me. She asked me to get in and she drove me to the mall parking lot, so I could take a cool down period before going back to her house.

"I'm so sorry this happened to you. I knew about Chris, but I thought Stacey was through with him. Listen, your pain will pass. I know because I've been there. Your heart's broken, but Stacey really loves you. She doesn't love Chris like she loves you. He's just better for her right now. He's older and on his way to college. You understand, right?"

"No."

"Yes, you do. Just be patient because there's someone real special out there for you."

"That might be true, but right now Stacey's all I want. No matter what, this is hard for me to deal with. She's all I know and we shared so much together."

After a few hours I finally got myself together. Tammy and I went back to her house. We stayed up all night talking like we used to do. We talked a little more about Stacey. Later, I changed the subject to my Aunt Helen. I talked about how good she was to me when I was younger. Aunt Helen made staying at her house so much fun. She always made sure we had our bacon, cheesy scrabbled eggs, pancakes and sausage every Saturday morning. We couldn't enjoy Scooby Doo without our breakfast. She always

31

made sure we had blankets and hot buttered Jiffy-Pop popcorn when we watched late night scary movies. Tammy had forgotten those little details about her mother and she broke down crying. Reminiscing about my aunt's life was like therapy for Tammy. I helped her recall pleasant memories of her mother. Tammy had almost completely blanked her mother out of mind. We agreed that her mother leaving home with her boyfriend had little or nothing to do with her and Charles. I was hoping I could be as therapeutic with Charles. I noticed he was a lot different compared to my first visit. I promised Tammy I would talk to him. It was morning and I needed to close my eyes. The funeral was at eleven o'clock that morning.

The family arrived at the church a few minutes before eleven o'clock. I noticed that my aunt's boyfriend wasn't anywhere in sight. I didn't blame him because he did the right thing by staying away. If he had shown up a riot probably would have broken out at the church. As the guests came around to greet the family someone grabbed me. It was Stacey crying and trying to hold me. I wanted to push her away, but I was better than that. I gave her a hug and I felt numb all over. Usually, I would feel sensations all over my body, but now I didn't. It had little to do with the fact that we were at a funeral. My feelings for her were gone. I'm not saying that I wasn't still in love with her. I just wasn't feeling her. The funeral lasted about an hour. It was the shortest funeral I've ever attended. Most black funerals last at least 2 1/2 hours. The most exciting and unexpected thing to happen was when Uncle Charlie stood up and spoke about Aunt Helen. He didn't try to portray her as an angel. He spoke straight from his heart. This was the first time we'd seen him cry for Aunt Helen. He said he didn't fully blame her for leaving home, but the manner in which she left hurt him. Uncle Charlie said no one there should hold anything in their hearts against Aunt Helen. Only he and Aunt Helen knew the true story of their relationship. He prayed that her soul was in heaven because she deserved to be at peace. It took a big man to get in front of a crowd and speak so well about a woman who made him look so bad. He did a great job at breaking tension in the church.

The next day we went home and I didn't see Stacey again. She continued to write me for awhile. Stacey called about six months later on a Friday night. It was actually good hearing her voice. She needed to talk. I could almost guess her next line. Chris had broken up with her. She caught him cheating with another girl in his dorm. I told her true love really hurts. We talked for about an hour. I explained to her how much I had changed. I told her I would always love her, but it would be best if she didn't call again.

I learned so much from this chapter in my life. I couldn't wait to close this chapter and move on to the next. I was Stacey's sexy little secret and I loved almost every minute we shared. Seeing Tammy and Stacey together remains my sexy little secret.

JUNIOR YEAR: 3

Trying to move on isn't easy, it's just something that has to be done. I tried focusing all of my energy into school and it went well. There were times that I actually missed my old school. I had no problem making the transition from private to public school. I did notice that the pace and teaching styles differed greatly and I felt like I wasn't learning as much. In each of my classes I had about ten to fifteen more students than at my previous school. This was exactly what my parents predicted would happen. I refused to tell them that they were right. I had already heard enough from them about me deciding not to play football. Although, I felt like I wasn't learning as much as I did at my previous school, Randallstown High was definitely the place for me. I made up the difference by teaching myself. I didn't need a school to teach me everything. Knowledge is everywhere and it's up to the student to know where to find it. I was taking all honors classes and was a straight "A" student. I attributed this to the pace of my new lifestyle. I decided to take some time off from dating to refine my skills. I was viewing love as a war of the hearts. My heart was wounded and I didn't want to carry any residual emotions into a new relationship. My parents had advised me to start a new relationship as soon as possible. For some reason they thought a new girlfriend would help me forget all about Stacey. I saw this as bad advice. I needed a whole new strategy. I'll admit that I was guarded, but for good reason. There was only one good thing that came from my broken heart. My emotions made me more creative in my poetry.

People always say when young people start having sex it's hard to go back to holding hands. This wasn't exactly true in my case. Broken hearts have turned the mightiest men into mice. I had planned to go back to the simpler things like holding hands and kissing. Although, I knew I was going to miss having sex. I really wanted to focus on developing a solid friendship first.

I had my eye on a girl I met in English class named Monica. She was also in my U.S. History class and sometimes we ate lunch together. I noticed her on the first day of school. She was the most beautiful girl in school. Monica stood out like a big-bright-beautiful sunflower in a barren field. Her beauty was far beyond physical. She was an excellent visual artist and poet. I liked to think of her as my little Renaissance woman. She was a very spiritual person. She was so deep that people referred to her as "Sister Mother Earth." This wasn't meant to be disrespectful in anyway. Monica was viewed as an African Princess. Her father's family was of Somalian decent. She had just completed a book of affirmations for people of color that she hoped to publish one day. I was really impressed with her artwork and writing.
Monica was unique in so many ways. She was a virgin and planned to stay that way until she was married. Monica and I started to develop a strong friendship. I felt like I didn't want to rush into a relationship with her. I feared opening up to someone too fast like I did with Stacey. Somehow, I had to trust in Monica. I needed to rid my heart of the emptiness. My heart was a lonely place and I wanted to let Monica inside my love. She offered everything that I was looking for in a girlfriend. Poetry was our

common connection. It was almost as if we communicated through poetry. The more time we spent together the stronger my feelings for her grew.

Jennifer was another girl I had my eye on. She was what I considered *simply sexy* and I liked her a lot. Jennifer was funny and just real cool to be around. I started spending time with her during and after school. We weren't a couple, but people thought we were. I hated the way people looked at us. They looked at us funny because Jennifer was white. I didn't feel like I had to explain shit to anyone. Our parents never questioned our friendship. But one day when we were at Jennifer's house she tried to seduce me. I told her that I just wanted to be friends, but she didn't understand why I wouldn't have sex with her. She thought it had something to do with the fact that she was white. I told her that I wanted to have sex with her, but I had my mind set on another girl.

Jennifer was hot and willing to do whatever I wanted her to do. She wanted to know who this girl was that had my attention. I trusted her, so I told her it was Monica. I made her promise not to tell anyone. I needed more time to make sure Monica was the right one for me. I told Jennifer that I would hook her up with my buddy Troy and she seemed fine with my suggestion. I didn't think her infatuation was all about me. Jennifer was just curious to experience sex with a black guy.

My life was almost back to normal. Well, it was as close to normal as it was going to get. After my experience with Stacey, my life wasn't the same. I wanted to spend some time with my next-door neighbor, Lisa. I missed her a lot. I had been too busy with my other female friends. Lisa was my best friend of all. She was a single twenty-one-year-old, living all alone in her parent's old house. Her father died about four years earlier from lung cancer. Lisa was his heart, so he left everything to her. She had it made. The house was already paid in full and her mother had remarried and moved to New York.

Lisa was a natural beauty who stood out in any crowd. She was about 5'8" with the body of a goddess. I was her workout partner. We used to power walk or jog at least three times a week. She wore her hair in long flowing dreadlocks. She only wore makeup on very special occasions. Lisa's knowledge was endless and I learned so much from her. She was actually the first girl I ever kissed. *She's going to kill me for this.* She was my sitter and she used to practice French Kissing on me. That was actually hard for me to admit. I've always been too ashamed to tell her that I still remembered. She probably thought I was too young to remember. It seemed like a dream, but it really happened.

Lisa's life long dream was to become a famous singer. She was already pretty well known throughout the Baltimore/Washington area. She was the lead singer for a local R&B/Jazz group called Soul Survivors. They did it all from music to poetry. I admired Lisa and her group. They had a major influence on me. Lisa helped me develop my poetry style and we even wrote music together. Sometimes she was like the big sister I never had. We spent lots of time together. I always saw the latest movies because she took me on opening day. I never had a birthday that Lisa didn't give me a present. That year she gave me my first copy of *The Autobiography of Malcolm X.* I don't think there was another seventeen-year-old in this country with social and political views as strong as mine. To some extent I was a militant teen. My parents were well aware of how much time I spent with Lisa, but they had no idea how much she influenced me. I loved talking to Lisa because she was a good listener and problem solver.

Lisa taught me not to refer to her as religious. She was a spiritual person. She said spirituality was based on an individual's own personal beliefs and religion was based on another man's personal beliefs. Lisa believed spirituality kept us strong and religion weakened black people. She believed in two basic principles, there was a God and that Jesus died for her. She stressed black pride and unity. Lisa was slowly molding me, but I didn't realize it then. She taught me that Malcolm, Martin, Marcus and Medgar were messiahs. She defined a messiah as a savior or liberator of his people. I didn't fully believe this, but I could see where she was coming from. Sometimes she was a little too deep for me, but I trusted and respected her so much that she probably could have told me anything.

Lisa learned most of her beliefs from her father. He was a Black Panther during the 60's and 70's. Lisa still had pictures of him from those days. She described her father as a visionary and a revolutionary leader. She told me never to refer to Malcolm as Malcolm X. She felt this connected Malcolm to America's stereotypical image of him. To separate him from that image, she referred to him by his Islamic name El-Hajj Malik El-Shabazz or simply Malcolm. We agreed that he was a far greater man than America ever gave him credit for being. Lisa and I used to go to all types of cultural festivals, events and concerts along the East Coast. When I went to places to hear her sing she would introduce me as her little brother. If she was in a discussion with her friends, Lisa would always have me add my opinion. She said a man with no voice was weak and a man who didn't vote was even weaker. She taught me the differences between race, creed, color, religion, culture, ethnicity, traditions and customs. She told me to never confuse the meanings. *I told you this girl was deep.* She was so proud of who and what she was. She told me to love and respect people of all colors, because we all needed one another. Lisa gave me an eye opening education.

I spent an entire day at Lisa's house telling her all the details. I mean, I didn't leave out anything.

She said, "Relax and tell me all about what happened to you in North Carolina."

Lisa's house had a pleasant atmosphere with soft mellow music playing in the background. She had candles and incense burning, which really added to the peaceful atmosphere. There were African sculptures and paintings all around her house. She had a large fountain waterfall in her living room. Lisa's house was unbelievable and I loved being there. Her house gave us inspiration

38

when we wrote songs or poetry.

"I can't believe Stacey played you like that. You didn't deserve that at all. I understand that you're hurting, but what doesn't kill you will only make you stronger. I guarantee you'll bounce back a better man." Lisa looked like she was deep in thought for a minute. "Take off your clothes."

"What?" I was completely thrown off guard. I thought she was joking.

"I wanna give you a massage with this African body oil to help you forget your problems."

In the past she had massaged my shoulder after a tough workout, but this was completely different.

"I know exactly what you need. You need a physical relationship based more on sex and less on love. This way your heart will be protected and you can still enjoy yourself."

I realized that she was trying to seduce me and I was getting weak.

I thought, *What about Monica?*

I was always attracted to Lisa and I thought this could be the start of something big. She was making me lose track of my new strategy. I trusted her and I didn't think she would go too far. I knew I was wrong, but I took off all my clothes down to my boxers. Lisa told me to lie on my stomach and I did. From my periphery I could see her taking off her top and bra. She told me to just relax and she straddled her body over mine. She started massaging my back. Her hands went up, down and side to side with slow rhythmic movements. This felt so damn good. She gently laid her breasts on my back. I could feel how hard her nipples were. She started massaging my back with her breasts. I was so turned on that I tried to turn over.

Lisa whispered in my ear, "I'm not finished yet."

She licked and kissed my back. I could feel her pelvis grinding in the small of my back. She was so hot that she just kept riding me until she came. I was impressed. I had never seen a woman do that before. She had an orgasm from the pressure against her clitoris

39

while riding my back. When I turned over she had the most beautiful breasts I had ever seen.

I thought, *Oh my God, this is the best foreplay.*

My penis was rock-hard. Lisa had me lay on my back and she massaged my chest. She straddled me from the front and we kissed. By no coincidence, we had the exact same kissing styles. She was my favorite kisser because she was the one who taught me. Lisa slowly pulled down my boxers and she looked like she stopped breathing when she saw the size of my fully erect penis. She began massaging my penis with her oil. Her hands felt so good that she made me come with magnum force. She just laid on top of me with her breasts slipping and sliding up and down my chest. Lisa was very creative. She told me to come back whenever I needed to talk.

When I got home I couldn't believe what happened. I almost had sex with my mentor. My conscience bothered me a little. I felt like I had been cheating on Monica. What was I doing to myself? Monica wasn't even my girlfriend. I made Lisa hot by telling her about what happened to me in North Carolina. I went to her house to talk about my problems, not to have sex. After a few minutes I was fine with the idea. I figured that Lisa had taught me almost everything else, why not the art of making love? I thought both of us were curious. I had to keep in mind that we never even had intercourse that day. Lisa made me feel so good that I couldn't believe that was just foreplay. All I could think about that night was how good it would feel to be inside her. I imagined how she'd look when I penetrated her for the first time.

I've always loved looking directly in a woman's eyes during sex. I get so turned on by her sounds, breathing and facial expressions. Penetrating a woman for the first time is like opening a present on Christmas Day. Each time after that it's still a gift, but it's more like opening a birthday present. At this point, I was about to have sex with my mentor, but I was still a militant teen focused on issues.

The next day at school I ran into Troy and Keith. I hadn't seen them in a few days.

Troy said, What's up, Eric. You been avoiding us or what?"

"No, females have just been keeping me real busy. Y'all have no idea how busy."

They laughed.

Keith said, "Yeah right. You've probably been real busy watching your father's porno movies."

"That was the old days. I'm into live action now." We all laughed. "Speaking of live action, Troy I got a real nice girl I wanna hook you up with."

"Who?"

"Jennifer Banks."

"The white girl?"

"Is that a problem?"

Troy smiled and said, "No, not at all. She's fine as shit."

"She is fine, but get ready for some nasty stares from the sisters around here."

"I ain't worried about them, I can handle it."

Troy and Keith were on the football team that year. Troy was a big heavy set offensive and defensive lineman. He looked a lot like the rapper Heavy D. Keith was a tall slim J. J. Evans lookin' somebody. He was a wide receiver with excellent hands and speed. Keith was definitely one of the best high school athletes in the state. I was a good running back, but I lost interest in football. I still worked out with them to keep in shape just in case I decided to play football during my senior year. I can still see Troy and Keith walking around school like celebrities in their football jerseys. I thought that was real cool. On game days they wore their jerseys around school all day to impress the girls and it worked. They got lots of attention. I can't lie, I wanted some of that attention too, but I just needed to stay focused on school and Monica. Lisa was cool, but Monica was better for me.

I was always closer to Troy than Keith. We were all like brothers, but I felt like I had to look out for Troy. Even though girls surrounded him, Troy was still a shy fat boy. He probably wouldn't have had a girlfriend that year if I hadn't hooked him up with Jennifer.

I was even close to Troy's family. I loved his grandmother like my own. Since, both of my grandmothers had passed Troy's grandma called me her grandson. His grandmother lived in Baltimore City. Troy, Keith and I loved going to her house all year long. This was our only real exposure to ghetto life. We were really rich spoiled preppy kids from the county. But we loved the corner stores, block parties, ghetto games and the neighborhood people. We used to play all types of sports against the neighborhood kids. It was like Baltimore City vs. Baltimore County. Even though we had more money, better educations and better houses, we never acted as if we were better than those kids. The funny thing was that they made fun of us. They said we talked, dressed and acted like white boys. They didn't realize it, but they were equating ignorance and poverty with being black. This was pitiful and it bothered us a lot. We didn't act or speak in any special way. We were only being ourselves. They respected us for the way we played sports, but when we were done explaining to them why they had the wrong mentality, they respected us even more. Keith was a Muslim, so he took his time breaking it down to them. I told them to fade to black. This represented all black people coming together and trusting one another. Also, it meant breaking away from jealousy, envy and fear. I noticed a lot of other neighbors of all ages paying attention to what I was saying. I told them I could express my point better with a poem called *Fade to Black*.

It's a Black thing
So you should understand the plan
Political, economic and spiritual freedom
I've seen the light
So fade to Black

Wake up to consciousness

42

Our world's smoked up and cracked up
HIV positive in a negative way
Inhale life...not death
Inject yourselves with consciousness
Darkness can be the light
So fade to Black

Malcolm "X" marked the spot
The tree was planted a long time ago
So trace the roots
To know the roots is to know you
To know you is to love you

In search of Africa...Africa
Where can you be
Deep inside of me
It's time to be seen and heard
Consciousness is the word
Took my culture, religion and name
Now I'm wise to the game
So fade to Black

No shame in ghetto games
The world's a ghetto
But poverty ain't pretty
Black is power...money is power
But which is happiness
Black power's in the hour
But time's running out
So fade to Black

I felt like I put my all into instilling Black Pride in that group. I prayed that my point got across and I think Lisa would have been proud of me. The crowd gave me hugs, handshakes and a thunderous round of applause. I even brought tears to some of their eyes. My friends and I felt proud and we actually made friends that day. We brought a couple of the guys back to our neighborhood to show them that all black people weren't poor. Troy's dad ran his own advertising firm and Keith's dad was a lawyer. I introduced them to my father and he loved this because it gave him the opportunity to tell them about his famous success story. I had heard it hundreds of times, but I still listened because I was proud of him. I wouldn't have had such a wonderful upper-class lifestyle if it wasn't for him. Watching as the guys listened to him made me realize how blessed I was. My father told me that he would be honored to speak to anyone we thought he could help.

He said, "If I can talk to ten kids and just get through to at least one, then I've done good."

My father was so motivated.

The person from the city that I was most impressed with was Troy's older brother, James. He was a notorious drug addict living with his grandmother because the rest of his family had turned their backs on him. I liked talking to James. He was a drug addict, but he full was of knowledge.

Seventeen years earlier he was an outstanding high school football player. He won the Outstanding Scholastic Athletic Award twice. This was an award given to top athletes in the state with the highest grade point averages. This award almost automatically gets a person an athletic scholarship. This was a big deal to me because I was an athlete. James knew all about sports. He was like a sports historian. He used to dream of becoming a professional football player. He said that he was still the best quarterback in the city. Troy didn't like me talking to James so much because he was ashamed of him.

I did make fun of James sometimes, but it was never for his drug problem. James had the worst smelling feet. I said he must have had a recipe for those stinking feet. They smelled like he soaked them in vinegar for an hour, then sprinkled powdered cheese on them. In reality, we all made fun of each other's family members, but I genuinely liked talking to James. I asked him all types of questions about his life. I asked him if he had any dreams. He said he would like to become a sports commentator or coach a professional football team. I asked him how and why he ever started using drugs. James said he started hanging out with the wrong crowd. He started smoking marijuana in high school and hanging around some older guys from the neighborhood that sold and used drugs. One night he was with the drug dealers and one of them talked him into trying some heroin. After the first time he couldn't stop. He said he's been chasing that first high ever since. Those guys helped to ruin his football career and his life. James never even finished high school. He dropped out of school during his senior year and the sad thing was that colleges all over the country wanted him. There was a good chance that he would have made the NFL. I was so much into health and fitness that the idea of mixing drug and athletics was totally foreign to me. I asked James why didn't he stop using drugs. He said he didn't want to stop. It was something he needed to do to keep from getting sick. He wasn't even getting high from the heroin. He had to mix cocaine and heroin together to feel anything. He showed me all his track marks and sores that came from injecting drugs. I thanked him for talking to me and being so real. I thought it was best for me to learn from his mistakes instead of making my own. I wanted to save him, but he was a brother that didn't want to be saved. Three weeks later James was found dead in an abandoned building. I was sad, but I thought James was probably better off that way.

After James' death I wanted to go back to that neighborhood to help young people like he helped me. I went to the neighborhood recreation center to see if I could start a mentoring program. I even got my father to help. Troy and Keith's parents got involved and my friends helped out whenever they got the chance. We got the program started quickly and everything was going well. One of the local television news stations did a segment on the program. A reporter interviewed me. He introduced me as the founder of the program. He asked me about two or three questions and I answered each question with a quick and intelligent response. I was excited about seeing the segment. The camera crew filmed footage of me reciting a poem to the group of kids. The reporter told me to look out for my segment on the eleven o'clock news.

At eleven o'clock the news opened detailing all the murders committed in the city that day. Our segment aired last. Instead of airing the entire segment all they showed was some short footage while the anchorman did a quick voice-over. He simply mentioned that a teenager, Eric Brown Jr., started a mentoring program for boys and girls at the Mary E. Rodman Recreation Center. The entire segment lasted about ten seconds. No one even heard my interview. I asked my parents why couldn't our story had been longer or in the headlines. My father gave me a quick and simple answer. We were saving lives not taking them.

Lisa called me and had the same shocked reaction. I told her everything was fine and I wasn't going to let this discourage me. Monica called to let me know that she saw the segment too. She said such hard work deserved more recognition. She was impressed with how motivated I was and asked if I would be interested in joining a poetry club at school. Monica had been advertising the club around school for a few days. I told her it was an excellent idea. I was willing to do anything to spend more time with her. I wondered what she thought of my friendship with Jennifer. She had seen us together a few times. She probably thought I was really into Jennifer. I had to come up with a way to show Monica that I was more interested in her than Jennifer, so I wrote a special poem for her.

Lisa was still on my mind, so I called her back to tell her that I needed to see her. She told me to come right over. I sneaked out of the house through the backdoor. Lisa was at her backdoor waiting for me. It was late, but sleeping was the last thing on my mind. It was a Friday night and I didn't have anything to do. Lisa told me she wanted to give me an herbal bath to help me relax and release toxins from my body. Going to her house was always a memorable

46

experience. Lisa undressed me and had me get into the bath water. She started singing to me. Her voice was sultry, seductive and sexy. She had me in a trance. Lisa was getting herself worked up too. She slowly undressed herself. I watched her as she stood there totally nude singing and doing a slow sexy dance. She began to masturbate and pretty soon she was enjoying herself too much to sing or dance. I laid back in the tub, watching as she pleased herself. She was making me hot. This was a beautiful thing to witness. Before long I started masturbating too. She noticed what I was doing and I think it turned her on even more. I started talking to her. I told her how beautiful she looked and how much she turned me on. I was about to reach my peak when I saw her tightening up. This was too intense. I knew what was about to happen. Her moans got louder and louder. I asked her to come for me. We were having mutual orgasms and it felt too good to stop. The sight of Lisa masturbating drove me crazy. I went straight for her and we kissed. She wanted to go to her bedroom. The foreplay continued. She told me to look in her closet and grab whatever I thought she'd like. I opened her closet door to a full arsenal of sex toys. I must have had a weird look on my face.

Lisa said, "It can get lonely sometimes."

I said, "I understand, but do you need so much company?"

She had me use a vibrator on her. We both were really into it. I wanted to be inside of her so bad. I felt her hand stroke my penis. That was nice, but I needed more. I repositioned myself on the bed putting my feet towards the head of the bed. Lisa shifted her body. I instantly felt a warm wet sensation. She was performing oral sex on me. She was good. She stopped me from using the vibrator on her, so she could give me all of her attention. Lisa kept going faster and deeper. She made me come again. Lisa was trying to make me fall in love with her. We laid there kissing and caressing for hours. I still wanted to be inside her. I didn't say anything, but I figured that she was more into foreplay than the actual act of making love.

BEAUTIFUL IN BLACK AND WHITE: 4

A week later we had our first poetry club meeting after school. Seven people showed up including Monica and myself. We were about to begin the meeting when a blonde girl stepped into the room. When my eyes focused, it was Jennifer. She asked if this was where the poetry club was meeting.

I thought to myself, *Oh hell no not today.*

I didn't want her there because the poem I was going to recite involved her and Monica. When it was my turn to recite my poem, I was a little hesitant. But Jennifer was a good friend, so I felt like she would understand what I was doing.

I said, "My poem is entitled *Beautiful in Black and White.*"

Long blonde hair with blue eyes
Skinny thighs and hips with no twist
Thin lips with a long thin nose
No doubt...this is beautiful
What we always see
But has no future with me

I try to define beautiful
In my mind I see images of you
I see afrocentric sculptures depicting the
Natural beauty I see in you
Long black hair with brown eyes
Shapely thighs and hips with a sweet ass twist
Lips that speak to me in a warm wet way
Kiss me...lick me...love me

I am the beholder of your beauty
A beauty which is far beyond physical
A beauty illuminating deep within
In your eyes I see our future
I'm in search of a queen
My queen of the unseen
Co-ruler of our black kingdom
Take your place upon your throne
I'm talking futuristic
Queen of our future
I'm the king of our destiny

Now that I have you
I'm living the impossible
The immeasurable is within inches
You add power to the plan
Strength to the vision
An easy decision to make you my queen
I love you down to your core
Like I said before
Your beauty is far beyond physical
I'm not trying to redefine beauty
But trying to refocus certain eyes

The room was filled with different reactions. I looked at Monica first. She didn't say a word and didn't have to. She had the most beautiful and glowing smile on her face that I'd ever seen. Next, I discreetly looked at Jennifer. She was a little red in the face. She smiled and nodded like she approved. That was a relief to me because I valued her friendship.

It was Monica's turn to recite her poem and I knew she had something heavy prepared. Monica and I definitely had the best poems. After her poem I didn't need to hear anyone else's poem. Monica's poem was so hot that it left me wondering if she was really a virgin. She had such raw talent that she didn't even realize how good her work was. I don't think I heard anyone else's poem because Monica's poem had such an affect on me. Intelligence has always been a major turn on for me. I think Monica felt the same way about me. I was hoping that I was the guy she mentioned in her poem. The poetry club planned to meet again the following week.

The next night I finished reading *The Autobiography of Malcolm X*. This was the most powerful book that I have ever read. Malcolm's story was so motivating to me. He made me look at life with a new vision. He had a positive influence on me. Malcolm brought many evils to light, but he never made me hate anyone. I learned to be strong and to defend what I knew was right. Malcolm's goal was to improve the rights of all Black Americans. He planned to make social, economic and political improvements. Anyone could see that he was a brilliant man. I'll admit that the pre-Mecca Malcolm was a dangerous militant leader, but he was only a threat to those who tried to violate his rights. After his pilgrimage to Mecca, Malcolm was a changed man. When he found true Islam he changed his name to El-Hajj Malik El-Shabazz. He then considered himself a human rights leader. This meant that he was for the rights of all people regardless of color. America has distorted the image and views of El-Hajj Malik El-Shabazz. That's why most people still refer to him as Malcolm X. We always refer to other well-known Muslims by their Islamic names. Two good examples are Muhammad Ali and Kareem Abdul-Jabbar. America wants to remember Malcolm as a violent, hateful and militant Black leader. Some of our former presidents were slave owners, but they aren't remembered for that. El-Hajj Malik El-Shabazz was murdered by three assassins: ignorance, greed and envy.

My U.S. History teacher was a white man named Mr. Wallace. We all knew that he was a racist. It only took the one question that most white U.S. History teachers resent. I asked why he never mentioned Malcolm before in class. He politely announced to the class that this was an U.S. History class and not an African American History class. He was setting himself up for disaster, but he was too stupid to realize it.

I asked, "Isn't Malcolm part of U.S. History?"

Mr. Wallace said, "Not in this classroom or curriculum. Maybe, I'll mention him next February during Black History Month along with Martin, Rosa and Harriet."

I was so mad that I walked out of his class and went to the principal's office. When I looked, Monica was right behind me. We waited for like an hour to talk to the principal. We explained to Principal Thompson what Mr. Wallace had said and he felt like we were overreacting.

Mr. Thompson said, "I've known Bill Wallace for almost twenty years and you're trying to make him sound like a racist and I know that's not true."

Our principal was mainly concerned with the fact that Monica and I had walked out of class. I couldn't believe what was happening. Mr. Wallace and Mr. Thompson were fucking with the wrong roster of students.

We intentionally did little things to aggravate Mr. Wallace. We refused to sit during his class. We all stood in a circle around the classroom and hummed every time he spoke.

Mr. Wallace said, "I don't care if you don't want to learn. I'll still get paid anyway."

When other teachers or students walked by they thought we were doing some kind of special class project. This was kind of fun, but it didn't really do anything. We decided to go to the Vice Principal, Mr. Walker, who happened to be a black man. Monica and I explained to him exactly what had happened. We came up with a plan to have Mr. Walker and two administrators stand outside of Mr. Wallace's classroom door to listen to our class. The next day when class began we formed our usual circle. This time we didn't hum when Mr. Wallace spoke. From the moment I walked into the classroom I was ready for a showdown. By this time the message about what Mr. Wallace said had traveled throughout the school. We learned that Mr. Wallace's other classes started forming the same famous humming circle during his other class periods. Mr. Wallace was starting to look worn out and I thought that he was probably at his breaking point. Over time, the little silly things we did began to have a major impact. I looked directly in his face and he looked in mine.

I asked, "What's *Black Rage*? Where did it start?"

Mr. Wallace didn't say a word. He had no idea what I was doing. I just needed him to listen.

Long gone but not forgotten
Worked in fields of corn, tobacco and cotton
Taken from my home to carry the weight
Of your world on my shoulders
Built an entire country for free
Maybe you've heard of me

Taught me to hate my own...over skin tone
Deep feelings of mistrust
What the hell have they done to us
Take me back to my past
I have no future in America
Take me back to Africa

Where I was completely free
Home...where I was me
Never got my forty acres and a mule
Did you think it was too cruel?
Too cruel for one mule to work all that land
Trust me...I understand

All work with no pay
Your heaven on earth has been my hell
But one day you'll pay
Maybe my heaven will be your hell
Nobody knows...Only time will tell
Why do you hate me so
To this day I don't know
Black rage is real
Black rage is what I feel

I asked, "Mr. Wallace can we please talk about Malcolm today?"
Mr. Wallace yelled, "I told you, we weren't talking about that
nigger in this classroom, now sit your black ass down!"
Needless to say Mr. Wallace never taught in a Maryland
classroom again. The next year we had a new principal and a new
African American History class. No matter what, we would still
have to deal with racism again regardless of what accomplishments
we made. Maybe we would encounter racism at a different time or
place, but we would encounter it again. Where do we truly fit in the
American scheme? We all are victims of *America's Transplant*.

After all this time
I still haven't assimilated to your culture
America the beautiful hasn't been so pretty to me
We're as different as night and day
The differences in our flavors

Go deeper than chocolate and vanilla
My likes are your dislikes
My dreams are your nightmares
If we sang the same song
You would sing it to a different tune
We even dance to a different rhythm
No matter how hard I try to keep up
With the pace of your world
Something always holds me back

You've had generations of wealth
I've had generations of heartaches and struggles
I want a piece of the pie
But all I seem to get are crumbs

Commit a crime
You may get time
I'll get 25 to life or even death
You so-call defend, you judge and you sentence me
That's American Justice at its best
Keeping the peace
Patrolling the beat
Controlling the pace of my world

I'm a Transplant in the belly of the beast
No matter how hard you try to deny it
I'm a part of you
The part you love to hate
God bless America...I love America
But I hate the evil it does

The school year had drawn to an end I sat in my bedroom
rearranging things and getting rid of junk. I reached into the back
of my desk drawer and felt something. I had almost forgotten about

that stuff. Stacey's old letters and pictures were still in my drawer. The worst thing I could have done would be to read them. Something inside of me forced me to unfold one of the letters and start reading. Stacey's words were so beautiful. She really was in love with me. I couldn't stop wondering what we could have had. Even though I knew a long distance relationship wouldn't have worked for us. It's so hard getting over your first love. Who was I fooling? I couldn't lie to myself anymore. After all that time I was still in love with Stacey. I truly gave her my all. If I could have held her that night I wouldn't have let her get away from me again. I felt there was still a possibility that I could have gotten her back. True love never dies, it just lies somewhere deep in the heart waiting to resurface at the strangest moment.

I looked at Stacey's pictures. I missed her so much that I couldn't hold back my tears. I could still see her standing there. I had taken those pictures myself. We were so happy then, but nothing lasts forever. Whoever said that time heals all wounds was a damn liar. My pain was too deep. Stacey was mine only for a short time, a period in my life that I kept reliving in my mind. It's hard to share so much with someone and to lose them so abruptly. She was stripped from my life, but remained in my heart. I was an emotional wreck. I wanted to hate her, but my love for her was much too strong. I thought back to how we held each other crying in the rain. It was then that I realized she was deeply in love with me.

I could have thrown the letters and pictures away, but the love would always remain. It's sad, but I still have these letters and pictures to this day.

I promised myself that would be my last cry for Stacey. She was seriously messing with my mind. I had to get her out of my heart and off my mind. Her love was haunting me like a wicked ghost from the past. I wanted to call her just to let her know I still thought of her from time to time. I wanted to let her know I still loved her. I imagined that somehow she knew I still loved her. I thought my broken heart had mended, but I was wrong. I knew that

Monica was the best cure for my condition.

During this chapter in my life I dealt with so many different issues. I was trying to recover from a broken heart. Suddenly I was bombarded with sexual attention from a woman I admired all my life. I was trying to take things slow to capture the heart and mind of my true love, Monica. I battled racism. I was a mentor in search of my own identify. I felt like a twenty-one-year-old trapped in the body of a seventeen-year-old. I was living a fast and foul lifestyle. My conscience was starting to bother me and I wanted to devote all my time to Monica, but Lisa was too good to give up then. Monica and Lisa were my soul-sistas. We connected on a higher level. I always said that we vibed to the same righteous rhythm. Lisa and Monica were somewhat similar. They were intelligent and equally beautiful. Monica had my heart and that was a major factor. There was no place on earth that I would've rather had been than with her. Everyday I dreamed of making her mine. I had to make a move before someone else stole her heart. When I looked in her eyes I really saw a solid future. She was the queen of our future and I had our destiny in my hands. The love I had for her added strength to that vision.

People were right when they said that once you start having sex it's hard to go back to holding hands. This is true because sex is a *powerful* thing. Monica didn't want to have sex until she was married and the last thing I wanted to do was to corrupt her. I wanted to be good, but I seemed to be at my best when I was bad. I realized what Stacey was going through. She was in love with someone, but someone else was better for her during that time period. I was slowly learning what life and love were all about.

I felt like Lisa was in love with me. She spent so much time, energy and money on molding me into the man she wanted me to be. I thought back to how she used to take me to the movies and restaurants. I wondered if she saw these as real dates. I always felt like she loved me. It just took hearing about my sex life to bring out her true feelings. The thought of me having sex and her not being involved drove her crazy. I did appreciate all the things she did for me and to me. I loved her for teaching me how to kiss. I've been told over and over that I'm a great kisser. My kisses seem to take women on a journey, lost deep inside my love.

Lisa and I shared a special relationship and she knew all my secrets. We were sexually involved, but I felt like I could still talk to her about anything. Monica and Lisa knew a lot about each other, but they hadn't met. I knew that their meeting was inevitable. Lisa could tell by the look in my eyes when I mentioned Monica's name that I was in love with her. For some strange reason I agreed to set up a meeting between the two. Monica only thought of me and Lisa as good friends and I definitely wanted to keep it that way.

LISA: 5

Lisa was so in love with me. She never said it, but I felt it. This girl was loving me up and down. I mean, she actually kissed me from head to toe. I loved the way she gave me sweet little kisses all over my body. The way she looked at me said it all. She gave me eye contact that pierced down to my soul. Lisa was in tune to my every need. I wanted to return that same love, but it was impossible for me to equal the love she gave. She started calling me more than usual. I think she called just to hear my voice. I didn't say much to her on the phone because I was afraid that one of my parents would overhear our conversation. I asked her to stop calling so often. I didn't want to draw any additional attention to our relationship.

My parents were laid back and didn't suspect anything. If they found out about me and Lisa, she would have been facing child molestation charges. My mother would have died. I would have defended Lisa by saying she was a good woman with one minor character flaw.

I was in my bedroom studying my one-hundred-and-one sexual positions guidebook. I had been studying for my next sexual encounter with Lisa. I was going to blow her mind. My parents called me to their bedroom to talk to me. They were planning to go away for a week to a medical conference in Las Vegas. I didn't know it, but they had spoken to Lisa earlier that day about the possibility of me staying with her while they were away. They gave me three options, going to the conference, staying home alone or staying with Lisa. My father said he didn't care what I decided. My mother preferred that I stayed with Lisa.

I thought, *Are they joking?*

I called Lisa right away to tell her my plans.

Lisa took me to an African cultural store. We picked up some extra body oils and incense. Lisa surprised the hell out of me when she handed me the keys to her Volvo. She knew how much I loved her car. She was too good to me. Her Volvo was fully loaded. Just to name a few features, it had a power sunroof, AM/FM stereo cassette player, air conditioning, leather interior and chrome wheels. Lisa was trying hard to make me fall in love with her.

My parents were scheduled to leave the next morning. My father left me with five hundred dollars to feed and entertain myself. As soon as they left, Lisa scooped me up and we headed to the mall. She wouldn't let me spend any of my own money. Lisa picked out a beige Claiborne suit and shirt with a pair of black leather Kenneth Cole shoes for me. She was about to spend well over four hundred-dollars on me.

"I can't let you pay for my clothes. My father left me some money. I don't have enough to get all this, but I really don't need a suit. How can you afford to spend so much money?"

I was trying not to draw any attention from the salespeople or the other customers, but they looked at us anyway.

"My dad left me very well off and money is the least of my worries. I wanna do this for you. You deserve it. So, at least try the suit on before making a decision."

I smiled. "Okay."

Lisa handed me the suit and to my surprise she followed me into the dressing room. Lisa actually helped me try on the clothes. This was a bold and sexy move. I thought the other customers and salespeople were under the impression that Lisa and I were brother and sister. Her joining me in the dressing room and her making such a big fuss over me definitely changed their impressions. I know they saw us as lovers. We did make a very attractive couple. I wasn't too far from eighteen, but I thought I could pass for older. Lisa was twenty-one, but she could pass for eighteen or nineteen. She was only about an inch shorter than I was. Sometimes, I could see how we could pass as or be mistaken for a real couple. When I finally put on the suit I really liked the way I looked. Lisa couldn't stop telling me how sexy I looked. The suit added about two years to my appearance and I felt good in it. As we stood in the dressing room in front of a mirror, Lisa wrapped her arms around me.

"Like I said before, you deserve this suit and I can afford it. Now, I'm going to take you out to dinner later to show you off to everybody."

"Okay, I gotta have this suit. I like the way I look in this. If you buy this suit for me, you'll have to let me pay for dinner tonight. Is there any other way I can repay you?"

Lisa winked her eye and said, "I'll definitely let you know later."

When we left the mall Lisa asked me to drive her to the supermarket. We were just like a real couple. I was starting to get used to the idea of being with her. She made me feel like I was the man. I loved driving Lisa's car. Her Volvo was so smooth that it felt like we were riding on air. I looked so damn good behind the wheel. Lisa gave me a key to her house and that made me feel like I was officially her man. I was driving a fancy car, I had a pocket full of money and I was spending the evening with a sex goddess. I was about to spend the night with Lisa and I didn't have to worry about my parent's consent. I kept thinking that we had the entire house to ourselves and an entire week of uninterrupted sex. I was excited. What more could I ask for? The only thing I didn't like was I had a woman taking care of me. It was only temporary, but I really wanted to be a little more independent.

When we got back to Lisa's place we showered together. We did some of the most passionate kissing ever.

"Wanna see me get myself off?"

"Damn, you know that's my weakness."

We had reservations and I didn't want to be late.

I thought, *What the hell, we're black, we're supposed to be late.*

I needed to see Lisa get herself off. I watched as she lathered her body up with liquid body wash. She took the lather down to her sensitive spots. I looked at her wondering where she came from. I'd never seen a woman with so much sex appeal. She lathered my body up and down. I loved feeling her nails as she ran them all over my body. Lisa went back to pleasing herself.

"You're the rainmaker. Ooh, baby you make me so wet."

I was so into this. In my smoothest voice I freestyled a poem.

"I come to you when you need me most. Making your hot summer nights wet. I'm the rainmaker. Giving you relief from your heat. Rain for me. Rain til it's dripping wet. I'll make you wet... I'll make you sweat. Let it rain...let it rain. So beautiful...so wet. Flow for me. Let it go...let it flow. I wanna drown in your emotions. See the rain...be the rain. I wanna get deep in your water...lost inside your love. Do you like the flow? I'm the rainmaker. Making you wet. Giving you relief from your heat. You'll never have a drought as long as you have me."

Lisa rushed me to her bed.

I asked, "What's your fantasy?"

"I want you inside me. Do me slow and hard."

When I penetrated Lisa, she looked like I was a lot more than she anticipated. Her breathing pattern changed. I ran my tongue all around her neck and gave her little kisses.

I said, "Talk to me. Is it good to you? This thing's good for you."

"Forget doing it to me slow. Give it to me fast, deep and hard."

All I heard were screams of pleasure. We reached our climaxes together. We were a sexual match made in heaven, blessed with the skills to please one another. Lisa held me so tight she wouldn't let me go. Her body was shaking.

She said, "I love you...I love you."

"I love you too. You're my sweetheart."

Lisa and I laid there for hours lost in ecstasy.

61

The next morning we made love again in front of a mirror. It was a beautiful sight to see. Needless to say, we never made it to dinner the night before. I called and made reservations in my name for that evening.

Lisa said, "We needed to stick to our normal workout routine."

I smiled, "I thought we already had a good workout."

"That was a good workout, but we still need to go jogging or something."

Lisa got out of bed to walk to the bathroom and almost fell on her face.

I cracked up laughing. "You're talking shit because you're too weak in the knees to even walk to the bathroom. I think you had your workout for today."

"You might be right. Now, help me to the bathroom."

We laughed. I got up and helped Lisa to the bathroom.

We eventually got ourselves together and went power walking. I was Lisa's man and I liked it. We were having an incredible time together. When we got back from walking. The phone rang and Lisa answered.

She said, "It's Monica."

I forgot that I had given her that damn phone number. I was worried Monica's call would spoil the mood. Lisa never left the room, so I felt limited in what I was able to say.

"Hello."

"Hi, Eric. How's everything going?"

"Everything's going pretty good. So, what's new with you?"

"My parents bought me a brand new Honda Civic."

"That's real nice. What color is it?"

"White. When are you gonna come see my car."

"Soon, real soon."

"Are you okay?"

"Yeah, it's just that Lisa has to use the phone."

"Okay, I'll be in touch."

"I'll talk to you later."

I was happy to hear from Monica, but I had to cut the

conversation short because I was too uncomfortable talking to her with Lisa on my back.

Lisa laughed at me. "I had to use the phone, what a weak line."

"What did you expect me to say with you all on my back like that?"

"Oh, if you needed some privacy all you had to do was ask. Anyway, later for her. You're all mine this week."

Lisa and I decided to go to the movies. We had a lot of time to kill before dinner, so we went to the Harbor Park Movie Theater in downtown Baltimore. After the movie we went to a seafood restaurant overlooking the inner harbor. The restaurant was what I considered elegant. Our waiter reminded me of a fake-ass Mr. Bentley from the *Jefferson's*. I think he intentionally made his accent heavier to give the restaurant more of an international appeal. I wasn't impressed by his accent at all, but the food was impressive. We had crab cakes for our appetizer and jumbo lobster with steamed vegetables for the entree. Lisa drank a glass of white wine. I ordered a ginger ale and a virgin strawberry daiquiri. We had a hot dinner conversation about the love we made the night before. Talking to Lisa about sex was foreplay in itself. We made each other hot just by talking. We went on and on talking about sex. All of a sudden Lisa had serious look on her face.

"I wanna be honest with you."

I thought, *Oh, no.* "I'm listening."

"I never told you this before, but I have a boyfriend."

I thought, *Not this shit again.* "Who is he?"

"Mike and I have been dating for a few months."

I knew him, but it was hard for me to imagine them together. She hardly ever saw him because he lived in Washington, D.C. He would be in town in a couple of days for a show Soul Survivors were doing at a restaurant. I did appreciate her honesty because she really didn't have to tell me.

"That's not all. We've had sex a few times and I'm not sure if I'm going to stop having sex with him."

That made me mad. I had to calm myself down because she told me from the start that this wasn't going to be a serious relationship. Lisa's announcement knocked the wind out of me, but I was okay. Monica was starting to look better and better. Lisa really spoiled the mood. I was glad she didn't try to deceive me. A part of me wished that she had just kept the news to herself.

"Thanks for being honest with me. Anyway, you said this was just a physical thing."

After dinner Lisa and I walked around the harbor for awhile. I couldn't think of anything to say to her. I could tell that Lisa felt bad about what happened.

"I'm sorry, Eric."

"There's no need to apologize because you didn't do anything wrong."

I gave her a hug. "Can we just go home?"

I needed to sleep this off, then I would be fine.

When we got home I had my confidence back.

I looked at Lisa and said, "Fuck Mike. You're all mine tonight and what I'm gonna put on your ass, he won't take off. Skip the foreplay I want you right now."

We undressed each other quickly. I picked Lisa up and laid her out on the bed and gave her a deep kiss. I put her legs in the air and I penetrated her so deep that I could feel her cervix. I made her scream from pleasure and pain. She looked like it hurt so good. I grabbed her foot and put her toes in my mouth. I kissed, licked and sucked all her toes. The sexual beast was coming out of me. I wanted to override Lisa's system with pleasure. I turned her over and started hitting her hard from behind.

"Does Mike fuck you like this? Does he give it to you this good?" Lisa screamed, "NO...NO!!!"

I made her take every inch of me. She was so hot. Lisa was about to release her sexual beast. She motioned for me to lie on my back. She got on top of me and rode me like she was in the home stretch of the Preakness. I pulled over a chair and had her straddle me. She was in for a long hard ride. We liked to call this position the "Rugged Raw." I grabbed her by the ass and made her ride me

64

faster and faster. I asked her if she had any other fantasies. She had me lay on the floor on my back. She straddled my face. She did more straddling that night than a cowgirl at a rodeo. I liked this a lot. I couldn't breath, but it really turned me on. Lisa reversed her position into a 69. Now, we were both giving and receiving pleasure at the same time. I loved her for being such an unselfish lover.

At first, I was a little intimidated by Mike. I soon forgot all about him. Lisa was mine and nobody could tell me any different. We had sex like this almost every night.

The next day Lisa and I just stayed home and chilled. We rented some videos and ordered pizza. We lived like lazy bums that day and we loved it. My parents called to see how things were going. I told them things couldn't have been better and I wasn't lying. They said they would see me in a few days.

I felt so mellow. Lisa had that affect on me. It was her, the house and her overall lifestyle. She was incredible and I was in love with her no matter how hard I tried to deny it. Monica was in trouble. I felt like I couldn't give Lisa up even if I wanted. She was too good to me.

WHEN NIGHT FALLS: 6

Lisa had to go meet up with the band for a rehearsal. I didn't want to go, so I told her I would see everybody at the restaurant the next night. I used the time that Lisa was away to call Monica. I needed a Plan-B just in case this thing with Lisa didn't work out. Monica seemed surprised to hear from me. I told her I was going to see her soon. At first I wasn't trying to see her until my parents came back home. I wanted to ride my experience with Lisa out to the end. I came up with an idea to have Monica meet me at Lisa's house. I wanted her to go with me to the restaurant where Soul Survivors were performing the next night. Lisa said she wanted to meet Monica and I couldn't think of a better time. Lisa was going to have Mike and I didn't want to be alone.

When Lisa got back from her rehearsal she was so excited. The group's manager had booked dates for the next two months for them to perform at some local clubs. She was really excited because they were going to perform at two local festivals, Artscape and Afram. They were now on the same shows with some nationally known acts. I was happy for Lisa and I encouraged her to do something solo. I felt she would have a better chance of making it big by going solo.

"I invited Monica over tomorrow evening so the two of you can finally meet."

"Ask her to join us at the restaurant for the show."

"I did already."

"Oh."

"Is that a problem? Don't tell me you're getting jealous."

She smiled and said, "I'm happy you have a little girlfriend." I left that alone because I wasn't in the mood for an argument. That was her little way of saying she was going to be with Mike anyway. I couldn't wait to see Monica. I was getting tired of Lisa's shit. I had to be around Mike and act like everything was okay. I gave Lisa space that night. I had no idea what she and Mike had been doing earlier. I imagined they had a little quickie somewhere. I had to stop because I was making myself mad.

Monica came over and she looked so damn good. That was exactly what I wanted. I wanted Lisa to see that my other girl was no joke. I told Monica to have a seat while I got Lisa. I felt like I had invited Monica to the scene of the crime. I was praying that Lisa would be nice. She had the power to ruin me. Earlier, I'd practiced my facial expressions in the mirror. I didn't want anything to give me away.

Lisa looked pretty damn good herself. I told her that Monica was there waiting in the living room.

When Lisa came into the living room I said, "Monica this is my good friend Lisa and Lisa this is my good friend Monica."

They smiled and seemed to hit it off well. They complimented each other from head to toe. Monica told Lisa how beautiful her house was. They kept going on and on talking amongst themselves not saying a word to me. I swear, they talked so long that I thought they were exchanging beauty secrets or something. I felt left out for a minute. I liked seeing the two of them together. They were quite similar. Monica was just a few shades darker and a few inches shorter. I began to zone out into a fantasy of the three of us having a ménage `a trois. I thought of how sexy a triple kiss would be. I was getting rock hard from my fantasy.

Lisa said, "Eric, let's go."

She must have read my mind. She looked right at me and noticed how hard I was. Because of my hard-on, I walked by Lisa like I was crippled or something. When Monica wasn't looking, Lisa copped a quick feel. I think her freaky-ass mind was probably on the same thing I was thinking. Dirty minds always think alike. Lisa left ahead of me and Monica because she was due at the restaurant at 6:30 p.m. We planned to arrive around 7 p.m. Soul Survivors were scheduled to go on at 7:30 p.m.

We arrived at the restaurant and right away we noticed the place was packed. Blackness was in full effect. My people were representing and I loved the way most of the crowd looked. A few people looked like they were trying to keep most of the top fashion designers in business for at least another year. I saw one guy in a tight-ass white suit with white shoes. He really didn't have to match that well. Another guy made me laugh with his cheap lookin' three piece lavender suit. I couldn't understand why people felt like they had to wear their Easter suits when they went out for an ordinary evening. I looked casual in my khaki pants and Polo knit shirt. Monica wore a pretty summer dress accented with earthy colors and her afrocentric jewelry. We looked appropriate for this type of gathering. I noticed Mike up front. I went over to speak and to introduce him and Monica.

Mike said, "What's up Eric, I reserved a table for you and your date."

I thought, *Damn, why does he have to be so nice?*

I shook Mike's hand and thanked him for reserving our table. I introduced him to Monica.

"You've got good taste."

I thought, *I know I'm fucking your girl.*

I said, "Thanks, good luck tonight."

Mike walked away with a goofy grin greeting other people. He was a cool guy, but I couldn't see what the hell Lisa saw in him. Monica and I sat back, relaxed and ordered drinks and appetizers.

The bandstand was empty until a guy stepped up to the mic.

He said, "Pabulum's is proud to present Baltimore's own Soul Survivors."

The crowd went wild. I was so proud of the group. The band came out first. They started playing a smooth instrumental tune. They got halfway through the song when Lisa appeared out of the darkness. She looked totally different from earlier. She had on a multicolor dress with a matching head wrap that she made herself. Her dreadlocks flowed from her head wrap. Her makeup was very tasteful. She was barefoot with a toe ring on each foot and an anklet. The band was kickin'. Mike played the bass like he was making love to the strings. Kevin beat the drums like they owed him money. Stanley blew the hell out the sax and Malik made a killing on the keyboard. Lisa's voice was as sultry and seductive as ever. She sounded so good that she give me chills all over my body. The girl could sing. Soul Survivors did about seven songs before they stopped for an intermission. The band blew the crowd away with their sound.

Lisa said, "We're gonna take a break, but before we break, I wanna bring to the stage a young man who's gonna set your souls on fire with his poetry. Eric, come bless this stage with your lyrical presence."

I thought, *Where the hell did this come from?*

Monica said, "Oh Eric, I didn't know you were part of the show."

Under my breath I said, "Neither did I."

I was mad. What was I going to say? I kept thinking I'm a poet...I'm a poet...I'm a poet. I was so nervous that I didn't even remember standing up to walk to the stage. When my vision cleared I was standing in front of a restaurant filled with people staring directly at me. The band started playing a smooth mellow groove.

I took a deep breath and said, "Good evening. This poem was inspired by true love. I'd like to dedicate it to my future wife. Wherever she is. My poem is entitled *When Night Falls.*"

When night falls
Black love's on the rise
The look in your eyes...a simple translation of love
Red, black, and green set the scene
Darkness made beautiful by candlelight
Silence amplifies the sound of I love you whispered gently in your
ear
Tonight actions speak louder than words
In an instant two bodies become one
Let me take you on a journey led by love
We'll explore the pleasure in your valley
Taking you to the mountain top
Black love...black beauty
Both symbolic of the motherland

When night falls
Black love's on the rise
No surprise God brought us together
Tonight we'll fulfill our true purpose
As we combine to create
I'll plant the root
You'll bear the fruit
Together we'll spread the seeds
We lust...we love...tonight and forever
Our passion's hot as hell but heaven sent

I said, "I'd like to thank God for this gift and Soul Survivors for
letting me share it with you. Goodnight and God bless."
I gave Lisa a hug as she walked to the mic.
I whispered in her ear, "I'm going to kick your ass."
Then, I turned and smiled to the crowd as I returned to my seat.
Lisa said, "Did y'all feel that or what? I told y'all he was all that.
Show him some love. That's my little brother."
The crowd applauded. I heard a few whistles and yells.

Monica said, "That was so beautiful."

"Thanks. I think I did good considering I was unconscious through half of it."

I had to thank God because I really didn't know how I did it. I was never so nervous. I wrote that poem for Monica about a month earlier, but she'd never heard it. I had never even recited it before that night. It was the only poem I could think of at that exact moment.

Monica and I had finished eating dinner by the time the band came on again. The second half of the show was even better than the first half. They truly gave the crowd something to remember. At the end of the show I told Lisa to never ever do that to me again. I actually gave her a little kick in the ass.

"What if I didn't have anything prepared at all? You would have made a fool of me."

"A true poet is always prepared."

Lisa was right, but she made me sick because she always had an answer for everything. I wasn't really mad, I kind of liked the exposure. I just needed more notice.

Mike came up to me and gave me a hug. I was as stiff as a board. He said, "I wish I had skills like you."

He was so goofy. He kept setting himself up. I almost said, "If you had my skills your girl wouldn't be fucking me." Instead, I said, "Thanks, brotha."

The other guys in the band told me what a good job I did being put on the spot like that. Lisa pulled me to the side to tell me that she was going out with the band and would be home late. I was fine with that because I still had about two hours or more to spend with Monica before she was due home. I had a lot of respect for Monica's parents and I didn't want to keep her out too late. They didn't know she was out with me. All they knew was that she was having dinner with friends.

Monica and I went to my house. I didn't feel right taking Monica back to Lisa's house without her being home. I missed my house. I hadn't been there all week. Monica and I sat in a dimly lit living room watching a movie and sharing a bag of microwave popcorn. The television was the only sound in the room until Monica spoke.

"So, who was this wife you mentioned tonight?"

"Nobody, I was just saying something to peak the crowd's interest. I needed to take up a little time and to inspire myself."

"Who do you think she'll be or who would you want her to be?"

Monica knew it was her. She just wanted to hear it come out of my mouth.

I looked into her eyes and said, "I've heard good things come to those who wait and I've waited a whole year. My time has finally arrived. I can't hold back any longer. My inspiration for the poem was you. Monica, you're the inspiration for everything I do. You're a part of me. I've loved you since the first time I saw you."

Monica was speechless.

I asked, "Can you say something?"

She softly said, "I love you too. I've loved you for a long time. All this time I've wondered how you felt about me. I hoped you felt the same way. It's nice to hear you say you love me."

I was so relieved.

"I want to give you my heart. You're my precious sunflower." I pulled her close and caressed her. "You're so beautiful."

I kissed her gently on the lips. I felt Monica's tongue slide across mine. She was ready. I could tell that she was nervous. I felt her heart beating against my chest. I slowly ran my hands up the sides of her face. With her face in my hands I pulled her in closer and gave her a deep passionate kiss. I felt sensations all over my body. I laid back on the sofa and Monica laid on top. Her body melted into mine. We were both feeling it. We were on a straight love high. Our bodies felt like one. Chest to chest and hand in hand gripped in a lovelock. Nothing could separate us until I realized what time it was.

I said, "It's getting late. I have to send you home before your parents send the cops out looking for you."

Monica laughed, but she knew I was right. "Thank you for such a

72

lovely evening."

With a smile I said, "It was all my pleasure. I'm looking forward to doing this again."

We kissed goodnight and I walked her to her car.

I thought, *Simply unbelievable.* She was sweet, beautiful and classy...a real lady. I loved the way Monica carried herself. She was well worth the wait.

I went back to lock my front door and headed back to Lisa's house. I didn't notice Lisa's car. I went inside her house. She wasn't home yet. Mike must have gotten lucky. I headed straight for Lisa's bedroom. I took a shower, then watched some television. I was so tired that I fell asleep within minutes. I woke up at 4:30 am. and Lisa still wasn't home. I was pissed. I was worried something bad might have happened to her. I got up and went downstairs. I was on my way to the kitchen when I noticed the basement light was on. I opened the door and peeked down the steps. I expected to see Mike and Lisa fucking like sweaty dogs, but to my surprise the basement was empty. Lisa or I forgot to turn off the damn light.

Lisa walked in the house about an hour later. I was wide-awake. She looked at me with a weird facial expression.

She said, "What's up, Shorty."

"Take your drunk ass and go sleep in the guestroom. You should be ashamed of yourself."

I was in her bed butt-naked talking shit. Lisa was so drunk she actually went to the guestroom to sleep. The next morning I let her sleep until 11 a.m.

I yelled, "Lisa, I'm going out."

I was going to meet up with Monica at her house, so we could wash our cars together.

Monica looked even prettier than I remembered. I helped her wash her car first. I showed her all the intricate details for keeping her car looking and smelling new. I was saying a bunch of nothing, but she paid attention to me like I was revealing life's greatest secrets. I could tell that she really liked me because she kept staring

73

at me. I knew what she wanted.

"Let me show you how to clean up under this seat."

She got inside the car and I pulled her down low enough so her parents couldn't see us kiss. After we finished washing the cars we went to Druid Hill Park in my car. I picked out a nice spot under a tree. We stayed there for about an hour kissing, holding hands and talking. I got aroused, but I knew this was as far as it was going to go. I was fine with that. I had a lot of respect for Monica. I asked her if we could hook up and go to the movies later. We had to go home and get out of our car washing gear. I asked if she minded if I invited Troy and Jennifer to the movies with us. She said it sounded like a good idea. I wanted to do something different. I decided that we should go to Georgetown for dinner and a movie. I called Troy and he liked the idea. I asked him to call Jennifer and fill her in on all the details. I was excited about all of us going out together on a double date.

I went back to Lisa's house and she was finally up.

She asked, "Where have you been?"

"I went to wash my car at Monica's."

She looked kind of upset. "What?"

Lisa rolled her eyes.

"You stayed out all night and all I did was wash my car with Monica. How the hell can you be mad at me?"

"I just wanted to spend time with you today."

"You were too hung over to do anything. I asked you to get into bed with me last night and you marched your ass right to the guestroom like you were mad at me. I was worried all night that something happened to you."

I was able to keep a straight face even though I lied about the whole guestroom thing.

"Please forget about that. I want to do something special tonight. Your parents are due back in the morning."

"I made plans to go out with my other friends tonight. You understand, don't you?"

"No!" Lisa smiled. "I'm just playing. So you finally made a move

74

on Monica?"

"Yeah, something like that."

Lisa laughed. "I guess she fell for that future wife line."

She made me laugh. "It was a lot more than that line, but the line did help. I have to get ready."

Lisa gave me a kiss and told me to be good to Monica. That was too easy. I thought this was her way of telling me we were done. Sometimes you don't have to announce a break up. The signs are so obvious. Lisa was spending more time with Mike and I wasn't so interested in making love to her anymore and I'm sure it had a lot to do with Goofy Mike. All Lisa was ever used to was short-term relationships. She tried to act like her heart wasn't involved in our relationship, but I knew different. I just wanted to be the best I could be to Monica. Thanks to Lisa, I still had hundreds of dollars in my pocket. I was going to show Monica an unbelievable evening.

Monica was going to meet me at my house. Before she arrived I wanted to get her some roses. I went to a florist to pick up a dozen mixed roses. The bouquet was a perfect arrangement of red, white, pink and yellow roses. Monica was the first girl I had ever given flowers. I knew she was going to love this. I was happy that she was meeting me at my house, because we didn't want her parents to know we were dating. Monica told them that she was just going out with friends. We wanted our relationship to appear as innocent as possible.

When Monica arrived she gave me a sexy little kiss. She was so surprised when I gave her the roses. When I looked at her she had tears in her eyes. No one had ever given her roses. The roses were a nice touch.

We had to wait for Jennifer and Troy. When they arrived we decided to go in separate vehicles. I liked that idea because Monica and I could have privacy. The ride to Georgetown seemed shorter than usual. Maybe, it had something to do with the fact that Troy and I raced most of the way.

We parked in a garage and took a horse and buggy to the theater.

I thought that was a real classy move and the girls loved it. Troy looked at me like he was thinking, *I ain't paying for this shit, man.* Of course, I paid for the ride. In the movie theater, Monica and I sat away from Troy and Jennifer. We drank soda, ate popcorn and kissed throughout the entire movie. I peeked over at Troy and Jennifer and they were enjoying the movie. I mean, they were more into the movie than each other. When Troy noticed me looking at them, he gave Jennifer a quick little kiss on the lips. He was too funny. After the movie we walked across the street to a restaurant. Troy looked at me with that same crazy look from earlier. This time he whispered in my ear.

"Man, it's a McDonald's farther down the street and a Burger King about two blocks over. I already paid Jennifer's way to the movie and I need gas money to get back home."

I pulled him to the side.

"I'll pay for the girls, but I ain't feeding your hungry ass."

Troy shook my hand and gave me a hug.

"Hey, act like you got some class."

I was willing to do whatever it took to show Monica a good time. She deserved to be catered to and pampered. During dinner Monica kept running her foot up and down my leg. She looked so seductive eating dinner. She was a little freakier than I thought. I was getting turned on like crazy. Alarms were going off in my head. *Danger-Danger, Monica's playing with fire and has no idea that my shit's the bomb.* When I looked at her again she had this I-wanna-fuck look on her face.

I asked, "Was dinner good? Did everybody have a good time? I'm gonna pay this man and we're gonna get the hell out of here." Monica looked ready. We left the restaurant and I flagged down another horse and buggy to take us straight to our cars.

When we got back to the cars I said, "Troy go 'head and we'll catch up with y'all tomorrow. Goodnight Jennifer."

I opened the car door for Monica. As soon as I got in the car we attacked each other. Monica was hot. I had never seen her like this. I started the car and drove to a less populated area of the garage.

Monica took my hand and put it down her panties. Oh my God, she was dripping wet.

Monica said, "Please, put your finger inside."

This was like a dream because she was so different. I loved this so much. Monica closed her eyes, clinched her fist and teeth real tight. She raised her head and body slowly.

Monica screamed, "I'm coming!!!"

I was in shock. She grabbed me and held tight. She was breathing like she had just finished a marathon.

I said, "Damn, that was good. I don't mean to sound stupid, but are you really a virgin?"

"Yeah, I'm in training for the real thing. I taught myself how to come like that."

My mouth fell open and my tongue hit the steering wheel.

"You like to masturbate?"

"Yeah."

"Can I watch you one day?"

"Yeah, I'd like that."

"I love you."

"I love you too."

We kissed.

Monica slept the entire way home. When we got back home I gave her the sweetest goodnight kiss. She was my new sweetheart. I couldn't wait to see her again. Lisa wasn't home, so I wrote her a note saying that I was going to spend my last night alone at my house. I missed sleeping in my own bed and I slept like a baby. My parents were due back in the morning. I had to savor those last few minutes of freedom.

The next morning after my parents got back home, I decided to go over to Lisa's house to sit in my favorite spot in her living room and write poetry. Her living room was the perfect place for inspiration. Lisa's front door was locked and I didn't want to wake her, so I used my key. As soon as I opened her front door a naked, bony, yellow ass greeted me. I swear the asshole winked at me. I caught Mike in an up stroke. He was giving Lisa a little pleasure.

I said, "I'm sorry. I was looking for inspiration to write."
I was in the right place, but definitely at the wrong time. Mike and
Lisa were in the living room having sex in my former favorite spot.
Lisa was so embarrassed that she hid her face behind Mike's arm. I
don't know how I looked, but I laughed my ass off when I got
outside. I was so embarrassed for Lisa. I guess she forgot that she
gave me a key. Lisa and I ended on such a positive note, but Goofy
Mike had to show his ass.

MONICA: 7

My parents returned from their Vegas trip energized and all in love. I hadn't seen them that happy in a long time. My mother was glowing. My father must have put it on her real good. He probably tried some new shit he picked up from one of his freaks. It was good to see them so happy.

My father said, "Eric, we're going to skip the annual family reunion. Your mother and I are going to Jamaica. Would you like to go?"

I wasn't trying to go back to North Carolina. I had no real desire to relive that shit again. Stacey was history. Lisa and I were done, no real desire to stick around with her. I didn't want to leave Monica behind, but I wasn't going to worry too much about her.

I said, "Hell yeah dad, I'm going!"

I was so excited about an idea that popped in my head that I cursed in front of my parents. I pictured myself in Jamaica with Monica by my side. My parents just looked at each other and ignored my small use of profanity.

I called Monica as soon as I finished talking to my parents. I wanted her to come to my house to spend time with me and my family. I wanted my parents to get used to her being around the house. I had big plans in store for us. When she arrived at my house my parents greeted her at the front door with smiles. They knew how much I liked her, but they were just a little too overjoyed to see her. They didn't know that we were already dating. I feared she would think something was weird about them. I didn't want them to scare her away from our house. I needed them to tone it down a little. My parents were excited about seeing Monica again because they hadn't seen her since we started the mentoring program. My mother invited Monica to stay for dinner. My parents bought up the trip to Jamaica. I asked my parents if Monica could join us in Jamaica. Everyone looked so surprised that I asked that question. My parents told Monica they would be glad to have her join us. My father offered to pay for her airfare. She would have her own room in our private villa. I figured that if I put my parents on the spot they wouldn't let me down. Now we just had to sell this idea to Monica's parents.

My parent's went to Monica's house with us to help persuade her parents. Her parents were good people. Her dad was a graduate of Morgan State University and a local talk radio host. Her mother was a graduate of Spelman College and a top real estate agent. Monica had told them what a nice person I was and they thought the world of me. They always talked about seeing me on the news for mentoring program. They were impressed with the work we did with those kids. For some reason, Monica's parents saw us as having a brother-sister type relationship. Maybe it was because they really saw me as a nice guy. I was hoping Monica and I gave them the brother-sister impression. That must have been the case because they gave Monica permission to join us in Jamaica. They said it would be a good experience for her. My parents promised to supervise us at all times. I knew that Jamaica was a beautiful and romantic place and it was going to be hard for us to resist one another. I respected Monica and didn't really want to corrupt her, but she would be lucky to leave Jamaica with her virginity still intact. I didn't know if she could hold out for marriage or not. As my girlfriend, she would be doing great to keep her virginity until her eighteenth birthday. I was bad and I knew it. I was happy that Monica was going with us to Jamaica. I made my move on her at the right time.

I told my parents that Monica and I started dating while they were away. They were excited for me. My mother gave me a hug and my father gave me a high five. It took them a second to process what I said.

Together my parents shouted, "Don't be a fool in Jamaica."

My father said, "We're going to watch the two of you like hawks."

My mother asked, "Have the two of you had sex yet?"

I shook my head. "No, we haven't had sex yet. Monica's a virgin. She plans to stay that way until she's married."

My mother said, "That's good. You better leave that girl alone. Don't force her to have sex."

My father started in on me next. "You better take your time. You've got a lot going for you. Don't mess around and become a teenage father. You're going to be a doctor. What would you like your specialty to be?"

I thought he was joking.

I said "I'm not sure right now."

I didn't have the nerve to tell him I had no plans of becoming a doctor. I was tired of hearing about all the sons and daughters entering and graduating from medical schools. My father was a graduate of the University of Maryland School of Medicine.

He said, "When the time comes all you have to do is apply and you're guaranteed a spot in medical school. Surgery is where your focus should be. I've started a great legacy. I want you to follow in my footsteps. Doctors get so much respect from everyone. If you become a surgeon you'll receive twice the respect of a general practitioner. Being a surgeon is the best career you could ever have. What if your son becomes a doctor? We would have three generations of excellence. We would go down in University

Hospital's history. Become a doctor, son, and the world will be yours."

My father wanted me to come down to the hospital to observe and meet some important people. He was so set on me becoming a doctor that it was like a sickness. I only saw myself going to college long enough to receive an undergraduate degree. I was seventeen and four years of college even seemed like a long time. I couldn't even begin to think about medical school. I didn't want the stress or responsibilities of being a doctor. I didn't want to carry a pager and be on call like my father. I agreed to go to the hospital just to keep the peace. Maybe I would see something or meet someone to change my opinion.

The next morning we left for the hospital around 6:15 a.m. My father was scheduled to work a 12 hour shift that day. He introduced me to so many people that I was sick of smiling and shaking hands. Some people I recognized from previous visits to his job. Others I didn't know, but they recognized me from meeting me years ago. They treated me like royalty since both my parents worked there in top positions. My father had to rush off for an emergency surgical case. He told me I could stay around the operating room or go to the emergency room to find my mother. I headed straight for my mother's office. She was the nurse manager of the emergency room. My mother was surprised to see me and asked if I was enjoying myself. I told her I was having the time of my life. She told me she had two very important people she wanted me to meet. The first person was a young black guy named Terence Stevenson. He was the nurse manager of the medical-surgical unit. Terence was the first male nurse I had ever seen. He was built like an athlete. I couldn't figure out why he was a nurse. Terence was a Naval Hospital Corpsman before going into nursing school. He said Hospital Corpsman were like unlicensed nurses in the military. Corpsman were mostly males, but there were some female Corpsman. I had never heard of them before this. He served in military hospitals, ships and as a Marine field medic. He took me on a tour of his unit. My mother knew I didn't want to be a doctor and I was starting to see what she was doing. Next, she took me to the Family Health Clinic to meet the nurse manager. Corey Jones was another young black male nurse. He wasn't as fit as Terence, but he was a big guy. It was strange seeing two male nurses. Not only were they nurses, but they were straight young black men running shit. I was real impressed. Corey took me on a tour of his clinic. He explained that the clinic was intended to serve the city's underprivileged population. I noticed a young boy named William from my mentoring program. He was there with his pregnant girlfriend. They were only fifteen years old. When William noticed me he ran over to greet me. He seemed happy to see me and told me he was doing well.

He was fifteen in the eighth grade. He had become discouraged and planned to drop out of school when he was recommended for the mentoring program. The program helped to encourage him to stay in school and also helped him study. The principal, teachers and counselors saw a dramatic improvement in him. They recommended he be put in his right grade. William was an intelligent boy who simply lost focus. He said the mentoring program put him back on track and he would be starting high school in the fall. William made me feel real proud. I wished he hadn't made his girlfriend pregnant, but at least he was back on track with school. He made me look really impressive in front of Corey. He congratulated me on my success with William. Corey and Terence were nice guys and I appreciated what they did for me. The hospital looked like a beautiful place to work. The women outnumbered the men twenty to one. Women were everywhere. I imagined that male nurses were a hot commodity around the hospital. I was starting to feel like I could do this nursing stuff. I still needed more information. I knew my mother was going to fill me in on all the details. My father would be pissed off if he knew what I was planning. He would probably disown me if I became a nurse.

When I went back home my father said he would set up another day for me to return to the hospital. I told him I'd seen enough. I hated to disappoint him, but I was pretty sure about my plans. I had to keep my plans to myself because if I had told him what was on my mind he would have killed me. I was his only child and I felt like he was putting too much pressure on me. He never asked me what I would like to be. I really wanted to become a writer. I was blessed with the ability to write short stories and poetry.

History always has a way of repeating itself. Years ago before my grandfather died he wanted my father to take over his business. My grandfather owned and managed residential and commercial real-estate properties. My father refused to take over his father's business because he dreamed of becoming a doctor. My grandfather still supported him and paid his way through medical school. It hurt my grandfather, but he respected my father's dream. They were able to compromise and my father promised to keep the business in existence whether he managed it or not. How could I compromise with my father?

My future was important to me, but I wanted to focus on summer fun with Monica. I called to fill her in on my new revelation. I told her all about my day and Monica thought it was a good idea for me to become a nurse. She agreed with my father that doctors were well respected. She said it could be very profitable. I told her that I had definitely decided to attend the University of Maryland at Baltimore, the same place my mother went to school.

Monica was undecided on a school or a major. She wanted to attend Spelman, Morgan or Maryland. Spelman was her first choice and definitely my last choice for her. The idea of her being that far from me drove me crazy. I told her I needed her close to me. I had no intentions of going to school out of state. I didn't want to talk about college anymore, so I asked Monica if she would like to go to Pabulum's to see Soul Survivors again. They were also having an open mic poetry night. I didn't want to recite anything, I just wanted to listen to other people.

Pabulum's was one of my favorite spots. Pabulum actually means food for thought and that's what they offered food for the mind, body and soul. I could feel the spiritual energy from that place from miles away.

We arrived to another packed house. This time was not quite as dramatic. We had a table in the back and I liked that better. Something very different happened that night. The group was announced as Soul Survivors featuring Lisa Ashford. Oh shit, Lisa was taking my advice. I predicted she would leave the group by the end of summer. I think the success and attention was starting to go to somebody's head. Mike and Malik started the group, but they needed to change Lisa's name to Soul Survivor because she was the only member who was going to make it. I swear it looked like Mike and Malik were checking the crowd for a replacement lead singer. You could hear and see the confidence in Lisa's performance. She always looked very professional when she performed. I knew it was just a matter of time and I was sure that they felt things coming to an end. During the intermission they opened the mic for poetry. For a second it looked like no one was going up until Monica jumped out of her seat. She shocked the hell out of me. I was nervous for her.

Monica stepped to the mic and said, "Good evening, the title of my poem is *Black*."

His love swept me off my feet
Picked me up and gently brought me down
Somewhere between the love we made last night
And how love came storming in
Love was the wind
I was rain
And he was the thunder

I dig his beautiful Black figure
In my eyes there's nothing bigger
He's my man and I love him
There's no brotha above him
He's captured my heart

85

So other brothas ain't got nothing coming
They just can't compare to his love and intensity
Black is my man
And my man is Black

His love has taken me to levels I've never known
Winter, Spring, Summer and Fall...this brothas got it all
So strong...so Black...so beautiful
I long for his love
And his love is long
He taps all my dimensions
Mind, body and soul
He loves me down to my core
His love keeps me warm and makes me hot
He gives me safety and security
Love and belonging
My days are filled with...Ooh
My nights are filled with...Ah
My dreams are filled with loving Black
I'm his queen of the unseen
He's the king of infinite wisdom and possibilities
If love was a house
Then his heart would be my home
Black is my man
And my man is Black

I was completely blown away by Monica's poem. I had never
heard her poem before. She always added a sexual element in her
poetry. I bet the entire crowd thought I was tapping that. Her poem
even made me think I was tapping that. The sweet thing was that I
really tapped her heart. She was in love with me. It was right then
and there I realized that Monica was really mine. My first exclusive
girlfriend. No other guy was going to pop up and claim her. She
was all mine. As Monica approached the table I stood up and

applauded. I give her hug a kiss on the lips. I had to play the part of the smooth lover man. I heard women cheering and guys saying, "Yeah Black!" I picked up the nickname Black and from that night on my friends referred to me as Black. It started to grow on me after awhile.

Monica and I didn't stick around to talk to Lisa or the band. We decided to head back to my house for awhile. I kept staring at Monica all night. I was trying to predict her next move. When we got my house I laid on the sofa. She crawled on top of me and we started kissing. Monica worked her tongue deeper and deeper. She tasted so good that I wanted to eat her alive. I was hungry for her. I thought I had to play it cool because my parents were home. They were in for the night, but I figured they were upstairs making love. We were all the way in the family room. To be on the safe side I pulled the double doors to the family room closed and locked them. Monica was all mine. She felt good when I cuddled up next to her. I ran my fingers through her hair gently massaging her scalp. I whispered in her ear as I massaged her.

I said, "I love you so much."

I nibbled on her earlobe. She could hear me breathing.

I whispered, "I want you so bad. I wanna touch you in every way."

Monica's long black silky hair felt so good to me. I was putting her at ease. I moved my hands from her hair to her temples. She loved the way I kissed her neck. I moved back to her hair, down to her neck and back. Her breathing was so intense. She sounded almost orgasmic. I turned her over and slowly began to unbutton her blouse.

I asked, "Can I taste you?"

She unsnapped her bra.

I said, "I wanna kiss you from head to toe until my tongue gets jealous. Then I'll lick you just like you like it. Am I making you hot? Is it getting wet?"

Monica smiled and nodded her head. Monica's breasts were beautiful. Round mounds of pleasure with sensitive peaks. I licked

87

my fingertips and ran them across her nipples making circles around them. I teased them with my tongue just enough to moisten. Her nipples were so hard. I gave her a little more tongue. I gently blew on her nipples for a chilling effect. Then I warmed them with my entire mouth giving a sucking sensation. I ran my lips around her breasts with little passionate kisses. With my hands I cupped her breast letting her nipples peak through my thumb and index fingers. I began to suck them again. She began to moan as if she needed special attention somewhere else. I let my tongue drop slowly down her abdomen and down her sides. I pulled up her skirt and began to kiss and suck her inner thighs. I worked my way down to her feet. She could feel my hands running up and down her legs. I began to massage her feet and she seemed surprised when I licked all over them. I took her right big toe and began to suck it and she moaned.

Monica said, "I can't take it. It feels too good. Please don't stop. You make me feel so good."

I worked my way back up to Monica's inner thighs.

I said, "I wanna be your everything. Your first, your last, your best and your one and only. Can I make you come?"

Monica said, "Yes, *please*."

I pulled down her panties with my mouth and dropped them on the floor. From her inner thighs I slowly made my way into the center. Up, down, and side to side. I hit all the right spots. This was her first time experiencing this. It started getting real good to her. Monica grabbed my head guided my tongue to her most sensitive spot.

She began to tighten up and scream. "Oh my God! That's it!"

Monica had to bite down on a sofa pillow to keep my parents and neighbors from calling the cops. I enjoyed giving her pleasure. She wanted to start up again on me, but I had to get her to her car. It was getting late and she had to get home. She couldn't stop telling me how good she felt.

As I walked back to my front door, I looked over at Lisa's house and she signaled for me to come over to her house.

88

I said, "No, I can't. I'll call you."

I didn't want to get too close. She would have been wondering if it was love in the air or just raw sex. I called her when I got inside my house. The first thing she mentioned was about Monica.

Lisa said, "I guess little Monica is getting real good to you by now."

"Yeah, she's my good thing...my sweet thing. I do miss your flavor a little."

I surprised her with that line.

"Well come get some."

"Mike's been beating my time. Punching the hell out that clock."

"Please, he couldn't work this shit if he wanted. I fired his ass last week."

"Bullshit, that's just a temporary lay off. He'll be back on the J-O-B next week." She knew I was right.

"Congratulations, Soul Survivor. Soon you'll be the only one left standing."

She laughed, "I'm taking your advice, remember? That's not important now. I still can't believe you walked in on me and Mike."

"I can't believe I did either. I thought I was blind for a minute."

"Fuck you."

"We'll talk about that tomorrow."

We both laugh.

"Let's go jogging in the morning."

"That's fine with me because we still need to talk about your career."

The next morning I met Lisa at her house. The weather was perfect for jogging. It was one of those clear sunny days that was filled with nothing but sunshine and fresh air. We jogged around the neighborhood instead of going to the high school track like we usually did. I apologized again for walking in on her and Mike. She begged me to forget about it. I needed to know her status with the group. Lisa said she was going to do a solo demo. She was getting so much attention that she told Mike to change the name of the group or she was out.

Lisa said, "It's time for a change. I'm on an entirely different page from the rest of group. They don't have big dreams like me. They're more focused on their jobs than their music. I'm doing most of the writing and singing. I really don't need them and I'm so tried of Mike I could scream."

"I'm glad you've finally taken my advice. I'm sure you'll make it big. One day Lisa Ashford will be a household name, but don't forget about me."

"No matter what happens I can't forget you. I'll take you on tour with me one day. Maybe I'll put you in one of my videos."

Lisa and I kept going on and on dreaming. I knew that Lisa was talented enough for all that to happen for real.

When I got back home Monica had called. She wanted to have lunch with me. She met me at my house and we went to the mall. She asked where I had been this morning.

I said, "I went jogging with Lisa. Would you like to join us one morning?"

"No, once in awhile you need time and space away from me. I like Lisa, but I've noticed something about her."

I had no idea where she was going with this.

"Don't get mad. I know she's your friend, but she's hot for you. I can tell by the way she looks at you. I think she's in love with you."

I was speechless and tried my best to keep a straight face.

Monica said, "I trust you and anyway I can't tell you who you can or can't see. She's your buddy and you've known her forever. Could you ever imagine having a relationship with Lisa?"

"She's intelligent and very attractive, but she's like my big sister. I couldn't imagine messing around with her."

I hated lying to Monica, but I had to lie. If she ever knew the truth about my relationship with Lisa, we would have been finished. I was so happy when Monica changed the subject. We saw a movie and spent the rest of that day shopping.

Sunday morning my mother asked me to go to church with her and my father. I hadn't been to church since Easter of the previous year. My mother said the church was giving a trip to an amusement park. She wasn't sure which park, so she told me if I went to church I could find out. The trip sounded nice, but I still didn't want to go to church. I felt bad when I thought about it, so I agreed to go with them. There was a good turn out that Sunday. I noticed a sign advertising a trip to Kings Dominion. I imagined how much fun Monica and I could have. The trip was less than a week away. We had until two days before the trip to purchase tickets.

There were lots of the church girls checking me out. I heard there were some freaky girls at that church, but I wasn't interested. My favorite part of the service was hearing the choir sing. They were a lot better than I remembered. There were some new faces in the choir. They made me remember how much I loved gospel music. During the announcements the lady asked all the visitors to stand. I hadn't been there in so long that I almost stood. I almost forgot that I was a member. If I would have embarrassed my parents like that, they would have killed me and held my funeral right there in church.

The pastor came on next. His sermon happened to be on fornication. I had this instant feeling of guilt come over me. It felt like he was preaching directly to me. I think he looked at me a few times and he made me uncomfortable. He kept huffing and puffing. He got on my nerves. I found myself zoning out into a flashback. I was twelve years old sitting in my mother's car. We were parked on a shopping center parking lot. The next thing I remembered was seeing the pastor of our church pull up in a parking space across from us. We were about to get out of the car until my mother noticed a woman, who was a former co-workers of hers and church member pull up next to the pastor's car. I was getting impatient. My mother told me to shut up and sit still. I had no idea what was happening until I saw the lady get into the pastor's car. They embraced and kissed. I knew exactly what was going on then. This was starting to look like a scene from a soap opera. I knew that woman wasn't the pastor's wife. They started the car and left the parking lot. My mother was like a private investigator on duty. She followed them to a stoplight. They were about to make a right turn into a motel parking lot. My mother pulled up to the pastor's car. She said, "Hi Pastor."

The pastor looked so nervous I know he pissed in his pants. The woman recognized my mother right away and sank down in her seat like she was melting. They didn't have to do anything else, because they were obviously guilty of something.

There was one other incident that came to mind. We had a Boy Scout troop at the church around that same time. The men of the church started the troop. These guys were mostly regular members or deacons under the pastor's supervision. There were almost thirty scouts in our troop. At first, I had so much trust and confidence in this program. I think the whole thing lasted about four weeks. The scout leaders used to pray with us and give us spiritual guidance. The pastor even showed up at a few scout meetings. They did a great job of building up our trust. We never went camping or to the big Boy Scout Jamboree that they always talked about. We only went on a little hiking trip to Patapsco State Park. The scout leaders were too old and tired to hike for long distances. We cut the hike short and returned to the park and ate hot dogs. Wow!!! This was so much fun for a group of boys ranging in age from 12 to 15. The only other things I remembered were two fundraisers. The first was a candy drive, which ran for the course of the entire program. The second was a car wash. Both were huge successes. We turned in our candy money on a Tuesday night. Each scout sold at least one hundred dollars worth of candy. We must have washed at least fifty cars in one day at five dollars each. I begged my mother to take me to J.C. Penney to buy my first Boy Scout uniform. The next week I put on my uniform and marched down the street so proud. I was on my way to Troy's house so we could go to our meeting together. Troy's mother told me how sharp I looked in my uniform, but the meeting had been canceled. I never heard that it was canceled. I went back home and my mother called the church.

She knew that some people would be there for choir rehearsal or bible study. The person she talked to checked around and said there wasn't anyone there for the scout meeting. The following week no one showed up except the scouts for the meeting. The next Sunday my mother asked around about the Boy Scout troop. They said it was canceled, but they were going to restart it soon. Soon never came and if it did nobody told me. The pastor and his deacons took our damn fund raising money. Only God knows what happened to that money. We never saw that jamboree they used to tell us about all the time.

I noticed that the pastor was finishing up his sermon. I sat there looking at him thinking *why*. I sat there thinking about how much wrong this man had done. I prayed that God would remove any ill feelings I had in my heart against the pastor. I knew fornication was wrong and I wasn't trying to excuse my sins by recollecting the pastor's sins. He was such a hypocrite. It took a wicked person to judge others knowing that he had done such evil. This was only the evil I knew about. I hoped he had changed. The pastor was one major reason why I lost the desire to go to church. I really wanted my parents to move on to another church. They stayed because they felt like the pastor was a good man. My mother was a good woman because she never told anyone except my father what we saw. Now, I'm putting it in a book and I don't know what that makes me. They were so forgiving, but I wasn't. I felt that I believed too much in God to believe so much in fools. That church wasn't the place for me.

That afternoon Monica came over to spend the rest of the day with me. I told her about my experience in church. She told me the best thing for me to do was to find another church on my own. We went into our sunroom to listen to some music. All of a sudden it started to rain. This was no quiet storm. Outside there was a thunderstorm raging. The sights and sounds of this storm were kind of romantic. The sky turned dark with bolts of lightning dancing across the sky. The roar of the thunder frightened Monica. She cuddled up close to me and I held her tight.

Monica said, "You make me feel so safe in your arms."
The rain was so soothing as it ran down the glass of the sunroom.
The storm calmed to a gentle summer rain with an occasional clap
of thunder. We sat there watching the rain and listening to soft love
ballads by Luther Vandross. His music was so relaxing and it
almost went perfect with the flow of the rain. I wanted this moment
to last forever. I asked Monica to close her eye and let my love take
her to her favorite place. The rain seemed to bring out a different
side of me. I began to run my fingertips gently up and down her
neck, back and arms. Her skin was so sensitive to the touch. I
raised her arms above her head like a perfectly choreographed
ballet move. I felt her goose bumps as I ran my finger tips down
her arms. I found that her most sensitive spots were her neck and
the inner aspects of her arms. Little kisses really brought on the
goose bumps even more. I wanted to give every inch of her body
special attention. Monica was such a part of me that I felt like her
body was my own.

As the rain continued to fall I continued to take note of her
beauty. I thought of God when he created the heavens and the
earth. I wanted to know his exact thoughts when he created
woman. Nothing I knew or will ever know compares to this
creation. Each and every woman has her own unique qualities,
which make her beautiful. The ability to bring life into this world is
incredible. I began to recite a poem called, *You.*

"Bone of my bones...flesh of my flesh. I believe you are the most
precious thing on God's green earth. You're like something from
my dreams. An intense mixture of fantasy and reality. A beautiful
personalized gift from God. You are the air I breathe. You're my
inspiration, my best friend, my sexy lover and my sweetheart.
You're everything I could ever dream of and more. You are you
and that's what I love most...I love you."

Monica tried to speak, but I kissed her before she could get a
word out of her mouth. God truly gave me a gift when he brought
Monica into my life. Nothing could top the feeling I had in my
heart that day. I cherished each day we shared, but that day was one

I always remembered. Nothing beats the feeling of being young and in love. The fun was just beginning.

STRICTLY FOR FUN: 8

Young love was spreading all over the place. Troy and Jennifer were still dating. Their relationship seemed to be growing stronger. Keith started dating a girl we all knew from school named April. I called Troy and Keith to see if they were interested in going on the trip to Kings Dominion. I had them on a three-way call. Troy said he wanted to do something fun like that with Jennifer. He felt like she deserved something nice for all the things she had done for him. Keith said it sounded like a good idea and April would enjoy hanging out with all of us. Troy had something he needed to get off his chest.

He said, "I hate the way people stare at me and Jennifer. We don't deserve that shit."

I said, "I told you."

Troy said, "Yeah, but black women look at me like I did something to them and white guys look at me like I stole something."

Keith cut in and said, "You did steal something. You stole their opportunity and black women, they see you as a lost brotha. I don't have anything against Jennifer, but I could never see myself with a white girl. My family would disown me."

I felt bad for Troy. I wanted to make him fell more comfortable with his situation.

I said, "If you really love Jennifer make things work. Don't let ignorance destroy what you have."

"You hooked us up 'cause you didn't want sisters lookin' at you like you sold out for a white girl."

Troy was so dumb. I was trying to help him and he was trying to make me look bad.

I said, "That's not true. It had nothing to do with black or white. I wanted Monica. That's why I hooked y'all up. Anyway Jennifer seemed like she was ready to give it up and I called myself looking out for you."

"Yeah, she was ready to give it up and it was good. Good looking out, Black."

Keith laughed and said, "Y'all are two mixed up brothas."

I had to get in Keith's shit real quick.

I said, "It's just a matter of time for you my Muslim brotha. If you make it to the NFL you'll have a white girl on your arm in no time. That's like part of the contract in professional sports. You'll get a multi million-dollar contract, a signing bonus, a big ass house, fancy cars and a white woman. You can't escape it."

Keith was digging for a comeback.

He said, "You're just mad cause me and Troy are getting ours and Monica ain't giving you shit."

I said, "I have a lot of respect for Monica. It's just a matter of time. We're going to Jamaica with my parents in two weeks."

Keith and Troy didn't know what to say.

Troy said, "Her parents must be retarded letting her go with you to Jamaica."

Keith said, "Yeah, I wouldn't trust your nasty ass in Jamaica with my crippled grandmother."

They thought they knew me well. I guess they were right.

I said, "Your grandmother wouldn't have anything to worry about, but I couldn't guarantee your mother's safety. I know I'd try to get some from her."

Troy said, "Yeah, your mother is kind of sexy."

We went on back and forth like that for awhile. They were my boys and I missed hanging out with them. Now that we all had girlfriends I planned to spend more time with them. I figured it would be fun to have everyone together. I kept giving the females in my life top priority with my time. I forgot how much fun I used to have with Troy and Keith. Monica and Jennifer planned to go shopping that day. I hooked April up with them and they all went out to dinner. I told the guys about a strip club downtown that I knew would let us in. We headed for the club later that night. The bouncer at the door asked if we had ID. We all flashed our driver's licenses and the bouncer signaled us to go inside the club. Somebody said the bouncer never looked too close at ID's because he wasn't smart enough to calculate ages. The club was dark and smoky. We knew we were the youngest guys in the club. I think other people were fine with us being there as long as we didn't try to drink any alcoholic beverages. I had a roll of one-dollar bills and some five-dollar bills for the girls that did special tricks.

The first girl who came out went by the name Chocolate. She was a thick dark skinned girl with a hair weave down to her butt. When she smiled I noticed two gold teeth in her mouth. I hated to see women with gold teeth, but when she started taking her off clothes I never looked at her teeth again. Chocolate had a nice body. She was thick, but well proportioned. She danced her way over to us shaking all her stuff. She had a big round ass and nice breasts. Her best trick was making her butt cheeks clap. She got money from all of us for doing that. It was good trick, but not good enough for me to break her off a five dollar bill. I gave her like four ones for her performance.

The next girl who came out was named Precious. I could see why, Precious was beautiful. She seemed a little classier than Chocolate. She was obviously a real dancer at some point in her life. This girl was too fine to be a stripper. She had prettiest little breasts with big brown nipples. She was sexy with her little round butt. Precious reminded me of Stacey. She worked her way up and down the pole.

She straight up worked the hell out of that pole. Precious was my sexy little dancer. I gave her two five-dollar bills.

Juicy, a.k.a. The Loose Lady, was up next. Her name made her sound like she had a problem with her bowels. Right away we found out how she got her name. She was doing splits all over the stage. She did a full split and made her butt cheeks bounce up and down off the stage. Juicy was pretty, but she wasn't Precious. She did have a tight body. Juicy laid on her back and put her legs in the air. She made a V with legs and pulled tight on her G-string. We saw everything. Instantly money flooded the stage. I gave her ten dollars. She had talent.

Phat Nikki was the next dancer. She was nasty. I mean, she looked nasty. She had been in the game way too long. I think her butt had like four sections. Her stomach looked like she just had a C-section backstage. She must have worn a triple E bra cup 'cause her breasts were gigantic. The guys in the club went crazy for her. She had all the old dudes yelling for her. I couldn't understand it. What did they see? Her stretch marks had stretch marks and every ounce had bounce. Phat Nikki was the showstopper for sure. I saw a man on his knees banging a fist full of dollars on the floor. She got everybody's money. She did a pretty good job when I thought about it. I gave her three dollars. That was a lot more than what I was going to give her at first.

The finale was when all four girls were on stage together for a dance off. I picked Precious as the winner. After the show some other dancers that weren't part of the main show came out to join the others for lap dances. All the guys were signaling for Phat Nikki. She went right over to Troy and started grinding on his lap. The funny thing was that Troy didn't even signal for her. Keith and I died laughing. Troy looked like he didn't know how to handle all that ass. Keith got a dance from one of the unknown dancers. She was nice looking and Keith looked like he enjoyed her. I noticed Precious coming my way. I whipped out most of my money and signaled her. She looked even better close up. I guess she was about nineteen or twenty. She noticed my money and went to work on me. I had her straddle me. She put her pretty little breasts right in my face. Her skin was soft and she smelled nice. I knew she could feel how hard I was. Precious really started putting it on me then. My first lap dance was the bomb. She asked if I wanted to join her in the champagne room. I liked her, but I had to get back to reality. I figured most dancers and prostitutes had venereal diseases, so I told her thanks for the lap dance and gave her twenty dollars. For a little more money I know I could have gotten a whole lot more from her, but I never wanted to be with a prostitute. I never felt the need to pay for sex outright. Prostitute or not I wasn't trying to cheat on Monica. I was so worked up that I had to get the hell out of there before I did something crazy. I was missing my sweetheart anyway.

Monica and I were excited about our trip to Kings Dominion. The night before the trip we went to the supermarket to buy snacks. We prepared sandwiches, fruit salad, soda and chips for the road. I woke up at 5:30 a.m. the next morning in order to make it to the bus by 7:00 a.m. Monica was supposed to meet me at my house at 6:30 a.m. It was a job getting up that early. Since school was out I didn't get out of bed until 9 or 10 a.m. I did some quick stretches and push ups to get my blood flowing. By the time Monica arrived I was feeling fine. She greeted me with her usual glowing smile. I give her a warm hug and a kiss. She had a single red rose, a gift box and a card in her hands for me. I had no idea what this was about. She said it was something to show her love for me. Monica was so sweet and sincere. She was always giving me gifts. Even if it was as simple as a daily affirmation to make my day pleasant. She made the card herself out of some fancy thick paper. I always thought homemade cards showed originality and intelligence. This card meant so much because these were Monica's own words. The card read:

Thinking of love
Dreaming of you.

On days when it feels like the entire world is closing in on you and it seems like no one's on your side, always remember I've got your back. I promise that together we can conquer the world.

Love Always,

MONICA

Monica's words went straight to my heart.

I said, "I love you and always know I've got your back too."

She gave me a kiss and handed me the gift box. I opened the box and there was a red, black and green beaded necklace with a silver ankh.

"I made it myself. The ankh is an ancient Egyptian symbol for life. The red, black and green beads represent the colors of Africa. Together they are symbolic of Egypt, Africa's stolen legacy. This is to remind all those who didn't know that Egypt is and will always be part of Africa."

"Thank you for everything. Your card was beautiful. You're really special to me. I'll always wear this necklace. I've always hated the fact that my teachers and history books made Egypt seem like it was separate from the rest of Africa. I'll never forget these gifts. You're the first person to ever give me a rose and I like it. Now, let's hurry up and get to the bus. I can't wait to see which couple is dressed alike from head to toe."

Monica set the tone for the rest of that day. I loved her so much. When we got to the church parking lot Keith and April were already at the bus. Troy and Jennifer pulled up about a minute later. They stepped out of the car dressed exactly alike from head to toe. They had on white Nike T-shirts, multicolored Bermuda shorts and blue and white track Nike's. They looked so cute together that I almost died laughing. Monica pinched me to make me act right. It was too hard to hold my laugh in. They didn't know that I was laughing at them. They thought I was just real happy about the trip. We all boarded the bus and somebody had a huge boom box playing Run-DMC and LL Cool J. I was expecting a big yellow school bus, but instead we had a nice plush charter bus. We headed straight for the back of the bus. There was something about the back of the bus that attracted all of us. Monica sat in a window seat. We noticed the bus had a commode. For some reason, I felt that wasn't a good idea. We had a pretty respectable group, so I figured we were safe. Some church lady stood up and introduced herself. She gave us some basic rules and regulation. She then asked us to join her in prayer. I thought that was an appropriate gesture, simply because we were entrusting our valuable lives in the hands of a man who looked like a recovering drunk.

The bus was noisy from the boom box and everyone talking. Monica and I tuned everything out. We were in a world of our own. The sun was shining right through Monica's window and it gave her an amazing glow. I asked her what she thought of me the first time that she saw me.

Monica said, "I fell in love with your eyes. You gave me a nice friendly smile. I thought you were really handsome and you had a nice body. You looked nice in your clothes too. You looked like the only guy that I wanted to make my boyfriend. I needed to get to know you better. I thought you only liked me as a friend. What did you think of me?"

"I thought you were absolutely beautiful. I instantly saw a big, bright and beautiful sunflower in a barren field. The other girls looked okay, but you, you were the finest thing I'd ever seen. No one could compare to you. I thought to myself, this girl has no idea how good she looks. If she was mine I'd make her a star. In time she'll be mine. Your innocence was a major turn on for me too. You seemed confident, but somewhat shy. I knew you would be mine one day."

"You were that confident?"

"Yeah, and I still have that confidence and one day you'll be my wife."

102

"Ooh, I like that. Kids and everything? What about a white picket fence?"

We laughed.

"Whatever you want. I'll do it for you. 'Cause I love you."

"I love you."

Monica and I fed each other fruit salad.

I said, "I wanna fill your life with love, romance and excitement."

"You're doing a great job already."

"When can I make love to you?"

"I promised my parents and myself that I would remain a virgin until I got married and I plan to stick to that."

"Don't you ever wonder how good it would feel to have me inside you?"

Monica's tone dropped as if my question took her breath. "Yes, all the time. Sometimes I want you inside me so bad I could scream. You make me so hot."

"I don't ever want you to feel like I'm pressuring you to have sex. I love and respect you. I know you're well worth the wait."

"I don't feel like you're pressuring me. I like everything you do to me."

"And I like doing it. I'm still going to check in with you from time to time to see if you've changed your mind."

"Okay, but I won't change."

Monica laid her head on my shoulder and we fell asleep holding hands. I had a dream that Monica and I were making love on the beach in Jamaica. When I woke up we were probably about an hour from Kings Dominion. When I opened my eyes the first thing I focused on was Troy's Nike's.

I said, "Troy I like those Nike's."

Monica pinched me on the arm. I thought she was sleep. I just wanted to joke Troy a little. I wanted to tell Monica about my dream, but she would think all I thought about was sex and more sex. I thought it was strange when Monica said she had a dream about me.

I asked, "Was it hot?"

"It was about to get hot. Then I woke myself up. I dreamed you cheated on me with another girl."

My eyes got big. "It was just a dream."

"If you ever cheated on me I would die. I can't imagine you with another woman. The thought makes me sick."

"Well stop thinking about it. You're everything I need. You have one hundred percent of my love, which means I have none to share with another woman. Remember one hundred percent. All my love all the time."

"I feel the same way. I'm sorry, this is new for me. I've never been this deep in love with anyone. My heart is a fragile thing and my inner peace means everything to me. I need to be honest with you. I'm a little insecure about your relationship with Lisa."

"She's nothing more than a friend to me. I spend a lot more time with you and that's never gonna change. I love you. Anyway, Lisa is deeply in love with Mike and he loves her."

"I'm sorry. I really need to let this go."

"It's okay, I think the dream had a lot to do with your feelings."

Monica had some kind of sixth sense that helped her pick up something between me and Lisa. I still liked Lisa, but Monica was truly my focus. I pulled out some travel brochures on Jamaica to help take Monica's mind off of Lisa. Jennifer turned in our direction and noticed the brochures.

Jennifer said, "I heard y'all were going to Jamaica. How the hell did y'all pull that one off?"

That question got everyone's attention.

I said, "If you were my girl I could make a lot of unbelievable shit happen. You're not so stay out of our business."

I said that to be mean, but everybody started laughing. I was glad they took my comments as a joke because things could have gotten real ugly. A few minutes later we arrived at the Kings Dominion.

Our chaperon told us to meet back at the bus at 10 p.m. according to her watch.

She said, "Set your watches to 10:15 a.m. If you are not here at 10 p.m. you will be left behind."

104

The bus driver had this look on his face like he was thinking, *Don't believe that shit.* I grabbed Monica and we headed off the bus. The park was hot and crowded. We all planned to stay in a group of six. I noticed some other couples in the park dressed a like.

I said, "Look Troy those couples are dressed alike too." I jumped away from Monica just in time so she couldn't pinch me. I thought it was funny to see guys dressed like their girlfriends. I imagined their girlfriends picking out their outfits. Then telling their man, "You're gonna wear this to Kings Dominion and we're gonna look so cute together. Everybody's gonna to be so jealous of us."

Everyone wanted to head for the Rebel Yell and Grizzly roller coasters first. Our first stop was the Rebel Yell. The line moved pretty fast. Monica was excited. She loved roller coasters. I wasn't so excited about riding a roller coaster. I was wishing we could have started with the Scooby Doo roller coaster first. Then we could work our way up to the bigger, faster and more dangerous looking coasters. I rode the Rebel Yell with my father years ago. I remembered it like it was yesterday. We rode in the front car and I was terrified. I figured I would be fine as long as Monica and I sat somewhere in a middle car. As the line moved forward I noticed that Monica had a big smile on her face.

She said, "Good, we're going to be in the front car."

I just smiled and nodded my head like I really wanted to be up front. I couldn't let her know I was having second thoughts. I just kept smiling. We hopped in the car and the coaster operator gave us some instruction. The bar was locked in place and we took off. I was doing fine. I actually liked the speed of the ride. I was thinking, this isn't so bad. Our car slowly climbed the incline. Monica looked at me with a smile.

"When we drop, put your hand in the air and scream."

"Okay."

When the car dropped all I remembered screaming was, "Oh shit!!!"

Monica looked over at me and died laughing. I must have looked so stupid. I was so scared I had to laugh at myself. Halfway through the ride I was having fun. Monica's happiness was infectious. I wanted to put my hand in the air, but they wouldn't let go of the bar. When the coaster stopped Monica was still laughing at me.

Monica said, "You were so scared."

"I was just playing."

She said, "Let's get on the Grizzly next."

We headed straight for the Grizzly. I did much better this time around. I actually put my hands in the air. I was starting to look like the rest of the coaster freaks. I wanted to try some water rides next. The rest of the group agreed and we headed for the White Water Canyon Ride. This was my favorite ride of all. We got soaked on that ride. Monica looked sexy wet. I loved the way her hair looked when it was wet. She put her hair in two long Pocahontas braids. When I looked at Jennifer she was trying to do the same thing with her hair. April saw the look on my face and we both burst out laughing. I loved Jennifer. She was just trying to fit in with the group.

I looked at her and said, "Go 'head Pocahontas."

She just smiled and finished braiding her hair. Since we were already wet we headed for the Shenandoah Log Ride. Monica and I kissed as we rode through the dark tunnel. The worst part of the ride was an unexpected drop that made my stomach drop like when I was on the roller coasters. The heat made our clothes dry fast.

Troy yelled, "Let's go back and ride the Grizzly to help our clothes dry faster."

I wanted to pick another intimate ride so I could kiss Monica again. After the Grizzly we headed for the Time Shaft. This was a fun ride. It spun us around and the floor dropped out from under our feet. When we got off that ride we walked around for awhile. We smelled pizza, burgers and fries. After all that we all were starving. Monica and I had pizza with the works and French-fries from one of the outdoor restaurants. We fed each other and shared a jumbo soda. We stopped by the gift shop. Monica and I bought our parents little Eiffel Tower replicas, some giant multicolored lollipops and T-shirts. We decided to break the group up for awhile. We all wanted private time with our dates. We all agreed to meet up at six o'clock in front of the Eiffel Tower. There was a country band appearing live at the park, but none of us were interested. Patti Labelle was scheduled to appear there that following week and New Edition was there two weeks earlier. We said the church picked the wrong weekend to have the trip. We couldn't complain too much because we were having a ball.

Monica and I went to play some games. I won her three stuffed animals. We probably looked silly walking around with giant stuffed animals and eating cotton candy. I noticed some girls looking at us.

I overheard one of them say in her southern accent, "He luv her." I smiled and said, That's right I luv's my baby."

Monica covered her mouth and closed her eyes. We burst out laughing together. She said, "You are so stupid. You don't know what to say out of your mouth, but I luv's you too."

Monica was so beautiful that she made me look extra good. I think girls paid more attention to me when I was with her and I liked it. I loved showing my girl off in public.

We picked an intimate spot so we could kiss. Before I knew it we had a long passionate kiss going. I felt like I was in one of those chewing gum commercials. People could still see us, but we didn't care. We sat by a fountain to rest and talk for awhile. I took out my camera and had Monica pose for me.

I said, "Give it up baby. Make love to the camera."

I was really thinking. *Give it up baby. Please, make love to me.*

At six o'clock we met up with the others again. Keith and April made a record together at a recording booth. Troy had won some stuffed animals for Jennifer. I pulled out my camera and had some guy take a group picture of us. We went to the top of the Eiffel Tower and I took more pictures. When we got back to the ground we headed off for more rides until it was time to leave.

At nine thirty we started to wrap things up and head back to the bus. Everyone was exhausted. I was so tired that I felt like we had been there for two days. I was starting to get the impression that Troy and Keith were seriously in love with their girlfriends. It was hard to believe we were almost adults. It was funny seeing Troy and Keith so into their girls. A year ago they didn't even have girlfriends. They were getting their thrills listening to me talk about my love life. I thought it was funny how they thought that they were getting more out of they relationships than me. Monica and I may have not been having intercourse, but the passion was there. My girl was real sexy and she was giving me her all. Their relationships probably didn't reach the levels that ours did. I still wanted to make love to Monica, but I decided to lighten up the pressure a bit. I had to respect a girl that got my tongue in her hot spot and still didn't give it up. She was truly committed to her beliefs. Someday soon I wanted to tell her parents about our relationship, but I wasn't trying to do that before our trip to Jamaica. If Monica didn't give me what I was dying for in Jamaica, my next big opportunity was starting to look like senior prom. If that was what it took, I was willing to wait. She was too special to lose over sex. I felt like she was holding on to the world's greatest treasure. There weren't too many virgins around in our age group. I knew that a girl like Monica only came along once in a lifetime. She was a brilliant star and all other girls paled in comparison.

I was deep in thought until Monica grabbed me by the arm. The other people from our bus started to surface and we began to board the bus. Everyone looked worn out. I think everyone was feeling mellow and wanted to cuddle up with their boyfriend or girlfriend. Out of nowhere the guy with the boom box started blasting Run-DMC again. He was about to catch a quick beat down. He quickly found Howard University's WHUR 96.3 F.M. in the middle of the quiet storm broadcast. 95 North was backed up for miles because of an accident. A tractor-trailer had collided with three cars and caused a hazardous spill that closed three lanes of traffic. Luckily no one was killed. The delay didn't bother us because the music

108

sounded so good. The only thing that was missing was a gentle rain. The next thing I heard was a boom of thunder. I've always loved the rain. There was a little chill in the air from the bus' air conditioning. Monica and I cuddled up tight. All of a sudden the bus was totally quiet. The soft music and rain put everyone to sleep.

We got back to Baltimore about 2:30 a.m. I thanked my crew for going and I told them we had to hook up again real soon. Monica and I headed back to my house. I gave her a special thanks.

"You made this day absolutely perfect. I love you so much."

"Thank you for showing me such a good time. I love you."

I gave Monica a goodnight kiss and told her that I was going to tell her parents about us soon. I was tired of sneaking around. I felt bad that she had to drive herself home so late at night. All that would change after our trip.

The next day I went to Lisa's house to see if she wanted to workout. She answered the door looking like she already had plans to workout.

I said, "Hey, do you wanna workout?"

"Yeah, but what I wanna do doesn't have anything to do with running or walking."

I gave her a funny look.

Lisa said, "I'm just joking. I'm in the mood for some power walking."

We got in my car and headed for the high school track.

"So did you fuck Monica yet?"

"What's wrong with you and where the hell did that come from?"

"I'm just wondering if you got her little cherry yet."

"No, she's still a virgin and I'm fine with that and you should be fine with it too."

"How are you making it? If you get tired of choking your chicken you can always come back home."

Lisa was actually sitting there touching herself. She was starting to get to me a little. She looked a little sexy-sexy.

I said, "We need to get out and walk."

"Did I do or say something wrong?"

We got out of the car and started walking to the track.

I said, "I'm still attracted to you, but I can't ever do anything sexual with you again. Monica has some kind of sixth sense. She can feel the chemistry between us. Her dreams are telling her something."

Lisa laughed. "You better hold on to her. She sounds real special. Ask her if her sixth sense can tell her tonight's lottery number. She can make us all rich one day."

"Go straight to hell. I'm serious."

"I believe you, but what proof does she actually have."

"None. I just don't want to deceive her in anyway. She's my soulmate."

"There's no such thing as a soulmate. You come in this world alone and you leave it alone."

"No, your soul's alone in this world because you haven't found the right man yet. Monica and I are soulmates vibing to the same rhythm. I love her. You wish you could understand this love thing."

"Love is so played out. I told you to protect your heart and stick to the physical. Don't let you emotions get in the way. If and when Monica breaks your heart don't look to me to pick you up. I shouldn't say that, I'll always be here for you."

"Thank you. You helped me out a lot when Stacey broke my heart, but Monica's different."

"So, you think I really bother Monica that much?"

"Shut up and keep walking. I'm gonna have a get together at my house tonight. If you can, bring Mike."

We kept walking for awhile. I wasn't mad, just tired of talking. Lisa was so silly and carefree. She was too stubborn to admit that she had real feelings for me. She tried to act so tough, like I hadn't touched her heart. All that nonsense she talked was caused by her emotions getting in the way. It was hard to accept the fact that she was a woman who lost me to a teenage girl. Monica was too bugged out to see that she had all of me. I did have feelings for

110

Lisa, but those feelings didn't compare to what I felt for Monica. This was such a strange situation for me. I knew all the reasons why I was in love with Monica and I knew why she was in love with me. Lisa, on the other hand was a different breed. The love she was giving me was weird. I had no way to label it. She promised to always be there for me, but why? The best question was why did I love her? The answer was simple. Her love for me was limitless. She was always there for me. She picked me up when I was down. Lisa was so special to me. If I asked her to, she would have walked through hell for me. I owed her the same in return, but I just couldn't. And that's the reason why I was with my sweet Monica. No matter how strange things got, I planned to stay with Monica.

When I got home I called my friends and asked them to come to my house later that night for my little get together. Monica came over early to help me set up for our friends. This was a get together for couples only. Troy and Jennifer were the first to arrive. Keith and April arrived a little later. I told April that it was cool to bring her sister, Diane, and her friend, Sean. We were eating and listening to music when the topic of marriage came up.

I said, "Monica and I will probably get married after college and have two kids. Little Eric first then pretty little Erica. Of course we have to name them after me."

Monica looked like she liked the idea of marrying me and having our kids. I thought she was going to object to the names, but she didn't say a word. Monica had so much class. Even if she disagreed, she would never have made me look bad in front of our friends. Another girl would have started going crazy about me making plans without her input. Monica realized these weren't official plans just my way of being creative.

Troy said, "I'm never gonna get married. I just want me and Jennifer to live together."

Jennifer said, "That fine with me because marriage ruins relationships. My parents are a perfect example of how a marriage can ruin a relationship. They're still together, but they always complain about their personal time and space. I think marriage limits what they can do."

Monica said, "No, they limit what they can do. If they trusted one another things would be a lot smoother."

Jennifer said, "I can see your point. You may be right, but marriage still isn't for me."

I didn't comment because for all I knew my father was probably out fucking one of his girls as we spoke.

There was a knock at my door. I had no idea who this could be. Everyone I invited had already arrived. I opened the door and it was Lisa. I forgot that I told her about the get together. Lisa and I stood in the doorway mumbling.

I said, "Hi, where's Mike?"

"He's still unavailable. I just wanted to come over to tell you how hot I am for you." Lisa yelled inside. "Hi everybody. Hey Monica." She turned to me and asked, "What do you think Monica's thinking?"

"She's thinking you need to get a life and I need to shut this door. You're too wild. Come in."

Lisa walked with me into the living room.

"Everybody this is my friend Lisa from next door."

"Hi, I just stopped by 'cause I wanted y'all to listen to my demo."

I said, "For those of you who don't know, Lisa is the lead singer of a group called Soul Survivors. Now, she's planning to go solo."

I played her tape and it sounded real nice. She was definitely ready to do the solo thing. Monica seemed like she was fine with Lisa being around. If she wasn't I knew I was going to hear about it later. Lisa was ready to go after we listened to the tape, but everyone including Monica asked her to stay. Keith picked up the conversation where he left off. He said he planned to marry April after college. April wanted to marry him too and have two or three kids. Sean said he was too young to even think about marriage. Diane agreed with Sean.

Lisa said, "It's nice being single and I never plan to get married. I can come and go as I please. I can leave the country tonight and I

112

don't have to get an okay from anyone."

I wanted to mess with Lisa and ask about her lonely nights and how a husband could help fill the gap, but that was a little too dangerous to play around with that night. I feared her answer.

The group started to break up. Soon it was down to Monica, Lisa and me. Monica started telling Lisa how she couldn't wait for our trip to Jamaica. Oh no, I forgot to tell Lisa about our trip. She looked a little jealous as Monica talked about the trip, but Lisa played it off well. We had a serious love triangle going on. Something had to give sooner or later. Everything seemed okay, so I stepped out of the room.

I overheard Lisa say, "Monica, have you ever been so in love with a man that you could feel him even when you were apart? I'm talking about a man that stays on your mind day and night."

"I know exactly what you mean. Black is all that and more to me. I see, feel, smell, taste and hear him when were apart. I've never been so much in love before."

"Have y'all made love yet?"

"That's none of your business, but I'm very proud to say I'm still a virgin. We don't need to have sex to express our love. We have something very special right now. When the right time comes we'll make love. Black has shown me a whole new world. When he introduces me to the other dimensions of his love, our world will be that much more special. Time always has a way of making things so much better."

"I'm sure Eric can give you all you're looking for. He's special to me too, but in a different way."

"The thing I like most about Black is that he gives me so much of his time. I have access to him whenever I need him."

I had heard enough. I said, "My mother asked if all my company was gone. I told her that everyone was gone, so please don't make a liar out of me."

Lisa said, "Thanks for inviting me I had an interesting time. Have fun on your trip. Peace."

I wanted Lisa to leave hours earlier. She was becoming a real troublemaker. I was proud of Monica for standing her ground against Lisa. I'm sure Lisa's plan was to intimidate Monica, but it didn't work. More than anything, Lisa fired up Monica.

I said, "I'm glad she's gone."

"I don't mean any harm, but I don't like Lisa. She might as well have said I'm in love with your man. I know she loves you, but she can't have you."

"Thank you, but I don't want her anyway. I heard part of your conversation, but I had no idea where it was going."

"I knew exactly where it was going and I'm glad she didn't take it there."

I walked Monica to her car and kissed her goodnight. I knew that something had to give sooner or later and I felt like this was just the beginning. Lisa was dangerous and I had to keep her away from Monica. I'm glad I stopped Lisa when I did. She was crazy enough to tell Monica what she was missing and how good I was in bed. The last thing I needed was to lose Monica. I was mad at Lisa for cutting things so close. She was such a selfish individual. One way or another Lisa had nothing to lose. In her mind she probably thought she had more to gain by breaking up my relationship with Monica. I said it and I meant it, Lisa was never getting anything from me again. All I had on my mind was being in paradise with the love of my life. Monica and I were just days away from our Caribbean paradise in Jamaica.

JAMAICA EVE: 9

The day before our trip, Monica and I went shopping at the mall. Shopping was one of our favorite hobbies. Not only did I like to undress Monica, but I liked to dress her too. I loved helping her pick out clothes. We even shopped at thrift stores sometimes for those hard to find fashions. Monica was the type of girl that looked good in anything. The clothes didn't make her, she absolutely made the clothes. During this trip to the mall we picked up things like shorts, shirts, tennis shoes, sandals, bathing suits, swimming trunks, beach towels and more. I even picked up a waterproof camera. Monica was without a doubt my best friend. I never dreamed we would share so much so soon. The idea of her parents letting her go to Jamaica with me and my parents was totally unbelievable. This was too good to be true. Monica's parents, Mr. and Mrs. Cameron came over to my house to talk to my parents. My father told Monica's parents he would take care of all her expenses. My father arranged for us to stay in a villa at an all-inclusive resort in Montego Bay. I imagined this was a very expensive vacation for my parents. They acted as if it was no sweat to cover Monica's expenses. I was sure my parents could easily afford to pay for Monica's accommodations. I figured they saved a lot of money over the years, considering I was their only child. In addition to that, ordinarily I never asked for much. Mr. Cameron repeatedly asked my father to let him pay for something.

Mr. Cameron said, "We've been to Jamaica and I know that this is an expensive trip."

He slipped Monica an envelope of money that my father had refused to accept. Monica asked if she could spend the night at my house. My parents were fine with the idea. I thought she had lost her mind asking her parents a question like that. When I thought about it, spending the night at my house wasn't a big deal. After all, Monica was about to spend a week in Jamaica with me and my family. Her parents agreed to let her stay since we were leaving so early in the morning. I took Monica home to get the rest of her things. I got to see Monica's bedroom for the first time. Before that moment, I felt like her room was a restricted area. I thought I had stepped into a bedroom from a model home display or a page from *Better Homes and Gardens.* Her bedroom looked like no one had ever stayed in it. She was too neat. The rest of the house was nice, but Monica's bedroom was immaculate. Seeing Monica's room made me want to rush home and do some extra cleaning in my bedroom. Monica's bedroom was her private studio and art gallery. I noticed a painting turned backwards on her easel.

"What's this all about?"

"Oh, that's not for your eyes right now. Check these out first."

The first piece she showed me was a portrait of Prince. Her work was excellent. Her portrait was so life-like with unbelievable detail. The Prince portrait was an original. It was unlike any album cover or poster I'd ever seen. Monica had an awesome portrait of Malcolm on her wall. I was impressed. She framed it in a fancy gold frame that set the picture off perfectly. She had a very unique piece she called Old Glory. It was an image of the United States flag. The flag was red, white and blue fading into red, black and green. Instead of stars it had rows of black people depicting the way slaves were arranged on slave ships during their transatlantic journey to America. I loved her portrait of the beautiful and legendary singing sensation from Baltimore, Billie Holiday. I couldn't think of a better tribute to Ms. Holiday. She did a portrait called Four Jazz Greats. In the center Dizzy Gillespie and Miles Davis played their trumpets and by their sides Charlie Parker and John Coltrane played their saxophones. My favorite piece was a breathtaking portrait of Jesus. His eyes and facial expression spoke to me. It was so life-like that it gave me chills.

"Your portraits are awesome."

"Thank you."

"Your portrait of Malcolm is impressive, but the portrait of Jesus is definitely a masterpiece."

"Thanks, I spent months working on it."

"You pay lots of attention to detail and that's important. Are any of these portraits for sale?"

"No, I wouldn't even know how to set a price for them. They're mostly for show."

"You're incredible."

We had finished gathering Monica's things when her parents stepped into her room.

Mr. Cameron said, "I know you guys are going to have a nice time in Jamaica, but please be very careful. Eric your parents are nice people and I think they've done a fine job raising you."

"Thank you."

Mrs. Cameron smiled and said, "I agree you're a fine young man and we'd love to have you as a son-in-law one day."

"Ma, what are you talking about?" Monica was embarrassed.

Mrs. Cameron said, "We're happy you have a boyfriend."

I was shocked that Monica's parents mentioned anything about me being her boyfriend. Actually, they made me feel real special. I felt like they had started to scrutinize my relationship with their daughter a little closer. Maybe, my parents had accidentally given up some information. I had the feeling that my parents had opened their mouths. Monica's parents had known me for awhile and this was the first time they'd ever had a talk like this with us. If my parents did give up some information I hoped they tried to reassure

117

Monica's parents that she was in good hands. Monica was too quiet. She looked like she wanted her parents to go away.

I said, "Well, to be honest I planned to have a talk with the two of you after our trip. I would love to be your son-in-law one day. I knew this was going to come up sooner or later, but this is a lot sooner than I expected. I hope this won't change our vacation plans."

Monica cut in before I could get my next word in. "Black, I mean, Eric and I have been dating for about a month now. That's all we have been doing. We're just really good friends."

I continued. "Yeah, I have lots of respect for Monica and myself. We plan to take it slow. I would be lying if I said I wasn't curious, but I promise you nothing's going to happen here for a long time."

Monica looked like she was getting upset.

She said, "I promised the two of you I would remain a virgin until I was married and I'm sticking to that."

Mr. Cameron smiled and said, "We believe you and we trust the two of you."

Mrs. Cameron looked a little upset too. "We don't plan to change your vacation plans at all. We feel like if you were going to have sex you're going to do it regardless of where you are."

Mrs. Cameron looked at me and said, "We've raised Monica to be a respectable young lady and we believe in her."

Mr. Cameron shook my hand. Mrs. Cameron actually had tears in her eyes when she gave me a hug. I stepped out of the bedroom as they said their sad good-byes to Monica. I didn't want to watch them get so emotional. I carried Monica's bags to my car. I could understand what they were feeling. This was their last time seeing Monica for the next week and they were also dealing with her growing up. Their only little girl was beginning to look more and more like a woman. It must have been hard sending their daughter away with a young man and his family. Monica was seventeen and I was her first boyfriend. She was a very attractive young lady and I'm sure that her parents feared the day when Monica got her first boyfriend. They knew this experience was going to come up someday. I think they handled it well.

Monica and her parents finally came downstairs. Everybody looked better. I was starting to feel guilty for taking their baby away.

"Mr. and Mrs. Cameron thank you for trusting us. I promise we won't let you down."

Mr. Cameron said, "We know she's in good hands."

I opened the passenger side door of my car to let Monica in.

Monica looked up to her parents and said, "Thanks, I love you guys. See you in a week."

I said my final good-byes. I hopped in my car and we took off. I bet her parents beat themselves half to death for letting Monica get away like that. They made a tough decision, but I guess deep down inside they knew that they had to trust Monica. I liked the point Monica's mother brought up. If we were going to have sex we could have done it anywhere.

"I love your parents."

"I love them too, but I thought for a minute that they weren't going to let me go to Jamaica."

"I really promise to be good."

"How good?" Monica had a devilish look on her face. She was trying to change up what I was saying and I was crazy enough to fall for it.

"I'm gonna be real good to you. You know my style."

We went back to my house and my parents were still up doing some last minute packing.

My father asked, "What took you two so long?"

I said, "We had some things that needed to be ironed out before we could come back."

He had no idea what I was talking about. He was bright enough to know that I wasn't talking about ironing clothes.

I said, "We'll be up in my room."

In a forceful tone my father said, "Yeah, with the door open."

I laughed, "Yeah, with the door open. Goodnight Ma and Dad."

My father asked, "Monica, you know where the guestroom is,

119

right?"

"Yes, Sir. Goodnight Mr. and Mrs. Brown."

Monica and I headed up the stairs to my room. When we got to my room I turned on the television and Purple Rain was on. This was one of our all-time favorite movies. Monica was excited. She said, "I love this movie."

"I know. Me too. This is the best movie soundtrack I ever heard."

"Prince does a good job acting too."

"Yeah, he's does okay, but Apollonia is the star."

"Shhh."

I've never considered Prince anything less than a musical genius. His music's a perfect mixture of sex, love, and spirituality. Purple rain was a sexy flick. The music put me into a sexual trance, especially *The Beautiful Ones* and *Darling Nikki*. Prince's music had a big influence on me. As a student of love, seduction has always been important to me. There's truly an art to seduction and I consider Prince a modern day master. Sometimes overall appearance alone is enough to seduce a woman. Non-verbal communication is my favorite form of seduction. For example, I have this way of licking my lips that sends a sexy message. When I met Monica all it took was eye contact and a smile. Any brother can come up with corny lines or pretend to be someone he's not. My best line has always been, "Hi, I'm Eric." That line is short, sweet and right to the point. Most importantly, I'm just being myself and there's nothing fake about that.

The movie and the music were starting to affect Monica. We were getting hot. She slowly pushed the door shut with her foot.

I said, "That's good, not all the way. Let my father think he can still see us. Come here."

I tongued Monica down. Before I knew it I had her on the floor. I was hovering over her like a hungry beast about to move in for the kill. I played it cool and continued to drop kisses down on her wherever it felt good. The action in my room started to look hotter than the action in the movie. We were fully clothed, but I took my time and gave Monica's body the same attention as if she was

120

completely nude. Monica could feel my hands all over her body as we kissed. I loved our deep passionate kisses.

It began to sound like a lot more than kissing was going on. The right pressure in the right spot can surely make a woman reach her climax. I can't lie I wasn't too far behind. The movie was over and we still kept going. We had to shower and get ready for bed. Monica left my bedroom, but returned to say goodnight. I put on my Purple Rain soundtrack and she ended up staying a little longer. We stayed up talking about our trip. Neither of us had been to Jamaica before, so we had no idea what to expect. We could only go by what our parents had shared with us about their trips. I couldn't resist touching Monica through her pajamas. We had to stop at some point. It was almost 4 a.m. when we went to sleep.

That night I had a sweet sexy dream about me and Monica. We were on a beach of silky jet-black sand. The beach had chocolate covered trees with cocoa leaves. I had everything I needed at my fingertips. We laid there diggin' a tropical scene. Monica was right by my side looking sweet and sexy. My chocolate covered cherry treat with a special flavor that I loved to savor. Sweet as I can remember from January to December. No matter the season she was good all year long. She was a tasty treat I loved to eat. Good to the last drop. It was something about that beautiful dark skin that drove me crazy. When we kissed she wrapped her chocolate legs around me and pulled me in deeper. All I heard were moans of pleasure and screams of passion. This was the reinvention of hot chocolate. Slowly Monica's blazing hot chocolate body was melting into mine. I ran my tongue all over her sweet chocolate body. To my surprise she poured champagne on me and licked it off. I was spellbound by her beauty...mesmerized by her eyes...captivated by her touch.

I whispered in her ear. "Welcome to my love. Let it take you to levels you've never known. You're my sweet thing and I love you. Thank you for making my erotic exotic fantasy come true."

I woke up with a smile on my face. Sex on the beach, I was tripping hard. I was having champagne wishes and chocolate dreams. I wanted Monica so bad that I was beginning to have crazy dreams.

JAMAICA: 10

The next morning we all got up around 5 a.m. Monica and I did pretty good to have only gotten a little over an hour of sleep. We departed BWI airport at 7:30 a.m. We flew on Air Jamaica flight #240. Our take off was pretty smooth and so was most of the flight. Monica and I were really tired because we stayed up too late the night before, so we slept most of the flight. The landing was rough and it upset most of the passengers. The most important thing was that we made it to Jamaica safely. We arrived in Montego Bay about 9:45 a.m. Right away I could see how beautiful Jamaica was. There was a shuttle bus from the resort waiting for us. In Jamaica they drive on the opposite side of the road. My father had no intention of renting a car because he feared driving in Jamaica. The bus driver was seated on the right side of the bus. After everyone boarded the shuttle we sped down the left side of the road. When we arrived at the resort the social director greeted us. His name was Thomas. He was a tall thin clean-cut Jamaican guy about thirty-years-old. He told us he would give us time to settle in and he would be starting a tour of the resort in an hour. The resort was really nice. My parents went all out for this trip. We were rolling with the big shots and stomping with the big dogs.

The resort was a kaleidoscope of beautiful Caribbean colors. There were tall palm trees swaying in the breeze. It was about 86 degrees. People were complaining about the heat and humidity. Obviously, they weren't from the southeast region of the United States. The heat and humidity in Jamaica were tame compared to what we had just left. The main lobby of the resort was filled with exotic tropical trees and plants. I didn't see many black faces around the resort except for the staff. I didn't say anything because I didn't think anyone was in the mood to hear my righteous views. So, I kept them to myself. I felt privileged and inspired to be in the homeland of Bob Marley and Marcus Garvey. I noticed that the resort was full of rich white people. I didn't feel out of place because not only did we look rich, but we were rich. I thought we represented Black America real well. Our villa was located on top of a hill less than a mile from the main lobby. In reality it was just a short walk, but the staff arranged for us to be dropped off. The resort had hotel rooms and suites, but I liked the villas a lot better. We went directly to our villa after checking in.

We instantly fell in love with our three-bedroom villa. It was really luxurious with all the conveniences of home plus a Jacuzzi. The living room had an entertainment center with a color TV, VCR and stereo. We loved the decor of the villa. The bright colors of the furniture and walls added lots flavor to the place. I sat back in a chair and kicked my feet up on the ottoman. We were living like rich white folks from a popular soap opera or television series. I just wanted some blacks there to enjoy all this with us. I hopped on the sofa to see how deep it would allow me to sink. The sofa was so tight it held me up like I was weightless. My father taught me how to tell the difference between a quality sofa and a piece of junk. This was definitely a quality sofa. The entire place had class written all over it. From the living room we had a perfect view of the resort and the beach. I stepped out on the balcony. I saw

124

sailboats, wind surfers and water-skiers. The balcony was neatly furnished with tropical plants and a hammock built for two. There was even a heavy steel and glass table with four chairs. This was a perfect set up for a romantic dinner or for lounging on a lazy Sunday morning. This place was guaranteed to cater to our every need. Back inside, the dining area had an expensive looking antique wooden table with six wooden chairs. The bedrooms were nice too. The master bedroom suite was all that and more. It had a king sized bed, a 27" floor model color TV, a spacious master bath and Jacuzzi. I wanted to bump my parents out of the master suite, so Monica and I could move in. I guess they deserved the master suite since they were paying for everything. Monica and I were still tired. I felt like going straight to bed, but I knew my father wanted us to take the tour of the resort with him and my mother. My father was probably the most excited of all. He promised to keep us busy all week long. The first day we planned to stay in Montego Bay and hang out around the resort. Monica was so impressed with the place that she almost forgot to call her parents to let them know we had arrived safely.

We all met up with Thomas in the main lobby. He seemed to be a real cool guy. I noticed how he was checking out all the ladies around the resort.

Thomas said, "Again, welcome to MoBay. I guarantee you'll enjoy your stay here."

Thomas guided us throughout the resort. He gave us a brief history of the resort as we headed for the beach. The beach was covered with white sand. I smiled because I was having a flashback of my hot chocolate dream and the jet-black silky sand. I liked the sand even though it was the complete opposite of what I saw in my dream. Jamaica had the most beautiful white sand and crystal clear water I'd ever seen. It made all of the stateside beaches back home seem dirty and contaminated. The resort had four restaurants featuring Jamaican and American cuisines. The beach pavilions were preparing lunch during our tour. The bar was up and running serving drinks. They gave us refreshments including these delicious tropical fruit drinks. This resort had it all. An Olympic size pool, tennis courts, a fitness center and an 18-hole golf course. The complete tour took just over an hour. Thomas said a shuttle bus would be leaving for Dunn's River Falls in Ocho Rios at 9 a.m. the next morning. We planned to go to Ocho Rios. I asked my parents if it was okay for me and Monica to go down on the beach. Monica wanted to go back to the villa to do something. She said she had a surprise for me.

I went to the bathroom to put on my trunks. When I came out Monica was standing there in a two piece bikini.

Monica said, "Surprise!!!"

"You look so good. Let me get a closer look."

I grabbed Monica and gave her a kiss on the lips.

"You're so beautiful."

"I picked this one out when I went shopping with Jennifer. We knew you'd like it."

I smiled. "You're gonna turn a lot heads on the beach. You need to cover your butt, so I won't have to knock anybody out."

"What, my butt doesn't look right?"

"I'm just joking. You look sexy."

"I'm gonna wear my sarong anyway."

When we got on the beach guys were eyeballing Monica real hard. There were people on the beach reading, tanning and simply relaxing. Further down the beach there was a volleyball game going on. We sat down next to an older white couple. They acted as if they didn't see us, so I made them speak.

I said, "Hello."

The man looked at us like we were doing something wrong. I felt like he thought we were resort staff members taking an extended break. His wife actually spoke to us.

She said, "Hello, are you staying here?"

I thought, *I knew it. What the hell do you think?*

I said, "Yes, we are. If you look up on the hill just to the right between those palm trees, at the white villa with the charcoal colored roof. Can you see it?"

"Yes."

"That's where we're staying. My father happens to be one of the top surgeons in the United States."

I made that up, but it sounded good. Monica kept quiet and just smiled. The woman's face became blushed.

"That's wonderful."

Her husband really didn't have anything to say then. I could tell his wife was impressed. My intent wasn't to impress them, but instead to let them know that I wasn't just some freeloading peasant. I never asked what they did for a living because I could tell from their reactions that they weren't really big shots. They probably won a trip or were using the husband's boss' time-share. After awhile, I did notice a few more black people other than the resort's staff. I know the woman's husband noticed them too.

I heard him say, "Honey, I've had enough sun."

His wife looked at me and said, "It was nice meeting you."

"I'm sorry I didn't get your name." Like I really cared.

"That was very rude of me. I'm Catherine Schafer and this is my husband Henry."

"Hi, Mr. Schafer. I'm Eric Brown and this is my girlfriend Monica Cameron. My friends call me Black."

Mr. Schafer looked at me like he had some other names he wanted to call me. I couldn't believe this guy still didn't know what to say to me.

Mrs. Schafer said, "It was nice meeting you Monica and Black, but we really do have to go."

She did a good job of saving her husband from an awkward situation. And I did notice that she referred to me as Black. I guess she was a lot cooler than I gave her credit for being. As they walked away we noticed a young black couple approaching us. When I looked again I figured that they were brother and sister. I thought the girl was cute, but there was something awkward about the guy. He was walking on the beach sipping what looked like iced tea through a long straw.

He said, "How y'all doing?"

I said, "Pretty good." I smiled. "How are you guys doing?"

"We're doing good. Did y'all just get here?"

"Yeah."

He said, "I'm Daron and this is Missy. Is that your girlfriend 'cause y'all make a cute little couple?"

"Yeah, I'm Black and this is my girlfriend Monica. So, Missy's your sister, right?"

"Oh, so like I can't have a girlfriend or something."

All of us had to laugh at that.

"No, y'all just look a lot alike. That's all."

"Yeah, she's my sister."

I don't know who Daron thought he was fooling. We all finished greeting and Daron stepped over to Monica and touched her hair.

"I know you got Indian in your blood. You got good hair. I do hair, but I'm really a dancer/choreographer. And I gotta beautiful singing voice too."

This guy obviously had a little too much *sugar* in his iced tea.

I asked, "Where are you from?"

Missy answered, "We're from Howard County in Maryland."

"Seriously, we're from Randallstown."

Daron goes, "Oh my God, for real."

We sat and talked to Missy and Daron for awhile and they finally had to meet up with their parents. It was nice to meet them, especially since they were around our age and happened to be from our home state. They arrived at the resort along with their parents the day before we did. Finally, I was alone with Monica. We moved some chairs to a nice little spot on the beach. We were trying to relax. All I wanted to hear was the ocean and I didn't want to talk to anyone else besides Monica. The sun felt nice beaming down on us. We rubbed each other down with sunscreen. I removed one of Monica's sandals and gave her a serious little foot massage.

"I want to pamper you all this week."

"That sounds nice. I have some special stuff planned for you too."

"Oh, really. I can't wait to find out what you have in store for me.

You look so good that I can't help myself."

Monica's stomach looked so tight and sexy that I had to sneak in a little kiss to her belly. The beach was so relaxing. The atmosphere was taking over me. I felt a calming sensation come over my body. If I had died at that exact moment, I would have gone peacefully. Monica and I laid on the beach holding hands trying to compose a poem describing the Caribbean and the sensations we felt. Nothing I could think of except an orgasm could top what we felt. The Caribbean atmosphere was incredible. I felt like I was falling in love with Monica all over again. We laid there for hours. At first I was worried about getting too dark, but I loved my dark complexion and I felt that the sun was only enhancing what God had naturally given me. I thought about something that Lisa used to tell me a long time ago. The darker the berry the sweeter the juice and the darker the skin the deeper the roots.

Monica and I were getting hungry, so I gave her a piggyback ride up to the pavilion for lunch. We sat at the table and were served right away. We ordered Jerk Chicken with black beans and rice. We ate fresh fruit and I had to have another tropical fruit drink. I started wondering what our friends were doing back home. I wished we all could have been there together.

Thomas walked over to our table.

He said, "How's everything going?"

"Good, everything's fine. We already know your name. I'm Black and this is my girlfriend Monica."

"It's a pleasure meeting you. Monica, you're a very beautiful young lady."

"She knows she's beautiful, I tell her all the time. Thanks a lot."

Monica smiled like she had just won something. Thomas was trying to use his smooth Caribbean appeal on my girl. For a minute, I thought it might have been working a little.

I thought, *Give me a break...back the fuck up, you Shabba Ranks lookin' bastard...I mean, like you're not getting enough from the other tourists.*

About six women greeted him in an extra friendly way as he sat there talking to us. Not to mention the ones I noticed greeting him during the tour. Another guy walked up to our table as we sat there talking.

Thomas said, "Black and Monica, This is my brother Preston."

Preston looked like Thomas, but a little younger with shoulder length dreadlocks.

He said, "Hello." He shook my hand and said, "This how we do it in Jamaica."

Preston made a fist and pounded it up and down against mine. I thought that was all right, but I didn't like what I saw next. He held Monica's hand a little too long for me.

"Monica's my girlfriend."

Preston said, "And she's very beautiful. It's a pleasure meetin' ya."

These brothas were starting to get on my nerves. Damn, how would they treat her if I wasn't around? They were a little too forward for me. I wasn't intimidated. I just wanted some respect. I tried acting normal like they weren't pissing me off.

I asked, "How's the Blue Mountain tour?"

Thomas said, "Listen don't go to no mountains. I live here and I don't go to no mountains. They'll rob your ass mon. Stay outta Kingston too. There's some bad spots in Montego Bay, but you're safe at this resort. I'm not trying to scare you, but there's lots of poor people here."

"I understand and thanks for being honest."

Thomas said, "We gotta go now, but Black ya might wanna check out the fitness center. We gonna be there shortly."

Preston asked, "Do ya like reggae music?"

I said, "Yeah."

Preston said, "Come check out my band tonight down there." He pointed to another pavilion. "I'm gonna be performing."

The waiter finally brought out our food, and thank God. Thomas and Preston left us alone so we could eat. I could see my parents making their way over to the pavilion.

130

"Hey Ma. What's up Dad. Y'all just missed these Jamaican gigolos trying to pick up my girl right in my face."

My father said, "I know, I can't leave your mother alone for a minute. It's only going to get worse when we leave the resort and hit the town."

My mother said, "Don't you know Jamaican men love American women?"

Hey, I was beginning to think my mother had a lot more than mothballs in her closet. The skeletons were starting to break loose.

I said, "I'm going to the fitness center to workout. Monica, do you want to go?"

Monica said, "No, I'm going to stay here with your parents."

"I'll meet y'all at the villa in about an hour."

I didn't need to change. I had on shorts and a T-shirt and that was fine to wear for a workout. When I got to the fitness center Thomas and Preston were already there.

Thomas said, "What's up Black. Come on over." They were lifting weights.

"Hey what's up?"

"Do ya like it here mon?"

"Yeah, but I didn't like the way you and your brother were flirting with my girl."

"No disrespect. We treat all da ladies like dat."

Preston looked at me like he didn't care.

He said, "We can't help it. American women love Jamaican men and we love them. We party with them all da time. White, black, young and old."

"Yeah, so what. I've noticed all your women. Monica's mine and respect that."

Thomas said, " It's okay, mon. Why do they call ya Black?"

"Monica gave me that name."

"Well Black, hang with us and you can get all the girls. We'll take you to see *real* Jamaica. This ain't Jamaica, this a damn resort. You ain't seen nothing till ya come with us."

I said, "I'm trying to go to Sunsplash in a couple of days."

Thomas said, "Cool, ya gonna be with us."

Preston stopped working out and said, "Check dis out. It's only August and I've had 'bout a hundred women this year." Preston started laughing. "I can sing their panties off. Mon, don't never trust your girl in Jamaica alone. If she get fucked, she ain't never gonna tell ya da truth. What happen in Jamaica stay in Jamaica and she just come back home to ya happy."

I said, "Bullshit, not my girl."

Thomas laughed, "We gonna school ya. Show ya how rude boys run things."

"I believe y'all, but we need to finish working out. Fuck all this talking."

I knew they weren't lying. I saw so many women in their faces all smiling and flirting. They had it made. Any handsome young black man who wanted to be a gigolo needed to be in Jamaica, it was definitely the place to be. There were horny women all over the place waiting for some good sex. I felt like I could pull it off. After one day I was already developing an accent. All I needed was some ganja and a Red Stripe Beer to put me at ease.

After my workout I was feeling good. I met up with Monica and my parents at the villa. They were getting ready for the nighttime reggae party. I wanted to have a private party with Monica, but we had to spend time with my parents. Earlier that day they had been out shopping at one of the local craft markets. They picked up some nice wooden carvings and T-shirts. Monica and I planned to go with them the next time. I really didn't mind spending the evening with my parents, but I did need some private time with Monica because she was looking real good. Jamaica made her look like an exotic beauty. Even in the Caribbean no one could compare to her beauty.

We all were ready for the reggae party. The resort looked even better at night. When we got down to the beach the entertainment was just starting. Preston's band was performing. Most of the crowd were American tourists, but there were some Europeans mixed in the crowd. I could see a lot more black people now.

132

Preston's band was pretty good. Of course, they did some Bob Marley songs. They mostly did original songs, but when I really listened they were doing American Pop and R&B songs to a reggae rhythm. I liked that a lot. Monica asked me to dance with her. I didn't get up right away, so she pulled me by the arm and I finally gave in. I had fun dancing with her. This was the first time we'd ever danced together. My parents got up and were dancing next to us. They looked like old pros on the dance floor. They were world travelers and had been to the Caribbean many times. Preston noticed us and gave Monica and me a shout-out. I saw Daron and Missy come up with their parents. All of a sudden, Daron broke out dancing. He could dance his ass off. Pretty soon people stopped dancing to watch him. He was stealing the show from Preston and his band. I think Preston started getting jealous because he started dancing harder and faster. He got the crowd's attention for a minute until Daron stole Preston's moves and did them twice as good. Missy came over and started dancing with her brother. They were both dance students with an unfair advantage over everyone else that was bold enough to continue dancing. When the music stopped I think Missy and Daron got more applause than the band. I invited Missy, Daron and their parents to join us at our table. We introduced our parents. Everyone was having a good time. Preston had to give it to Daron. He kicked his butt dancing. Preston called Daron up on stage to dance. Preston had no idea what he was starting. Daron was a real showoff. He grabbed the mic from Preston and said something to the band. The next thing I knew Daron was singing Michael Jackson's *Billie Jean* to a reggae beat. This fool even moon walked across the stage. I laughed so hard my throat hurt. After about three songs Daron finally returned to his seat. He really helped liven up the party.

We ate curried fish and chicken for dinner. Monica and I had more tropical fruit drinks and my parents drank rum and beer. Things slowed down after awhile. Monica and I went down to walk on the beach. This was a beautiful night. The moon was reflecting off the ocean. We could hear some slow reggae music playing in the background. Most of the couples were on the beach or in the gazebos. There were torches lit up along the beach. The moonlight, fire, the gentle breeze and the sound of the ocean set a perfect romantic scene. Monica and I picked a remote spot on the beach. I wanted to get my feet wet, so I sat down right at the edge of the beach. Monica took off her shoes and sat between my legs. This was real nice. The water came up a little further than we expected, but we didn't mind. I held Monica tight between my legs. I pulled her hair to one side and gave her kisses on the back of her neck. We sat on the beach for awhile until we noticed there was no one in the gazebo. We rushed right to it. The gazebo gave me a better angle to kiss Monica. I put my arm around her and she cuddled up close to me.

"I can't believe how the sky looks."

"It's so clear. I can see almost every star. I'm going to get up early tomorrow and paint the sunrise."

"Um, that sounds real nice. Wake me up when you finish."

"No, you better be right on the beach with me."

"You know I'm kidding. I'm down for whatever makes you happy."

"I love Jamaica."

Monica made me think about what Preston and all the things he told me about American women in Jamaica.

I asked, "Would you ever come here alone?"

"No, I couldn't enjoy all this without you. What made you ask that?"

"No real reason. I was just asking. I love you."

"I love you too."

"We should head back to the villa if you still plan to paint the sunrise in the morning."

"Let's stay a little longer."

Love was in the air and I swear I was deep breathing. Monica had me on a serious love high. The Caribbean air must have been an aphrodisiac because my hormones were raging. I kissed Monica like there was no tomorrow. She loved it and so did I. All I had on my mind was making love to her. Everything was perfect. This was the place where I wanted it to happen. Monica cuddled up closer to me. I didn't want to ask if we could make love. I knew what her answer was going to be. I figured if it was going to happen it would happen naturally and that's how I wanted it to go down. It never hurt to ask, but the last time I asked it did hurt. The word "No" echoed through my head. I wasn't going to let the word "No" spoil our mood. Since we weren't going to make love I needed Monica to use her hands as a substitute. It was like she read my mind. I felt her hand slide down my abdomen to my pelvic region. She was somewhat scared.

"People will notice."

"They can't make out what's going on over here."

Monica moved her hands into position. She admired the length and the width.

"Uh yeah, that feels good...up a little...ooh right there faster... yeah faster...ah yeah, that's it."

Monica started tonguing me down. She was being more aggressive than usual and I liked it.

"That was good. I'm better now. A man can go crazy without any release."

"I guess I can relate a little bit."

We headed back to the villa to get some rest for an early start. Monica really wanted to paint the sunrise and we had also planned to go to Ohco Rios the next morning.

I felt kisses to my forehead, cheeks, lips and neck. I opened my eyes and it looked the same as it did when I closed them hours earlier. This was Monica's special wake up call. It was time for us to go to the beach. I promised her that I would, so I had to go through with it. I wanted to see the Jamaican sunrise at some point anyway. I needed a few minutes to get rolling.

Believe it or not there were other people on the beach already. A few of the people looked like they had been there all night. As we set up Monica's equipment people watched us like they were completely puzzled. It was about 5:10 a.m. I was surprised that no

135

one else thought about painting the sunrise. I kicked back in a chaise lounge and found myself drifting off to another world. The morning sky and the sound of the ocean put me to sleep like a soft lullaby. The next thing I remembered was getting my right big toe plucked. Another wake up call from Monica. I'd take the kisses over the pluck anytime. She was making progress. We could see the sun's first rays pierce through the horizon. The light glistened out on to the ocean. Monica was capturing all this on canvas. Looking at her picture was like looking at the actual sunrise. This was the first time I'd ever seen Monica at work. The people on the beach were impressed with her work. They kept commenting on all the detail her painting conveyed. Yellow, orange and a brilliant white blended together to form the sunlight, which emerged from the blue-black darkness of the horizon to bring this picture to life. Each time I thought Monica was drawing to an end, her brush continued to stroke. She gave life to the clouds that arched the horizon like a giant brow. Breathtaking. She had captured one of God's finest works and claimed it as her own. The skills Monica possessed were natural and no one could ever have taught her this technique. The sun rose, shined and blazed its way all over the canvas. Monica strictly painted for her own pleasure and at the same time she created something so appealing to others. I was beginning to understand why it was hard for her to set a price for her work. In just a few minutes she created a priceless beauty. Some of the spectators asked if they could buy her painting. She quickly told them her work wasn't for sale. No one saw the sunrise like Monica did that morning. I noticed a Polaroid shot of the sunrise that someone had taken. It only captured ten percent of the sunrise's natural qualities. Monica was able to reproduce every natural essence that the sunrise had to offer. Her eyes, mind and hands moved in perfect unison anticipating the suns next move. The camera failed miserably, it simply produced a still photo with a limited spectrum of the true colors of a much more vivid sunrise.

   On our way back to the villa I reminded Monica that we only had a few hours before our trip to Dunn's River Falls. We got my parents and we all went to breakfast in the resort's main dining room. There was a very appetizing breakfast buffet set up for everyone. We ate a traditional Jamaican breakfast of ackee and saltfish with Johnny cakes. My parents drank authentic Blue Mountain coffee. The coffee beans are only grown on Jamaica's eastern mountain slopes. My parents called it the world's finest coffee. Monica and I drank fruit juice because we didn't like coffee. Our breakfast was hot and tasty, but my attention was focused somewhere else. I overheard four young attractive white women at the table across from us talking about going to Negril to a nude beach. That sounded real nice to me, but I wasn't sure if I had enough dick control for a nude beach. No way was I trying to walk around with a rock hard Willie in front of a bunch of nude blushing white women. Nobody was getting a free Mandingo fantasy from me. I wondered how guys could be so limp around so many attractive nude women. If I was on the beach everyone would think of me as a disgusting low-class pervert. Somehow, I'd let them know that this pervert had plenty of style and class.

Everyone at my table was quiet so I entertained myself. I had to bring my focus back to my plate. I was easily distracted by anything dealing with nude women. I was having second thoughts about where I wanted to spend my day. A part of me wanted to hop the bus going to Negril and skip Dunn's River Falls. After breakfast we went looking for our bus. I saw Thomas and he directed us to an old beat-down-ass bus.

The driver asked, "Ya goin' to da falls, mon?"

I said, "Yep."

The other shuttle bus that picked us up from the airport was a piece of shit too, but this one couldn't win third prize in a junkyard contest even if it was only going up against two other buses.

The driver had some cool reggae playing. This kind of took the emphasis off the crappy-ass bus. We were speeding down the road and from where I was sitting it felt like the bus was out of control. We were in for a ninety-minute ride to Ocho Rios. The main road was fine. Once we got off the main road the others were a little messed up with giant potholes. The driver swayed to avoid them at the same time swaying back to avoid oncoming traffic. There were kids everywhere walking or riding bikes along the road. They seemed to have no fear of the traffic. I saw shacks along the way. Some were houses and others were shops or restaurants. The reggae music seemed to add a theme to the trip. The music made me feel like we were in the middle of a music video shoot. From the road we had a nice view of the endless blue sky, turquoise ocean and green countryside. Dunn's River Falls was located in a well-maintained park. We could hear the falls as we entered the park. My father described the area as a tropical rainforest with exquisite wildflowers. He was right. I had my waterproof camera with me. I photographed the other tourists, trees, ferns and orchids. The sound of the falls got even louder. We could hear people yelling, laughing and having a good time. The area was full of tourists from local resorts and cruise ships. Right away I knew this was going to be a very unique experience. The falls were naturally formed tiers of limestone with cool white water running down. The tall rainforest shaded the falls. We had to wait in line to climb the falls and we all formed a human chain and tried to maintain our balance while scaling the slippery limestone. We laughed watching people slip. After about an hour or so, we finally made it to the top of the 600-ft. falls.

There's a craft market at the top of Dunn River Falls. My parents went down to the beach where we planned to meet them later. Monica and I wanted to see what the market had to offer. My parents warned us about the vendors' aggressive sales tactics. They told us never to pay the asking price for anything. The craft market was full of tourists. I'd never seen so many crafts in my life. I could see that the crafts were deep-rooted in African tradition. The first stall we walked up to had woodcarvings of Jamaican men and women. The vendor was a friendly woman who greeted us with a big smile.

"Sweetie, can I sell ya somethin'?"

She pointed at her carvings and started explaining them. "These are made of mahogany, ebony and this rose colored wood is called lignum vitae."

Her carvings were nice, but we wanted to look around a little more. Her carvings ranged from $25 to $75. I thought that was the right price range for her crafts. I thought about what my parents said and we walked away.

The lady said, "Give me ten-dollar for dis or thirty for dis one." I said, "We'll be back."

A Rastafarian with long dreadlocks ran the next stall we walked up to.

He said, "I got the best crafts at the best price. Take a look, mon."

"We'll be back."

"Take a look at dis!"

"We'll be back."

His stuff was good, but we didn't have much time to stop at every stall and talk. At the next stall there was a woman who tried playing on our guilt.

She said, "Hello Sir, can ya buy somethin'? I'm a poor mother of five and I need help. Can ya buy somethin' please sir?"

The woman's story almost worked on us. Monica asked if we could buy something.

"We'll be back."

I noticed this cool Rasta playing an old beat up guitar. He was singing a reggae song I think he made up himself. He stopped singing when he spotted us. He tried selling us some ganja.

"Whatcha know 'bout dis mon. How many spliffs ya need?"

I said, "None, thanks for offering, but I don't smoke."

"Lord have mercy. Ya don't know whatcha missin'."

Monica and I laughed and got the hell away from him real fast. We ended up going back to the pitiful woman and buying some beaded necklaces, shells and straw baskets. We did go back to the first stall and got two wooden carvings. Monica and I got something to eat from a jerk chicken stall. After all that we went down to the beach with my parent. We told them they were right about the vendors. An hour later it was time to go back to the bus.

The ride back to the resort seemed shorter. We still had plenty of daylight left, so we went snorkeling when we returned to the resort. I think our busy pace was starting to catch up with us. We all were tired, but we went back to the villa and got dressed for dinner. My dinner was out of this world. One thing I could honestly say was that I enjoyed every meal. For dinner that night everyone except my father had curried lobster with potatoes, steamed broccoli and carrots. He ate curried goat with rice and peas. I couldn't eat goat even if I wanted. By this time I had even stopped eating beef. After dinner Monica and I went back to the villa. My parents went to the bar for drinks. They said they would probably stay out for a few hours partying with Missy and Daron's parents. It was hard to gauge exactly how long they would be gone. Monica and I wanted to get a little freaky, but we had to play it safe. After our showers we just chilled out in the villa. Monica had on her sexy black pajamas and robe. All I had on was my pajama bottoms. Monica told me to lie down and she started kissing my chest. We almost forgot about the Jacuzzi. I was about to strip down and jump in the Jacuzzi.

Monica asked, "If your parents walk in, how are we going to explain being in the Jacuzzi butt ball naked?"

"Damn, you're right. We'd be busted. Put your bikini on and I'll put on my trunks. Monica, grab that basket of fruit from the kitchen on your way back."

We got into the water and fed each other mangos, guavas, grapes and June plums. We were about to get something started when we heard my parents come into the villa. At first, they tried to sneak in the room.

My mother yelled, "I hope everyone's decent."

I yelled back, "Not yet give us a minute. I'm just playing come in."

My parents looked worried, but all they saw was me and Monica in the Jacuzzi in swimwear eating fruit. To their surprise we looked completely innocent. They told us to make sure that was all we did. They stayed for a few minutes then went back to their party. I gave

Monica a high five for suggesting that we put something on. We got out of the Jacuzzi dried off a bit and went out on the balcony. We picked up where we left off before my parents rudely interrupted us. I was looking out on the beach when Monica came up behind me. She had a small bottle of baby oil with her. She wrapped her arms around me and ran her soft oily hands all around my upper body. She grabbed my right hand and put my index finger in her mouth. She looked me in the eyes and started sucking my fingers. My little seductress was doing a fine job at turning me on. With my free hand I untied her bikini top and pulled her closer uniting our bare chests. We probably looked like exhibitionists half-naked on the balcony kissing. I don't think anyone saw us. Even if someone did see us it was a pleasant sight to witness and one not so foreign to the Caribbean. Monica and I laid on the hammock and fell asleep in each other's arms. The next thing I remembered was my parents waking us. I panicked for a minute. I looked at Monica and to my surprise she had on her bikini top. I guess I dozed off first and she slipped the top on again. My parents directed us to our rooms and I was off to sleep again.

The next day I woke up to the sounds of calypso music. I stepped out into the living room to see what was going on. I saw my parents dancing, laughing and having a good time. They woke up early to practice dancing for the resort's calypso night. I thought they were funny because they were so serious about entering a dance contest. It made me feel good seeing the two of them so happy together. Seeing them together like that made me wonder how my father could ever cheat on my mother. She was a beautiful intelligent woman with so much to offer. I came to realize he was actually very happy with my mother. It was rare to hear them argue about anything. His cheating had little to do with what she did, but more to do with him having his cake and eating it too. Infidelity is a touchy subject, which isn't easily explained. One thing that came to mind was my insatiable sexual appetite. I was sure heredity had some part to play in that. I could almost see where my father was coming from with his extra-curricular activity. I didn't approve of what he was doing, not even his sexual appetite could justify his infidelity. I was sure my mother knew my father had been unfaithful, but she was incredibly happy. The happiness was probably superficial and the hurt was buried deep inside. I stood there and in just a few seconds I somewhat desensitized myself to my father's cheating. For a long time his cheating bothered me. At that moment I understood, but I still didn't approve. I analyzed my parents and myself and came to the realization that it was best not to analyze their situation any further. My father was always discreet with his dirt. People talked, but no one had any concrete proof. Not only was my father smooth with his dirt, but he was pretty smooth on the dance floor.

Too bad I was going to miss calypso night. I was going to Sunsplash with Thomas and Preston. This was supposed to be their opportunity to teach me the art of being a Jamaican gigolo. That sounded like fun, but I wanted to experience Sunsplash with Monica. Thomas called me to meet up with him and Preston. I told him I was bringing Monica along and he sounded happy to hear that. On the way down to the lobby we ran into Missy and Daron. I invited them to join us like I was driving or something. Thomas didn't mind the added company, so the six of us crammed into his little car. Sunsplash was held at the Bob Marley Centre in Montego Bay. That year Sunsplash featured acts like Ziggy Marley, Shabba Ranks, Shinehead, Steel Pulse, Third World, Sugar Minott and so many other talented acts. Sunsplash was the biggest reggae festival anywhere. There were tens of thousands of reggae fans from all over the world in town.

We were standing in a huge field filled with people jumping up and down dancing all over the place. I liked to see Jamaicans dance. All I can say is that it was almost X-rated to watch. We called it dry sex. There was scaffolding set up in the middle of the field with soundmen, equipment, lights and cameras. People were puffing ganja like cigarettes. I never used drugs before, but that day I caught a serious contact. Monica was feeling it too. We got caught up in a cloud of smoke. Missy and Daron didn't complain at all. They were enjoying the contact. Monica and I didn't want to seem like party poopers, so we didn't complain. The music was out of this world, but the smoke did take away from my fun. Before going to Jamaica I was already a big fan of reggae music. I could see and feel Bob Marley's influence everywhere. I wished that I could have had the opportunity to see him perform live. I knew a lot about the people of Jamaica. The entire day Thomas tested my knowledge and gave me additional lessons on the people, food, drinks, music and heritage of Jamaica. I saw white Jamaicans for the first time. It was strange hearing white people speak with Jamaican accents. Thomas referred to the white people born in Jamaica as Jamaican whites. Some of those people looked like they were passing. After so many years on the island their blood had to be mixed. He said the white people of Jamaica were divided into two groups. The other group of whites were European immigrants mostly from England. He referred to them as white Jamaicans. It was strange being in a country where black people were the majority. While I was at Sunsplash I really looked at the people. I looked at all the different skin tones, hair textures and body shapes of the people. Looking at the people there made me want dreadlocks. That day I realized black people were the same regardless of what country we were from. People of color from all over the world could relate to reggae music, especially to Bob Marley's songs of oppression, rebellion and freedom. I was impressed with Rastafarians. To my surprise Thomas was a Rastafarian. I was under the impression that all Rastafarians smoked ganja and had dreadlocks. But Thomas proved to be different. He told me about the philosophies and traditions of Rastafarians. I already knew quite a bit about them and their ties to Marcus Garvey, Haile Selassie and Africa. We stayed at Sunsplash almost fourteen hours. Overall, I had a very enlightening experience. We all had a really good time. Thomas and Preston actually showed me the respect I had been looking for when it came to Monica.

When we returned to the villa my parents told us that they won

143

third place in the dance contest. They looked disappointed for some reason. They actually had their hearts set on winning first place. I was proud of them for just placing in the contest. I made them realize how good they had done. I was sure they faced some stiff competition. I wasn't trying to stay up too late trying to convince them how good they were. I needed a vacation from my vacation. I found myself constantly on the go.

The remainder of our stay in Jamaica was nice. We saw more of Montego Bay. We visited the legendary Rose Hall Mansion, which is supposed to be haunted. Our days were filled with sightseeing. We went downtown to the craft markets and experienced more harassment from the vendors. We rode taxis to get around town. These taxis were unlike any I'd ever seen. One was so bad that I couldn't tell the color, make, model or anything else about the little four-door piece of shit. All I knew was somehow it ran and it was fast. We spent lots of time walking up and down Gloucester Ave. looking at hotels, restaurants, cafes, stalls and storefronts. We also got the chance to visit Doctor's Cave and Cornwall Beaches. Our resort was so sheltered that it felt good for us to move around the Montego Bay so freely. One of our taxi drivers, Solomon, was extra friendly to us. I guess it had a lot to do with my father tipping him so well. Solomon offered to take my parents out to a popular dancehall later that night. They were so wound up that they agreed to go. I guess they couldn't get enough of Jamaica's energetic nightlife.

Our last night in Jamaica Monica and I had dinner with my parents. After dinner they went out and we went back to the villa to pack. A few hours later they returned looking like they had been chased home by a ghost. They had me worried.

I asked, "What happened?"

My father said, "I don't want to talk about it."

My mother said, "You wouldn't believe what happened."

Monica and I became more anxious.

Monica asked, "Is there anything I can do?"

My father held up his bare left wrist where his gold and diamond

Rolex used to be.

"Damn, they got robbed," I said in a low tone.

My father said, "We were robbed."

I asked, "Was it that taxi driver?"

My mother said, "No, but I'm sure he had something to do with it."

Monica looked worried. She asked, "Are you two okay?"

My father said, "No, but we'll be fine. It's all my fault. I don't know what the hell I was thinking. Why was I wearing that watch anyway? I thank God because we could have been killed. That damn Solomon lead us to a table in the back of the dancehall and left us. We weren't even sitting there a minute when this guy came up and pulled out a gun. I can't even remember what he looked like because it happened so fast. All I remember seeing was the handle of the gun before he pulled it out of his pants. Then, I saw that long black barrel. He asked for my watch and all of our money. He got about $225 from us. That's nothing, but my watch meant a lot to me." He grabbed my mother. "But you...you mean everything to me."

My father became overwhelmed with emotions at the thought of what could have happened and headed to the master bedroom.

My mother said, "Don't worry we're going to be fine. I'm so glad we're leaving in the morning. No matter what I still love Jamaica. Goodnight, I love you two."

It was hard for me to process what happened. The robbery was so sudden. Things were going too good. The most important thing was that my parents were safe. My father's pride was hurt. He was having so much fun that he forgot about his and my mother's safety. That was totally unlike him and I think that's what hurt him so bad. If this had to happen I was glad that it happened on our last night. My father was so upset that he probably would have been ready to cut our vacation short. I just wanted to sleep this off.

The next morning our flight left at 9:15 a.m. My father was quiet for most of the flight. Eventually, we all agreed with my mother that we loved Jamaica and would gladly return. I couldn't stop thinking about my father's Rolex. It was worth thousands and the idiot that stole it would probably only got a hundred dollars for it. With all those diamonds on that watch, the thief would have had a hard time convincing someone that they were real and an even harder time proving that it was an real Rolex.

My mind was so busy worrying about my parents that I actually lost focus of Monica. She was so sweet. She knew I had a lot on my mind. I felt her grab my hand. She started massaging my hands with lotion. The hand massage was soothing to me. Before I knew it Monica was giving me a manicure. She was spoiling me. Men love shit like that. Sometimes it's the little things that mean the most. I realized that I failed to fulfill my mission of making love to Monica. The more I thought about it, I realized that we made all the love we needed. Monica and I made love each and every time we looked at each other. We made love each and every time we touched. We had definitely made love. We just never had intercourse with each other.

EXTRA SEXUAL: 11

During the entire flight home I was tormented by turbulence. Things got so rough that the fasten seatbelt sign lit up and the pilot ordered everyone to return to their seats. I closed my eyes and pretty much accepted my fate. I seriously thought we were going to crash. I prayed to God that he would let us make it home safely and he did. When the plane landed I was so happy I almost kissed the ground. After we went through customs Mr. and Mrs. Cameron greeted us at the terminal. They looked so happy to see Monica and she looked equally happy to see them. I wasn't sure how my face looked, but I wanted Monica to stay with us. Monica's parents embraced her and then they hugged me. They made me feel like part of the family. They thanked my parents for everything. All of a sudden I felt sad from the thought of them taking my sweetheart away. I was completely spoiled. I had gotten used to being close to Monica everyday. We were under the same roof for a week and now it was almost back to business. I still needed more time with her even though I was going to see her later that day. I felt terrible when we separated. Monica hugged me and whispered I love you in my ear. She thanked me and my parents for a wonderful and unforgettable time.

Every time I'm away from home for awhile I have to get used to my house all over again. My house looked so different. My father was in the kitchen sorting through a pile of mail. He handed me two envelopes. The first envelope contained my class schedule. I was going to be in Mrs. Porter's homeroom class. I had no idea who she was. The second envelope contained a generic looking store-bought greeting card that simply read "Happy Birthday." It was the type of card which was intended to have a message written in it, but whoever sent this card didn't even sign it. There was no return address. I checked the postmark. It was from North Carolina. STACEY!!! I had this feeling that the card had to be from her. I was excited. I put the card down and decided to call Monica to compare class schedules. When I called Monica her mother said that she was asleep. The card stayed on my mind. What if it was from one of my relatives in North Carolina? For all I knew it could have been from my great grandmother. I did send her a card for her ninety-first birthday. She was probably getting senile and forgot to sign the card. What the hell was I thinking? Deep down I had a gut feeling that it was from Stacey. I bet the card was blank because it was too hard for Stacey to come up with the right words to say to me. I felt like she didn't sign it because she didn't know how I would react to getting a card from her after all that time. Stacey was probably at home missing me and having flashbacks of our last love making session, which happened to be on my last birthday. I tried calling Monica back, but she was still asleep. I wanted to talk to her to get my mind off that card. I sat there and actually started writing a reply right on the card.

Hello Stacey,

No words are necessary-it's okay. It must be hard finding the right words to say after all this time. I understand what you're feeling. This time last year was unbelievable. My world was wrecked when I lost you, but my heart has finally found peace.

Her name is Monica. She's absolutely incredible.
Don't worry you'll always be a part of me. You have an
eternal space in my heart. First loves are always special. The
last time we spoke I know I was bitter and I'm sorry. I can honestly
say that I never hated you. The love I felt for you was far too
strong. I still feel your love and that's probably why I'm doing this.
I often see you in my dreams.
Neither time nor distance will ever change what you mean to me.
This card was a very special gift.

I love you now and 4ever,
Eric

I called Monica for the third time and finally she was awake. I
was glad she answered the phone because I know her mother was
getting tired of me calling.
I asked, "Did you get your schedule yet?"
"Yeah, I'm going to be in Mrs. Porter's homeroom. Do you know
her?"
"I have no idea who she is. She's probably new. I miss you. Can I
come over?"
Monica said, "I miss you too. Come over as soon as you can. If
you want you can have dinner here." Monica's phone beeped.
"Hold on somebody's on the other line." There was a click, then
she clicked back. "It's Jennifer on the other line. Come on over."
"Alright, see you in a few minutes."
I grabbed Stacey's card. On the way over to Monica's house I
planned to stop by the post office. I wanted Stacey to get that card
as soon as possible. When I walked out of my house I noticed
Lisa's car in her driveway. I had to stop in and let her know that I
was back. Before I even knocked Lisa opened the door. She was
excited to see me.
Lisa yelled, "Hey baby!!! I missed you."
She hugged me.

"I missed you too. Damn it seems like we were gone forever. You look good."

"So do you. Black is a good name for you 'cause your ass is black for real."

"You try lying in the sun for all those hours and see how dark you get. I knew some ignorant ass person was gonna say something smart. I thought about you when I was in the sun. Remember what you said about dark skin. The darker the berry the sweeter the juice and the darker the skin the deeper the roots. Do you remember that?"

Lisa smiled and gave me a kiss on the cheek. "You know I love your sexy black ass. Let me be serious. How was Jamaica?"

In my best Jamaican accent I said, "Lord have mercy, girl. Jamaica was all dat."

"I know Monica had a good time."

"And you know that. I gotta run. I'll see you later."

"You better. Tell Monica I asked about her."

"Call me. Maybe we can go walking."

I hopped in my car and headed for the post office. I was so excited that I whipped my car out of my driveway like pimp driving a 1977 Cadi. I felt like I was in high demand, like all the ladies wanted me. I was cool, but feeling a little cocky. I thought about sending Stacey's card priority mail, but that would have looked like a desperate move. I figured it was more than enough that I had made a special trip to the post office. Stacey would receive the card within two days. I couldn't wait to hear from her. When I dropped the envelope in the mailbox I wished that I had taken my time to think things through a little more. I let my emotions get the best of me. It was kind of cruddy sending my old girlfriend a card while I was on the way to my new girlfriend's house. I kept beating up on myself the entire way to Monica's. How could I do something so impulsive? Stacey still had an unexplainable spell on me. There was no way Monica would understand what I had done and there was no way I was going to tell her what I had done. At least I represented Monica well on the card in my little message. Well, I tried to represent her to the best of my ability considering my weakened mental state. It's hard to explain exactly what happens to the male mind when attractive females are involved. I was a young hungry extra sexual beast and Stacey turned my mind to mush. It was a short drive to Monica's and I hoped she didn't pay attention to how long it took me to get there. When I saw Monica my mind instantly regained its solidity.

She asked, "Hey what's wrong?"

"Nothing. Why'd you ask?"

"You have a crazy look on your face."

"It's nothing. I was just missing you."

We kissed.

"Good. I missed you too. I changed my mind about staying here for dinner. Jennifer told me about a bookstore downtown that's having a poetry reading this evening. There's going to be some friends from school there and I heard some of the best poets from this area are going to be there. We'll have more freedom there than at Pabulum's. So you wanna go?"

"Sounds good to me, but don't put Pabulum's down. That's my spot."

"I wasn't. I love that place. That's where we got our start. I want to take you there tomorrow night for your birthday."

We kissed again.

"I love you."

"I love you."

"I asked, "Do you plan to recite anything?"

"No, I just plan to feel the crowd out."

"Scared?"

Monica said, "No, I might be intimidated a little by the crowd."

"Not me. I don't care. I can flow with the best of 'em.

"Ooh, you sound ready."

"I am. Let me holler at your people then I'm ready."

"My people? You mean my mommy and my daddy."

"Yeah."

I went to say hello to Monica's parents. Then we headed

151

downtown. We had passed Timbuktu Books hundreds of times, but never went inside. We were about to find out what we had been missing. Before we went inside I grabbed my notepad from the backseat of my car. I had no idea what I was going to recite. I never liked reading directly from a pad. Whatever I did I wanted it to be good because Timbuktu's looked like the major leagues. We stepped into a very impressive establishment. Timbuktu's was an independently owned African-American bookstore. We had no idea how nice and comfortable the interior was. The owner went all out to create a comfortable atmosphere. The place was decorated with fancy brass reading lamps, leather chairs and sofas. Along the walls were picture of famous African American writer and poets. The bookstore was configured in a huge L-shape.

I remembered going there as a child with my parents when the building was used as a bank. The gothic architectural style of the building was still very much alive from the cathedral ceiling, high sculptured arches and columns, down to marble floors. As we walked through the bookstore I glanced at several books. The back of the bookstore was set up for the poetry reading. There were several chairs set up, but a few people chose to sit on a carpeted area on the floor. There were a lot more people present than I had expected. The crowd was mostly black, but there were a few whites and Latinos sprinkled throughout the building. The majority of the crowd was older. Besides a small group of teens the crowd's ages ranged from 25 to 40. Jennifer and Troy were there with two other people from our poetry club. I was surprised to see Troy there because he wasn't really into poetry. Troy was just there to keep an eye on his girl. He was so damn sprung. He would have followed Jennifer's sexy little ass to hell and back. I sat down next to Troy and Jennifer. I talked to them and flipped through my notepad at the same time.

I said, "Hey Jennifer. What's up Troy."
Troy said, "Chillin."
We shook hands.
Jennifer said, "Hi Black." She started talking to Monica about

152

school.

Troy asked, "What's up with you? I heard you were gonna be here. You gonna read some poetry or what?"

"Yeah, something like that. I'm gonna let a few people recite then I might do a little something. I want to recite this one, but it's incomplete. I'm gonna recite it, but I have to freestyle the rest."

"You're good enough to do it. How'd you like Jamaica?"

Troy could see how busy I was, but he kept talking.

I said, "Loved it. We lived like celebrities. I wanna go back. I'll tell you more about it later. They're about to get started."

The mistress of ceremony welcomed us to Timbuktu's Black Love Poetry Night. She started the night off with a poem of her own. Her poem was about all the things her man does to her body. I thought her poem was sexy. She didn't hold back at all expressing her feelings.

This pretty young girl went up next. I didn't notice her at first, but I recognized her from elementary school.

I was louder than I wanted to be when I said, "Hey, I know that girl. That's Robin from my kindergarten class."

Monica looked at me and said, "It takes you to remember something like that."

"I'm serious. I remember her for real. I used to eat her cookies."

Troy burst out laughing and Monica had a strange look on her face.

Jennifer said, "You're so nasty."

I said, "What? I didn't say I ate her pudding. I really did eat her cookies and I sipped her milk too."

Monica looked at me and said, "Please be quiet. What he's trying to say is that he had his first crush on her and they shared refreshments."

I said, "Yeah. That's all I was trying to say. Damn you know me like you own me."

Monica smiled and said, "I do."

I liked the little bits and pieces of Robin's poem that I heard. I wanted to say something to her, but I knew she wouldn't remember

153

me. I thought about how cute she used to look with her three pony tails, her little dresses with matching hair ribbons and her black strap over patent leather shoes with gold buckles. Now, who could forget a girl like that?

The next guy to take the mic was named Rodney Jordan. Everybody called him "Poppy" because he looked Puerto Rican with his light skin and he had what they called good hair. I had never seen him or heard his poetry before. Lisa knew of him. I heard he tore Pabulum's apart with his poetry in the past. Lisa said he was the smoothest and deepest poet she had ever witnessed. Poppy ripped it again. His poem was animated and he was straight up dramatic with his vocal tones and body language. When he finished the crowd went wild. He got mad snaps for his poem. The mistress of ceremony took the mic to invite the next poet to the stage. The crowd was hushed. Nobody wanted to go up after that. I felt Monica tap my arm. I had to go up after I talked all that mess earlier about flowing with the best of 'em. I wasn't trying to look weak in front of my girl, so I stepped up and grabbed the mic.

I said, "What up y'all. My name is Eric, but I go by the name Black. I'm gonna change the pace up a little. No need to rush, right ladies y'all know what I'm talking about." The women cheered and clapped their hands. "And for the fellas that don't know what I'm talking about just sit back and take note. I'd like to dedicate this to my girl."

I didn't say my girl Monica because all my girls inspired my poem. My inspiration was like a mixture of Stacey and Lisa topped with a whole lot of Monica.

"My poem is entitled *Extra Sexual*."

She doesn't quite understand what she does to me
Her love seems to bring out the best in me
Or should I say...she brings out the beast in me
When it comes to her love
I'm in so deep it's like I'm running in my sleep

154

'Cause sleepwalking just can't compare
To the speed of my dreams or the pace of my reality
My mind races taking me to places I've never been before
I'm feeling high...but this high
It ain't got nothing to do with drugs
She's got me on a straight love high
She makes me extra sexual and you know that's hot
I'm nasty even when I think I'm not
Nasty as I wanna be
Nasty as she needs me to be
Anyway we look at it...it's all the same
I wanna make love to her in so many ways
Like mind, body and soul
As I lay her down I completely take control
Extra sexual fantasies are what I'm all about
I can't exactly define extra sexual

It's whatever she needs me to be
Her ups...her downs...her ins and outs
I can be that brotha to hold
Or that someone to simply listen
I can be her walk on the wild side or
That long hard ride
I'll even whisper extra sexual fantasies in her ear
I'm her 100% man equal to her every need
Whenever she hungers I will feed
Extra sexual fantasies making her crazy hot
I'm extra sexual even when I think I'm not
Together our love turns mighty rivers into streams
And nightmares into wet dreams
Extra sexual fantasies making us hot
This extra sexual stuff sho'nuff hits the spot

The crowd showed me love. It seemed like all the ladies got my point. Extra sexual goes beyond the physical needs of a woman. It's about meeting all of a woman's needs. Like being in tune to her emotional needs as well as physical needs. Being creative, fulfilling fantasies, taking extra time to pay attention to little details and taking a woman to new levels. That what I'm talking about. I didn't get the same love the crowd showed Poppy, but that was fine with me. Poppy was a lot older and he had seen and experienced so much more than me. I was only 17 years old and he was like 31. I knew my style was only going to get better with time. My crew loved my work. Monica smiled and praised me.

Monica said, "I liked that a lot. God definitely blessed you with talent. You stole the show."

I didn't know if she was telling the truth or just stroking my ego. Whatever it was I appreciated all the love.

We hung around until the last poet went up. These were the most talented poets I had ever been around. I think I enjoyed listening to the other poems more than actually reciting my own. Most of the poems recited that night were pretty explicit and intended for an older crowd. No one did or said anything to make the younger crowd feel uncomfortable. In Baltimore when there's an older crowd they hardly ever want a younger crowd around. They often refer to unwanted young people as "hoppers." I'm not sure if they were aware of our ages, but I never heard the term used. Instead of alienating us, they made us feel welcomed. I felt like we made major contributions and kept the night flowing. Being around the older poets somewhat nurtured our skills. We were the ones who were going to keep this genre alive and I'm sure that the older crowd knew it. Overall, everyone had a good time. When I dropped Monica off she reminded me that we were going out for my birthday and she had some special surprises in store for me.

The next morning I laid in bed thinking about the poem I recited the night before and how I came across to the crowd. I tried to think of ways to improve my skills. I laid there reciting poetry to myself and thinking about how special my gift was to me. Poetry was my life. I could write about whatever I wanted. Not all of my poetry was meant to be viewed or heard by others, but for the most part I liked sharing my poetry. I thought about my life and what it meant to be eighteen. I was an adult and I thanked God for allowing me to see it. I was happy with my poetry and my life. One thing did bother me. My parents had delayed my life for an entire year. I hated thinking about what they did, but it was reality. When I was in the third grade my parents had my teacher hold me back because I had problems reading. Comprehending what I read was my biggest problem. I could read an entire book, but wouldn't be able to explain shit about the book. I saw books as collections of words without any meaning, no rhyme or reason. Where would I have been if my parents had let my teacher pass me to the fourth grade? More than likely I would have been an illiterate kid bullshitting my way through life. The only thing I regretted was the fact that my parents didn't give me any choice in the matter. I thought I would have done fine in the forth grade with a tutor, but my parents actually did me a favor by holding me back. Repeating one year turned me into an excellent well-rounded student. Nobody ever noticed my slight age difference when I was in school. So, I guess that one year really didn't matter much. I was still only eight months older than Monica.

I laid in bed thinking about something I couldn't change, when my parents knocked on my door.

"Hold up." I slipped on my pajama pants because I always liked to sleep naked. "Come in."

They walked in with a birthday cake singing happy birthday.

"Y'all know I'm too old for this."

There I was lying in bed with a rock hard Willie. I'm talking morning wood to the maximum and my parents were singing happy birthday to me and my big grown ass.

"This is really nice, but please stop."

My mother was carrying the cake and my father was carrying a box, which held my brand new VCR. My father handed me a small box. When I opened the box there was a stethoscope was inside.

I thought, *Oh no, not this doctor shit again*. I was just going to save the stethoscope for nursing school.

"Let me guess the VCR is from mama and the stethoscope is from you."

My father said, "No, I helped pay for the VCR too. And that's not just any stethoscope. It's a Littmann the finest stethoscope on the market."

I almost told him that I didn't want to be a doctor, but I didn't want to ruin my birthday. The phone rang and my mother answered it.

My mother said, "It's Grandma Edith and Tammy."

She handed me the telephone.

I said, "Hi Grandma."

"Happy birthday Junior. You're an old man now."

"Yes ma'am. How you feeling?"

"I feel good for an old woman. God's been good to me."

"I wish I could have seen you for your birthday, but my parents wanted me to go to Jamaica with them."

"I understand. When are you coming to see me?"

"I'm not sure. We go back to school in a few days."

"That's good. Are you ready to go back?"

"No. Not at all."

"You're a smart boy and I know you'll do well."

"I will. This is my last year of high school. I hope you can come up for my graduation."

"If I'm feeling good enough I wouldn't miss it for the world."

"I hope you can make it 'cause that would be real nice."

"Okay darling, you have a wonderful birthday. I love you."

"I love you too."

"Hold on here's Tammy."

She said, "Hey cuz! Happy birthday!"

"Thanks."

"How you doing?"

"I'm good."

"I messed up real bad."

"What did you do?"

158

"I went and bought a box of those cheap greeting cards and let grandma send it herself."

"Oh my God!!!"

The next thing Tammy heard was a dial tone. I hung up the phone right away. I couldn't talk. Damn, I made a complete ass of myself. I was glad my parents walked away while I was on the phone. I jumped the gun sending the card. I felt so small that I could have hid in a crack in the wall. I laid in the bed balled up in a knot trying to soothe myself. The longer I laid there thinking about what I had done the better I felt. What did I really lose or gain? I had Monica and I was happy as long as she never found out that I sent the card to Stacey. I was ashamed because I was so sure Stacey had sent that card, but it was no big deal. All this meant was that Stacey knew I still had feelings for her. There was no way I was going to act on my feelings. I felt stupid for being such a cocky bastard. The phone rang again. This time it was Lisa.

Lisa said, "Happy birthday, Shorty."

"Thanks."

"I am going to see you today, right? I've got something special for you."

"Damn, you never forget me."

"How can I forget you? We need to power walk or jog today."

"Yeah, let's do that. It's been a while. I need to talk to you anyway."

"About what?"

"I'll meet you in thirty minutes then I'll tell you."

As soon as I hung up the phone it rang again. This time it was Monica.

Monica said, "Happy birthday."

"Thank you."

"You don't sound like you're having a happy birthday."

"I'm fine. I just woke up."

"Are you coming over here to get your surprises or do you want me to come to you?"

"I'll come see you. I really had a good time last night."

159

"So did I. The next time we go to Timbuktu's I have to recite something."

"Yeah, I was surprised you didn't. I'm getting ready to go power walking with Lisa and as soon as we're done I'll be over."

"Don't take too long because I'm really looking forward to seeing you."

"I won't be long."

"Okay, I love you."

"I love you too."

I hurried up and got dressed. By the time I got outside Lisa was already in her driveway stretching. She looked as beautiful as usual and nothing could ever change that.

I said, "Yeah, I like that stretch right there. Don't move just let me look at you."

Lisa smiled and held her position. "Don't torture yourself like that. I can't wait to hear what you want to talk about?"

"Not so fast. Don't you have something for me?"

"That's the only reason you're here."

"No it isn't. You know I love you."

"Come inside and I'll get it."

I followed Lisa into her living room. She opened her backpack and pulled out a card and a small box wrapped in blue paper with a gold ribbon. I knew exactly what was in the box. I opened the box and it was a Guess watch. Exactly what I needed because my Citizen was tired as hell. I almost forgot to open the envelope with the card. I think I was starting to have something against birthday cards. Lisa put a fifty-dollar Macy's gift certificate inside the card.

I said, "Thanks for everything. You love spoiling me. We can power walk around the neighborhood and I'll tell you what's on my mind."

As soon as we got outside I said, "The thing I need to talk to you about has to do with a birthday card I received from North Carolina."

"Don't tell me it was from Stacey."

I smiled. "No, but I wish it had been from her."

"So was it from one of your relatives?"

"Yeah, my grandmother."

Lisa looked at me with a confused expression on her face. "So why did you want the card to be from Stacey? Don't tell me you still have feelings for her."

"I do."

Lisa shook her head.

I said, "For some reason I can't get over her. That's not really the issue here. When I got the card I automatically assumed it was from Stacey. So, I wrote a little message in the card and returned it to her the same day."

"Why? You big dummy it was from your grandmother. What made you think it was from her? Don't you know your ninety-one-year-old great grandmother's handwriting from Stacey's?"

Lisa seemed to catch a funky attitude.

I said, "I know it's hard, but can you calm down? I was confused because the card wasn't signed and there was only a forwarding address on the envelope. In the past when Stacey sent me mail she never used a return address. For all I know Tammy could have addressed the envelope for my grandmother. Keep in mind I'm not a handwriting analyst. Anyway, I was so excited from the thought of Stacey sending me a card I was blinded by emotions."

"Have you heard from her yet?"

"No. I really don't expect to hear from her."

"I don't understand why you did what you did. Why would you want to communicate with Stacey after all she put you through? I thought I helped you get over her."

"I'm not trying to take anything from you or Monica, but I fell in love with Stacey first. She was the first girl I ever made love to. You know it's not easy getting over your first love. I love being in a monogamous relationship with Monica and I don't plan to go anywhere."

I think I struck a nerve because our pace slowed.

Lisa said, "Monogamy isn't reality. Why do you think marriages don't work? It's human nature to be attracted to more than one person and to pursue your desires. That's why you're in this situation with Stacey. Eric, you still desire her little fire. You might not like me saying this, but that's why you're with me now. I think you're still hot for me. Evidently, I give you something that you can't get from Monica. I'm not exactly sure what that is. All I'm saying is I really believe you can be in love with more than one person at a time. I actually miss being with you sexually. You did things to me and for me that other guys never thought of. I hate making comparisons, but Mike always skipped foreplay and you gave me special attention he's never even dreamed of."

"I understand what you're saying and thanks for the compliments. When I think about it I believe we would be a couple if I didn't fall in love with Monica. The whole thing with Mike messed me up a lot. I think I could have taken you from him. I felt like eventually my age would have presented a problem. It was hard for me to see where we were going and I could see a clear future with Monica. I miss being with you sometimes, but I love times like this too. You're like my therapist. I need you in my life and I hope you need me."

"I need you too. I told you, I'll always be here for you. It's too hard for me to find all the qualities I'm looking for in one man. You might not believe this, but you are the closest thing to my Mr. Right I've ever known."

"That was sweet. I like that a lot. Well, basically you molded me into your Mr. Right."

Lisa laughed because she knew I was telling the truth. She was kind of crazy, but she had a way of making me think. I hated sharing so much with Lisa and hiding so much from Monica. I knew I was in love with Monica so why couldn't I clear my head and just be honest with her? The truth was, if Monica ever found out about all the things I was hiding, she would drop me like a hot rock.

I wanted to hurry up and get to Monica's to see what surprises she had for me. All that talk about love and relationships made me

162

want to do something special for Monica. As soon as Lisa and I finished our walk I went home, showered and headed to the mall. I walked around the mall for almost an hour like I was lost. I really didn't have anything particular in mind for Monica until I walked up to Victoria's Secret. Monica only wore Victoria's Secret underwear and I knew she would love to have something new. I had never been to Victoria's Secret without Monica. I thought I would feel uncomfortable in a lingerie store without her, but things actually went okay. I had been there so many times with Monica that I knew my way around like I was home. The salesladies almost fought each other to assist me. I knew Monica liked Victoria's bra and panty sets, so I picked out two sets for her. The saleslady was impressed by the fact that I knew Monica's size. Most guys she dealt with would have to use her or another woman as a model to figure out their girlfriend's size. I had my girl's stats down. All of the women in the store seemed impressed seeing me buy lingerie for my girlfriend. They smiled and watched me as I moved from rack to rack.

I was extra late getting to Monica's. She opened the door pulled me inside and laid a serious kiss on me. Mrs. Cameron was in the kitchen and she yelled happy birthday to me. I didn't even get a chance to see her because Monica grabbed my hand and led me up to her bedroom.

"Look what I have for you."

She had two easels set up. Monica painted a portrait of me. As usual her work was outstanding. I figured this was the picture that she had on her easel turned backwards the last time I was in her room.

"I love it. I've never seen anything like it. You did a good job. Did you use oil paint?"

"Yeah, you're getting good. I'm glad you like it. Look at this one."

The next picture was an acrylic painting of the two of us.

"I like your watch. Must be from Lisa."

"Yeah, How did you know?"

"Just a good guess. Here open this."

She handed me a small box wrapped in blue and silver paper. I opened the box and it was a thick, heavy, sterling silver bracelet. I was excited.

"I can't believe you got this. Thank you so much."

"I knew you wanted it. I saw you looking at it at the mall."

"Thanks for everything. I have something for you."

I handed Monica the Victoria's Secret bag.

"I was hoping this was for me." She pulled out the sets. "Ooh, thank you. You're so sweet."

"I want to see you in those."

"Wanna see me in one tonight?"

"Try one on now."

"You must be tripping."

"I am. I can't help myself. At least let me take you out to dinner tonight."

"I'm supposed to pay since it's your birthday."

"Thank you, but you've done more than enough."

We hung out at Monica's house for a few hours, then we went to Pabulum's for dinner. The restaurant wasn't so crowded. This was an entirely different pace for us. There was no live band or anyone reciting poetry. There was only soft music, candlelight, my sweetheart and the poetry running through my head. The atmosphere was relaxing to us. Monica looked so sexy that I wanted to pick her up and gently lay her out of the table and go to work. Our waitress walked up and spoiled my fantasy. She took our orders. We both ordered Blackened Cajun Catfish. Pabulum's catfish was the best I ever had. I couldn't wait to get Monica back to my house because I knew my parents wouldn't be home.

After dinner we went to my house. This time I took Monica by the hand and led her to my bedroom. I put on some of Bob Marley's music to get that Caribbean flow going again. Monica laid on my bed like she was ready for some action. I climbed on top and kissed her.

"I wanna make love to you until you just can't take it. I wanna

164

hear you scream my name."

I wanted to use a different type of foreplay. Earlier, I had taken a porno movie from my father's collection and loaded it into my VCR. Monica had no idea what was about to pop up on the screen. When the movie started Monica sat up on the bed not saying a word just taking note like the fine student she was. I knew this would have some type of affect on her. I wasn't interested in watching the movie because I had already seen it like three times. I moved closer to Monica and kissed her neck. She sat there almost numb as if none of this was having an affect on her. Maybe, the movie wasn't working. I figured she needed some live entertainment. I stood up and began to undress. I had been working out for years and finally I had achieved the results I had been looking for. My body looked tight. My muscles looked defined. My chest looked massive and my rippled washboard abs caught Monica's attention. All that hard work was about to pay off. I felt Monica's tongue slide up and down my abs. She kissed, licked and sucked my chest. Monica slowly lowered my pants. She lifted the leg of my boxers with one hand and massaged me with the other. Her touch felt so good. I could feel the texture of her tongue glide up and down my inner thigh. I was so turned on that I could barely fit in my boxers. Monica helped me slide them down. She laid on the bed. I dropped to my knees and returned the favor and began kissing her inner thighs. I slid her panties to the side, so I could feel her juices. Oh my God, she was creamy wet. I moved her back on the bed and positioned myself between her legs. I pressed my hardness deep into her pelvis. I loved it.

I said, "Oh shit!"

If it wasn't for Monica's panties and her strong will I would have been deep inside. I continued to press against her clitoris. Up, down and side to side. Then I held constant pressure to one spot.

"Is that it? Is that your spot?"

"Yeah. Oh yeah."

"Come for me."

Monica tightened up like she was about to explode. I got pleasure

165

from seeing her so aroused and when she reached her climax I almost did too. I still needed a little more attention. I had an erection that just wouldn't go away.

"I need to be inside you so bad. Are you ready for this? Look, I've got a condom if that's what you're worried about."

"It's not that. I want you so bad, but not tonight."

"It's my birthday and you can give me a gift I'd never forget. I wouldn't forget this in a million lifetimes. Who are you saving this for?"

"My husband. You know how important this is to me. I have to save it for him."

"I'm that man." I thought, *Maybe a little poetry will do the trick.* I said, "If you give me tonight I'll give you a lifetime. Let me serve you I deserve you...like no one else does. I promise you an everlasting endeavor of love...to have and to hold. How does that sound to you because I mean every word?"

"I can't."

"That's not what I wanted to hear, but I understand. I'll wait. I won't worry 'cause this love ain't going nowhere."

Monica held me tight and we kissed. She lowered her hands and touched me like I needed to be touched. I had no idea where she had learned her massage techniques, but she laid down all the right strokes. Monica was good at calming me down. Whenever my testosterone levels got too high I would do or say almost anything to have sex with her. I meant everything I said about giving her a lifetime. She was all I needed for the rest of my life. She was the half that made me whole. I couldn't ask for a better friend. What I told Monica was the truth, we had no need to rush because our love wasn't going anywhere. That summer we connected in so many ways. From Kings Dominion to Jamaica, we had the summer of our lives. I hated to see that summer end. In a few days we would be starting our senior year and I planned to make it extra special. During the previous school year Monica and I made some important individual accomplishments. I couldn't wait to see what was in store for the next school year.

The Truth: 12

As usual Monica and I were up to one of our favorite hobbies.
We were two days away from the start of our senior year and we
had to do some intense last minute school shopping. This time
around we invited our mothers to join us. This gave us all a good
opportunity to bond. Mrs. Cameron and my mother had become
good friends and they actually had a lot in common. They were
both professional shoppers with their own hidden agendas. Monica
and I were school shopping, but our mothers actually ended up
with more clothes than we did. I almost got everything I needed in
one day. Monica got a lot of clothes too, but for some reason Mrs.
Cameron said they were going to finish Monica's shopping the
next day. Whatever I didn't get on that trip would have to wait
until after the start of school. This was an endless day that started
to frustrate me. We went to three malls and probably went into
about fifty different stores. For the first time in my life I hated
shopping. Going shopping with three women is an overwhelming
experience for any man, especially when he's asked to carry tons of
bags and chauffeur his mother, girlfriend and girlfriend's mother
all around town. I couldn't wait for the madness to end so I could
have some time to myself.

That night I was home alone in my basement working out when the phone rang. My parents had gone out for the evening. I answered the phone.

"Hello."

"Hi Eric, how are you?"

I paused.

She asked, "Do you know who this is?"

"Hi Stacey."

I should have waited for her to identify herself first because I ran the risk of blurting out the wrong name, but Stacey had an unmistakable accent. I lied to Lisa when I said I didn't expect to hear from Stacey. I knew she couldn't resist responding to my card.

"How could I not recognize your sweet voice? So, you got my card?"

"Yeah, but at first you confused the hell out of me. It took me a minute to figure out what was going on. When I realized what was going on I laughed."

"Thanks a lot. Believe me it wasn't a joke."

"No, trust me I don't mean it like that. I'm curious to know what made you think the card was from me?"

"I was confused. This is embarrassing."

"It's okay. Tell me."

"When I saw that the card was post marked from North Carolina, I instantly thought it was from you. The thought of you sending me a card was exciting. The card wasn't signed. You know your style. You never used a return address in the past. Anyway, I imagined you lying around having flashbacks of my last birthday. 'Cause I did."

"Oh really. Well, let me be completely honest with you. The last time we spoke you had a shitty little attitude. The thought of sending you a birthday card never crossed my mind."

"I'm really not in the mood for this. I don't need to hear this at all."

"Let me finish. I told you I never meant to hurt you. I had my heart broken too and I never want to go back there again. Your card

168

completely caught me off guard. It actually made me cry. For so long I needed to hear those words from you. On your birthday I did have flashbacks of the two of us together. You're a part of me that I'll always cherish. I never stopped loving you and you said everything I needed to hear in that card. I don't know exactly what Monica means to you and I really don't care. Take a minute to think about her kisses and think about mine. Think about her love and think about mine. Do you remember the first time we made love?"

"Yeah, I can't forget."

Stacey had me under a deep spell. She continued to mesmerize me.

"I'll always remember the first time because it plays in my mind over and over again. Eric, my body aches for you. I wish I could have you inside me right now. Tell me you don't want me and I'll never call you again."

"I'm so confused right now. I know exactly what I need, but I do miss you. I miss everything about you. Your lips, your sweet kisses and your smell. I miss running my hands up your smooth sexy legs and grabbing a hand full of your ass. It would feel so good to be inside you."

"Relax Eric. I don't want to put any pressure on you."

"Pressure, are you joking? If you were here I'd show you pressure. Listen, I still love you, but Monica is my everything. When I say my everything, I mean it with all my heart. I love that girl."

"I won't call you anymore, but when you're ready, you know exactly where to find me. No matter what's going on in my life I'll make time for you. Goodnight my love."

"Wait, before you go, thanks for calling. I hope we'll always be friends."

"We're much more than friends and you know that. Since we're friends tell Monica you had an interesting conversation with a friend."

"Goodnight. I have to go."

169

I hung up the phone. My mind was all screwed up. I wasn't sure if Stacey was convinced that I wanted to be with Monica. The main thing was that I was convinced that I wanted to be with Monica. Stacey's spell was as strong as ever. The thought of being with her again turned me on. She knew how deep my love was for Monica and I guess that was the reason she finally surrendered.

Before I could even clear my mind the phone rang again. I picked up.

"Hello."

"Hi Eric."

"Hi Lisa. Please, can I call you back tomorrow?"

"This won't take long."

"Alright."

"You sound tired, but this good news will pick you up fast. You'll never guess what happened."

"What?"

"I got a call from MCA Records and they want me."

My stomach dropped. "They want you? I told you it was coming."

"Yeah, they loved my demo and they want to sign me. You were right. You've got a good ear for talent."

"Congratulations. I'm so happy for you."

"You don't sound so happy."

"I'm okay."

"The record company wants me to move to New York and I'm leaving in the morning."

"Are you driving up?"

"Yeah, the record company booked me a flight for Tuesday morning, but I can hardly wait another day. I'm not sure what I'm going to do with the house here, but I'm going to find a place in New York. I didn't tell you but, when you were in Jamaica I went to New York to visit my mother and we dropped off a copy of my demo at the record company. I didn't mention it because I didn't know how things were going to turn out. Now, I can finally breathe again. I can't believe they want me. My dream is finally coming true. I'm gonna be a famous singer. Soon Lisa Ashford is going to be household name. Thanks for believing in me, Eric."

I was silent. I couldn't get myself together. I was trying to process too much information.

Lisa said, "Eric, say something."

"Good luck I knew you could do it."

"Are you sure you're okay? "

"Yeah, I'll see you tomorrow before you leave."

I wanted to get off the phone because there was a lump in my throat that wouldn't go away. I had predicted someone would discover Lisa's talent soon. It just never occurred to me it would hurt so bad. I understood that this had to be done and there was no way Lisa was going to let my feelings stand in the way of her future. I knew this was the best thing for her. No matter how I looked at this situation it still hurt. Lisa had been by my side for my entire life and I had to get used to her being away from me. I felt my eyes fill with tears and at that exact moment nothing mattered to me. All I wanted was my sweet Monica. She had a way of smoothing out all the rough spots. I was sure that Monica was all I needed and I planned to channel all of my love and energy her way. I wanted to call her, but I really needed to get some rest. I had developed a pounding headache thanks to Stacey and Lisa. My mind had a lot to process. Lisa's news had the biggest impact on me. I was happy for her, but on the other hand I wanted her to stay at home right next to me. Who was going to be my workout partner, my confidant and my personal problem solver?

Early the next morning I went over to see Lisa off. She actually seemed sad. It seemed as if we both knew that things would never be the same with us again. I refused to be sad. I gave Lisa a big hug and an innocent kiss on the lips. Then I helped her load up her car. I didn't look when she drove off. I just headed back to my house and went to bed.

A few hours later Monica called to let me know she would be spending most of the day shopping with her mother. She invited me, but I declined the invitation. I wanted to hangout around the

171

house and workout because Stacey had interrupted my previous workout. I started my workout in my bedroom with push-ups and crunches. Then I made my way to the basement, where I did my circuit training. My workout consisted of weight training, jogging on the treadmill, jumping rope, riding my stationary bike and kickboxing. My workout went on for hours, but I did find time to jot down some thoughts that were flowing through my head. I was still trying to process all of the information from the night before. The most important thing to me was that I still had Monica in my life.

After my workout I took a hot shower. I put on my pajama bottoms and a robe. I heard my mother in the kitchen, so I went down to speak to her. A few minutes later my father came home. They wanted to know why I was home so early wearing pajamas. I told them that I was taking it easy since I had to go to school the next day. I talked to them for awhile, but I didn't tell them about Lisa because I didn't want to let on that something was bothering me. I went back up to my room to iron my clothes for school. I've always liked the smell of new clothes being ironed.

Someone was at our front door. The next thing I heard was my mother telling Monica it was fine to go up to my room. My mother didn't give me any warning. I could have been up to something very personal. Monica knocked on my open bedroom door.

"Hi Eric can I come in?"

I gave her a big smile. "Hi, it's open come on in."

Monica walked right up to me and gave me a kiss.

"Ooh, you look sexy in your robe. You don't need to wear that around me. Take it off so I can massage your chest."

We laid on my bed and Monica began to massage my chest.

"When was the last time I told you, you were beautiful?"

"I'm sure we were in Jamaica."

"It's been too long."

Monica laid her head on my pillow.

"You are so beautiful. I love the way you look in my bed. I named this pillow you're laying on after you. I hold it every night and I

172

dream of you. It gives me comfort, but it doesn't even compare to the feeling I get from the real thing."

"That was really sweet. I loved that. You're so different from other guys your age. Sometimes you say some corny stuff too, but most of the things you say to me are sweet. You write and speak poetically and I like that."

"You bring out my creative side. I love you so much. Thanks for the massage. I worked out for hours today. You always know what my body needs."

"It's funny you mentioned that because I had a hot dream about us last night."

"I wanna hear all about it."

"We pretty much lived my dream the other night, but in my dream we were in my bed and I let you penetrate me."

I got excited. Hearing Monica talk about me penetrating her sounded so good.

"I'd love to penetrate your world. Did you like the way I made you feel in your dream?"

"Yeah. The only thing I didn't like was the guilty feeling I had afterwards."

"What was that all about?"

"Well, it didn't have much to do with you, my parents, or me. I felt like I let God down. I hate disappointing you so much. Sometimes I get weak and I wanna give in. That's when I ask God to give me strength."

"That's too heavy for me. I'm not gonna touch that. All I can say is I hope I've haven't done anything to ruin your image in God's eyes. You're a very spiritual person and I don't want to change that. Don't worry about disappointing me, always keep God first."

"I think about God a lot."

"So do I."

"If you had the chance to ask God a question, what would you ask?"

"I'd like to know if he was happy with me. What would your question be?"

"I'd ask how long I had to live or how I could find peace in the afterlife?"

"To me it's not important to know when I'm going to die, but finding peace in the afterlife is important. Also, keep in mind it's not how long you live, but how you live and the lives you impact."

"I don't mean to change the subject, but we need to discuss the future. I had an interesting conversation with my mother about my future today. We decided that it's best that I go to Spelman for college."

Something inside me snapped. "I don't believe you. How can you just leave me?"

"I'm not leaving you. It's called growth and I think it will be good for us."

"What do you mean good for us? I bet your mother told you to say that. I can't believe you want to break my heart. First Stacey, then Lisa and now you."

Monica looked pissed. "Hold on, somebody doesn't belong in that line up. What do you mean Lisa broke your heart. You're in love with her, right?"

"No."

"Well, What's going on? I want to hear the truth."

I was tired of lying to her. I looked in Monica's eyes and I felt like she wouldn't have believed anything else but the truth.

"I don't know how to say this. I'm going to be honest with you. Lisa and I had a relationship before you and I started dating."

"What! Did you sleep with her?"

Monica already knew the answer because her eyes were flowing with tears.

"Yeah. I did."

"Oh my God! How could you? Why did you lie to me for so long? No wonder you like spending so much time with her."

"It's not what you think. I kept the truth from you, but I didn't sleep with her at any point during our relationship. That all happened in the past. We're just friends now, that's all. Please believe me."

"Remember the other night when we talked about me saving myself for my future husband? You said you were that man."

"Yeah."

I started to think some things were better left unsaid. Sometimes the truth actually hurt worse than a lie. Now my lie had become our bitter reality. I never intended to hurt Monica. I could see our world crumbling and Monica's heart breaking into tiny pieces.

In a sad tone Monica said, "You're definitely not that man. You lied to me. I asked you not to hurt me and you did. So fuck you. Don't call me or come around me. I don't want to see or hear from you."

Monica took off out of my room, down the steps, and out the front door. I grabbed my robe and ran behind her. I grabbed her by the hands bringing them up my lips to kiss them. She tried pulling away, then she stopped.

I said, "Monica, please listen to me. I know you're really upset. Since I've known you I've never heard you curse. It hurts me to my heart that those words had to be directed at me. Please give me another chance. My lips may lie, but my heart doesn't. My eyes don't lie, these tears are real. You can look at me and see how awful I feel. I never meant to hurt you and I promise it'll never happen again. Please forgive me. I need you in my life right now more than ever."

It was as if Monica didn't hear a word I said.

She said, "I sensed something was going on with you and Lisa. I asked you on more than one occasion if something was going on and you lied every time. I can't trust you, so I don't need to be with you. I can't be your fool any longer. Goodbye Eric, I hope you'll be happy with Lisa."

The look in her eyes said it all. She was through with me. Monica got in her car. I kept trying to convince her that I never cheated on her, but nothing worked. She drove away. I walked back towards my house with my vision blurred from tears.

175

THE DARK SIDE: 13

Was this my introduction to the lonely life? I felt as if loneliness and heartache laid next to me in my bed embracing me like old familiar friends. I could hear them whispering in my ear. "We're back 'cause Monica doesn't love you like we do." Being without her nearly drove me crazy. I refused to let this situation get the best of me. Monica was my everything and it was hard for me to accept how things went down. No matter what I said to Monica trying to smooth things out, she just wouldn't listen. I knew my relationship with Lisa would come back someday and somehow to bite me in the ass. And this thing really took a chunk out of me. At first everything seemed so perfect, but it all slipped away so fast. Tomorrow was just inches away and it was too hard to say goodbye to a yesterday filled with so many special memories. Wanting to hold on to the past and wanting to hold on to Monica, I held my pillow tight taking a deep whiff of her fresh scent still on my pillow. I was trying to find comfort, but nothing worked. My problem was that I feared the future would bring more sadness my way. The worse had already happened. I lost my soulmate.

By the time morning rolled around my mind was clear and so was my conscience. For so long my conscience was stained with my dirty little lie. My grandmother always said what doesn't come out in the wash comes out in the rinse. I simply told Monica what I felt she knew all along. Her sixth sense was right on target. She felt there was something strange about my relationship with Lisa. The fact that I hung out with Lisa so much didn't help things at all. I was sure Monica pictured Lisa and I having sex all those times we were together. Lisa always had a certain air of arrogance with Monica when it came to me. I understood Monica's hurt and anger, but at the same time my emotions kept shifting. I started turning things around. One minute I understood Monica and the next I was mad at her for wanting to leave me. She seemed so accepting of the idea. Somehow I had to accept change because my soul-sistas were making moves all around me. Monica and Lisa were my strength and my fear of change was my greatest weakness. In reality Monica and I were too young to be so serious. Our lives had so many changes to undergo and at this point our future plans clashed. I didn't want to dwell on what happened too long. Monica seemed set on the idea of going to college out of town, so heartbreak was an inevitable thing in our relationship. She just brought the issue to light months ahead of time. I figured time was on my side. My plan was to give Monica time and space. I missed her and for all I knew Monica was probably missing me too. Even though we were apart, Monica was still mine. She was just temporarily on out of my reach.

I woke up extra early the next morning to analyze my situation. I must have awakened with the devil because all I could think about were all the new opportunities and untapped territories at school. I was thinking along the lines of Kim, Stephanie, Tracey, Tonya, Renee and Pam. In reality none of them compared to Monica, but I could still have fun flirting and teasing.

Senior year came in with a boom. It was the sound of a thunderstorm. There was a chill in the air and my bed started to feel too good to part with. I didn't want to get up and leave a warm bed to go out on such a cold gloomy day. All of a sudden I thought, *Ain't no sunshine when she's gone*. It took everything in me to get up. I hopped out of bed with a serious case of denial. My mind shifted from being Mr. Monogamy to being a true Playa-Playa. I arrived at school early. Monica's car was already on the lot. We were in the same homeroom and we had a few classes together. I was going to stay outside and wait for my friends, but I wanted to see Monica. I walked in the building and down the hallway imagining Monica sitting in homeroom. I looked in the main office and there she was. Instantly everything seemed to be in slow motion. Monica was in the office talking to the secretary. There was something different about her. This was the new Monica, the one without me. I stared at her with a look of love that a blind man could see from a mile away. Usually my mouth would water seeing Monica look so beautiful. This time my mouth was dry as hell. I missed my water and now my well was dry. That's when it hit me. Monica was in the office getting her schedule changed. She made my heart hurt so bad. For the first time I felt like there was a chance someone else was going to take my place. All that hard work had gone to waste. My worse fear was some other guy coming along and getting that booty after one date. I had really fucked up. Payback's a bitch. Monica wasn't actually the type that was out for revenge. I knew she had too much pride and self-respect to have sex with anyone before marriage. Any type of revenge dealing with another guy would have killed me. I stood there in a broken down pose watching Monica, but she never looked my way. I just picked myself up and walked down the hall. The hallway was becoming flooded with students. I headed to my class feeling like the wind had been knocked out of me.

My classroom was empty, so I sat in the back of the room. About a minute later Troy, Jennifer, Keith and April walked in the room. That's when it really hit me. Monica was gone. Monica and I belonged in their happy little group. April and Jennifer never acknowledged my presence. This meant that they knew what happened and they were on Monica's side. Troy and Keith came back to talk to me. They greeted me like they always did even though I hadn't seen or talked to them for awhile.

Troy said, "We heard about what happened. Monica called Jennifer last night." Before I could respond Keith said, "Yo, I can't believe you fucked Lisa and didn't tell us."

He gave me a high five and so did Troy. They wanted to know how I enjoyed being with Lisa. Troy and Keith actually expected me to give them play by play details. I told them I wasn't in the mood for bragging. When I looked up this gorgeous young woman with a beautiful golden honey brown complexion walked in the room. She wore a very sophisticated looking navy blue shirt suit that fit her like it was tailor-made for her shapely petite frame. She had her straight shiny black hair back in a neat ponytail. I looked her up and down and smiled. This woman was so fine that she had everybody's attention.

She said, "Good morning everyone. For those of you who don't already know me, my name is Mrs. Porter."

My smile got even bigger.

I thought, *Who said ain't no sunshine when she's gone?*

Mrs. Porter was a star. There was no way the school's administration should have allowed this pretty young thing to teach around all those young horny guys. Then again, each and every guy was going to give her his full attention. Without a doubt she had mine. Mrs. Porter looked so familiar. I couldn't remember where I'd seen her until Jennifer opened her mouth.

Jennifer turned around and said, "Remember her from Timbuktu's."

I wasn't sure if she was talking to Troy or me. I appreciated Jennifer's help, but I didn't acknowledge her. I just kept my eyes on Mrs. Porter. The thought of seeing this gorgeous woman everyday made me excited. School was going to be fun after all. I wondered if Mrs. Porter remember me from the bookstore. I stared at her for awhile trying to remember the poem she read. How could I forget her? Mrs. Porter was Debbie, the mistress of ceremony from Timbuktu's Black Love Poetry Night. Mrs. Porter had this Superman/Clark Kent thing going on. She was a sex fiend in disguise. She recited that poem I liked so much about all the things

179

her man does to her body. I wondered if she remembered me and if she liked my poem *Extra Sexual*. If she did that meant we vibed to the same rhythm. I remembered her poem like she was talking directly to and about me.

Mrs. Porter checked attendance and when she got to my name she gave me a pretty smile with extended eye contact. I felt like she was sending me a nonverbal message. The first period bell rang. I wanted to say something to Mrs. Porter, but she got caught up talking to other students. I was going to see Mrs. Porter again later that day and I couldn't wait. She was my last period English teacher.

Around lunchtime I saw Monica walking down the hallway. The hallway was mostly filled with underclassmen going through their lockers or just hanging out talking. If Monica caused a scene it really didn't matter too much to me because those kids didn't know us anyway. I approached her from behind giving her a soft tap on the shoulder. She stopped walking.

I said, "Hi, I missed seeing you in homeroom this morning."

Monica gave me a sharp killer stare. If her stare was a blade, I would have been instantly decapitated.

"I told you I don't want to see or talk to you."

"Damn, you can't be that serious."

"Well, I am."

Monica started walking away.

"Hold up. I need you and I'm not giving up on you that easy. I thought about giving you time and space. You know, just enough so you could miss me a little."

I smiled trying to lighten the mood.

Monica paused looking me up and down. She said "Give up."

"I'll give you a little more time and I'll call you real soon."

"You are so ignorant."

"Ignorant, you called me ignorant? I'll show you ignorant. I never wanted things to be like this between us. You're taking this somewhere we really don't have to go."

Monica ignored me.

I said, *"I love you too."*

Monica walked down the hall like she could care less about seeing me again. I knew I had done wrong, but she didn't have to be so mean to me. She was sending me serious hate vibes. I was evicted from her heart...exiled from her world...suspended from her love. At some point she had to realize that I wasn't perfect. The underclassmen in the hallway had no idea what they had just witnessed. No one had to explain shit to me. Monica's message was loud and clear. I just walked my ignorant ass down that long hallway trying to keep myself together.

The rest of my day actually went pretty good. It was going to take a lot more than Monica's attitude to break me. Heartbreak had victimized me before and I was a lot stronger. The thought of seeing Mrs. Porter again seemed to give me a boost. I walked into Debbie Porter's class like I was the man. My same seat from homeroom was open. Mrs. Porter greeted the class. She handed out some paperwork about classroom rules and regulations and a class syllabus. Debbie walked up to my desk handing me the paperwork. She gave me that same pretty smile from earlier.

Mrs. Porter asked, "How's your day going so far?"

She shocked me with her forwardness. I was tongue tied, but I didn't think she noticed.

In a slow deep tone I said, "Sweet, real sweet. Thanks for asking."

Monica was supposed to be in that class with me. Right then and there, I was glad she wasn't around. Again, Debbie had my full attention and I didn't see anyone else in that room.

Mrs. Porter started telling the class about herself.

She said, "I'm a graduate of Randallstown High and Howard University." She didn't say what years she graduated from high school or college. This was her way of keeping her age a secret. "I've been married for three years and I have an eighteen-month-old daughter. My hobbies include reading, writing, reading and writing. It's late and that was to make sure everyone's still paying attention. Also, I'm fluent in Spanish, French and German. I would

181

like to go around the room and have each of you give a brief intro, but we really don't have the time. I'm sure most of you are familiar with one another. Since I'm new I need your help. Please take out a sheet of paper. Write a brief intro including your goals, hobbies and anything else you think is important for me to know. When you have completed this exercise fold your paper and pass it to the front."

I pulled out a sheet of paper and wrote my name, age, goals and hobbies. Under hobbies I wrote, my hobbies include writing poetry, reading poetry and reciting poetry. Mrs. Porter-I'm just trying to make sure I have your attention. You've got my full attention. Check out this poetry sample entitled *The Dark Side*.

THE DARK SIDE

Have you ever seen the other side of the moon? I'm talking about the side where telescopes never zoom. You know the side where people deep in love rarely care to focus. It's called the dark side and that's where I'm focused. Even when I look directly into the light...darkness is all I see. Staring directly into the sun doesn't even hurt my eyes. Heartache is the only pain I know. Love has completely changed my vision. Heartbreak helped bring the dark side into focus. Now, this reality is far too clear. I now cry invisible tears and you would too if you could see what I see...on the dark side. If women are from Venus and Men are from Mars then my head must be somewhere lost in the stars, 'cause I don't understand a damn thing. One night we were heavenly bodies in flight. The next night we came crashing down to earth. Everyone falls in love sometimes, but I never want to fall again. Love comes and goes and now love's out the window. It's been kicked to the curb. I'm looking out that same window, but I refuse to lean too far. You see, I just might fall right back into love again. And I'm not quite sure that's where I really want to be.

After all our papers were passed forward everyone started doing class work. I found myself staring at Mrs. Porter as if she could read exactly what was on my mind. She was amazing. Her little body was perfect. Her lips looked like they were made for mine. I noticed that her eyes were fixed on me. I wanted to seduce her with my stare. With my eyes focused directly on her, I clinched my teeth sucking in air making a sound like I could feel her soft sexy body all over mine. She watched as I ran my tongue across my top lip, then sucking my top lip a little. Her eyes widened. I released my top lip and ran my tongue across my bottom lip, then sucking my bottom lip and releasing with a kiss mouthing the word *sexy*. The whole time I never lost eye contact with Debbie. She gave me a peculiar look almost as if she was embarrassed, but at the same time somewhat curious. I wanted to make her hot and I think it worked.

At the end of the class period Mrs. Porter asked if she could talk to me. Monica was right, I was ignorant. I actually sat in class trying to seduce my teacher. I walked up to Mrs. Porter's desk.

I asked, "You wanted to see me?"

"Yes, just a minute."

Mrs. Porter stood up walked to the door and waited until the last student left the room. She closed the door and returned to her desk. I knew she was about to let me have it. She didn't crack a smile or say a word. I sat on the student's desk closest to hers with a worried look on my face.

"Mrs. Porter, I'm sorry if-"

"Relax, that's not what this is about. I know quite a bit about you Eric, or should I call you Black."

"Eric is fine."

She smiled and I felt relieved. Maybe this was going to be a lot easier than I thought. Debbie was probably curious after all. She sat there rubbing lotion on her hands in a seductive way. Damn she looked sexy. The thought of her running her lubricated hands all over my body ran through my mind. Instead she was selfish and used all of the lotion on herself.

Mrs. Porter looked up at me and said, "I read your intro and it was very impressive. Did you make up your poem while you were sitting there?"

"Yes, it was easy. I was inspired by my weird emotions. I'm going through something right now."

"I understand. I'm not supposed to say anything to you about this, but I know about your break up with Monica Cameron."

"How did you find out about that?"

"Monica transferred into my third period English class and she mentioned you and the break up in her intro."

"Really."

Mrs. Porter was giving me the inside scoop. This was a sign that she trusted me.

"Monica's hurt and angry, but she still loves you. I'm familiar with the two of you. I was at Pabulum's the night she dedicated her poem to you. And I was at Timbuktu's when you read *Extra Sexual*."

"I can't believe you remembered the title."

"Everyone was impressed with your poem. As a matter of fact, we want you to come back."

"Give me a little time. I know it's rude to ask a woman her age. But how old are you?"

"I don't mind. I'm twenty-eight."

"I'm sorry for the stares and gestures earlier. It's just that you're so beautiful."

"Thank you. And you're a very handsome young man. It's okay, I've been getting stares, smiles, winks and whistles all day. No one else took things to the level you did."

"I'm sorry. I'll try to control myself. It's just that beautiful women bring out the beast in me."

"I already know I'm going to like you. If you have any uncontrollable urges try to control yourself, especially in a classroom full of students."

"Are you saying you can help me control my urges in private?"

I was being forward and Debbie didn't seem to mind. Just my way of testing the boundaries of our relationship.

"Not quite. I know exactly where you're going. Keep in mind I'm married and I'm your teacher. I would like some private time with you to tap your mind a little. You have a special gift with the spoken word. My husband would get a kick out of meeting you."

"I'm not sure about that."

"It would be fine. He's a writer, poet and community activist."

"What's his name?"

"Jonathan Porter."

"He's your husband? He's old."

We burst out laughing. I wasn't about to apologize. He was old enough to be her father.

Mrs. Porter said, "He's old but he's a good man."

"No doubt. Basically, I've patterned my life after his. I'm very familiar with his work. You have to know my friend Lisa. Her father was a Black Panther and he was best friends with Mr. Porter at one time."

"You're talking about Lisa Ashford, right?"

"Yeah."

"That's my girl."

"Did you know Lisa got a record deal and moved to New York?"

"No, but I'm happy for her. She must have just left for New York because I saw her over the weekend and she didn't say a word to me about that."

"I don't think she wanted anybody to know, so can we keep it on the hush?"

"Oh, that's not a problem."

"Back to us, six degrees of separation kept us apart, but now nothings going to keep me from you."

Debbie smiled. "I like that six degrees line. We are together and all, but we could never have what you want. You're a very attractive young man, but you want something I can't give you. Remember I'm married and I'm your teacher."

"I just want to get to know you better. I only know bits and pieces

185

about you Mrs. Porter or should I say Mistress Debbie?"

"Mrs. Porter is more appropriate for now. What do you plan to do about Monica? What about this broken hearted soul you mentioned in your poem?"

"I love Monica, but I think I'm just gonna sow my wild oats for awhile. My heart is truly broken, but I can't let it get the best of me. I'm interested in spending time with you. You make me feel good and you help ease my pain. The best thing for Monica and me right now is space."

"Are you sure?"

"Yeah. I'm sure and to prove it, here's my number. Feel free to use it anytime."

"You just don't give up, do you? I suggest you focus more on Monica and a lot less on me. We can still be friends. Maybe we can meet at Timbuktu's or Pabulum's for poetry readings sometimes." Mrs. Porter paused for a few seconds. "Don't you still live with your parents and what would they think of me calling?" I think she forgot how old I was for a minute.

"My parents wouldn't think anything out of the ordinary. They'd think you were just a friend. Don't think of me as a kid. I'm very mature for my age. I really want to hook up with you."

"I'll be in touch. We have to be very discreet about our friendship. I can't ruin my career."

"No problem. We basically hang out at the same spots. Nobody would suspect anything. You'll be in your car and I'll be in mine. After a poetry reading we could meet up at another spot afterwards?"

"Slow down a little. I can't promise you anything. It's getting late and we have to get out of here."

Mrs. Porter headed for the door and politely assisted me with my exit. Actually, I think she was a little uncomfortable with me and she was putting my ass out of her classroom. I walked to the door sticking my head out and looking up and down hallway to make sure the coast was clear. The hall was all clear.

In a whisper I said, "I'm sorry for coming on so strong. I didn't mean any harm. I'm really flattered that you wanna be my friend. Let me know when it's convenient for you and I to get together." Debbie put on that pretty smile that I was accustomed to seeing. Her comfort level seemed to be restored.

With her soft voice Mrs. Porter whispered. "Now that's more like it. I can meet you at Timbuktu's Friday night at 10 p.m. for our Erotic Poetry Night."

I sneaked in a quick hug and said, "Stay sweet and dream about me. I'll see you in the morning."

Mrs. Porter was sending me mixed signals. No matter what she said or did, I knew she wanted more than a friendship. I scared her by being so aggressive, but I knew in time Mrs. Porter would show her true colors. She could definitely get the "Rugged Raw" anytime she wanted. In the meantime I planned to chill. I had to get started on my homework and I needed to work on a new erotic poem for Debbie.

My parents came home expecting to hear a full report of how my first day of school went. I gave them a brief synopsis of my day. Of course, that wasn't good enough for them. My mother got a call at work from Mrs. Cameron. All of a sudden, I didn't like their friendship. She wanted to know if my mother had any details about my break-up with Monica. My mother was clueless. Mrs. Cameron wanted my mother to pump me for details since Monica refused to give up any. There was no way I was giving up the real scoop.

"Monica and I decided to slow down a little. She wants to attend Spelman College in the fall and I want her to stay here with me. All these colleges here and she wants to go out of state. She has her mind set on going away and now I don't want to be bothered with her. Mrs. Cameron helped Monica make that decision and I don't want to be bothered with her either. She happens to be a graduate of Spelman and now she wants her daughter to follow in her footsteps."

I put those bits of the truth together so well that I almost believed it myself. My parents sure fell for it.

My mother said, "I think it's wrong for her to leave you. But she needs to do what's best for her future."

My father said, "I think it's a good thing the two of you broke up. You need to get out and meet other girls, anyway. You two were too damn serious to be so young. And it's time you started making some serious moves. You're only a few steps away from college. If you look closely medical school's right around the corner."

He made sense at first, but the medical school thing made me mad. I had plenty of time to think about medical school. All I knew was that I was tired of this man planning my future.

I said, "It's only the first day of school."

This fool yelled at me. "And the first day of the rest of your life."

My mother and I looked at my father like he was crazy.

He toned down. "I realize I never gave you the opportunity to choose a college."

"Actually you never gave me the opportunity to choose anything."

"What do you mean?" He said, with fire in his eyes.

"You've chosen my college and career. To be honest with you, I don't want to be a doctor," I said loud and clear.

Now that fire in my father's eyes was an inferno. "Well, what the hell do you want to be?"

"A nurse."

We now had a raging inferno on our hands.

My father yelled, "Over my dead body. There's no way in hell I'm going to let you do that."

"You didn't let me finish. I want to be a writer too. Maybe, one day my work will get published."

"Don't expect me to put out one shiny nickel for your education. As a matter of fact don't expect anything else from me."

"I'm a man now. I'll make my own way."

"How the hell can you pay for anything?"

"There are thousands of scholarship programs I can apply for."

"You better start applying because I mean what say and I said what I mean."

"For once can you just believe and trust in my decision making.

188

This is my life."

"I guess asking you to follow in my footsteps is asking too much. I bred and fed your ass for eighteen years and now all of a sudden it's your life."

"That's how it is."

"Well, if that's how it is, you're eighteen and you can move yourself right up out of here."

My mother jumped in. "I've heard enough. If Eric wants to be a doctor, nurse or a writer you should support him. If you don't, I will. He never gave us a day of trouble and you should thank God. He wants to do something productive."

"Productive." He laughed. "That's for illiterate children without any hope or potential. But this boy has endless potential and intelligence. Why settle for a standard occupation like nursing when he can be a doctor and have it all?"

My mother had the fire in her eyes now. "You consider nursing a standard occupation. You must be joking." She took a breath to calm herself down. "Well, Doctor, I've had more than enough of you tonight. Eric, if you want you can stand here listening to this mess. I'm going to my room."

My mother and I headed upstairs. My father continued to mumble something, but we refused to listen. The next thing I heard was the front door slam.

My father didn't know that my mother already had a Plan B. We had tons of scholarship information. His money didn't mean shit to us. He didn't know that my mother had some money stashed aside for me. She knew important people too and it was almost a sure thing that I was going to be accepted into University of Maryland's School of Nursing.

PLAYA-PLAYA: 14

By chance I ran into Stephanie on the parking lot after school. She happened to be the most popular girl in school. Stephanie didn't gain her popularity from being a brilliant girl, from sleeping around or from athletics. She was the girlfriend of the legendary Curtis Williams. Curtis was the quarterback of two championship football teams from Randallstown High. He graduated the year before and was the new starting quarterback for Hampton University. Too bad he wasn't around when Stephanie's car wouldn't start. She asked for my help and I was ready and willing to assist her. I looked under her hood and found that her alternator belt was broken. I tried giving her a jump, but her battery was totally dead.

Stephanie asked, "Can you give me a ride home? I'll get my father or brother to get my car towed somewhere later."

"I'd love to give you a ride home."

We smiled. There wasn't any need to say anything else. We both felt an undeniable attraction to one another. I opened my passenger side car door for her. She got in looking at me with a smile. Stephanie was impressed by the fact that I was such a gentleman.

She wasn't used to a guy opening a car door for her.

During the ride to Stephanie's my mind was going a mile a minute and I felt like hers was too. She was too quiet, so I broke the ice.

"How's Curtis doing?"

Stephanie looked surprised by my question. "Okay, I talk to him almost every day."

"I've never been one for long distance relationships. How's it working for you?"

I was being down and dirty exploiting an obvious weakness in their relationship.

"It's fine. We see each other like twice a month. It's not what it used to be, but I'm happy."

Stephanie was saying one thing, but her face told the real story. I smiled and shook my head.

She asked, "What?"

"Nothing."

We pulled into Stephanie's driveway.

"Wanna come in for a minute?"

"Yeah."

As we walked up to her front door I looked around making sure nobody from school saw me going in her house.

Stephanie looked back at me and said, "I know you're not scared."

I didn't know if she was asking if I was scared of her or someone telling Curtis about us.

"I ain't scared of shit. You know how people like to talk."

"Don't worry. People on this street don't know my business. Come on in. Nobody's home. My brother will probably be home in about an hour. My parent's schedules are too unpredictable. More than likely they won't be home for hours."

"This is a nice place."

Their house was neat and nicely decorated. Her parents obviously had a lot of money or a lot of credit card debt. Stephanie acted like her house was no big deal.

"I'll tell my parents you liked the place. Do you want something to drink?"

"Yeah, what you got?"

Stephanie opened the refrigerator door and looked inside.

"We got Coke, water, orange juice, milk and some ghetto-cherry flavored Kool-Aid."

"Gimme some Kool-Aid, Shorty. I can't believe you offered me milk."

"I love milk. Don't you know? Milk does a body good."

"I see. And it did your body real good. You must have been a Similac baby."

"You know that's right. How you think I got a booty like this?"

"Let me see." She turned around. "Ooh yeah, definitely a Similac baby."

My little flirting made Stephanie think about Curtis.

"What made you ask about my relationship with Curtis?"

"I was just trying to see if you were happy."

"I am. I'm going to Hampton next fall. Me and Curtis will be together all the time."

"I've heard that same song and seen that same dance before. It's the same old routine."

"What song and dance?"

"Exactly, he's got you going so good that you can't even see it. Curtis is probably fucking every girl in sight. He's in Virginia, the black college booty capital of the world. All those girls from Virginia State, Hampton, and Norfolk State. Take it from me. I know how this stuff goes down."

"You don't know my man," Stephanie said defensively.

"He's got a dick, right?"

"Yeah."

"He's the starting Quarterback at Hampton. You can bet your sweet ass he's gettin' busy."

"I ain't trying to hear that."

Stephanie finally poured the Kool-Aid.

"You might be right about Curtis, I don't know."

My Kool-Aid was so sweet I thought I was going into a diabetic coma.

"Y'all must be all out of sugar."

"Why'd you say that?"

"'Cause somebody put all of it in this Kool-Aid. But it's good though."

"Thanks smart-ass, I made it."

"Are you interested in anyone besides Curtis?"

"Not really." With a twisted grin on her face she said, "You wanna fuck me, don't you?"

"You know I do."

"Why didn't you just ask? Did you think getting me upset about my boyfriend would make me want you?"

"You're right, I'm sorry for the mind games. I've liked you for a long time. Too bad it took your car breaking down for you to notice me."

"That's not true. I always speak to you."

"That's all you do. You never took the time to get to know me."

"You always seemed so conceited."

"I'm not conceited. Just confident and picky about the girls I talk to."

Stephanie sipped her Kool-Aid. She asked, "Wanna taste my Kool-Aid?"

I reached for her cup and Stephanie burst out laughing.

She said, "Kiss me stupid."

Our lips slowly connected. My hands moved from Stephanie's face, through her hair, around to her breasts and finally resting on her ass. Stephanie's hands were on the back on my neck pulling me in deeper. My tongue was gently massaging hers. Stephanie's tongue made that Kool-Aid taste even better...even sweeter. We got totally lost in that kiss. I backed Stephanie into the wall. The room temperature seemed to rise. Stephanie was about to get a sample of how good my hardness felt pressed against her body. It felt so good pressing my body against hers that I almost lost control. Stephanie's body had a slight tremor when I touched her in

193

certain spots. She wasn't used to being touched like that. Curtis wasn't giving this girl what she really needed. She was an incredible kisser and she liked to be kissed slowly. With my tongue and fingertips I scanned her body for more of her sensitive spots. I thought she was about to reach some type of climax. She started to moan and shiver even more. Our kisses became wetter and sloppier. Stephanie unzipped my pants and guided her hands to my fully erect penis. She did this nice little stroke and used her thumbs to massage my penis. Our breathing became more intense. I sucked her lips and she sucked mine. I picked her up and she wrapped her legs around me.

She said, "I want you."

"I want you too."

I lowered her to the floor and got on top of her. I could see her nipples through her shirt. She completely unbuttoned her blouse. I kissed her breasts and slid my tongue across her hard nipples. Stephanie stopped me.

"I don't want to stop, but we have to. My brother will be here any minute."

"Let's go to my house."

"I'd love to have sex with you, but I can't. I'm scared Curtis will know something's up."

"What? How would he know?"

"I don't know. He said he has a way of knowing if I had sex with somebody." Stephanie was buttoning her shirt and trying to regain her composure.

"He would never know," I said as I grabbed a hand full of myself.

"I can hear him saying, 'If it doesn't fit like a glove somebody's been gettin' my love.'"

"That's a myth. Your stuff will fall right back in place and it will be as tight as the day he left it. Here, take my number. When he does you wrong and you want revenge call me. He will do you wrong and I hope you know that."

"We'll see." Stephanie gave me a goodbye kiss. "Thanks for the ride home. I really enjoyed you."

"I really enjoyed you too. Thanks for the Kool-Aid. It was the best I ever had. When you see me in school don't just speak, actually talk to me."

"I will. I promise. See you sexy."

The art of being a playa, the price of being a playa and the karma associated with being a playa all crossed my mind, but the fun of being a playa stuck like glue. If I wanted I could have a different female friend every night. Not for sex, mostly for companionship. Every night the chance to experience a different flavor. Chocolate, honey, brown sugar and caramel. Just to name a few. Vanilla??? Each night a different personality offering different concepts and new exciting ideas. I wasn't sure if this new playa lifestyle was for me or not. There was only one way to find out. I had to live it to the fullest.

The next night was Mrs. Porter's turn. I was in rare form dressed in all black. Timbuktu's crowd had no idea what they were in store for. The place was filled with what looked like a real artsy type crowd. There wasn't a familiar face in the crowd. This made me somewhat nervous until Mrs. Porter walked up and gave me a friendly welcome hug.

"Hey Eric. You ready for this?"

"Call me Black. And you know I'm ready."

"Wait until you hear my poem."

"I can't wait. Is it hot?"

"*Hot,*" Mrs. Porter said in a sexy tone. "I'm about to get things started."

"Go 'head, Mistress Debbie and do your thing. Just do me one favor and let about three or four people go on, then give me a real nice intro."

"You got it." Debbie made her way to the stage. "Good evening. I'm Mistress Debbie and I want to welcome you all to Timbuktu's Erotic Black Poetry Night." As usual Debbie opened with a poem of her own entitled *Erotic Images (portraits of love)*. Her poem was hot for real. She left the mic smoking. Debbie's poem reminded me of something that Lisa would have recited or something Monica would have recited after she lost her virginity and experienced about three real good love making sessions with me.

After the third poet completed his poem I knew Debbie was ready for me. That guy Poppy wasn't anywhere in sight. Good. The night belonged to me and I was about to prove it. I not only planned to recite my poem, but I planned to put on a performance.

Debbie said, "Please help me welcome a young man who is known as the poet, Black. He has a true gift for the spoken word and he's developing a reputation for his erotic poetry and I know we're going to love his poem tonight. Give him a warm welcome.

I made my way to the mic. "Thanks. My poem is a little different. It was inspired by a close friend of mine that hangs with me all the time. I guess you can say he's a major part of me. If y'all don't know what I'm talking about, you will. My poem is entitled *Can you feel me.*"

I took my time starting. I had to unbutton my shirt so the ladies could get the full effect. My red, black and green beaded necklace with the ankh laid perfectly on my bare chest right between my pects. My abs looked real tight. A full six-pack of ripped muscles. Most of the women liked what they saw. My goal was to make them feel me through my words, gestures and physical presence.

Can you feel me baby
'Cause I damn sure want to feel you
I'm the greediest neediest sex fiend around
I'm talking foot fetish and all
My tongue has a mind of its own
Reading your mind like an open sex book
Giving you everything you need
And shit you didn't even know you was missing
I wanna planet rock your world
On and on to the break of dawn

196

Indeed...giving you what you need
I won't fake the funk
So don't sleep on this gift
I'm here to put in work
So note the length and the width
You'll never have to beg for this third leg
It's long dark and handsome
Larger than life...cutting like a knife
Big Willie, Chief rocker, Daddy long leg, Big dipper, Deep stroker,
Hoochie choker
You're in for a long hard night
Tomorrow you'll forget all about Tom and Harry
You'll strictly have Dick on your mind
Your appetite's large and I'm gonna feed it
With our bodies closer than close
Hand in hand gripped in a love lock
Chest to chest as I press and press
Switching positions like a sex guide
Slow or fast...I'm pleasing your ass
Hitting hard from behind on an incline
Then you on top...I yell-Don't stop

I wanna scream your name as you scream mine
Come with me...as we journey together in ecstasy
What I put on your ass tonight no man will ever take off
Can you feel me baby
'Cause I damn sure feel you

   The women in the crowd went absolutely crazy. They wouldn't
let me sit down. I started to button up my shirt and Debbie stopped
me.
   She yelled, "Show that body off."
   Mrs. Porter obviously forgot who she was for minute (a married
woman and my teacher).

I never expected the response the audience gave me. At first, I thought the women would find my poem lewd, obscene and just down right offensive. Instead, I was received with so much love. Words like powerful, charismatic, creative genius and sexually appealing came to mind. Finally, I felt like I had left a lasting impression. They loved me. The next thing I wanted was to have some panties thrown my way. But it didn't happen. Debbie calmed things down.

She said, "Black is the man. Thank you for warming the place up. You made it real hot up in here. Who's up next?"
None of the other guys moved. They were intimidated by my poem. They probably wanted to rethink their approaches. And that's exactly how Poppy made me feel my first time at Timbuktu's, but I still recited my poem. It was early and things were starting to slow down. Two women recited their poems and everything came to an end.

On my way out of the bookstore a group of extra friendly women both young and old bombarded me with questions. I answered as many as possible. Nobody asked for my phone number and I didn't offer. Most of them wanted to know when I was coming back. My poetry was helping me develop a fan base and I loved it. Debbie caught up with me as I was about to go to my car. She was still excited.

"Thank you for making my night."
Instead of acting like my teacher she was more like a giddy little schoolgirl. I played it cool.
"It was nothing. I had a good time. Thanks for inviting me."
"I had no idea you had a body like that."
"I'm glad you liked it. Thanks again for everything."
I started towards the door, still acting cool and very nonchalant.
She asked, "Is someone expecting you?"
"No."
"Well, can we talk for a minute?"
"Sure."
We went outside towards the parking lot. Debbie moved close to

me. She closed her eyes and took a deep breath.

"I can't believe I'm telling this. I'm so attracted to you. If you weren't one of students I'd probably give you a kiss right now."

I laughed. "I can always transfer to Mrs. Robinson's class."

"It's not that simple. You'd still be a student at Randallstown."

"I can always go back to my old school."

Mrs. Porter was ripe for the picking.

I said, "I dream of making you a star."

"What do you mean, a star?"

"I'm talking about directing a love scene anytime or anywhere starring you and me. And together we'll bask in the afterglow. Look at the sky. Stars have that glow you can see from miles away. A bright, beautiful, shining, glistening star. That's exactly what you are and I wanna give you that special glow for everyone to see."

"That sounds good. Do you really think you can do all that?"

"I can promise you that."

"Oh my god, this is dangerous. I have to let you go. I'm going to get myself in some serious trouble."

I said, "We should-"

Debbie leaned in and gave me quick kiss on my lips.

I said, "That was real nice, but a little too quick. I need to feel you."

"I have to get away from you now. Thank you. Have a good weekend."

She actually started running away. What a silly woman.

I yelled, "Slow down let me give you a ride to your car."

"I'll be fine. My car's parked right over here."

After all that I was going home alone. I watched Debbie get into her car. Oh, the things we could have done that night. It was still early, but there wasn't really anywhere for me to go. So, I headed home. On the way home I stopped at the McDonald's on Liberty Road near Rolling Road. For some reason, I had a craving for some hot salty fries, a garden salad and a Coke. The drive-thru was packed, so I decided to take a break from the norm and go inside.

When I saw the cashier I was happy about skipping the drive-thru. She gave me a friendly smile and took my order. She was the prettiest little thing. I noticed her nametag.

I said, "Marcia, that's a pretty name."

She gave me a simple thank you. When I handed Marcia my money our hands touched. Her hand was so soft that I copped an extra feel and it made Marcia smile. She stepped back to gather my order. She thanked me again and handed me my food.

"Have a good night."

I grabbed the bag, thanked her and headed towards the door wishing she had given me something like her phone number or address so we could hook up. Then, I noticed her reflection in the door. Her image was so clear that it was almost as if I was staring her right in the face. Marcia had no idea I could see her. She gave me a little wink and blew a kiss.

I thought, *That's my girl.*

I stopped dead in my tracks and did an about face. This was perfect. She was interested in me after all.

"Marcia, I'm Eric."

I extended my hand taking her hand into mine. We talked for a few more minutes and exchanged numbers. This was the start of something sweet. I had to make this 5'3" hazel eyed honey-brown a star.

MARCIA: 15

I told Marcia I had a private phone line in my bedroom and it would be fine to call me whenever she got in from work. It was about 2:15 a.m. when I got her call. Both of us were too anxious and excited to get any sleep. Late night telephone conversations are usually hot. Late nights seem to bring out the freaky side in most people. That's exactly what I was in the mood for, some freaky shit. Not quite phone sex, but more like telephone foreplay. I wanted to test Marcia out with a little sex talk. We talked for a couple of hours, but the conversation stayed pretty basic. Marcia practically told me her life story. She talked openly like we had known each other for years. She was a seventeen-year-old senior at Milford Mill High School. Marcia's thirty-five-year-old single mother was raising her. She described her mother as a beautiful young hard-working woman. Marcia's mother worked full-time and went to school full-time. Her parents separated when she was about twelve-years-old, but they never divorced. She hadn't seen or heard from her father in six years, until he made a recent surprise visit. Her father claimed to have found Jesus and he wanted to get his family back together. Marcia's mother told him that Jesus was never lost and neither was she or her daughter. If he wanted to see them anytime over the last six years he always knew where to find them. They were actually doing better without him. Marcia and her mother lived in an apartment complex off Liberty Rd. She said the apartment was good for them because it was practical and located right off the bus line. They didn't have a car. Their apartment was less than ten minutes from my house. Although, we seemed to be from two opposite ends of the spectrum, I hoped that wouldn't present a problem. I really didn't give up a lot of information about myself. Just basic stuff. Marcia never asked what my parents did for a living and I didn't volunteer any information. I really didn't want to seem like I was bragging. She had recently broken up with a guy from her school named Jeff. I briefly told her about my break up with Monica. I asked Marcia if I could pick her up around 7 p.m. for a date she would never forget. I could see her smile through the phone. She seemed to be the type of girl I could have a good time with.

The next morning I was in my driveway washing my car and the strangest thing happened. Jennifer pulled up right behind my car.
Jennifer got out of her car and said, "Can I be next."
I didn't know if she was talking about herself or her car. Jennifer had a lot of nerve. She hadn't talked to me since school started and now she was at my house smiling and joking like she was my best friend. I played it cool. There was no reason for me to act a fool.
I said, "What's going on?"
"Nothing. We haven't talked in awhile."
"No shit. I'm surprised you still remember my name."
"Sorry. I was wrong. But you know how girls stick together."
"I understand that, but what's going on."
"Your girl's not interested in the poetry club anymore and it's time for us to get things started."
"First of all Monica's not my girl. Second, I'm not really interested myself. My plate's full. I've got food fighting for position and gravy dripping right over the edge of my plate. Monday evening I'll be back at the recreation center working with

202

the kids again."

"I can't believe you're not interested in the poetry club."

A sad expression covered her pretty face. Jennifer was really a sweet and sincere person. She meant well.

I said, "Okay, put some flyers together and I'll do my best to help. To be honest, the mentoring program has more than enough volunteers now. They really don't need me there as much."

"So, can I count on you?"

"Yeah. Just let me know when and where."

"That's not all. I need another favor."

"You must have been saving all this up for awhile. 'Cause you got a lot to say all of a sudden."

"This is serious. Troy's been cheating on me with a girl named Cassie."

"Oh my God, I know her. He's cheating on you with another white girl. That brotha's tripping."

"You act like the only thing he's doing wrong is dating another white girl. This is a major catastrophe. A travesty. A transgression-"

"Hold up. It's not that serious. Do you have any proof?"

"Yeah, she's at his house every night."

"That's proof enough. The brotha's hooked."

"Hooked?"

"Yeah, hooked on white girls."

"See that's what I don't like about you. Last year I wanted to be in a relationship with you, but you couldn't handle my skin color."

"You might be right. Dating you would have gone against everything I represent. I'm trying to uplift my race. My main focus is black unity. Now, how would I look dating a white girl? That wasn't even the main issue. I liked Monica more and that's why I hooked you up with Troy."

"And I regret ever being hooked up with him. If you weren't so black or so proud, we would have been a couple."

Jennifer was teary eyed and as she spoke her voice cracked. "I loved you, but you broke my heart. I bet you didn't know that, did

203

you?"

"I had no idea. I loved you too, but as a friend."

"I was in your life first. Do you have any idea how hard it was seeing you and Monica so happy together? When she called me, I was actually happy when she said your relationship was over. I'm her friend, but it's been hard keeping this charade going."

"I'm completely at a lost for words. Please don't tell anyone what you just told me. Things are fucked up right now, but if Troy or Monica found out about how you really feel about me, things will be much worse."

Jennifer looked so upset. "Is there a chance we can get together?"

I thought, *Not a snowballs chance in hell. I can't get down like that with a gringo.*

I held Jennifer in my arms for almost a minute trying to comfort her.

"You know my position and I can't change."

"Well, can you talk to Troy for me?"

"For what?"

"I guess I'll try to get things back to normal. I still need to be with him. If not I'll have to give him that threesome with Cassie he's been begging for."

"What?"

I thought, *Lucky bastard. I'm not saying shit to him. A threesome? Why didn't I have a girl willing to do stuff like that for me?*

Jennifer gave me a kiss on the cheek, got into her car and drove away. I finally finished washing my car. I tried not to give too much thought to Jennifer's dilemma. I liked Jennifer a lot, but she was weird and miserable at the same time. She was trying to play on my feelings in hopes of becoming my girl and there was no way that was going to happen. Her heart was broken, but I couldn't accept full responsibility for that. Jennifer made me realize that I was a heartbreaker. My mother said when I was a baby people looked down at me and said I was going to be a heartbreaker. I think it's funny how people have a way of saying that like being a heartbreaker is a good thing. Little did those people know, they cursed me. Most of the time we go through life not knowing how many hearts we've actually touched or broken. It's not easy to come right out and say, "You broke my heart." Most people keep that hurt bottled up and carry that pain into their next relationship. But that hurt came spurting out of Jennifer like an uncorked wine bottle. She couldn't keep it bottled up any longer. I felt sorry for her and the rest our group. We were once a group of teens in love and time had transformed us into a junior soap opera.

Through all the madness my mind was still on my date with Marcia. I had a bouquet of long stem red roses delivered to her apartment. The delivery thing was a more subtle approach. I didn't want to show up on her doorstep looking like a cornball with roses.

I went to Cooper's Barbershop to get my fade tightened up. Cooper's was like most inner city barbershops. There were three barbers at Cooper's and they were as different as morning, noon and night. Mark was one of the barbers there, who jacked up almost every head he tried to cut. He was an apprentice, so most of the time the master barber fixed his mistakes. Larry was the barber in the middle. He was a neat freak and a perfectionist. Larry was probably the best barber there, but he was the worse if you had somewhere to go. One day I watched this fool spend two hours on one person's head.

My barber was the owner, he was an older man named Mr. Cooper. He had about three customers ahead of me. On Saturdays there was hardly anywhere to sit. I called this place information central. Men always complain about gossiping women, but these were the most talkative men I'd ever been around. This was the spot to hear the latest sports commentaries, international, national and local news. And of course, the hottest neighborhood gossip about who was sleeping with who, who got shot, who got *got*, what was up and who was down. I knew most of the guys there, but I didn't do a lot of talking. Mr. Cooper had a huge stack of old *Ebony* and *Jet Magazines*. Most of the magazines were like five to ten years old. The guys who didn't have much to say would sit around reading those same old magazines every week like they were current issues. The shop had an old broken floor model television with a 13" black and white television sitting on top, which no one paid much attention. The television just added extra noise to an already chaotic atmosphere. No matter what went down, Cooper's always remained a respectable establishment. Mr. Cooper still had old advertisements for black hair care products posted on the walls. Next to one of the advertisements was that same old poster found in every black barbershop displaying those same old haircuts nobody ever asked for. Occasionally, there were a few women at the shop. Some women were there for haircuts or eyebrow arches. Some guys would bring their girlfriends by just to show off. In most cases, single mothers were there with their sons.

I waited about an hour and fifteen minutes for my cut. In the past, I had asked Mr. Cooper to use an appointment system to cut down on his client's wait time. He was too stubborn to change anything about his vintage shop. As usual Mr. Cooper hooked me up with a tight cut. That was the main reason I loved going to Copper's. I later realized vintage was good and change wasn't for everyone.

As promised, I arrived at Marcia's at 7 p.m. I expected her mother to answer the door, but Marcia answered the door looking more than ready. She looked beautiful. Her hazel eyes were the first thing to snatch my attention.

"Hi, Eric. Thank you for the roses. They're beautiful and you look real nice."

"Thanks. You look nice too, with those pretty eyes. And I love your outfit."

"Thank you. Come in and have a seat. I just need to grab my purse."

"I'm glad you liked the roses. They're just the beginning. I've got a lot more in store for you." I wondered if we were alone. "Where's your mother?"

"Working."

"I was looking forward to meeting her."

"Maybe next time."

That was a good sign, Marcia was already planning for our next date.

I sat down and looked around. The smell of fresh potpourri filled the room. Marcia had the roses I sent centered on the coffee table. Their apartment was small, but really neat and clean. They had pictures all around the living room. There were plenty of brass, porcelain and crystal figurines around the room. Somebody collected elephants and giraffes. I could tell that they put a lot of time, energy and pride into keeping their place clean. Marcia stepped back into the living room with her purse. I looked her up and down. She was fine from head to toe. We were both dressed in black. Marcia had her hair back in a wavy ponytail. She wore a pair of black slacks, a black silk blouse and a black leather jacket with nice soft black leather shoes. My favorite girl was covered in my favorite color.

I had made reservations for us at Clyde's Restaurant in Columbia, Md. Clyde's is located right off the lake. We had the perfect romantic location for a first date. The weather was nice. It must have been about 65 degrees with a little chill in the air. The kind of chill that would make a girl want to cuddle up close to her man as they walked along the lakeside.

The date was going well. The food was good and so was the conversation. There was a candle on our table and the flame danced in Marcia's hazel eyes. I couldn't take my eyes off her.

Marcia looked at me and asked, "What is it?"

"You're beautiful. I refuse to fall in love again, but you're making it hard."

Marcia smiled. "I feel the same way about you. So, are you looking for a girlfriend or just looking for a friend?"

"Actually, I'm looking for a close friend and a sexy little plaything. You know, somebody I can make feel good and somebody who can do the same for me. I don't want to get caught up in titles again. Anyway, love is too played out. Don't you agree?"

"Yep. I like how open and honest you are. Love hurts too much and I just want to have fun without being so serious."

"That's good to know. Seems like we're on the same page. You look so young and innocent."

"I'm young, but not so innocent."

"So, what's your story? Been around the block a few times or what?"

Marcia gave me a strange look. "I couldn't tell at first, but now I know you're crazy."

We both laughed.

"I had to make you laugh somehow."

"You're too smart. I've never been around the block before. Maybe a few stops here and there, but never around the block. What about you?"

"Same for me, a few stops here and there."

"You look like a good boy, a nice church boy."

"Good, I like when girls underestimate me. I'm at my best when I'm bad and I'd love to give you a sample."

"Not tonight, I'm a good girl."

Marcia made me laugh with that line. I looked down at her plate, then at her lips.

I asked, "Can I feed you?"

"No. Your food's gonna get cold."

"So, tonight it's all about you."

Marcia paused and gave me the cutest facial expression. She asked, "Can it be about us?"

"That sounds better, doesn't it? Whatever you want we can do."

Marcia gave in and let me feed her. Feeding her got kind of sexual. Regardless of the size or consistency of the food, she did her best to seduce me. She even had a very subtle and seductive way of mimicking oral sex with her straw. A few minutes later, Marcia started feeding me. She was a lot of fun. We eventually zoned out into our own little private world. We weren't aware of who was watching or what was going on around us.

208

After dinner, Marcia and I walked down by the lake. We stood around holding hands, talking and watching a group of ducks play in the water. There were only about three other couples in the area taking in the romantic scene. We watched the moonlight shimmer off the calm water of the lake. There was a chill in the air, so I took off my jacket and wrapped it around Marcia. I put my arm around her and she didn't seem to mind at all. We walked a long the lakeside until we came upon a really intimate spot. Marcia didn't say a word she just stared deep into my eyes. I pulled her closer and gave her a long passionate kiss. By this time, it was actually cold out, but we kept each other warm with our body heat. I started to recite some samples of my poetry and Marcia seemed to like that a lot. Sweet words for a sweet girl. This was definitely the start of something special.

Our first kiss was nice, but the goodnight kiss was even better. Our date ended rather abruptly for a few reasons. Marcia was scheduled to open at McDonald's early the next morning. I wanted to take Marcia to my house, but I didn't know what kind of mood my father would be in. He hadn't really given me two words since our argument. After Marcia and I left the lake we went to Patapsco Valley State Park. The park was closed and dark as hell. There was a big sign that read, "Park closed from dusk to dawn violators will be prosecuted."

I thought, *Yeah right.*

Marcia and I were in the backseat of my car making out hot and heavy, when we noticed a bright beam of light aimed on us. There was a young white policeman standing at my window tapping on the glass. He asked to see some ID and simply asked us to leave the park. He was real cool about the whole situation, but we left in a hurry and didn't stop until we got to Marcia's apartment complex. When it was all over we joked and laughed about the whole thing. I told Marcia I was going to give her a date she would never forget and I'm sure she never forgot that night.

Marcia reminded me of a lot of Monica, probably a little too much. It was both a good and bad thing depending on how I looked at it. I had to stop myself a few times from calling her Monica. Maybe it was the fact that their names were similar. I even saw Monica a few times when I look at her. Marcia had such a good time that she never knew that I was a little uncomfortable. Marcia was beautiful, passionate and romantic. She had all the same qualities that made me fall in love with Monica, but I wasn't trying to fall in love again. I liked Marcia, but I was still in love with Monica. I just needed to give my relationship with Marcia more time and Monica wouldn't be on my mind so much.

On Sunday I went over to Troy's house to watch football games all day with him and Keith. We were kickin' it in the basement watching TV and listening to KRS-ONE and Public Enemy. We had a good time acting like fools. Keith and Troy rapped and I was the DJ. Keith was like Rakim on the mic and I was better than the real Eric B. on the turntables. Troy was without a doubt the overweight-lover Heavy D. We had fun putting lyrics and dope beats together. When we finished rockin' Troy's house, I told them a little about my date from the night before. I asked Troy what was up with him and Jennifer. He said he was tired of her shit. Jennifer was too controlling and she wasn't giving him what he needed. He didn't have to say what that need was. I knew he was pressuring Jennifer to have a threesome with him and Cassie. Of course, Troy never mentioned anything about that. Keith said his relationship with April was going real well. He was sure they were going to get married someday.

Keith said, "Florida State wants me real bad. I know that's where I'll end up going. Anyway, they need a wide receiver with skills like mine."

I said, "It's good you can choose a college and career for yourself without your parents interfering. My father has pretty much planned my entire life for me. He kind of disowned me because I don't want to follow in his footsteps and become a doctor."

"My father wants me to follow in his footsteps and become a lawyer. But he doesn't sweat me because he knows that if I make it

210

to the NFL I'll make more than almost every lawyer at his firm," Keith said with an extra proud look on his face.

Troy didn't take his eyes off the TV, but he was paying attention to the conversation.

Troy said, "I'm going to Morgan State. After that I'm working for my dad's company and one day I'll run the company."

I was starting to realize that my father was an evil dictator or either he had some type of mental imbalance. A lot of men who are unable to fulfill their life-long dream due to some shortcoming usually live through their sons. This wasn't the case with me and my father at all. My father was a well-respected surgeon, who placed overwhelming demands on me. He knew I had the potential to do anything under the sun and to be successful at it. I wanted to do my own thing, at my own pace and when I was ready. This shit bothered me because I loved my father and wanted things back to normal.

That night I had an incredible revelation. Most of the time my best ideas came to me late at night. My creative side was in overdrive. Instead of the poetry club I thought it would be best if we started a newsletter or magazine. The poetry club basically sat around in a classroom reciting poetry that people outside of the room rarely heard or read. We had too many innovative ideas going to waste. We not only recited poetry, but we discussed important issues and concerns that most young people could relate to. I figured most young people in our community would find a teen publication beneficial. I knew our club had enough brainpower to run a small country, so a newsletter or magazine wouldn't be too hard for us to put together.

I talked to Jennifer the next day in school. At first she looked like she wasn't trying to hear what I was saying. When I finished pumping her head with all of my ideas she was excited about getting the publication off the ground. All I wanted to do was to be in charge of one thing, the section called the Poet's Corner. I told Jennifer that we should name the publication *Imani*, which is a Kiswahili word meaning faith. She liked my ideas, but we had one problem. Randallstown already had a school newsletter. We decided not to make it a school newsletter. The Imani Newsletter was going to be a publication for young people all over the Baltimore Metropolitan Area. Jennifer took off to tell the other members of the poetry club about the newsletter.

I wanted to talk to Mrs. Porter about our relationship. We needed to slow down or end whatever we had started. I talked to her after school and she agreed with me. She was actually scared about where our friendship was going.

"Eric, you're such a powerful person. It's hard for me to even put into words the kind of energy that I get from you. I hope you continue to exude all the fine qualities you possess and one day you're going to make some lucky woman incredibly happy."

We embraced for a quick second and I thanked her for the kind words.

Later that night, Marcia called and asked if I could cut school and meet her at her apartment the next morning, so we could spend the entire day together. She surprised me because I knew exactly what she wanted to do. She had sex on her mind and as always, so did I. Her mother was going to be at school and work all day. We could really be alone. I had this deep burning desire inside of me to make love to Marcia. She was yearning, longing, desiring and aching for me to quench her thirst. Marcia hungered and I was definitely going to feed her need. All that night I thought about all the things I wanted to do to her.

Keeping with our schedule I arrived at Marcia's at 8 a.m. We greeted with a kiss. Marcia never had to say much to me. Her eyes said it all. She was blessed with the most beautiful bedroom eyes and an irresistible sex appeal that possessed my body. I picked Marcia up and carried her to her bedroom.

Marcia said, "Before we do anything, I want you to know something really important about me."

"What is it?"

"I've been with guys before, but I've never gone all the way."

"So, you're a virgin?" I said with a surprised, but happy look on my face.

"Yeah. Is that a problem?"

"No, not at all. That makes this even more special."

"I wanted to wait, but I feel like you're the right one."

How did she know I was the one? I spent months trying to convince Monica that I was the one. After one date Marcia knew I was the one. I thought she was incredible. There were more questions bouncing around in my head, but I was on the verge of something big and I didn't want to spoil it with stupid questions. I started to slowly undress Marcia.

I said, "You're beautiful and I can't put into words what this means to me." My tone dropped to a whisper. "Thank you."

I undressed myself as Marcia made her way to the bed. This wasn't going to be just ordinary sex. I wanted to make love to her soul and give Marcia a wonderful experience with lasting memories. I started with a kiss to her forehead and worked my way down to her pretty little toes. Marcia had an intense orgasm somewhere in the *middle* of the head and toe foreplay. I even turned her over, kissing and licking up and down her spine. When I turned her back over I checked to see if she was ready to receive my love and she was well lubricated. She was hot, tight, wet and ready to receive. I had a stockpile of pent-up sexual energy. I had to keep in mind that Marcia was a virgin. As slowly and as gently as I could, I penetrated her. I looked right in her eyes. She had a surprised look in her eyes. This was my Thanksgiving, Christmas, New Years and the 4th of July all in one day. Marcia let out a high pitched moan and gripped me tight. I kept going with a slow in and out motion. Deeper and deeper, she was able to take it all inside. We stayed in a missionary position most of the time. I just moved her legs further apart or up and down for a little variety. I put my hand under her ass for leverage. For a minute I forgot that she was a virgin until her screams reminded me.

In the heat of passion I yelled out, "Oh, Monica. Baby, you feel so good."

"I'm Marcia. My name is Marcia and don't forget it."

Marcia may have been mad, but the sex was too good to stop for one simple mistake.

I was breathing hard. I said, "I'm sorry, baby. I won't forget...I won't forget."

Making love to Marcia for the first time was an incredible experience for both of us. I held her close to me and she fell asleep in my arms.

THIS LOVE THING: 16

It was late May and for months Monica was like the invisible woman. I *never* got to see her. She must have had some special strategic plan to avoid me. Things were actually going pretty good for me and Marcia, but after all that time I couldn't stop thinking about Monica. I had a dream that I made love to Monica. The dream was so real that it made me want her with everything inside of me. My dream reminded me of how much I lived for her love. Monica was on hold, but I couldn't hold out any longer. For too long my stupid pride kept me from calling her. We were two days away from our senior prom, one week from graduation and four days away from Marcia's prom.

Our entire senior class was in the gymnasium practicing for graduation. There were so many people in the gym that I couldn't pick Monica out of the crowd. Our teachers were trying to bring order to the chaos. They were directing us to line up in alphabetical order. At first I couldn't see what was happening. My last name made me the last of the B's and Monica's last name made her the first of the C's. When I realized what was happening I turned around and was face to face with Monica for the first time in months. I was speechless. I just stared at her in awe. Time had

215

made her even more beautiful than I remembered.

With a smile Monica said, "Hi Eric."

I couldn't remember the last time that I'd heard her call me Eric. She was so formal. I wanted to hear her call me Black like she used to.

With a helpless look on my face I said, "Hi."

My mind was blank. I didn't know what to say to her after all that time.

I said, "I'm dying without you."

I'm not sure which of us made the first move, but we embraced and it felt so good. I realized Monica was the real thing and Marcia was just a stand in. I was home in her arms. We asked if we could be excused for a minute. The teachers all looked baffled like they couldn't process what was going on in front of them. Mrs. Porter knew exactly what was going on.

She smiled and said, "You've got ten minutes."

Monica and I rushed out into an empty hallway. The hallway wasn't as intimate as we would have liked, but it did give us more privacy than a gym packed with our classmates. All of Monica's hurt and anger seemed to have subsided. It appeared that time had healed her wounds.

"You've changed."

Monica smiled. "I've been missing you like crazy."

"I know exactly what you mean. It's so good to see and to finally hold you again. I'm so sorry for hurting you."

"Can we be friends again?"

"We can be whatever you need us to be. I was selfish. Spelman is an excellent choice for you and I think you should go. If we can get things back to where we were months ago, a long distance relationship would work fine with me. Like I've said so many times before, *This love ain't going nowhere.*"

"Thank you...thank you."

Monica was overwhelmed with emotions. We embraced again and I slipped in a kiss on her lips.

"I was too hard on you when it came to Lisa. You love me and I know you never meant to hurt me. Lisa always seemed to be competing with me over you and that made me mad. The thought of you two being together drove me crazy. It still upsets me, but I'm a lot better now. I let one mistake keep us apart too long and I'm so sorry."

"You don't need to apologize to me for anything. Can we just work on getting things back to normal?"

"I'd like that a lot. I'd like for us to go to the prom together. Are you available?

Without hesitation I said, "Yeah."

I was supposed to take Marcia. But I had my old girl back and that was all I wanted...all I needed for so long. I was whole again. Marcia and I planned to get a hotel suite and make love all night, but I was willing to give all that up for real love.

"I'm happy again. I've got my Sunflower back."

"I missed hearing you say stuff like that."

Monica and I went back inside the gym and everybody was looking at us. One face in the crowd really stood out, it was Jennifer's. She looked hurt with this it-should've-been-me expression on her face. There was nothing I could do about her broken heart. There was another heart on my mind. Ahead of me was a very dreadful task. I had to break Marcia's heart by telling her Monica was going to be my prom date.

I waited until around 7 p.m. to call Marcia. She answered the phone all excited.

"How was your day?"

"It went pretty good. I need to tell you something and I'm going to get straight to the point."

"Okay."

It was too hard to get right to the point. I thought of an easier way to start.

"Did you pick up your gown for my prom yet?"

"No, I'm going to get it tomorrow. I know exactly which one I want. I did get the gown for my prom."

"Don't worry about getting the gown for my prom."

"Why not?"

"You don't need it 'cause I ran into Monica today and she asked if we could go to the prom together. And I said we could."

"Oh my God! After your prom you and her can go straight to hell. That's so fucked up."

"It's our senior prom and we haven't seen each other in awhile. You understand, right."

"Wrong! I would never have slept with you if I knew you would go back to her."

"I made love to you."

"You sound so dumb. How did you make love to me, when you don't even love me? I couldn't make you love me even if I wanted to because you never stopped loving her."

"It's not really my fault. I told you in the beginning, I wasn't looking for love or a girlfriend."

"Why am I still talking to your dumb-ass? Forget all about me and my prom. You're going to get all this back one day. And I hope your dick falls off too."

Marcia slammed the phone in my ear. I deserved every bit of that. She had every right to hate me. My life was crazy and love was to blame.

I sat in my bedroom and started writing a poem entitled *This Love Thing*. It's about losing Monica, losing faith in love, being a playa, a heartbreaker, hooking up with Marcia and taking her virginity. Not to say that I was proud of what I had done, but these were just free flowing thoughts that I didn't plan on sharing with anyone.

I had a good thing
But now she's gone
So I'm just kickin' it
'Cause love's played out like an old 8-Track
And you know that shit ain't never making a comeback
I'm viewing life through the eyes of a blind man
I'm dead to her world but living day to day

218

I have sight but little vision
A one track mind
Call me a title taker…a heartbreaker
A thief in the night
Lover to many
But got love for none
If love stared me right in the face…I'd say
Don't try to step to me 'cause I ain't the one
I changed my number to 555-1234
'Cause love don't love here anymore
I know nothing lasts forever
And they say that all good things must come to an end

This love thing's just like a boomerang
Today something special happened
I got my old girl back
I thought it was over
But this chapter's just beginning
My life's an open book filled with blank pages
So Sweetheart tell me our love story
And this time I swear I'll listen
Love just made a comeback like an old Al Green 8-Track

Love and happiness
I'm still in love with you
Let's stay together

You're my lady and I love you
Take this love thing and put it to the test
I promise to give you nothing but my best
Here we stand together in love
Soul to soul and heart to heart

I should have read that shit at Pabulum's or Timbuktu's. I was so mad at myself for what I did to Marcia. She really deserved a lot better than what I gave her. Everything I did to Marcia was right in my face. I was drunk with guilt and remorse. When I turned on my TV, I thought I was drunk for real. I was watching Video Soul and there was this woman sitting next to Donnie Simpson, who looked exactly like Lisa. I turned up the volume on the TV and Donnie Simpson said, "Here's *Indigo Nights*, Lisa Ashford's world premiere video." I couldn't breathe. I felt like I was suffocating. How could Lisa steal one of my songs? I helped write that shit. And to top things off she never even called me to say how she was doing. At least she could have told me about her debut on Video Soul. She was beautiful and her voice was better than ever. She looked and sounded like a well-polished act. I got chills seeing her on TV.

Lisa was a celebrity soon to be a superstar. She was finally living out her dream and she forgot all about me. What about when we made love and she said she loved me? SHE SAID SHE LOVED ME! She promised to always be there for me. Where was she now? On the damn TV. I was going *crazy*. Tears started pouring out of my eyes. I was happy for her. At the same time I missed her and I felt like she forgot about me. I was getting payback for hurting Marcia already.

After the video Lisa started talking about the song.

Lisa said, "A good friend of mine co-wrote the song with me. Hey Eric, I know you're watching. I love you, baby."

Her greeting made me feel like a million dollars. My tears instantly dried. I regained my sanity. She didn't forget me after all and I loved her for that. Lisa made me feel like a celebrity too. This was the point in my life where I figured one day I would write a book about my life.

REUNITED: 17

Our prom was held at Martin's West, which was a popular local spot for proms. Monica and I finally arrived at the prom after taking about a hundred pictures at her house and then about a hundred more at my house. My mother looked out for us by letting me drive her Benz. When Monica and I pulled up to the building we noticed some of our classmates had rented limos. That was a little outrageous for my taste and Monica agreed with me. Speaking of outrageous, some of our female classmates designed their own gowns. A few of the girls incorporated too many different pattern ideas into their gowns. Like one girl who had ruffles, rhinestones, double splits, sequins and a giant bow covering her butt.

Forget the Prom Queen. Monica was my queen and she attracted everyone's attention. She wore a very elegant gold evening gown that noticeably showed off her mother's diamond necklace and just the right amount of cleavage. Her gown tastefully complimented her perfect shape. The Prom King, he didn't have shit on me. I wore a traditional Hugo Boss tuxedo with a black tie and cummerbund. Monica and I looked exceptionally stylish together.

We met up with Keith and April inside. They looked really classy together and so did Troy and Jennifer as they walked through the door smiling at us. Troy and Keith wore ties and cummerbunds that matched their date's prom gowns. Jennifer wore an emerald green gown and April wore a fuchsia gown. I was surprised to see Jennifer and Troy together. I couldn't help wondering how Jennifer pulled that one off. It was nice having the whole crew together again. Months ago I would have never imagined the six of us together, especially at our prom. We all entered the ballroom. It was early, but it looked like the entire senior class was present. To be honest, everybody looked nice. Even girls I never paid much attention to looked pretty. Like the female athletes, who shed they tomboy personas for the night. Their masculinity was hidden behind fresh hair-dos, prom gowns and makeup. I found myself eyeballing a few big girls that had a lot of cleavage showing. If I knew these girls could look that good, maybe I would have given them a holler when I was trying to be a playa. Then again maybe not.

Jennifer kept giving me this strange look that made me uncomfortable. She looked beautiful, but she scared me. She kind of looked like she could lose it any minute. I tried acting casual by putting my hands in my pockets and looking the other way. I slipped to Monica's side hiding behind her and shielding myself from our strange friend. There was a buffet set up, but none of us wanted to eat. We decided to head next door to the picture line so we wouldn't be at Martin's West all night. Troy and Keith pulled me to the side to tell me that they had reserved hotel rooms for the night. I was just happy to be with Monica. A hotel room with her was definitely out of the question. Making love to Monica on prom night was a long-standing fantasy of mine. I always saw prom night as the milestone event that would finally put me over the top. Sometimes senior prom is the event that propels young relationships to the next level. Troy and Keith were trying to get an idea of what Monica and I had planned for later. All I really expected from Monica was dinner and a goodnight kiss.

I said, "We definitely don't have any plans for a hotel. I've been dreaming about that forever, but I know Monica's not trying to hear it."

Keith asked, "So what you're saying is you've got reservations for two in your bedroom tonight?"

Troy laughed. "Yeah, him and his right hand."

I didn't find that funny at all. It actually pissed me off. Being with Monica meant a lot more to me than getting laid. A fact well proven when I replaced Marcia with Monica. Troy and Keith's little joke made me mad because they knew it's a touchy subject for a brotha not to get any play on prom night, especially senior prom. Troy and Keith were my boys, so I didn't stay mad too long. We walked over and rejoined the girls in the picture line. Each couple took individual pictures, then we all posed for a group picture. After taking our pictures I made a stop in the men's room. Monica waited for me and everyone else went back to the ballroom. Our class nerd, Eugene was in the restroom looking real nervous or like he was in a hurry or something.

"What's up *Eugene*?"

"Nothing. I asked everybody to stop calling me Eugene. My name's *Gene*. I don't have time to talk, man. I'm about to go get some pussy."

Everybody was getting some, even the class nerd. I wanted to punch him right in his damn glasses. I met up with Monica outside of the restroom. She asked what was wrong and I lied telling her everything was fine. As we walked back to the ballroom I noticed a group of girls around our age wearing regular street clothes walking in our direction. To my surprised it was Marcia and her girls form Milford Mill. I thought if I ignored them and walked by, they would do the same.

I heard one of Marcia's friends say, "Eric, you coming to our prom too."

When Monica heard my name called she stopped dead in her tracks. I tried pulling her along.

She said, "I think someone was talking to you. Do you know them?" With a smile on her face Monica asked, "Are they girlfriends of yours or something?"

I winked my eye and said, "No, they're just fans of mine."

Monica laughed like I said a real funny joke. I thanked the Lord that Marcia and her girlfriends didn't say anything else, they just stared us up and down, then walked away. For a minute I thought a fight was about to break out. I rushed Monica into the ballroom before anything else happened. The DJ was playing a slow song and I guided Monica to the dance floor. After the slow song the DJ played a head pounding club song with this annoying repetitious beat. We raced off the floor and went over the punch fountain. Someone tapped me on the shoulder. When I turned around Stephanie and Curtis were smiling at me. Of course that shocked the shit of me. Curtis and Stephanie were familiar with Monica. Everyone greeted. Somehow Curtis ended up in front of Monica talking to her and Stephanie was in front of me. She looked like she was having a good time.

Stephanie tipped her punch glass at me and said, "Hey, Kool-Aid. Does this remind you of anything?"

I smiled and said, "No."

My closet was loaded with skeletons and the closet door was slowly creaking open trying to reveal my secrets. I was determined to keep certain bones buried deep in the closet and Stephanie was one of them.

Stephanie whispered, "I'll be in touch."

I shook my head and raised my voice on purpose to make her go away. "Don't worry about it. I'm fine."

I was sure Curtis and Monica heard what I said. Monica grabbed me by the arm like she was reclaiming her prize and we said goodnight. I shook Curtis' hand and wished him good luck for his next football season. By that time, Troy and the rest of the crew had picked out a table for us. Monica and I walked over to the table.

Before I could sit, Jennifer jumped out of her seat. She grabbed me by the arm and asked me to dance with her. I pulled away from Jennifer like I was trying to get away from an over-zealous executioner. Monica told me to stop acting silly and dance with the girl. So, I gave in. Jennifer took me by the hand and led me to the dance floor. The song she wanted to dance to ended and one of my all-time favorite songs started playing. The DJ played an old school slow jam, *Fire and Desire* by Rick James and Tina Marie. This song really did something to me. I looked back at Monica and Troy and they were really nonchalant about the whole thing. Monica was smiling and blowing kisses at me. Troy was standing off to the side talking to two guys from the football team. Keith and April were at the table whispering stuff in each other's ears, probably whispering their prom night fantasies. I felt like none of them really cared what Jennifer was doing to me. Jennifer pulled me close to her, but I didn't want to get too close. She was about to get a surprise because that song was a straight-up aphrodisiac to me. Jennifer looked so good that she could have turned me on without that song. She was gorgeous. I never denied the fact that she was a very sexy girl. Jennifer looked extra sexy in that emerald gown. The gown helped enhance her beautiful eyes and skin tone. To top things off she had an ass like a black girl and I loved that. My hand was in the small of her back and I wanted to ease it down a little lower. Jennifer laid her head against my chest and shoulder. She started stroking the opposite side of my chest. Monica couldn't see what was happening. Even if she could see, she would have thought that Jennifer was just being silly. Jennifer moved in closer. I didn't move away and she could feel how hard I was. Her breasts felt so good against me.

Jennifer whispered, "If I die tonight and don't make it to heaven. I can say I had a sample of heaven right here on this dance floor."

That really got to me. I thought her words were sweet.

"You really love me, don't you?"

"I do," Jennifer said in a very euphoric tone.

She made me think of how things would have been if I didn't have that black-white hang-up. Jennifer was really sweet and most of the time I didn't even see her skin color. I was at my senior prom on the dance floor with my best friend's girl with a hard-on.

We were in view of her boyfriend and my girlfriend. Only I could experience some crazy-shit like that. When the song was over Jennifer asked me for another dance. If I didn't have Monica, she would have been a sweet little prom date. I told Jennifer that the dance was very enjoyable, but I had to get back to Monica. Jennifer smiled, thanked me for the dance and we went back to our table.

Our class president, Carlos Peterson took the microphone to make some comments and to announce the prom King and Queen. Monica and I knew we didn't stand a chance of winning. If there was a category for comeback couple of the year, we definitely would have won. Carlos took his time announcing the winners. I guess he called himself letting the suspense build. He was starting to piss off the entire crowd because everybody had other plans after the prom. Monica had made reservations for us at Sabatino's Italian Restaurant in Little Italy. Sabatino's was probably the number one after prom spot in town and that's why I wanted to go somewhere else. Anyway, I've never been a big fan of Italian food, too much damn garlic. Carlos got serious after a few threats. He finally announced the winner, Keith Muhammad and April Anderson. We all were happy for them. This was a big surprise because nobody from our crew expected to win. Keith and April were an excellent choice. From the time they started dating, they always seemed to have a strong and healthy relationship. We all agreed that they deserved to be king and queen.

We all joined in with the king and queen for our last dance of the night. It was a good thing we decided to stay long enough for the announcement of the king and queen. Originally we all had planned to leave early.

Monica was the most beautiful girl at the prom and I was so fortunate to be with her. Jennifer had temporarily stolen the spotlight from her, but Monica was my leading lady...my sexy little star. This was our reunion and dancing with her took me back to Jamaica. She had that same happy glow I saw surround her as we danced on the beach. That glow was nothing but love and I was the reason for it. At first, I questioned Monica's motives for asking me

226

to the prom. For so long it seemed like she hated me. Then two days before the prom she was all in love again. This time around, if I could help it, I didn't want to get caught up so deep in her love. Soon she would be leaving me and I wanted to protect my heart to the best of my ability. All of a sudden, something came over me. I thought to myself, this night will never come again and I have to make the best of it.

I looked in Monica's eyes and said, "I love you."

"I love you too."

Then she held me tight. Monica was feeling the same thing I felt. We didn't want things to change and I think if that night could have last forever, we would have loved it. I stopped dancing and ran my hand down Monica's cheek. I held Monica's face in my hands pulling her in for a kiss that described exactly what she meant to me. I forgot where I was or just didn't care. Everyone around us stopped to take note of what was happening. We were submerged in a kiss, submerged in passion and most of all submerged in love. The Prom King and Queen didn't have shit on us, we stole the show.

For so long I dreamed of having sex with Monica on prom night. We didn't have sex that night, but what I did get meant so much more to me. Monica and I re-established what was on hold for so long. *An undying love.*

SUNFLOWER: 18

I got my letter of acceptance from the University of Maryland. Troy was on his way to Morgan State. Jennifer was accepted to Towson State University. Like Keith had predicted, he was on his way to Florida State University on a full athletic scholarship to play football. I was happy to learn that he wouldn't be going alone. April was also accepted to Florida State. And of course, my sweet Monica was accepted to Spelman College. I tried with all my energy not to think about her leaving me. We both knew that dreadful day was quickly approaching. After graduation our lives seemed to have gone into an accelerated mode. It's funny thinking back on how much we all grew in a couple years. Monica helped define me. She claimed and named me. I was her man, Black. She helped to mellow me out and give my life stability. At the same time I added so much to her life. At first, Monica had difficulties dealing with my relationship with Lisa. In time she grew from a young girl with insecurities to a confident mature young woman. During our break-up Monica found herself and nothing could take away who she was. *I loved the essence of her existence.*

Monica invited me to go with her to Philadelphia to visit her maternal grandmother. I met Monica at her house and we hit the road about 10 a.m. On the way up to Philly we stopped and ate breakfast an IHOP. I had strawberry-topped pancakes and Monica had French Toast. We tried spending every little moment together. Neither of us had any exotic vacations planned for the summer. We basically wanted to stay home and enjoy the simple things like walks in the park, renting videos and eating shrimp pizza from Sorrento's on Route 40. Having a best friend on the verge of leaving really helps to put the simple things into perspective. I never focused on Monica's face so much. I was taking millions of mental photographs of her. Just my way of wanting to remember her exactly the way she was.

It was only a 90-minute ride to Philly. I had been to Philly a few times and I always felt right at home, it reminded me a lot of Baltimore. Monica's grandmother lived in South Philly, in a semi-detached brick row house with a large front porch and high brick steps.

When we arrived Monica's grandmother was sitting on the porch waiting for us. She was a very attractive eighty-three year-old woman with fine gray hair. Right away I could see very notable similarities between Monica and her grandmother. Looking at Monica's grandmother was like looking into Monica's face 65 years into the future. Monica resembled her grandmother a lot more than she resembled her mother. Monica and her grandmother embraced.

Monica turned to me and said, "This is my Grandma Rose." Before Monica could finish our introduction, Grandma Rose took over.

"Hi, Mr. Black. Monica has told me a lot about you," Grandma Rose said giving me a sweet embrace. She made me and Monica laugh.

"Eric, she knows your real name," Monica added.

I said, "Black is fine. It's a pleasure meeting you, Ms. Rose. Now, I see where Monica gets her beauty."

"Thank you honey, but call me Grandma Rose."

Grandma Rose led us inside her house. Her house smelled fresh like a 24-hour bakery.

"I baked a cake and some chocolate chip cookies. Go wash your hands and I'll give you some."

No matter how old grandkids get, grandmothers always remind them to wash their hands. Grandma Rose was so warm and friendly and she made me laugh over and over. I was so happy she wasn't a grumpy old lady, who mainly discussed aches, pains and her illnesses. Her house was sparkling clean. For an older woman, Grandma Rose got around well. She lived alone and was totally independent. She was a retired elementary school teacher. The elementary school she retired from was located right up the hill from her house. She used to walk to work everyday. It seemed like Grandma Rose had planned well for her retirement. Her house was far from a shabby little shack. I noticed her house had a certain modern appeal. She said her daughter helped redecorate the place the year before. They sold some of her antique furniture, but most of it was stored in the basement or attic. I think the modern atmosphere added to her vigor.

We sat in the living room on a sofa eating chocolate chip cookies and looking through photo albums. There were some very candid photos of Monica as a baby and as a little girl. She was so pretty.

"This is exactly how I want my little Erica to look," I said pointing to a cute baby picture of Monica with her daddy.

Monica said, "I'll see what I can do."

"You promise?"

"Marry me and we'll see."

Monica gave me a quick kiss.

Grandma Rose walked into the living room.

She said, "Monica you did all right for yourself. Black looks just like your grandfather."

Monica pointed to a picture of her grandfather, who was a tall light-skinned man. She laughed. "Black doesn't look anything like granddaddy."

Grandma Rose smiled and walked over to the stack of photo

albums. She flipped through a few pages.

"I didn't say he looked like your granddaddy, I said your grandfather," Grandma Rose said lowering the album and pointing to a picture of this handsome well-dressed dark-skinned man. The picture looked like it was taken sometime in the 1940's. This brotha was so sharp he could have stepped right off that picture on to the cover of *EM* or *GQ* magazines.

Monica had this who-the-hell-is-this look on her face. The man she knew as her granddad was really her step-grandfather. Monica's biological grandfather looked a lot like me. After all those year Monica's family should have told her the truth, instead of having her find out years later in the presence of her shocked chocolate chip cookie eating boyfriend. There was a temporary moment of embarrassment. When that moment passed, Monica looked at me.

"My grandfather was a very handsome man. You look just like him, Black. I guess I get my good taste from my grandma."

"That's right, baby. Nothing's better than a real black man," Grandma Rose said with a smile.

Grandma Rose was stroking my ego and scoring major points with me. She started telling us all about her first husband, Lewis. She met Lewis before moving to Philly and before going to college. In 1936, they met while working at a cigarette factory in Richmond, Virginia. They were married less than a year later. Grandma Rose said, "It was definitely love at first sight. He was the tallest, strongest and prettiest black man I'd ever laid her eyes on. With his deep voice, slim muscular frame, neatly trimmed moustache and soft smooth flawless black skin, he could charm the pants off a church girl."

Monica yelled, "Grandma!"

"I'm sorry, baby." Grandma Rose apologized.

"Anyway, church girls don't wear pants, especially back in those days they didn't," Monica said in a sure tone.

"Who's telling this story? You know what I mean. This isn't about pants or skirts."

In a low tone I said, "Yeah it's about drawers."
Grandma Rose was rubbing off on me. I said, "I'm sorry."
They laughed at me.
I said, "I just couldn't resist saying that."
Grandma Rose continued her story. "I packaged the cigarettes and Lewis drove the trucks. One day we went to work like always. This was around the spring of 1942. Lewis was late returning from his route. His supervisor assumed Lewis had run off with the cigarettes and sold them. He said, 'We'll probably never see that nigger again.' And in a way he was right." Grandma Rose's voice dropped and we could see the hurt and pain in her eyes. "They found Lewis' body on the side of the road still in his truck. All the cigarettes were gone. They tried to make it look like an accident, but I know he was murdered. My baby girl was only two years old. They killed Lewis and left us all alone. I'm sure someone ran him off the road. I heard people say Lewis was stealing cigarettes from the factory and selling them. If he did I never saw the money. Most people said the ones running the factory we worked for were the real crooks. I know he was set up to take the fall for a lot of bad people. I loved my second husband, George, but not like I loved Lewis. Those people took something precious from me when they took Lewis. As long as I live I'll never get over it."

My impression was that Grandma Rose married the second time for money. Her second husband was a wealthy well-educated man who moved to Philadelphia from Virginia. He raised Monica's mom and actually put Grandma Rose through school. It's funny how God works. For years Grandma Rose was so content working in a cigarette factory. It took the death of her first husband to change her life and guide her in another direction. Grandma Rose's true calling was to become a teacher and not to remain a factory worker. It took the loss of a life to have her touch so many other lives in a positive way.
    I offered to take Monica and her grandmother out to dinner. Grandma Rose got a little offended by my offer.

She said, "I cooks, darling. You need to taste my fried chicken."
I cooks meant she could put a hurtin' on some food. She not only
fried chicken, she put together an entire spread of soul food.
Grandma Rose was amazing. She could cook, she had a good sense
of humor and an impressive record collection too. During dinner
we listened to the Count Basie Orchestra, Billie Holiday, Duke
Ellington and Sarah Vaughn. Monica left the dining room for a few
minutes and Grandma Rose looked like she was dying to say
something.

She said, "I know my granddaughter and I'm sure you're getting
tried of just watching television all the time."
I knew exactly what she meant by that and she shocked the hell
out of me by mentioning it. Somehow, Grandma Rose knew that
her granddaughter was depriving me of sex. She was a slick old
lady. Grandma Rose made me realize that she hadn't been old all
her life.

A few days after our trip to Philly, Monica and her parents drove
down to Spelman to get her partially moved into the dorm. I
wanted to go, but Monica and her parents needed time alone. I
seemed to be monopolizing most of Monica's time. Her final move
date was actually a lot closer than I wanted to realize.
Since Monica was away I tried using that time to reconcile things
with my father. He was speaking to me again, but he still wasn't
saying much. My father did tell me that he was proud of me on
graduation day. He said I could make him even prouder if I wanted
to become a doctor. For some reason he just wouldn't let go of the
doctor thing. The more he mentioned it the more I was turned off
about becoming a doctor. He asked me how I planned to pay my
tuition and I felt like I was speaking to the enemy, revealing top
secret information. My mother and I kept certain information from
him. He was still my father and no matter how ridiculous he was, I
still had to respect him. I told him about the Maryland State
Scholarship I had been awarded and about the three other smaller
scholarships I was awarded. He looked mad, then there was a look

of defeat in his eyes. He knew with all the scholarships and my mother's financial backing that medical school was a far-fetched concept for me. I didn't like to see that look on my father's face, especially knowing it was there because of something I did.

"Maybe after nursing school I'll give medical school some thought."

My father lightened up a little. He could tell that I didn't truly mean what I said, but he perked up for a second just hearing me mention medical school.

About ten months after Lisa's departure, she finally decided to give me a call to let me know things were going well for her. She made me mad, but I was happy to hear her voice.

"I'm sorry I took so long to call, but I've been real busy in the studio."

"You must think I'm stupid or something. Two seconds are all you needed to say, I'm still alive. I was mad at you until you gave that shout-out on Video Soul and I saw my name on your CD for co-writing *Indigo Nights*."

"I told you I wouldn't forget you. You should be getting a check soon and I still want us to write some more songs together. You know if that song wins an award you'll get one too. Just think it's possible that you could win a Grammy or an American Music Award if that song is nominated."

"I never thought about that. By the way, you looked real nice on Video Soul and you interviewed well."

"Thank you. How was your prom and graduation? I'm sorry, for the first time I missed your birthday."

"Don't worry about my birthday. You hooked me up so much in the past I didn't even think about it. My prom was cool. I took Monica and we had a nice time."

"So, after all this time did she finally give you some?"

"She ain't got no ring on her finger. So, you can answer that question yourself."

"That's foul. How's she gonna go to a senior prom and not give her man some coochie. I would've hooked you up for real."

"I bet. You got a lot of nerve. You left my ass high and dry. And to top it off you didn't even call."

"You say that like I'm your woman or something."

"Yeah, you are something like that. You know what I mean. I missed you a lot. You wouldn't believe all the shit I've been through this year."

"I'm planning to come back to town around Thanksgiving and you can tell me all about it then. I have to go. Just remember I love you and make sure you keep writing."

"I love you too and I write something almost everyday. You better come see me soon."

Lisa had been gone so long that I was getting used to her not being around. She was full of shit, trying to act like she was so busy. I know she was busy partying and meeting new people. She really did look out for me because I only wrote a few lines of her song *Indigo Nights*. I missed her, but I missed Monica more.

Monica's last night in town was spent with me sharing dinner and laughs. I thought it would be appropriate to take her to Pabulum's for our last night together. To our surprise Soul Survivors were there providing some smooth sounds. They were doing mostly instrumental stuff. I guess they gave up their search for a lead vocalist. It was strange seeing the guys perform without Lisa. During intermission I went over to talk to them. Mike had changed his look. He had a lot more facial hair and he put on about thirty pounds. The other guys pretty much looked the same. Nobody even mentioned Lisa. I felt like she was a touchy subject with them, considering she left them behind in the minor leagues. I asked Mike if he would give me a smooth jazzy rhythm and a minute of his time to read a special poem for Monica. Of course he agreed because he and the other guy were kind-hearted individuals. Monica had no idea that I had a poem prepared. She figured something was up when she saw how long I stayed up front talking. I stepped on stage and Mike introduced me.

"Ladies and gentlemen we have a special guest here tonight who wants to share some love. I give you the poet Black."

"Thanks Mike. Good evening. Most of you are familiar with my work. But this piece is a little different. I'd like to dedicate this poem to the love of my life, Monica. She's on her way to Spelman and this is her last night in town. I thought it would be nice to share my poem entitled *Sunflower*."

From this land I wonder what really grows
What's it made of and how deep it goes
A barren field of dreams of what could be
This land is dry like the sands of time
Time on my hand and life on my mind
It's time to pull up the weeds and give life a chance
In this soil I'll plant my flower
My beautiful flower...my sunflower
With my love you'll never die
The sky is your target as you grow and grow
From this angle the moon doesn't seem so far away
The sun blazes you with love
The stars represent shattered relationships and shiny smiling faces
Though your head's to the sky
This mighty earth is still your home
Once a barren field of dreams of what could be
Now an abundant field of life
The grass is green and I am complete
Here today but gone tomorrow
My beautiful flower has been taken away
Picked from the soil of my soul...the center of my heart
Love gave you life but what took you away
In the place where you stood there's an empty space
A hole in my heart...Earth's vacant space
Your roots to my heart are far too deep
Not even time can break this inseparable bound
I'll flip the script and turn the page

236

Won't close the book
Just start a new chapter
In my heart I know what you're really after
Hope the grass is greener on the other side
No need to worry 'cause love ain't goin' nowhere

The crowd seemed to have loved my poem. Not everyone
understood it, but it wasn't really meant to be understood by
everyone. Monica got the message. She was in tears. I thanked the
crowd and the band for showing me so much love. I walked back
to our table, dropped some money to cover our bill. I took Monica
by the hand and we left Pabulum's. This was probably the saddest
night of our lives, but I refused to cry. Monica and I went to her
house to talk. We held each other, kissing and trying to find
comfort. I tried to stay most of the night until Mr. and Mrs.
Cameron reminded us that Monica had an early flight. Monica and
I didn't do any special goodbye kiss, we wanted to save our
goodbyes for the airport.

The morning that Monica left for school hit me right where it hurt
the most, my heart. She had a 7:45 a.m. flight. No matter what I
did, nothing could prepare me for that moment when I had to let go
of her. I considered it cruel and unusual punishment having to say
goodbye to the love of my life in a crowded airport. I held Monica
close to me massaging her back and stroking her hair. Mr. and Mrs.
Cameron did a good job hiding their emotions. I thought back to
the day when Monica and I were leaving for Jamaica. Her parents
were so emotional. This time, it seemed I had adopted their
emotions. Our little girl was about to start a new life hundreds of
miles away. I spoke to Monica like I was a concerned parent
instead of her boyfriend. I was being silly and it made her laugh.
    "Did you pack enough underwear?"
    "I did," Monica said with a pretty smile.
    "Make sure you drink plenty of water and eat your vegetables. Be

careful and don't talk to strange people. Look both ways before crossing the street. Say your prayers every night. And the most important thing." I paused listening to the attendant announce the boarding of Monica's flight. "Never forget me. Keep my picture in a frame in plain view, so everybody can see your man. I don't want to be tucked away in your sock drawer or in a box of old pictures."

I was joking, but very serious at the same time. People always make promises that things won't change, but they always do. Monica's flight started to board. Mr. and Mrs. Cameron stepped over to give Monica their goodbyes. They all embraced. I moved away to give them a family moment together. Monica's father signaled me to come back over.

Mr. Cameron said, "You're family and you belong right here with us in this family circle."

He said a quick prayer and then Monica's parents stepped away to give me and Monica a final moment together.

In a sad tone I said. "I don't think I'll ever love anyone like I love you. Even though we're going to be hundreds of miles apart, I still want things to be the same with us. You've given me so many special memories."

"Shh. You're making me cry. We said we weren't going to be sad. Thank you for being my everything. I love you with all my heart. We're making this real hard. Stay sweet and stay Black. Love you."

We embraced and I held her like it was going to be the last time. Monica's parents were watching, but I needed one last kiss. Our kiss was similar to the kiss I gave her on prom night. I felt her love surge through me down to my soul. When Monica let go and walked away I felt a piece of me descend down that corridor with her. After she boarded the plane I stood there watching until her plane took off.

Mr. and Mrs. Cameron tapped me on my shoulder and we walked back to the car. None of us said a word. When we got back to the car Mr. Cameron and I got inside. Mrs. Cameron went to the trunk. I looked up and she placed a large wrapped gift in my lap. I could tell it was a picture.

She said, "Monica wanted you to have this after she left."

I unwrapped the picture and it was the Jamaican sunrise picture that Monica did on the beach the year before. I almost lost it when I realized what it was. I sat there choked up looking at the picture with my lips tightly pressed together. Mr. and Mrs. Cameron thanked me for being such a good friend to Monica. I thought they were going to mess with me about the passionate kiss I laid on their daughter, but I was so upset, I guess they decided to leave me alone.

Monica's parents had successfully completed their mission. They had sent their daughter off to college with her virginity firmly intact and I'm sure they were proud. *Job well done.*

MR. WONDERFUL: 19

My classes had begun and I tried focusing more on myself, but at the same time Monica was still the center of my world. I was trying to make the best of our long distance relationship, which proved to be a lot harder than I ever imagined. If I had it my way Monica would have been a student at the University of Maryland right along with me. Even if she wasn't a student at Maryland, as long as she was at a local school I would have been fine. To help combat my loneliness I talked to Monica at least twice a week and we wrote each other, most of the time. Being alone allowed me the opportunity to really get deep into my thoughts. Some days I would go riding deep in the boondocks sightseeing or simply drive around the beltway for hours just thinking or listening to music. Driving can be stressful sometimes, but for me it's relaxing. It was my great escape. Driving helped me to zone out and forget my problems. I enjoyed the freedom, the speed and becoming one with the road. It's a guy thing. The relationship a man shares with his car is a sacred thing.

At this point in my life, my mother was an incredible source of support to me. She had become my best friend, mentor and guardian angel. I have to admit that all my life I've been a mama's boy. When I was younger I used to go everywhere with her. Before I was old enough to drive I used to be in her car right by her side riding shotgun. When I was old enough to drive I chauffeured her around most of the time. I've always been good to my mother. When I was in college there wasn't anything she wouldn't have done for me. She suggested that I get an apartment close to school. She helped me search for a place since she worked nearby and was so familiar with the area. We found a spacious two-bedroom apartment about four blocks from campus. At first I thought the apartment had a lot more space than I needed. A one-bedroom apartment would have been good enough for me. My mother said we were getting a bargain on the place. The apartment had been remodeled with a modern eat-in kitchen, refurbished hardwood floors and a fireplace. I could see that the place had lots of potential. My mother asked me to save room for her just in case she needed a get away. I wasn't sure if she joking or not. Either way she was paying the rent and I wasn't about to tell her that she wasn't welcome to crash at my apartment sometime.

My mother and I made a deal and this is pretty much how our deal went. If I stayed in school and maintained at least a 3.0 GPA my mother agreed to pay for my food, clothes, car payment, car insurance, rent and whatever else I needed. At first I was hesitant to agree. She was making me too dependent on her. The thought of someone paying all of my living expenses sounded good, but I feared that after a major fallout I would be cut off like an annoying hangnail. My mother promised me nothing like that would ever happen between us. I believed her because she was so sincere about helping me. She was also excited about the fact that I wanted to become a nurse. When my mother reminded me of all of the money I was saving her from my scholarships I didn't feel as guilty about accepting her help. She said I had already put in a lot of hard work and this was my reward. After hearing my mother explain all that, how could I turn down her offer?

For weeks my mother worked on furnishing and decorating my apartment. I really didn't care much about furniture or decorations.

All I wanted was a brand new big screen color TV and some new stereo equipment from Circuit City. When it comes to home furnishings, men always consider getting electronics before anything else. I was excited about having two bedrooms. I decided to make one room my bright bedroom and the other my dark bedroom to reflect my moods. My bright bedroom reflected my normal easy-going-everyday side. Light shined in through two windows enhancing my blue, gold and burgundy color scheme. This was my bedroom for slow lovemaking and romance. On the flipside, my dark bedroom a.k.a. the underground was the home of my alter ego. This room was where I could get raw. Let's just say you'd never find rose petals on the floor or between the sheets. I kept this room dark and the only light it had was a strobe light to add to erotic energy of the room. I had all these ideas bouncing off the walls of my spacious apartment, but no one to share my time or space. In my heart and mind Monica was right there with me enjoying my new place. In all actuality, she was hundreds of miles away.

When I started at the University of Maryland I planned to hang out mostly with male friends, but my life couldn't be that simple. Regardless of my situation, I had this inescapable urge to befriend the most beautiful women around me. There were three girls that caught my attention Leah, Nikala and Jasmine. The three of them had been friends since high school and they happened to be nursing majors. I ended up having sociology, psychology and biology with them. Right away they noticed how intelligent I was and they asked if we could form a study group. A beautiful image of the four of us in my apartment popped in my head. Leah was an eighteen-year-old Filipino beauty with a sexy little body. Nikala and Jasmine were glamorous model types. They were like life-sized Black Barbies. They were a little too glamorous for me. I liked women who wore makeup, but sometimes they over did it. Most of the time all they ever talked about was how good they looked or how they could improve their looks. It was fun hanging out with my new friends and that's all they were, friends. I made it clear from the start that I had a girlfriend. They thought I was special for letting them know that I had a girlfriend instead of frontin' like I didn't. Of course we talked about sex and relationships, but we never did anything out of the ordinary. They knew a lot about Monica because she was all I ever talked about. I did my dirt in the past, but that was all in the past. Though some times were *hard*, I was a new man, confident and focused on making a long distance relationship work.

One Friday I didn't have any classes and I didn't know what to do with myself. Monica was heavy on my mind and I couldn't stop dreaming about her. We hadn't seen each other in about eight weeks or more. My heart wore a serious frown. The last time we spoke Monica said that she would be coming home for Thanksgiving. Lisa gave me that same line, but I knew she wouldn't be coming my way for Thanksgiving, Christmas or anything else.

I was totally free for the weekend and that bothered me. There I was with nowhere to go, nothing to do, and no one to see. My mind started racing.

I thought, *If I leave right now I can be in Atlanta by 10 p.m.*

As crazy and as impulsive as that sounded the thought made me excited. Something was leading me to Atlanta. Thanksgiving was close, but not close enough for me. I packed some clothes and hit the road.

When I arrived at Monica's dorm she wasn't there. I ran into this girl in the hallway named Patrice. I asked if she knew Monica and luckily she did. "Monica just left a few minutes before you arrived, but she'll be back shortly."

Patrice was kind of cute. She called herself entertaining me while I waited for Monica to return. In a short period of time she talked me to death. She seemed to be a very analytical person. This girl was too smart for her own good. Useless information spewed out of her mouth like a toxic waste. She gave me the impression that she'd just smoked some weed or something. Patrice asked me to call her Pat. She wanted to know who I was and how I knew

Monica. She invited me down to her room, so I could be more comfortable, but I told her that the lounge was fine. She was trying to get way too personal with me. After about an hour Pat was really getting on my nerves. I decided to leave. I asked Pat not to tell Monica that I was in town. On my way out the door I saw Monica on her way up the steps. The happy look on my face quickly turned into an expression of anger. Monica wasn't alone. She didn't notice me right away because she was too busy laughing and playing with her fancy new friend. She was with some tall clean-cut looking light brown skinned guy carrying a pizza box and a two-liter Pepsi. He was older and very distinguished looking. He wore a nice suit and overcoat. He reminded of the type of guy Cliff Huxtable would have picked out for one of his daughters. But he was obviously a cheap bastard because he was having a pizza date with Monica in her dorm. To my surprise Monica gave this guy a kiss on his lips. When they noticed me standing there looking at them with this very intense angry stare, Monica froze for a few seconds. Her friend just stopped and stood by her side looking at me.

"Hi, Eric. It's good to see you," Monica said with this cheap-ass look on her face.

I hated when she was so formal calling me Eric.

I thought, *Call me Black like you used to. Don't change now, you little slut.*

Anger and betrayal were all I could think of. She looked and sounded guilty as hell.

I said, "It's good to see you too. Who's your friend?"

"This is a good friend of mine, Dr. Julian Catrell." She turned to him. "Julian this is Eric."

I was just plain old Eric. Not her boyfriend who loved her with all his heart and the man who had just driven over seven hundred miles to see her sorry-trifling-ass. She had a lot of nerve treating me like an average Joe. Julian Catrell was her good friend and I wasn't shit. To make matters worse her new man was a doctor. I was really pissed. Julian didn't say a word to me and I was glad he

244

didn't extend his hand to me for a handshake.

Monica asked, "What are you doing here?"

I took a deep breath trying to compose myself. "I came to see my girlfriend, but apparently she's not here. If you see her tell her I love her and I still need her. Tell her I'm sorry things had to turn out like this."

There was nothing else for me to say or do, so I walked away. Monica followed me down the steps.

"Eric, please wait a minute. Can we talk?"

"There's nothing to say. I need to get back on the road anyway."

"I'm sorry."

I didn't want to hear shit Monica had to say. My heart felt like it had been folded in half and ripped into tiny pieces. I thought I was her Mr. Right...her number one and only...her knight in black shining armor. In my eyes Monica could do no wrong, but she had really fucked up this time. We were only apart for about two months. In that short time I felt like she had forgotten all about me and everything we shared. At first glance she looked at me like I was a stranger, then that look turned into absolute guilt. We promised to make our relationship work regardless of time or distance. I had done dirt in the past and I just saw this as Monica's time to get a little grimy. I figured that this was karma paying me a visit. I broke hearts and did some other foul shit, but I never cheated on Monica.

On my way up I-85 North I saw a sign for Chapel Hill, North Carolina. The temperature outside must have been in the mid-thirties and the weather was getting nasty. There was a mixture or snow and rain falling. The roads were still a little too warm for ice to form. I was exhausted and my family had no idea that I had gone out of town for the weekend. I was listening to Sade's *Stronger Than Pride*. I found comfort in her sweet lullabies, but I was getting sleepy. I turned on the radio trying to find something more up-tempo and I cracked the window to see if the cold air would help to revive me. I started to worry about my safety. I was less than twenty miles from the University of North Carolina and less than twenty-five miles from Stacey. She said whenever I needed her I knew where to find her. This was impulsive, but I really did need her. She lived in an apartment complex close to UNC's campus. I wasn't exactly in the mood for anymore surprises and I was sure Stacey wasn't either. So, I pulled over at a gas station and called her.

"Hello."

"What's up Stacey?

"Sleep. Who is this and who died? It's 4 o'clock in the damn morning?"

"Sorry, it's Eric."

"I'm sorry Eric. Usually I'd recognize your voice, but it's after 4 a.m. and I can barely recognize my own voice."

"I need you, baby."

"How bad do you need me?" Stacey said in a very flirtatious way.

"I need you so bad I can be at your apartment in five minutes. I hope it's okay. I wanted to call to give you a heads up."

"Something must be wrong. Do you know how to get here?"

"Yeah and don't worry everything's fine. I just need you right now."

"Hurry up."

"I'm on my way."

Even though it was close to 5 a.m. in the morning, Stacey opened her door looking energized. She was a beautiful sight for my sore eyes. We hadn't seen each other in years, but there was still a powerful attraction between us. While on the road I was exhausted, but in Stacey's arms I was revived. Stacey wanted to know what was going on with me and why I was in North Carolina. I asked if I could explain things after a few hours of sleep, but Stacey wanted to know what was going on right away. After giving her all of the details she looked like she wanted to cry.

"I did the same thing to you and you didn't deserve it then and you really don't deserve it now. If there's anything I can do to help ease your pain don't hesitate to ask."

Stacey was so sincere and I didn't want to take advantage of her. I just needed someone to listen, someone to hold and a place to rest my head for a few hours. Stacey was about to let out her sofa bed. She asked, "Do you want to join me in my bed?"

I smiled, "I'll join you after a hot shower."

The shower warmed my body and being in Stacey's presence warmed my heart. When I got out of the shower Stacey helped dry me off. We laid in bed cuddled up in a spoon position talking for hours. I'm not sure exactly when I dozed off. The next thing I remembered was waking up to the smell of breakfast cooking. Stacey was frying eggs and bacon. I didn't have the heart to tell her that I'd stopped eating bacon. As part of my new health conscious diet, I stopped eating pork, red meat and I reduced my intake of fried foods. I hadn't had scrambled eggs in years and the sight of eggs nauseated me. Luckily Stacey made some grits and biscuits too. I ate half of the breakfast, so she was only partially offended.

Like typical folks, we both felt tired after eating breakfast. Stacey's apartment seemed to get chilly, but I asked her not to turn up the heat. We headed for her bed to made some heat of our own. Making love to Stacey was better than ever. I was an experienced lover with an extensive repertoire of sexual skills. One of my favorite positions was when Stacey straddled me and I gave her the "Rugged Raw."

I never stopped loving Stacey. And ironically after that weekend we re-established our long distance relationship. The distance between Maryland and North Carolina was a lot shorter than the distance between Maryland and Georgia and it proved to be a whole hell of a lot more satisfying.

Lisa had promised to visit me on Thanksgiving, but she didn't. I didn't really care because Stacey spent Thanksgiving with me and my family. This was her first visit to Baltimore and she loved it, especially my apartment. She actually got the opportunity to experience the magic and the mystery of the underground.

Monica was completely out of my life, but I knew she would forever be a part of me. Thanks to Stacey I could smile when I thought about Monica. I had very little ill feelings towards her. It's strange, but Monica helped me get back with my first love. If I hadn't gone to Atlanta that weekend I probably would have never looked Stacey's way again. For a long time Stacey walked around with her head to the ground because of her relationship with Chris. The funny thing was that Stacey felt like we were destined to get back together again. I had completely forgiven her for the incident with that no-basketball-playing-bench-warming-punk-ass Chris. I learned to forgive and forget, and to live and let go. Monica was gone, but maybe fate knew different for us. Stacey was my sweetheart and she called me her Mr. Wonderful.

My experiences with Stacey, Lisa, Monica and other females regardless of our connections inspired to write my poem entitled *Mr. Wonderful*.

Can you feel it
That's my love coming down
Spine tingling...backbreaking...earthshaking
Hittin' like a ton of bricks
Tight like a pair of new black dress shoes...from Easter of 1978
Don't even fake like you can't relate
My love will never leave you lonely
Like being up late night on a Friday night
Watching a love story dreaming you were the star
You can be sure that when it comes to my love
You'll be the star of every episode
I'll never leave you ass-out
Living on a one way street with your back against the wall yelling
Nigga please, life is too damn short
Instead you'll say shit like
Can I get a chance
If not, you got a brother, cousin or something
Your mama still making babies
'Cause I'll wait twenty-one more years for somebody like you

This may sound crazy but I'm a good man in search of a good
woman
So can you hook a nigga up...put a brother down
I never want to be left out there
With my rocks in a hard place
Stuck in the fast lane of life with four flat tires
You know a good man's hard to find
But I'm at my best when I'm bad
So consider me easy when you need a hit
And you know it's hittin' like a ton of bricks
Please don't judge me 'cause I know you do your dirt
Sistas are too judgmental
If you haven't heard a good woman is hard to find too
Like the saying goes
What's good for the goose is good for the gander
So when your goose is cooked
Don't worry, baby
'Cause it all taste just like chicken

LOVE LOSS: 20

There are many unseen forces that bear an impact on life. These forces in one way or another dictate the outcome our lives. Along with other forces irony and unpredictability seemed to dictate my life. In my wildest dreams I never imagined that Monica would ever call me again. Two weeks before Valentine's Day she called me at my parent's house to drop some heavy news on me that would alter the course of my entire life. I didn't realize how much I missed her until I heard her voice.

In a very warm and heart-filled way Monica said, "Hello, Eric. How have you been?"

I asked myself after all this time why would she care about how I was doing? Did I really care about how she doing? I did. I was just a sucker for her love, but she wasn't getting off that easy.

"How have I been? What an interesting question. Monica Cameron, my queen of the unseen...queen of my future. My question is how have you been?"

"You sound upset."

"Who me? I'm fine. What about you?"

"I've been doing good. I have some real special news."

"What?"

250

"Last Christmas I received a gift that changed my life. Well, to get right to the point, Julian proposed to me on Christmas day and we're getting married on Valentine's Day. And I'd love if you could be there."

I clenched my heart and tried to take a deep breath, but I couldn't because my sweet Sunflower had just taken my breath. At the same time, I felt like half of my life was taken away. Anger and resentment ran through my body like runaway slaves.

"You *must* be tripping. You got a lot of balls or something calling me with some shit like this. I wouldn't be there even if you and your man paid me. You must take me for a sucker. Why would I torture myself like that? I bet you just wanna see me drown in misery and self-pity. You know I still love you and the thought of you and him getting married isn't easy for me to accept. He's getting what I've been missing. And if he hasn't already gotten it, on your wedding night he'll be getting what I've been dreaming of...the good stuff I never got and I think that's fucked up."

"As a friend, I didn't expect you to react like this."

"Well, what the hell did you expect? It was hard enough for me to accept your relationship with him and now you drop this marriage shit on me."

"I'm sorry I called. I thought it would be better if you heard about my wedding from me instead of finding out some other way. I sent your parents an invitation. They should have received it by now."

"The mail came earlier, but nobody mentioned anything about a wedding invitation. Thank you for your phone call and your consideration."

I was about to hang up on Monica until I started have flashbacks of the good old days.

"You make me laugh. I remember how simple things used to be with us. Do you remember back in the days when you used to call me Black? You once referred to me as the king of infinite wisdom and possibilities. You told me a long time ago that when I felt like the entire world was closing in on me you had my back and together we could conquer the world. And I know we still can. I feel like the entire world is closing in on me right now. You still got my back or what?"

"You are so incredible." Monica's tone was one of amazement and fascination. "How do you remember things like that?"

"I never forget special things or extra special people."

"All I can say is that things change and so do people."

"But why? We didn't have to change. Let's get things back to the way we used to be. Fate made you call. I know you can see it. If you want I'll come down to Atlanta and make you my wife. Marry me."

"I don't believe you. Don't play with me. I have to go."

"I'm serious, let's get married. You and me against the world."

"I can't marry you. I'm already engaged."

"So what. I bet you're not even in love with him. Are you?"

"I can't believe you'd ask me a question like that."

"Are you?"

"Yes."

"No you're not, but I hope you'll be happy."

"Eric, I love you and I hope you understand this is something I really want."

"I love you too, but I'll never understand. Julian must be a good guy. I know he's lucky 'cause he's getting my favorite girl."

"So, does this mean you're coming to the wedding."

"Hell no! This means I'm trying to tell you goodbye and have a wonderful life with Julian. Ask yourself if you love him more than you love me and if so, go for it."

"I really do love you." There was a brief moment of silence. "Goodbye, Eric."

"Goodbye my sweet-sweet Sunflower."

I went down stairs to the family room to ask my parents about the wedding invitation. My mother looked like she wanted make up an excuse or lie. My father held up a stack of mail and in a real nonchalant way.

My father said, "You mean Monica and Dr. Catrell's wedding invitation. It's right here." He hunched his shoulders "I told you

252

women love doctors."

My father was so ignorant and heartless towards me that sometimes I wondered if he was really my father. The fact that Julian was a doctor seemed to give my father a new cause in his campaign to make me a doctor. I was so hurt, embarrassed and mad that I didn't want to hear another word from my father. He was lucky I didn't curse his ass out. I went to the kitchen to get a drink and my mother followed right behind me. She was so worried about me.

"Eric, I know you're hurting and it's okay to cry."

"I am hurt, but I'm not gonna cry over this."

"Come here baby."

My mother held me and patted me on my back like she was consoling a small child.

"It's okay let it out. I know you're hurting."

My mother wouldn't leave the crying thing alone. I started to cry a little, but at the same time I laughed out loud. I was hurt for real, but I thought about how stupid I must have looked in my parent's kitchen crying in my mother's arms. It was sad, but funny at the same time.

I sent Stacey a Valentine's Day card because I knew we wouldn't be together that day. I spent Valentine's Day with my friend from school, Leah. We had never been together before without Nikala and Jasmine. Nikala and Jasmine had hooked up with a guy we all knew from school named Dwayne. Dwayne was an older guy who had gone back to college to finish getting his degree. He liked for everybody to call him Big D. He used to say that he was a pimp back in the day. I can't lie some days Big D looked so out of place at school. After awhile we all got used to him with his jive talk, big gold tooth and gator skinned shoes. To be honest, he was a real intelligent guy and everybody liked him. He was on permanent disability, but he always had a lot of money. Around 1979 or 1980, Big D was shot several times by one of his girls. She left him incapacitated or what he used to call *in-ca-pimp-a-tated* for years. It wasn't unusual for "D" to treat a group of friends to food, drinks or even clothes. Some people saw this as buying friends, but his real friends saw it as Big D just being cool.

It was nice spending the day with Leah. She helped keep my mind off of Monica and Julian's wedding. We thought it was funny that we had spent a day meant for lovers together, a day which had no significance to us. I still called myself being in a relationship with Stacey, but I wasn't sure how committed we were to each other. Anyway, Leah and I were just friends and nothing more. I did like looking at her because she was such an exotic beauty.

A week later Leah and I went to a movie and dinner together. Afterwards we went back to my apartment to watch TV. We ended up watching black classic movies on BET. Leah knew all about Gordon Parks and his movie *The Learning Tree*. I've always considered Gordon Parks a creative genius for all of his work in photography, music, filmmaking and writing. Leah impressed the hell out me with her knowledge of Black History.

She said, "A lot of people don't know it, but my dad is black. I don't advertise it because I don't feel the need. I want people to like me for who I am not what I am. My parents met back in the days when my father was in the Navy. He was stationed in the Philippines for two years."

Leah gave the impression that she was very comfortable with me. My apartment was completely dark and we were sitting on my sofa pretty close together. I started to ask if we could pay my bedroom a visit. I knew we could have so much fun having sex under a flashing strobe light. Having sex under a flashing strobe light is like a natural high. It's an erotic and intoxicating experience.

"Have you ever had sex under a strobe light before?"

Leah laughed so hard that her head fell in my lap. "Where did that come from?"

"I don't know."

The next thing I remembered was Leah resting her head on my chest. I could smell the sweet fragrance of her hair. I put my arm around her and held her closer. This was it, the opportunity I'd been looking for. When Leah looked up at me I touched her lips

254

and ran my finger across them. I moved closer and gave her a gentle kiss.

I took Leah by the hand and led her to my bedroom...the underground, the place where stars were made and dreams came true. Before we could get anything started in the bedroom my phone started ringing off the hook. At first, I was just going to let it keep ringing since I was already with the person I wanted to be with, but something made me pick up the phone anyway. It was my mother calling me from work. She sounded like something bad had happened.

"Eric, I need you to get here right away."

"What is it?"

I was scared to find out what was really going on.

"Hurry up and get here. Be careful. I'll meet you at the shock trauma entrance."

"Okay, I'm on my way."

All I could think about was seeing my father seriously injured. Because of my family emergency, I gave Leah cab fare and told her I'd talk to her later.

The last time I saw my father I wished that something bad would happen to him. Now, I got what I asked for and I felt like it should have been me. He was a messed up individual, but he didn't deserve to be in shock trauma. My dad was a top trauma surgeon, he was supposed to be the one taking care of trauma victims. Now he was a trauma patient.

My mother was waiting for me at the shock trauma entrance. As soon as I saw her I asked, "How is he?"

My mother said, "Just come with me."

We walked down a long hallway through some double doors. When we got to the other side of the doors I saw my father standing there in his scrubs. I don't think I've ever been happier to see him. I had no idea he was okay. It was never easy for me to keep track of him. Most of the time he was working or out on the town with friends. But he was right in front of me. I gave him a hug.

"Dad, I thought you were in an accident or somebody did something to you."

I was so happy to see to my father that I forgot somebody was in the hospital seriously injured. I looked down the other end of the hallway and I saw Mr. Cameron coming in my direction with tears in his eyes. I hadn't seen Monica's father in months. Instantly, I knew it had to be Monica.

"Oh my God." And that was all I could say over and over.

My father said, "Son, I'm so sorry."

Mr. Cameron said, "Eric, it doesn't look good."

No one ever confirmed who I was actually there to see, but I knew it was Monica. My mother took to the treatment area.

Mrs. Cameron was standing at Monica's bedside crying and holding Monica's hand. I wasn't ready to look at Monica yet. I just embraced Mrs. Cameron. When I looked at Monica, she was lying there unconscious with a bandage covering her head and right eye. I felt so bad that I could hardly stand up straight. I was shaking and my arms and legs felt like spaghetti. It all seemed like a bad dream. All types of medical equipment surrounded Monica. There were tubes and wires everywhere. I noticed that she was on a ventilator. Mrs. Cameron looked like she couldn't take anymore, so she stepped out of the room. My mother explained what happened. She told me that Monica and Julian had returned from their honeymoon in Bermuda and were on their way back home from the airport when Julian somehow lost control of his car. It was hard to believe, but Julian died instantly from the impact of the crash. My mother said that Monica was brain dead and that the ventilator was doing all of the breathing for her. The doctors planned to take her off the ventilator soon. There was nothing else they could do for her. She was clinically dead. Monica had sustained some very fatal injuries. She had internal bleeding in her abdomen, which my father and the other surgeons were able to repair during surgery. She had a severe skull fracture and damage to her right eye. I could barely identify her. Monica's swollen face was covered with bruises and traces of old dried blood. My mother left the room to give me some time with Monica. I took Monica by the hand and laid my head on her chest. I refused to believe that she was gone. I felt my eyes water. "Monica don't leave me again. I need you right here with me. Why do you wanna leave now? I don't know if you can hear me, but I love you. I love you with all my heart. Thank you for all the special memories, especially our first kiss, that beautiful rainy day in my sunroom, Kings Dominion, Jamaica, senior prom and Grandma Rosa's house. I guess I have to let you go again to be with Julian. This time I promise not to be mad. God's going to take care of you, precious angel. I love you, but God loves you more."

Monica made a motion or maybe it was just some type of involuntary response with her hand. I noticed a tear pour down from her left eye. She was at peace and I was glad that I had that brief moment with her.

I didn't want to be around when Monica was taken off the ventilator. But she wasn't alone because her wonderful parents were by her side when she passed. I wished that somehow Monica could have lived. Regardless of her condition I would have been right by her side everyday taking care of her.

PART: II

TEMPTATION AND INFIDELITY

LIVING SINGLE: 21

I woke up on a gloomy Saturday morning to the sounds and smells of fresh grass being cut. Usually I prefer to sleep with my bedroom window closed to drown out the outside world, but for some reason I left my window slightly cracked. As I looked out of the window of my condo a little old black man caught my attention. He was on a riding mower determined to finish cutting the grass even though it was starting to rain like hell outside. He just kept going and going right along. That's just like me, not willing to give up...determined to finish no matter how hard the rain comes down. That's me and my life.

Monica's death really took a lot from me. Regardless of what's going on, time waits for no one. Not even the death of a loved one can change the fact that life goes on. Even after all these years I still dream of Monica. From time to time she visits me in my dreams. Sounds crazy, but it's true. She's much more to me than a pretty picture in a frame or the artist who painted the most beautiful sunrise I've ever seen. It's been hard getting over her death and the feeling that she should have been my wife instead of Julian's.

After Monica's death I continued to date. Leah and I dated off and on right up until we graduated from nursing school. After graduation she moved to New Jersey to work on a Neonatal Intensive-Care Unit. Even though she and I ended on good terms we don't keep in touch anymore. Truthfully, I can't say that I missed her either. I did run into her girlfriend Jasmine a few months after Leah moved to Jersey. Jasmine had put together a sweet proposition for me. She offered to pay me two hundred dollars plus tips to dance at her sister's bridal shower. It sounded like fun and I figured no harm could come from entertaining a room full of women. The more I thought about it the hotter it sounded. Jasmine gave me the date, time and location of the party.

I took a few days to put a routine together and practice dancing. I was an amateur, but I didn't want to look like one in front of all those women. Over the years I'd managed to keep my body in top shape. So, I didn't have a problem showing off my body. There was definitely enough muscle to capture any woman's attention. The next thing I did was come up with a character concept. I thought of how much women loved doctors and I came up with Dr. Make-'Em-Feel-So-Good. The Doc was about to make a special house call.

I knocked on the door of the hotel suite and two nice looking young women answered the door.

I said, "Hi, I'm Dr. Make-'Em-Feel-So-Good. I'm making a special house call for Brenda. She needs my attention right away."

The two women screamed.

I thought, *This is going to be too easy.*

When I saw Brenda, I recognized her right away. How ironic was this? She went to elementary school with me. Brenda happened to be the leader of a group of six girls, who held me down and stripped of all my clothes when we were kids. That was their way of getting payback for me stealing kisses or feeling their butts, then running. I was a nasty little booty bandit. The next day at school I told my teacher what the girls had done to me. He gathered the six of them and marched their butts straight to the principal's office. I didn't mean for things to get so serious. I thought my teacher

262

would just laugh it off, but he didn't. I had to explain to the principal everything that the girls had done to me. The principal called each one of the girl's parents and told them how their daughters held down a boy and stripped him. My teacher and the principal made me seem like such a victim, but I was far from a victim. I actually enjoyed the whole thing. That same day the story of six girls stripping me made its way around the entire school. Within hours I was an instant sex symbol.

As I got closer to Brenda, it took her about thirty seconds to recognize who I was. When she recognized me, she put both her hands over her mouth.

Brenda screamed, "Oh my God!"

She knew she was in trouble. I did a good job staying in character. I danced around for a few minutes. I reached into my bag for my flavored body oil. I took off my stethoscope, lab jacket and shirt. Brenda helped me rub the oil on myself, then we rubbed some on her. She was surprised when I licked the oil off her neck and chest. I was even more surprised when she licked the oil off of me. The other women in the room got real excited. They pulled me away from Brenda and I started dancing again. But they didn't want to see me dance. They wanted to see more of my body. I took off my pants and the women begin to feel all over me. I had about five or six women rubbing flavored body oil on me. They all felt me up and down. A few of them licked my chest and arms at the same time. Everybody was so worked up it was hard to tell who was having more fun, them or me. Before I knew it, all I had on was a custom made stocking over my penis. The women assumed it was stuffed. I tried to convinced them that it was all me. Of course they had to feel it to make sure I wasn't lying. They kept going on and on about my size. I tried to get back to my routine and give Brenda some more attention, but the other women wouldn't let me. They completely ruined my routine with their aggressiveness. The married women seemed more excited and aggressive than the single women. I think I was the only one who noticed or cared that my routine was ruined.

I enjoyed myself so much that I stayed until the end of the party. Brenda and I got the chance to talk for a minute. She and the other women at the party actually thought I was a professional stripper. Brenda apologized for what she and her little girlfriends did to me when we were younger. Brenda was under the impression that I stripped for a living. She thought that what she and her friends did to me in elementary school led me stripping. I laughed and told her that I was a trauma nurse at University Hospital. She looked impressed and relieved at the same time.

I made out pretty good for my first time dancing. I left the party with about three hundred dollars and seven phone numbers. I gave my number to a few women just in case they knew someone else who needed a dancer. I even offered to do private dances.

The next day I had three messages on my machine. One of the women from the party wanted to know if she could pay me to do a private dance. Another wanted to know if she could take me out to dinner. The last message was from a woman named Karen. She said she just wanted to hold me and make love to me all night. She had the sweetest and sexiest voice of all, so I went out with her. Actually, I went out with all three, but nothing ever came of those dates.

I still don't have a girlfriend. Stacey's still in my life and I'm blessed to have her. She's the closest thing in my life to a girlfriend. She's been with me through thick and thin. After she graduated from law school she moved to Maryland not necessarily to be with me, she landed a position with a prestigious law firm just outside of Washington, DC.

Stacey's a beautiful powerful attorney who wants to marry me. Occasionally, we do the booty-call thing and it's good every time. She's intelligent, successful and fine as hell. Even with all that, it's still not enough to make me want to jump the broom. I can't put my finger on exactly what it is, but something's missing. Maybe it's the fact that she doesn't stimulate my creative side enough and that's really important to me. When it comes to my other interests outside of her and my nursing career, she fails to give me any encouragement. Sometimes it's nice to have a woman giving those extra words of encouragement. A few years ago I started concentrating more on music. I learned to play a few instruments, which helped enhance my love of music. Stacey and I don't seem to have many of the same interests anymore. We continuously talk about marriage, but that's all we do is talk.

My girl, Lisa used to be real negative about marriage until she married her producer, Tony, about five years ago. She always gave everyone the impression that she never wanted to get married. Now, Lisa and Tony are happily married with two kids living in Southern California. Lisa put out two albums then slipped behind the scenes to be a full-time songwriter and producer. After having two kids she put on some extra pounds and became really self-conscience about her appearance. I'm sure that's why she stopped performing. I tried convincing her that she was still a beautiful sexy woman, but she said being behind the scenes was better for her and the family. Lisa didn't have to be on the road anymore and it allowed her more time with her family. We still keep in touch from time to time. Lisa kept her promise to look out for me. She used a few of my songs for herself and some of her artists. When she toured I always got free tickets and backstage passes. Thanks to her I've had the opportunity to meet a lot of celebrities.

My other girl, Jennifer, is married to a real cool brotha named Damon. They both were journalism majors at Towson State. They got married a few years ago and are currently co-owners of The Imani Magazine. Imani is a local African-American lifestyles magazine, which features music, art, poetry, health, romance, business and finance. Jennifer used the name of the newsletter she and I started in high school. Jennifer and Damon offered me the opportunity to be a partner in their magazine, but I turned them down. The interest just wasn't there for me. Occasionally, I freelance. I write poetry and health articles for their magazine. About a year ago, Jennifer and Damon won an award for a series of articles they authored called *Defending the Black Male*. Their series inspired me to write a poem entitled *There's a Burning Inside (A Black Man's Cry)*.

Open your eyes
Take a good look at me
Tell me what you really see
I'm no trifling dog or lazy scrub
My life is open
My mind is free
There's something burning inside of me

Broken dreams and bad memories are what I see
But I'm putting all that behind
I can bring the pain
But I feel pain too
I cry so many tears
I feel compassion, sympathy and empathy
So many emotions inside
Embrace all that makes me good and bad
Hold me and take away my pain
'Cause there's a burning inside

Less than a man in the new land
Head of the small house
Shackled and chained
Skin like the night
Why is my son white?
I stood by while Master had his way
So much taken away
Sometimes I feel I have nothing to give
I've been a slave
Living hell on earth
But all the time my head hangs high
There's an incredible burning inside

Fear me...fight me...hold me down
Centuries later I'm still around
Separate and unequal
Always 4 out of 5 or 9 out of 10
The majority of a minority
There's a burning inside

Understand that I live for you
I die for you
I'm the voice of millions
I remember the march
I have a dream...Keep hope alive
By any means necessary
Keeping it real for the brothas
From the heart for the heart
There's still a burning inside

Keith and April have been married the longest of all my friends.
They got married while they were still at Florida State.
Surprisingly, Troy was Keith's best man. I never even knew
anything about the wedding until months later. Keith and Troy
swore up and down that they did everything to get in touch with
me. I knew that was bullshit. They knew exactly where to find me,
but I try not to dwell on that anymore. They were probably mad at
me because I didn't keep in touch with them as much as I used to.
Keith suffered multiple knee injuries while playing college
football. He was still a top NFL prospect until he took an explosive
hit to his right knee that shattered his dream of playing professional
football. The whole incident nearly destroyed him. If April hadn't
been by his side he probably would have committed suicide. After
receiving their degrees from FSU, Keith and April decided to move
back to Maryland to start a talent and modeling agency.
Keith and April gave a party to kick off the grand opening of their

agency. They leased a huge office building in downtown Baltimore for their business. Troy and I went to the grand opening together because we heard there were going to be some fine-ass single women there, and there were. I'll never forget that day because it was the day that I met Candie and Tiffany. I walked out of the men's room on my way back to the party. At first, I didn't notice Candie and Tiffany sitting in a small waiting area to my left. But when I did, they looked so good that I did a double take. Candie was the more attractive the two. She instantly took my breath away. I've described a lot of women as beautiful, but Candie was extraordinarily beautiful, from her short sexy Halle Berry lookin' haircut down to her pretty manicured toes. She was a light-skinned sister with dark sexy features. Her most distinct feature was her dark eyes with those naturally arched eyebrows. I was diggin' the shit out of her, but she didn't give me any eye contact at all. She seemed to have a stinky little attitude going on. Her girlfriend Tiffany jumped out of her seat to introduce herself to me like she was seriously interested in me.

"Hi, I'm Tiffany."

"I'm Eric. How are you? Tiffany, who's your friend?"

Right away I tried to let Tiffany know I was more interested in her friend.

"Oh, that's my girl Candie."

With a smile I said, "Nice to meet you, Candie. I'm Eric."

Still with limited eye contact Candie said, "Nice to meet you too." And that was all she said.

Tiffany was beaming at me like she wanted to eat me alive. Candie had "heartbreaker" written all over her. She was so fine that I knew she could control me if she wanted to. A woman that damn fine could totally run and possibly ruin me. I liked her, but I wasn't sure if I was up to the challenge. Candie looked resistant to my charm anyway. I wanted to see Troy try to soften this one up some. I figured if he could work his magic then he deserved her.

I said, "Candie, I'd like to introduce you to a friend of mine."

Like clockwork Troy made his way down the hall to the men's

room to take a piss. I stopped him to introduce him to Candie and Tiffany. Candie seemed to come to life when I introduced her to Troy. She gave him this warm friendly smile. I couldn't believe my eyes. Candie actually seemed to like Troy's big Heavy D lookin' ass. Damn, Troy was the man.

Troy and I talked to Candie and Tiffany for awhile. When we got back to the party Troy asked which girl I wanted.

I said, "You take Candie, she looks like the kind of girl who would end up breaking my heart. Anyway, I already put in a good word for you, son."

"Good looking out. You still got my back. Remember the last time you hooked me up."

"Yep, I don't want to think about that."

"Why?"

"It was a long time ago, that's all."

Little did he know it was a lot more to the story than that, but I had nothing to say about his relationship with Jennifer.

Troy and Candie started dating and for some strange reason I agreed to go out with Tiffany. We did a double date with Troy and Candie. During dinner I couldn't take my eyes off Candie. Tiffany didn't have the same appeal to keep my attention. She was pretty, but looks alone have never been enough to hook me. I'm not saying that she wasn't intelligent. Tiffany was a sales consultant for a computer company, but common sense is a necessity when it comes to truly hooking me. Let's just say when God was giving out common sense, Tiffany was in another line getting a double dose of goofiness. Goofy women can be funny for a minute, but after an hour that shit is down right irritating. Candie was very sensible, laid back and cool. She was a physical therapist and with me being a nurse we could relate to some of the same topics. Actually, Candie and I had a lot in common. We did most of the talking at the table. Troy and Tiffany just sat back and listened to me and Candie talk. It was obvious that she belonged with me. I made a big mistake hooking her up with Troy.

I thought, *How could I have been such a fool passing up the*

269

opportunity to be with a fine woman like Candie?

From that point on I refused to go out with Tiffany again. I talked to Candie about Tiffany being so goofy and she knew exactly what I was talking about. Candie and I started to develop a special friendship. I was still very attracted to her, but I never told her. I didn't want to disrespect her or Troy. Candie and I started spending a lot of time together. I was spending more time with her than Troy did. We probably spent too much time together. The longer we were together the more interested I became in her. She was captivating. Candie and I could go almost anywhere and do almost anything together because Troy was always working at his father's advertising firm or away on business trips. Before long it was more or less mandatory that we saw each other everyday, especially for me. I was addicted to her and needed a daily dose of my true obsession. Candie was beginning to open up and tell me all kinds of thing about herself and in return I shared details about myself.

Candie was so appealing to me that she made me rethink my entire outlook on marriage and having a family.

Almost one year after I introduced Troy and Candie, Troy came to me explaining how he owed Keith a big favor.

Troy said, "Without a doubt you're my best friend. The man who introduced me to my lady. The man who always looked out for me in that department."

"Yeah, so what's your point?"

Troy pulled out a ring box and flashed a phat rock at me.

He said, "I'm about to propose to Candie."

Words can't express what I felt at that moment. All I could say was, "When?"

I said it like I wanted to know exactly when, so I could stop him from proposing or something.

"Tonight."

I gave him a strange look.

Troy continued. "Let me get this out. I was the best man at Keith's wedding."

"And you want Keith to be your best man at yours, right."

I didn't really care about being Troy's best man. All I wanted was to be with Candie. She was all I cared about. I didn't have time for that best man bullshit. Anyway, how would my toast to the bride and groom sound?

"I know it sounds crazy, but yeah. I feel like I owe him. You understand, right?"

"Yeah, it's okay with me. I'd like to be your best man, but I understand. Hey, if it wasn't for Keith's party neither of us would have met Candie. Keith's got my nomination for best man."

Troy and Candie have been married now for two years and I've never shared with either of them how I really feel about her or exactly what I've been going through.

AFRO-MANIAC: 22

Over the past few years Candie has added so much to my life. For years I was lost in things that had little or no meaning. For awhile I stopped writing poetry. I lost track of friends. To a point, I stopped caring about myself. My love for nice clothes wasn't the same. I still looked good, but not my best. I had almost given up. My focus was on saving and investing money for a bleak future. I had become one of the world's greatest penny pinchers. I lived in the same two-bedroom apartment for almost eleven years and drove the same old VW Jetta my parents bought me when I was sixteen. My car looked a mess and all I could say about it was, "At least it's paid for." The poor car started everyday, so I kept driving it...right into the ground.

Stacey was a big help to me, but she couldn't inspire me like Candie. Nothing's better than a beautiful black woman encouraging and believing 100% in a black man. A black woman is the strength of a black man. With a black woman's confidence and trust a black man can accomplish the impossible. Thanks to Candie's inspiration I'm almost exactly where I should be in life. I was offered a book deal for two books with the Sterling Publishing Group. My first novel *Love Ain't Going Nowhere*, is a romantic story about a young African-American couple and their dedication to staying in love regardless of the unrelenting challenges their lives are faced with. I wrote the manuscript right after college and buried it in a drawer. I never did anything with it until Candie read it. She instantly fell in love with the story and the characters. After reading the manuscript Candie knew I was on the verge of something big. Now, I have a website and an e-mail address for my readers. My first book-signing tour is about a month away.

I'm happy with my life again. I'm living life to the fullest. My new Lexus gives me the freedom I've always loved. My car helps me become one with the road again. When I first saw my car it was love at first sight. I named her my Sexy Lexy. She's a cold black beauty with lots of appeal. Her tires hug the road like they're completely in love. My Jetta was so old that I stopped going out for joyrides. Now, I kick back in my Lexus with her soft leather interior listening to my seven speaker sound system. My car even has a navigation system, just in case a brotha gets lost. I've come a long way since the days of riding in my old car. Candie talked me into getting the Lexus and she talked me into buying my condo, which happens to be in the same building with her and Troy. Candie helped me decorate my condo. She and I went to IKEA like a married couple picking out furniture for their new place. My condo is a more luxurious and a somewhat over-glorified version of my former two-bedroom apartment. It's what I like to call the new improved *Underground.*

My mother still visits me like she used to. I'm more of a Mama's boy than ever. My father's still his same stubborn self, just an older version.

Today, I sat in my living room writing poetry on my laptop and having a private concert listening to my queens Erykah Badu, Jill Scott, Lauryn Hill and Lisa Ashford. I love all of them for their creativity, positive energy and their natural vibrant earthy beauty. Their music inspires me in so many ways, but my true inspiration comes from Candie.

A couple of hours later Candie came over just to hang out for

273

awhile. When I opened the door she looked at me and smiled like she was happier than ever to see me.

I asked, "What's up?"

"Nothing. I had a dream about you last night."

My stomach dropped and seemed to by filled with butterflies or either I was getting sick from the Grilled Chicken Caesar Salad I had for lunch. I tried not to look too excited. I was hoping that Candie had a sexy dream about the two of us. We sat on my sofa and I focused all of attention on her. I couldn't wait to hear about her dream.

"What was it about?"

"I can't tell you. It wasn't good."

"Come on, you shouldn't have bought it up if you didn't plan to tell me. Did I die in your dream or what?"

"No, it wasn't anything like that. In my dream I came over to see you just like today and you gave me a kiss."

I smiled. "That's all. You said it was bad."

"It was bad. I'm not supposed to dream about stuff like that."

"Did we go any further than a kiss?"

"No, but in my dream I wanted to. I hope you don't look at me differently, but my dream was so good that it made me late for work."

"So, my kiss was that good."

"Yeah. I've never told you this, but I think you're sexy."

I was in shock and all I could say was, "Um...um."

"What the hell is um? Tell me what you're thinking."

"Um...this isn't easy."

"It wasn't easy for me to tell you about my dream either, but I did."

"Um...to be honest I have dreams like that about you all the time. The only difference is that in my dreams we actually make love. I've been in love with you since the first time I saw you. The thing I love about you most is that you have no idea how beautiful or how sexy you really are and that's a major turn on for me. You make simple things sexy, like the way you're staring at me right

274

now. You look so good. For three years I'm been fantasizing about you. I guess you can say I live for you. That's why I need to see you everyday. You're my greatest inspiration and I appreciate everything you've done for me. Thanks to you my first book got published. That day at Keith's party I wanted you so bad, but I didn't want to step up to the challenge."

"What challenge?"

"You resisted every attempt I made at you."

Candie laughed, "I liked you a lot, but Tiffany saw you first so I had to back off."

"What was up with that stinky little attitude you had?"

"Oh, that was because I wanted you for myself. The attitude was from Tiffany making me back off. I really liked you a lot when I first saw you."

"You liked Troy a lot when you saw him too."

"I thought he was funny. He was so nervous that it made him cute."

"He had to take a piss real bad that's all that was."

We laughed.

"I liked Troy right away. He was so sweet."

"He *was* sweet? So what, does he leave a bitter taste in your mouth now?"

"I don't wanna go there right now. It's strange that this conversation never came up before. What if you didn't give up on me so easily? We'd probably be a couple right now."

"Believe me I've been kicking myself in the ass everyday for two years thinking about what could have been."

"I know the feeling. Well, no use kicking ourselves over something we can't change. Maybe we'll meet again in another lifetime and then we'll be able to live out our fantasies."

"Why wait? We're here right now. I want you and I think you want me."

"I can't do that. I'm married to your best friend."

"You're my best friend."

"And you're mine."

275

I was tripping and saying whatever came to mind. "I'm sorry, but this open conversation took me somewhere else. My mind temporarily took me away from my boring reality."

"Yeah, and I need to get home back to my boring reality before I do something I'll regret."

"Give it a chance you might like it."

Candie looked down at her watch and said, "Oh my God, let me get out of here. Troy's flight landed over an hour ago. I'll talk to you later."

"I almost forgot, check out this poem I wrote for you real quick. It'll give you a good idea about what you mean to me."

I'm an Afro-maniac
You're my aphrodisiac
You got me hard as a pole
I wanna suck your soul

I wanna come inside
My love I can't hide
Your ass is in high demand
I'm your number one fan

Giving you ecstasy and sextasy
Tenderness and passion are my fashion
Silent screams of pleasure
Making you throb all over
Feeling beautiful from head to toe

Wrapping you up inside my love
Never ever letting you
You're my everything
My strength...my weakness
I like you...I love you
I want you...I need you

Every day...every night
No Nymphomaniac...Afro-maniac
A brotha crazy in love
A brotha deeply in love
Deeply in love with you

With my poem in her hand Candie looked at me with a smile. "I love this. It's really good."

"It's a little embarrassing having you read it, but I'm glad you did."

"I've never had anyone write poetry for me before."

Out of nowhere I said, "Have you ever thought about cheating on Troy?"

"No. Not until now." Candie smiled. "I'm thinking about how much I wanna kiss you. Eric, you make me feel so good about myself. I feel beautiful and you make me feel real special. You see something in me that other men don't."

"I see what your man doesn't see. You're everything I've dreamed of and more."

Candie had her back to the door. She reached for the doorknob looking like she was about to say goodbye, but I wouldn't let her. I moved in close.

Instantly, our world was in slow motion. I couldn't let her leave like that. Before she could say anything I laid a soft wet kiss on her lovely lips. At that exact moment it felt like the earth stood still. We took everything slow trying to enjoy every second of our heated encounter. Candie's kiss was so good to me that it didn't seem real. Stacey was good, but I hadn't felt passion that real in years. I hadn't felt a tongue like Candie's in years either. During our kiss I opened my eyes just to sneak a peek at her to confirm that our kiss was actually happening. Candie looked incredibly beautiful. This was a dream come true. Candie looked like she was in heaven and I know we both looked and felt the same way. We stopped kissing. I stood there just looking in her eyes, running my hand up and down her soft pretty face. I began to kiss her neck and unbutton her blouse. I could feel the sexual beast within me raging and dying to come out. We were about to take things to the next level. One of us had to be the voice of reason.

In a whisper Candie said, "No, no I gotta go. We can't."

"Please just one more little kiss. You're so beautiful." I looked at her and asked, "Why are you shaking."

"I'm nervous."

"Relax, you're safe here."

"Troy will be home any minute. I have to go." We kissed again. "Thank you. I needed that. I'll call you."

"Don't forget me. I love you."

"I love you too, Eric."

Candie was really nervous. She rushed off before we could get anything else started.

SCANDALOUS: 23

Candie wasn't the only one who was nervous. I didn't realize how nervous I was until she'd left my condo. When we were together I was more excited than anything. She has a powerful presence with a nice soothing effect on me. I hated the fact that she had to leave me to be with Troy. She was his wife, but when we were together she was all mine. Everything seemed to have happened so fast that I had to sit down and replay the scene in my head. A feeling of paranoia came over me. I jumped up and started checking the windows to make sure no one could see into my living room. Only God saw what Candie and I had done and I made no excuses. I felt bad, but God already knew where my relationship with Candie was going.

A few seconds later there was a familiar knock at my door. I opened the door and Stacey was standing there wearing an expensive looking black business suit with her briefcase in hand and a serious game face on.

I said, "Hey, what's going on. Bad day?"

She strolled inside not saying a word just looking around my place. I didn't know what she was looking for. She was probably looking for evidence to prove that I'd been up to no good.

I asked "What's up?"

"Oh, hey. I bet you had a good day. I ran into Candie on her way out of here. She looked nervous and didn't have much to say to me. I told you to leave that man's wife alone. So, are you screwing her now?"

Stacey was obviously jealous of my relationship with Candie. I had been spending so much time with Candie that I was starting to forget about Stacey and she could feel it.

"Okay, you just marched your way up in here like you own something and now you're accusing me of having an affair with my best friend's wife. You've got a lot of nerve. What the hell do you think of me?"

"I'm sorry, but you can't tell me you and Candie are just friends. I know y'all got that secret lovers shit going on."

"I'm not trying to tell you nothing. What makes you think Candie and I are more than friends?"

"How long have I known you? She's pretty, she's intelligent, she's got a nice body and all that in one package makes her your type. Shall I continue?"

"Go right ahead."

"You have to admit, you do have doggish tendencies."

"See you're wrong. That's it. I never direct any K-9 references towards you, if you know what I mean."

"I'd kill you if you ever called me a bitch."

"I've got too much respect to call you that. Did you come over to spend time with me or to ruin my evening?"

"It's not my fault you're living foul."

"This is the last time I'm going to tell you. Candie's just a friend."

"Well, somebody else is getting my time. I e-mailed you three times this week and I have yet to receive one stupid-ass response from you."

"I've been busy writing, okay. That's what I mostly use my laptop for anyway. I hardly ever go on-line anymore. And no one's getting your time."

"Something's wrong then. I miss the old Eric. I need my time with you."

"You don't act like it."

"Okay, I need my booty-call. Is that better?"

"I bet you think Candie's been coming over here for booty-calls too."

"Whatever man. Don't make me say it again."

"I think you should go."

"You don't mean that."

"I can show you better than I can tell you."

I walked over to the front door and opened it. I didn't feel like being with Stacey. It's hard to explain, but I felt like I was cheating on Candie just having Stacey around.

"Fuck you, Eric," Stacey said as she walked her fine little jealous ass out my door.

"You can, in your dreams. Goodnight."

I should have felt bad about putting Stacey out, but I didn't. She had to go because she was trying to ruin my happiness. I hate when people try to steal my joy. I was on a love high and it had nothing to do with Stacey. She sensed the energy between me and Candie and that's what bothered her the most. In the past I had given Stacey the impression that I was infatuated with Candie. I openly talked to Stacey about my feelings for Candie because not even in my wildest dreams did I ever imagine that Candie and I would ever have an affair.

My phone rang.

"Hello."

"Hey, Eric. It's me."

"What's up, Troy? How was your trip?"

I acted like I really cared. I wished he was still away. Far-far away.

"My trip was good, but I came home to a bunch of shit."

"What shit?"

I thought, *Oh no.*

"Did that wicked little yellow bitch get there yet?"

281

"Who?"

As if I didn't know who he was referring to. And I didn't appreciate him referring to her as a bitch either.

"Candie. I put her ass outta here and I know she's on her way down there to you to tell all our business."

"Look-"

I was about to get into Troy's shit.

"Sorry to come off at you like that. These are my issues and I know you always have my best interest in mind. If you get her calm enough, she can come back home tonight. If you can't calm her down, do me a favor and keep her little wicked ass down there with you."

There was a knock at the door.

"I think Candie's at my door right now."

"Oh man, don't tell her I called."

"Alright. I won't, peace."

I looked through my peephole and Candie looked more upset than I'd ever remembered seeing her. I let her in and we embraced.

"Are you okay? Troy just called to warn me you might be on your way down here."

"I hate his punk-ass."

"What happened?"

"It's just an ongoing argument that we've been having for about a year now."

"What happened, if you don't mind sharing?"

"I've shared a lot of things with you, but this is some crazy shit right here."

"I'm listening."

"Before Troy and I got married we agreed that we wouldn't have any kids. It's easy to agree to something like that until an actual pregnancy happens. Sometime in May of last year I found out that I was pregnant and it made me feel so good about myself. It really made me feel like a woman. The thought of becoming a mother excited me. I had the ability to bring a life into this world. Troy and I made a miracle that was growing inside my womb."

282

Candie stopped talking for a minute. She rested her head on my chest and cried.

I held her tight rubbing the back of her neck.

"Take your time. It's okay, we've got all night. When you're ready you can tell me what else happened."

"That bastard made me kill my baby. I had an abortion because Troy said we didn't have room in our lives for a baby."

"I can't believe he made you go through that. There's nothing I can say to make you feel better about your situation. There's no way to replace the baby you lost, but maybe one day you can have a baby with or without Troy. Just rest your nerves and I'll get some dinner going for us. I love you."

Candie looked pitiful sitting on my sofa crying. Somehow I had to make her feel better.

I made one of my favorite dishes, Jerk Chicken with black beans and rice. Candie enjoyed dinner and before long she cheered up and focused on a different topic. After dinner Candie asked if she could spend the night at my place. Of course I said it was okay. Basically, Troy said she could spend the night. She showered and slipped into my pajama top and a pair of my shorts. She looked cute in my clothes. She said wearing my clothes made her feel even closer to me. We sat in the living room trying to plan a nice relaxing get away just for the two of us. We needed to go to a place where we could have a good time and a place where no one knew us.

I said, "We should go down to Norfolk, Virginia for their Afram Festival. It's held at their Inner Harbor. Norfolk's harbor is the sister to the one in Baltimore. After the Afram we can head down to Virginia Beach."

"That sounds good."

After my shower I went back out to the living room to check on Candie. She was going through my collection of classic black movies. She picked out *Love Jones* for us to watch. She had excellent taste because that was exactly what I wanted to watch. We cuddled up on the sofa with a blanket and two pillows watching the movie and eating microwave popcorn. Halfway through the movie I went to my bedroom for some massage oil, so I could give Candie a full body massage. I wanted her to stay with me forever, so we could spend every night together. I had so many things I wanted to share with her. We looked too relaxed together. The lights were dimmed and we both were partially dressed. If Troy decided to stop by we would have had a hard time explaining what was going on.

My phone rang, but I couldn't answer it because my hands were covered with massage oil.

"Candie, grab that for me."

Even though my hands were oily, I should have just grabbed the phone myself.

When Candie answered the phone her voice sounded like she was getting something done to her that felt real good. As she talked I continued massaging her feet.

Candie said, "It's for you."

I whispered. "Is it Troy?"

Candie shook her head and put the phone up to my ear.

"Hello."

"Ooh, you're nothing but a scandalous dog. I told you she was your girl."

"Okay whatever. Goodnight."

I hung up the phone.

Candie smiled. "Stacey, right?"

"Yep."

"I forgot to tell you I ran into her down the hall."

"She told me she saw you. She said you looked nervous. She thinks we're having an affair."

"Whatever. She's always been jealous of our friendship. Sorry, but I couldn't help from looking nervous. I didn't expect to see her. She acted like she wanted to talk and I didn't have a damn thing to say to her. Your kisses had me messed up. You kiss nice."

"Your kisses were good to me too. Just the way I like my kisses slow, deep, wet and passionate." I gave Candie a kiss. "Don't worry about Stacey."

"I won't. Not one bit."

"I could get used to this. I'm really enjoying your company tonight. Why don't you leave Troy and move down here with me." I had a smile on my face, but I meant it.

"I'd have to move a lot further than down here. We'd have to live in another state if we ever hooked up like that. If our friends and family found out about us they'd die."

"No matter how hard I try to hide it, people can see how much I love you. There's no way to hide it anymore. Look, I'll pick a state and then I'll send for you. I swear, Candie I'm not joking, I love you."

"I believe you. I think you'd make a good husband."

"It's funny you mentioned that 'cause you're the only woman who can get me to walk down the aisle."

"I've always wondered why you never married Stacey? She's got a lot going for her."

"But, she's not you. Stacey's too busy and unstable for me. She will always be my first love. She's important to me, but she doesn't inspire me like you. I owe you big time for all you've given me."

"I don't know what you're talking about. Whatever I do is because I love you. Oh by the way, all the girls at work and at the salon love your book. Michele and Nikki even put up one of your book posters at the salon."

"Seriously? See that's what I'm talking about. You're not my wife, but you represent me well. My website's getting like a thousand hits a day."

"Eric, I'm so proud of you. You're going to have a bestseller on your hands for sure by the time you do your book signing tour. I saw your book-signing itinerary on your website today. I'm going to miss you when you go on tour."

"Don't remind me. You should go with me."

"I can't and you know why. Just don't forget about me."

"Never."

"I want to make love to you so bad, but not tonight. I wanna do

285

something in Virginia."

"I can't wait 'cause I know it's gonna be good. Our first kiss was explosive and I can only imagine how good penetration is gonna be. Where are you sleeping tonight?"

"I'm already comfortable, so I'll take the sofa."

"Come on and sleep with me tonight. I promise to be good."

"Don't say stuff like that. You make me wonder how good you'd be for real."

"You know what I mean."

"Not tonight."

I kissed Candie goodnight and went to my bedroom. Around 4 a.m. she climbed into my bed and cuddled up next to me. We both had the next day off. I woke up first and I just laid there staring at Candie's beautiful face and dreaming about making her mine. She looked like an angel at rest. I hated to wake her, but she really needed to check in with Troy.

The next day Troy thanked me for helping him out with Candie.

"Whatever you said to Candie worked. When she came home yesterday morning we made love like you wouldn't believe. I guess the time away made her miss me. Thanks again."

"That's what I'm here for, to help *you* out."

I thought, *Sorry bustard.*

"Between me and you, I don't get the opportunity to get a lot of ass. I thought married people fucked all the time, but I was wrong. Thank God for weekends and holidays. With my schedule the way it is, Candie's lucky to get a piece once a week. Sometimes I just don't have the energy. It's getting hard carrying all this extra weight around." Troy laughed like it was funny being overweight. He continued, "Next weekend I'm going to Dallas for four days. After that I'll be in San Diego for a week. We're expanding our firm. Most of our business is out west, but my dad wants our headquarters to remain on the East Coast. Right now my career is on fire, things couldn't be better. I'm telling you, business is good for real. I've got Candie chillin' on a back burner and she knows it.

The sad thing is I don't give a shit. I should've held off on getting married."

"Life's a bitch. Your life sounds difficult. I bet it's hard being you."

"Yeah, it is. I guess I'm turning into an old man now. By this time next year I'll probably need some Viagra to help get it up."

"That's sad. You should workout so you won't need Viagra."

"You ever try that shit?"

"Hell no. You?"

"Not yet."

We both laughed.

"You're too young to be living like you do."

Troy was probably the most naive or most confident man I've ever met. I thought he was a real asshole for not realizing what a gift he had. He didn't appreciate Candie at all, but I sure did. What man would trust his wife to spend the night at another man's place, especially after an argument? Sometimes Troy gave me the impression that he was having an affair with another woman, but it wasn't another woman. It was his career and money that he loved more than his wife.

I was mad at Candie for a minute for holding out on me that night at my condo and giving Troy what she should have given me. He was her husband, so I couldn't be mad too long. I had to learn to deal with my jealousy, but I didn't know how. It's hard being a single man in love with a married woman. If we both were married maybe my emotions would have balanced out somehow. All I could do was to take advantage of any opportunity I was presented to be with Candie. Troy had business trips planned and Candie and I planned to go to Virginia for a couple of days.

THE AFFAIR: 24

Since Candie wanted to see Troy off on his business trip, she and I arrived in Norfolk late Friday evening. Candie didn't give Troy any details about where she was going to be for the weekend. All she told him was that she was going away and he didn't ask any questions. They have a you-do-your-thing-and-I'll-do-mine type of relationship. Even though Candie and I had our thing going on, she still wanted to make her marriage work no matter how much Troy neglected her. I couldn't believe she actually wanted to see Troy off on his trip. She said if something happened to him and she didn't see him off she'd never forgive herself.

Candie and I had reservations at the Marriott in downtown Norfolk. The hotel is located about a block from the harbor. The Marriott was reasonable, but it still had a certain air of elegance about it. Our hotel room was a nice, but at the same time standard. Staying in a luxurious hotel room didn't matter much to us. To do what we had planned, all we really needed was each other and a little privacy. It made Candie feel better waiting a week before we had sex for the first time. I guess she thought I would look at her differently if we had sex in my condo on the first night we revealed our true feelings for each other. I've been in love with her for three years, so I wouldn't have looked at her any differently. Men and women have totally different perspectives when it comes to deciding on the appropriate time to have sex for the first time. For the average guy, it's never too soon to have sex.

Candie had me bring my little boom box along so we could make love to some of our favorite love songs. On the way down the highway she fed me strawberries and Hershey's chocolate kisses. She even had a single long stem red rose for me. She was trying to spoil me and it was working. For so long I'd been anticipating how good it would feel to actually make love to her and the time had finally arrived.

As soon as we entered the room Candie and I attacked each other. We laughed because there was no need for us to rush, we had the entire weekend to be locked up together. We didn't have Troy, Stacey, family members or any telephone calls to interrupt us.

Seeing Candie in front of me totally nude was the most beautiful sight I've ever witnessed. She was breathtaking. She was about to share something so special with me and I couldn't believe it. I was instantly turned on from the sight of her. We stood there holding each other, flesh to flesh lost in the most passionate kiss. I initiated the foreplay by giving every inch of her lovely body the attention it deserved. All of a sudden she flipped the script on me. A few days ago we talked about being unselfish lovers. We talked about all of our sexual likes and dislikes. To be honest I got a lot of satisfaction from giving Candie pleasure. Seeing her so aroused turned me on even more. Candie actually went into a take-charge mode showing me how unselfish she could be. She kissed, licked and sucked everything that made me a man. Being with her was totally different from anyone I've ever experienced. Candie and I didn't have any defined roles. We went back and forth from giver to receiver and it was *all* good.

As good as the foreplay was we were ready for my favorite part, penetration. Candie grabbed my long-hard-rigid penis guiding it to her soft-warm-wet canal.

To me a woman's eyes express her true feelings. Upon

penetration, I stared deep into Candie's eyes. When I penetrated her, Candie's eyes spoke to me. I saw forever in her eyes. Her eyes were like dark endless pathways to her soul that could take me anywhere I wanted to go. I've never bonded with a woman like I did with Candie. Making love to her was a complete exchange of spiritual, physical and emotional pleasure. This girl had it all. She was the total package. So special and satisfying to me.

Candie and I laid in bed caressing each other.

I said, "I'm loving...loving...loving you, Baby."

"And your love is ummmm...so...so good to me."

"What do you want to do now?"

"Is there anything else you'd like for me to do to you?"

"I'm good for now. You did me right. I'm really thinking about dinner."

"I've got everything you need to eat right here."

"You're nasty, but I like it."

We laughed.

"You're definitely the best I've ever had. You took me by surprise when you penetrated me. I didn't expect to get the whole thing so fast or so deep. You're a lot longer than I'm used to. That's why my eyes opened so wide."

She had no idea what I saw when I looked into her wide eyes.

"Sorry, but I couldn't wait to get inside. I like to go deep. You're without a doubt the best lover I've ever had. And the most unselfish."

"You know all the little hot spots that most men overlook."

We went on and on for about an hour caressing and critiquing our sexual performances and experiences. Candie and I never left our room for dinner, we ended up ordering room service. We continued to make love off and on for the rest of the night.

The next morning I woke up early to watch Candie as she slept. How could any man neglect this extraordinary beauty? The thing that bothered me the most was that Candie truly loved Troy. My worse fear was that she would never leave him for me. I put those thoughts aside for a minute and gently ran my index finger through her hair and across her eyebrows. My eyes fell upon her irresistible lips and I woke her with a kiss.

We got an early start on the Afram Festival because our checkout time was at noon. I left my car in the hotel's garage. Candie and I walked over to the harbor, where the festival was being held. I've always enjoyed ethnic festivals, thanks to my early days with Lisa. She used to drag me all over the place for festivals. My favorite festival of all is the annual Kunta Kinte Festival held in Annapolis, Maryland. What I love most about these festivals are the way that they display and teach our proud history, at the same time connecting the past, present and future. African-Americans have come a long way, but we still have a long journey ahead. I see ethnic festivals as a major stepping stone to uniting black people.

Candie gave me the impression that she had the same appreciation for the festival that I did. We walked around looking at all the people who had shown up. We noticed a few white families enjoying the festival too. It was starting to look like every black family from the area was there. Black people from different socio-economic backgrounds were interacting together like they didn't notice any differences. This made me think back to when I went to the Million-Man March. The diversity among black people is what makes us so unique. Black men are the luckiest men on this planet when it comes to our women. Within our race we have the widest range of beautiful women to choose from. No other men in the world have the variety of women to choose from that black men have and we still date outside of our race. All I'm saying is that black is beautiful and we have to recognize.

There were booths set up displaying all types of African arts and crafts. Vendors were lined up selling a wide variety of food and drinks. The local health department had a booth set up informing people of sexually transmitted diseases and performing HIV tests. Where else could we see live entertainment, learn African History, eat ethic foods, get financial advice and free health screenings?

My favorite vendor was from a local bookstore. Of course, they had copies of my book. No one noticed who I was until I

291

introduced myself to a woman holding a copy my book. She seemed excited to meet me. Her sister had read and recommended my book to her. I autographed her copy and helped sell about five more copies. I can't lie, I loved the attention. Candie just stood back and laughed at how excited I was. This was like a sample of my book signing tour.

Later that evening we headed down to Virginia Beach to the Marjac Suites on Atlantic Ave. We had a one-bedroom suite with an ocean front view waiting for us. After we checked into our room Candie had a craving for seafood from Red Lobster. I wanted to take her to a more exclusive and expensive restaurant.

Candie said, "Save your money. All that's not necessary. You don't have to impress me, I'm already impressed. If you feel the need to impress me just do what you did to me last night or what you did in the shower this morning."

"You got it. And I'll do it even better." We laughed. "You're too good to be true. I like Red Lobster and all, but I hate hearing *Happy Birthday* sang over and over to silly looking adults while I'm having dinner."

After dinner we took our shoes off and walked along the beach. It was a clear humid summer night and I was walking on the beach holding Candie, enjoying the feeling of being with her and the feeling of the ocean water and sand between my toes. The moonlight made a radiant sparkle in Candie's eyes. We slowed down to take in the atmosphere. As we walked along the beach we could see distant lights from ocean liners and cruise ships sailing along the coast line.

I said, "Maybe we'll take a cruise together one day."

"Now, how do you plan to pull that off?"

"You know damn well when Troy opens those new offices out west you're never going to see him. You'll have lots of free time."

That was probably mean for me to say regardless of how true it was.

Candie paused for minute. She said, "I hate to admit it, but you're right."

"He doesn't treat you like I do. Troy doesn't deserve you."

"That might be true, but he's still my husband."

"Just think, if we were together we could do stuff like this all the time."

Candie and I played in the water like two twelve-year-old kids. She splashed me and I did the same to her. There was lots of stuff going on around us. We could have gone to a club, seen a show or a movie, but we just wanted some time together on the beach. At one end of the beach people had gathered on the boardwalk to watch some Elvis impersonators perform. That wasn't our style, so we steered clear of that shit. Along Atlantic Ave. there were all types of street performers. We could hear a live jazz band playing from one of the beachfront restaurants. The music sounded so good that it made me hold Candie closer.

I said, "This weekend is slipping away so fast. Let's go back to our room and make love to something slow by Maxwell or D'Angelo."

"Ooh, that sounds good. I've got some new stuff I want to try on you."

"All I can say is that I adore you and I think I've finally found my sexual equal."

PEACE: 25

After my weekend with Candie I was more in love than ever. I was ready to surrender to her completely. She was the one. Candie had me spellbound. I wanted her so bad that I was ready to go right up to Troy and tell him exactly how I felt about his wife. In reality there was a small chance he would have just let me have her, but I wasn't really ready to press my luck like that.

For weeks regardless of whether Troy was in town or on a business trip Candie and I kept things hot. We made love almost everyday. Even if it was just a quickie or an all night thing we made the most of our time together.

Stacey was really pissed at me. It had been weeks since I'd heard anything from her. She had every reason to be mad at me. I guess she had enough of my shit and was ready to move on with her life. No matter how much I lied to her, she knew deep down inside that Candie and I had something going on.

I was beginning to hate my job with a passion. I questioned my reasons for still wanting to work. I received a nice advance from my book deal and I could make a decent living being a writer, but something kept me in nursing.

Being a trauma nurse is incredibly stressful, even when it's part-time. I was tired of seeing so many young black men die from gun shot wounds. My love for nursing was dying faster than all of those young black boys that we couldn't save. Baltimore's murder rate was at an all time high. The only war going on was on the streets. Things had gotten so bad that military physicians had come to our trauma center to get hands-on training for treating gunshot victims. I still loved the city, but it was turning into a battle zone. Too many people were dying over drugs.

My mother retired a year ago. My father still works in Shock Trauma. He's Chief of Trauma Surgery and a self-proclaimed God. He gets on my nerves so bad that sometimes I want to quit because of him.

I decided to go to work, but I swore if another young black man died of gunshot wound during my shift I was going to quit. A few people on my job saw me as a role model. Some people thought I was everything except a nurse. They thought I was a doctor or an orderly. That made me laugh because throughout all my years of nursing I've never even worked with an orderly. Some people treated me like they had never seen a young educated black man and that bothered me a lot. The women at work treated me real good. Even before my book was released they wanted to go out with me. After the release of my book it seemed like they wanted me even more. I think they started to see me as Marcus, one of the characters from my book. Everyone assumed that I had used that character to tell my life story. Maybe to a degree I did base my characters on myself and Monica, but the majority of the story was fiction. There were all kinds of rumors going around that I was having affairs with certain women on the job. I can't begin to imagine how those rumors got started.

That night I was busy as usual. Friday nights were always the busiest of all. Somehow I found time to take a phone call. At first I thought it was Candie calling to see how my night was going. Instead it was a guy.

He said, "Is this Eric?"

"Yeah."

"Eric Brown?"

"Yeah, who's this?"

"You don't know me and you don't wanna know me either. I know you know my wife, Sonia, and I'm tired of hearing shit about y'all."

"What? I don't know what you're talking about."

"Don't lie to me nigga. I know you know my wife 'cause you work with her. I'm only gonna ask you one time, no I'm gonna tell you one time. Stop fucking with my wife!"

"I'm not fucking with your wife."

"Why the hell does she talk about you so much then? All I ever hear is Eric...Eric...Eric. I know all kinds of shit about you. I'm tired of hearing about your damn book, how good lookin' you are and how all the women on the job like you. You're fucking with the wrong one now. I'll kill you. Stay away from my wife, Motherfucker!"

Before I could say anything else he slammed the phone in my ear. I was shaking like a little punk from his phone call. I never even saw his face. For all I knew he could have been a loudmouth midget. Regardless, I had an uneasy feeling. The thing that bothered me most was that I was totally innocent. Well, innocent with this maniac's wife. If the call had been from Troy I would have deserved every bit of that. I was friends with about a hundred women at work. Sonia was a nurse and just one of many women I occasionally had lunch with. She was fine as shit, but I never messed with her in an inappropriate way. I had no idea she went home and talked about me in so much detail to her husband. It was kind of flattering that she talked about me so much, but at the same time it was scary and weird as hell. I couldn't concentrate on work or anything else. I had to find Sonia and tell her that her crazy-ass husband had just called threatening my life.

When I finally found her, she gave me her usual pretty little smile and like a fool I smiled back.

Sonia said, "Hi Eric."

"Hey, guess what."

"What?"

"I just got a call from your crazy-ass husband and he threatened to kill me if I didn't stop fucking with you."

"Boy, stop playing."

"Look how I'm shaking. Do I look like I'm playing? He said he was tired of hearing about me. Did you tell him about me?"

"I did do that. He called you for real?"

"I play a lot, but this time I'm serious."

"Let me call him on his cell phone. I can't believe he'd call here embarrassing me like this."

"I can't believe it either. If I get killed, I wanna die for doing something I'm actually guilty of doing. He's accusing me of something I didn't even have the pleasure of doing."

Sonia acted liked she was mad at her husband. In reality she should have been mad at herself for being so stupid.

Sonia called her husband and said, "Did you just call here to speak to Eric?" He must have said he did. "Why'd you do that? He's my friend and we're gonna continue being friends."

I said, "Don't tell him that." This fool was trying to have me killed for sure.

Sonia turned and looked me. She said, "Shh. I got this." She continued with her husband. "Look, me and Eric are gonna be friends no matter what. How you gonna pick my friends for me? We'll talk about this when I get off, bye."

"Thanks a lot. Shit, you acted like you were going to straighten things out, but you just made things worse. Do me a favor, don't mention my name around your crazy-ass husband again."

"Don't call him that. He was just playing."

"Damn, you're crazy too. Please stay away from me. I don't need this shit in my life."

I had to hurry up and get back to my department. I made it back just in time to see an eighteen year old black boy die from a gunshot wound. When I got a closer look at him, he looked familiar to me. He had been to shock trauma twice within a year. This was his second and last trip to shock trauma. The last time he was there he had been shot three times. To make things worse I found a loaded 9mm handgun in his pocket.

We did everything we could to save him, but I wondered what we were saving him from. I felt like crying seeing his young lifeless battered body lying there. That was it. How could my night get any worse? I had two weeks off for my book tour and I had to make an important decision. I sat on the floor outside of my nurse manager's office and wrote my letter of resignation. I sealed it and slipped it under her door.

When I got off I felt beat down. I was so tired that I forgot all about Sonia's crazy husband. On my way to my car I noticed some people standing around it laughing until they saw me. I had no idea what was so damn funny. When I saw what they were laughing at I didn't find it funny at all. On both sides of my car in big red spray-painted letters my car...my Sexy-Lexy read *Stop fucking my wife*. All of my fear and frustration had turned to absolute anger. Some of the guys from the hospital security patrol came over and helped me cover up the foul message with newspaper and masking tape.

On my way home Sonia's husband's words echoed through my head. Stop fucking with my wife. Something wasn't right. Either I was a psychic or just paranoid. I didn't think Sonia's husband spray painted my car. This was something Troy would have done. He was the type of guy to do a weak act of violence like spray painting a car. I was fucking his wife and that's exactly what my car read. Sonia's husband was a thug. If he wanted revenge he would have come after me not my car. Troy probably figured out I was sleeping with Candie, but how would I confront him. Fuck it. I decided to just take my car to the dealer in the morning. Like old people say, you reap what you sow. It felt like my carefree fun with the ladies was starting to catch up with me.

Later that night I couldn't sleep. I felt like something bad was about to happen. It wasn't that I feared the unknown or dying, but I just wasn't ready to die. Death was on my mind so much that I laid in my bed and wrote a poem about my own death entitled *Peace*. Every poet writes about his or her own death. I guess it makes for good reading at the funeral.

I'm caught up going nowhere fast
I ask myself how long will this last
My fists are clenched
My jaw is tight as hell
Sweats pouring like the middle of July
I look down to make sure my feet are on solid ground
Darkness is all around
The sky is an angry black
Reminds me of a quiet storm

I look for lightning
But there's not a flash in the sky
I listen for thunder but there's no sound
I'm imagining the sun, stars, and the moon
But they're nowhere to be found
Maybe God hid the stars and the sun swallowed the moon
Everything's black like the back of my mind
Is this a dream

Or a simple escape from reality
Strange myths may come to be
But what does this have to do with me
I'm somewhere on the edge of time and space
Nothing really matters
I have no fear
I feel no pain
I'm gone from that place
That crazy mixed up world
A place I wished I could have flipped upside down and turned
inside out
I just wanted to find meaning to all the madness

Now I understand
I must be at peace
There's nothing to do but kick back and relax
How can I miss what I left behind
My journey's complete
God saved me from a world of sin
So don't cry for me...not one glistening tear
There's no coming back 'cause I'm at peace here
Rejoice in knowing that I'm at peace
Neither heaven nor hell
I'm at peace...I'm at peace

When I finished my poem I drifted off to sleep. I heard a booming
knock at my front door. I was too tired to answer. A child's voice
kept repeating, "It's the Second Coming," over and over again. I
laid in bed feeling confused. I opened my eyes to see what was
going on around me. The voice had stopped. My bedroom door
was open and my room was empty. All of a sudden I saw a bright
light coming from my stairway. When I looked again there was a
man levitating in my hallway making his way into my bedroom. At
first I was scared. When I realized who was in front of me
everything was calm and incredibly peaceful. The person in front
of me was Christ. I got out of bed to greet him. He extended his
hand to me. I touched his hand and a powerful sensation ran
through my body.
I asked, "Jesus, is it you?"
In a soft tone he said, "Yes it's me."
He looked like a young black man in his early twenties. He had
long black hair and a clean-shaven face with perfect skin. He wore
a glowing white robe. By any standard he was a handsome man.
I said, "You don't look like I expected, but I know it's you."
"You never know how I might look, but you'll always know it's
me."
I expected him to look like the picture on my great-grandmother's

300

wall. When I looked at him again he looked like a bearded white male in his thirties with long dirty blonde hair. I acted as if his change in appearance didn't bother me. It really didn't because I knew that he was still Jesus.

I said, "I know you're not happy with me. I wanna do right. Please make me a better person. Have mercy on me. "

"You're a good man and I know you can do better. I just want you to be careful."

"What should I do?"

"You already know what to do." He paused for a few seconds. "I'll see you again."

In a whisper I said, "Thank you, Jesus. I'm going to change. It's going to be hard, but I can do it."

There was flash of light and the next thing I knew I woke up in my bed under my covers. The image of Christ was so real that I actually had to convince myself that it was just a dream. But it wasn't just a dream. I asked myself how often did people dream about meeting Christ? I was visited by Jesus and he gave me a message. He was trying to save my life and I was going to take his advice.

LUVU4LIF: 26

Experiencing a night like I had and seeing my Savior face to face in such a realistic dream was enough to make me want to change my life. I wasn't ready to preach a sermon or join a church, but I definitely wanted to get my life on the right track. Although my relationship with Candie felt right, it was wrong. Somehow I needed to get things under control.

I called Candie first thing the next morning. I told her all about the night I had and asked her to come over because I had a lot on my mind. Candie was at my front door within minutes. We sat down in the kitchen and talked over breakfast. We ate grits, buttermilk biscuits and turkey bacon with Tropicana orange juice.

"I'm at a crossroads in my life and I have some serious decisions to make."

Candie looked concerned. "You quit your job already, what else do you have to think about?"

"This is a very desperate situation. This is probably my final plea." I paused "My life would be so much better if you were really mine, I mean all mine."

"I wish there was something I could do. We just need to be thankful for the time we have together."

"It's not enough for me anymore. You always have someone to cuddle up with at night. Meanwhile, I'm sitting around wishing and waiting for a day I know may never come."

"I'm trying. At least give me some credit. You don't realize how complicated it is trying to end a marriage. It's really not as easy as you think, trust me."

"What's keeping you with him?"

"I don't know. He's my husband and everyday isn't so bad. Troy's good to me and I love him."

"You're not in love with him and there's a big difference. I wanna give you true love, commitment and happiness. We can experience so much together. I just wanna love you. I need to see you, feel you and be with all the time."

"I want the same, but I can't give you all that right now."

"You know I'm scheduled to leave in the morning. My book tour starts in two days and I don't plan to come back this way anytime soon. This isn't goodbye, but I probably won't see you for awhile. I can't give up on you that easy. I just need to make some major changes in my life. There's so much more waiting for us somewhere out there and I wanna share it with you. I wanna give you the world. I want you to be my wife."

Candie began to cry. She felt like I was putting too much pressure on her at one time.

"I can't be your wife. Oh my God, if I could you know I would. I can't leave."

"But I need you. I need you right now. We can run away together and start all over again."

"Things are different with me and Troy now. Last night he told me that he's ready to start a family."

I bit my bottom lip and shook my head. "You're only going to make a bad situation worse. If you think Troy has you trapped now, once you have his baby you'll never leave."

"Eric, I don't want you to leave, but you have to get on with your life. You have a great talent and you deserve a woman who's going to make you happy.

303

"You're that woman. You make me so happy." I gave Candie a kiss. "You're everything I could ask for in a woman and more. Divorce Troy and let's do this right."

"You just had a bad night. I think you're being too impulsive. After your tour you'll be back to normal." Candie grabbed my hand like she was giving me a pep talk. "You're going to be a huge success. Just don't forget me and Troy."

"You and Troy? You're not understanding me. I can't ever forget you. I want you to leave with me tomorrow because I can't continue to live like this. To be honest, I never want to see Troy again. I can't face him again. I'm sure he knows about us by now."

"I told you he doesn't have a clue about us. If he suspected anything he would have confronted me right away."

"Was he home last night?"

"It depends on what time your talking about."

"I'm talking about whatever time my car was vandalized. I don't care what you say Troy did that shit. He's up to something. Why's he interested in a family all of a sudden?"

"People change."

"He's afraid of losing you to me. Making a baby is just a desperate last minute effort to keep you at home."

"It's obvious that you're a writer because you have an overactive imagination."

"I hope it's just my imagination. I know Troy's your husband, but you need to stop defending him. In time you'll understand exactly where I'm coming from."

After breakfast Candie followed me in her car to the Lexus dealership to drop off my car, so it could be repainted. It was going to take at least a week before the dealer could even start on my car. I told Candie I wasn't coming back home anytime soon, but I had too much unfinished business to take care of before I could make a permanent move. I wasn't sure if I wanted to sell or rent out my condo. No matter where I lived I still planned to continue writing for Jennifer and Damon's magazine. I could just e-mail my work to them from anywhere.

On our way back home from the Lexus dealership Candie was trying to make plans for what she thought was our last night together. Two of Candie's co-workers had told her about a harbor boat cruise featuring some local musicians and open mic poetry.

Candie said, "I told my friends I could get you to recite some poetry and possibly sign some books tonight."

"Do you know how long it's been since I've recited poetry?"

"I've never heard you recite in front of a crowd. I'd like that. You can do that for me can't you?"

"I have to finish packing for tomorrow."

"So, you're going to leave me just like that?"

"Yep, in a few days check the latest issue of *Imani* and you'll find a special poem I wrote for you."

"That's not good enough. I want to hear you recite it on stage tonight."

"I'm just giving you a hard time. I'd love to do something like that for you."

For the first time I felt kind of awkward being with Candie in public. I felt like everyone could see right through our little charade. As usual Troy was working late. When Candie told him that she was going out with me he seemed to have an attitude and that was highly unusual. Just another signal to me that he suspected Candie and I were up to something.

The Bay Lady had three deck levels of entertainment going on at the same time. Candie and I stayed on the main level, where we could enjoy a more mellow and relaxed atmosphere. I liked the entire set up, but the best entertainment was on the main level. A jazz quartet played music and between songs they stopped to invite poets up to recite. Candie introduced me to two of her female co-workers.

Candie's co-workers looked at me like I was something good to eat. Actually I was, but I was Candie's exclusive treat. Her co-worker, Joy refused to let go of my hand while she talked to me. Candie playfully karate chopped through our hands. Everybody laughed it out like it was a cute little trick, but I knew Candie was serious. She didn't want Joy to play with me like that. I suspected that Candie's co-workers sensed that she and I were more than friends. Joy looked at Candie with both admiration and envy. Candie's other co-worker, Nadine, had this I'm-gonna-tell-your-husband look on her face. Candie's co-workers made me feel uncomfortable, but I was put at ease when they pulled out copies of my book and asked me to sign them. After about ten minutes of small talk Candie and I got some drinks and made our way to our table. Candie surprised me with her boldness when she reached across the table to hold my hand.

I asked, "What are you doing?"

"Having fun making them jealous."

Candie pointed over to her co-workers.

"Okay, but I hope you know what you're doing. If you're okay with this I am too."

"Stop worrying. Let's give them something to talk about."

I glanced around the room for a minute and fixed my eyes on the buffet. I happened to look over my left shoulder. I couldn't believe my eyes. If I didn't consider myself a sane person I would've sworn I was hallucinating. Troy was standing at the door looking like a lost kid at the mall. He didn't notice me and Candie right away. I slowly pulled my hand away from Candie's before Troy noticed us holding hands.

"Candie, act natural. Don't look now, but Troy's at the door looking around."

Even though I said not to, Candie looked right at Troy.

Candie said, "Oh shit, here he comes."

I acted just like I never noticed him. Troy walked over to the table.

Troy said, "Hey I've been looking all over this damn boat for y'all." He looked at me with a smile. "You can't hide from me." For a second I didn't know if he was playing around or being sarcastic.

I said, "Yep, you're right, you got me. So, what you been up to?"

306

Troy shrugged his shoulders. "Same shit different day. You?"

"What can I say? Different day different shit, I'm moving on."

Candie asked, "What are you doing here?"

Troy said, "I missed you and I figured the least I could do was to surprise you. I made it onboard just in time."

I didn't have anything to say. I couldn't wait for the band to finish their long ass song, so I could get away from that damn table. I was ready to recite a poem, do a song and dance or whatever it took to get away from Troy. I hated looking at him. I stabbed him in his back and it felt like he was coming back for revenge. As soon as the band finished their song I jumped out of my seat.

"It's my time."

Troy looked at me like he wanted to say something, but I kept moving.

Candie said, "Good luck."

Some other guy tried to go up ahead of me, but I signaled him to sit down. I took the mic just like I used to back in the day, except back then I got a fancy intro from someone.

I said, "Good evening. I hope everyone's having a good time." I felt the need to talk before reciting my poem to combat my nervousness. "Some of you might remember me from way back as the poet Black."

The room was so quiet that all I heard was the music from the other level playing. I never got so many blank stares before. Those people had no idea who I was and looked like they could care less.

"Since nobody remembers that far back maybe you know me by my real name, Eric Brown Jr., the author of *Love Ain't Going Nowhere.*"

The brothas in the crowd still looked at me like they didn't know who I was and didn't give a shit. But a lot of the women warmed up when I mentioned my book. The crowd gave me a round of applause.

"Thank you. I'd like to dedicate my poem to a very special woman in my life. My poem is entitled *Luvu4lif.*"

Hold me down baby
And represent me well
You're my lady and I love you
I love the ground you walk on
Loving you step by step
I'll even kiss your feet if you need
Love's in the air and I'm deep breathing
Free falling into your love
The sun rises and sets in your ebony eyes

Your passion has ignited an eternal flame within me
My heat...my fire...my greatest desire
In your arm is where I find myself
No place I'd rather be
I need to have you...to hold you...to Luvu4lif
We share an unconditional love
More precious than silver or gold
Our love will stand the test of time
When silver turns to black and gold into green
I flip to the next scene

The greatest lovers of all time
Erotic dreams of you and me
Allude to multiple mutual orgasms
How do I love you
You know all the ways
With my eyes shut
I feel your beauty
With my bare hands
I describe it in a way only I can
Running my fingers through your hair
Caressing your scalp
Across your eyes
Down your nose

Around your lips
Cupping your chin
Giving you gentle kisses to your lips face and neck
I slide my tongue down your spine
I know every inch of your body as if it were mine
But it's yours to give
A gift I think God for everyday

Now ask yourself
Have you ever seen love
It stares you in the face when you're asleep
Wakes you up with a kiss
This is my love
Bathe in it
Let it caress you
Touch your heart

Warm your soul
It's deep inside
Let me take control
Love begins and ends with you
I love the life that I've been given
Love is life and I'm for living
Take all this love I'm giving
'Cause I'm gonna Luvu4lif

As I recited my poem I tried not to look at Candie or Troy. I
walked back to my table to the sounds of applause and whistles. It
felt good to get that love from a new generation of poetry lovers. I
noticed that Candie had tears in her eyes. She looked like she was
battling to hold back her tears.

When I took my seat Troy said "That was a nice poem."
"Thanks a lot. I'm glad you liked it."
Still teary-eyed Candie said, "That was so beautiful."

I didn't have to say a word because she knew it was for her. Troy looked at Candie then at me.

Troy asked, "Was that for Stacey?"

I paused for a second and smiled, "No, it wasn't."

I didn't offer any other information. Deep down I'm sure he knew who the poem was dedicated to.

As the night went on the three of us sat at the table acting like everything was okay. It was so hard trying to enjoy such an awkward evening, especially since I was trapped in the middle of the harbor with Troy. If we had been on land I would have called it a night and left Troy and Candie alone. Troy spoiled all of my plans. My explosive evening with Candie turned into a real dud.

When the boat finally docked Troy looked at me and said, "That's real messed up what happened to your car."

I clench my fist and imagined punching him right in his damn mouth.

Instead I said, "Just a minor setback. Whoever did it won't have to worry about me messing with his wife after tonight. I'm going to make a new start somewhere else. I'm about to visit some interesting cities and maybe I'll make one my home."

"Sounds like a plan. We'll miss you though. So, are you saying you're really messing around with somebody's wife?"

"I'm not saying all that."

"You know you're wrong."

"Right or wrong, sometimes we find ourselves in some of the strangest positions. I guess you can say I got caught up. It's a love thing and you know how that goes."

"Since you don't have your car tonight I'd like you to ride with me because we really need to talk."

Candie looked like she was about to choke. The last thing she wanted was for me and Troy to be alone talking. She feared what I might say.

"Troy, how are you just going to let me ride home alone? If you want Eric can drive my car home."

I said, "That's sounds better."

When we all got home Troy walked over to me.

Troy said, "I still need to talk to you."

"I'm too busy to talk to you tonight. I'll be free in a couple of weeks and we can talk then."

"I guess I can wait until then."

"Good. Now this isn't goodbye. This is more like, see you later."

I extended my hand to Troy for a handshake. He pulled me in close and gave me a big bear hug. He held me tight and patted me on the back. When I patted his back all I felt was the knife that I planted deep in him.

Troy said, "Good luck with everything. I love you, Eric."

I couldn't believe what was happening. I was so ashamed that I wanted to confess my sins and beg Troy for his forgiveness.

I said, "Troy, I love you too. You've always been a friend to me and I'll never forget it."

I looked over at Candie and she was crying a river. I don't know how she felt at that moment, but she looked like she was really hurting.

I took her by the hand and said, "You know this isn't goodbye." I whispered in her ear, "Luvu4lif. Check your e-mail, I'll be in touch."

Candie didn't say anything. She just nodded her head and gave me a hug.

Watching Troy and Candie walk down the hallway together hurt me to my heart. I wanted her to be in my arms so bad. As I walked to my condo a melancholy jazz tune by Miles blared in my head. The tempo started off slow and gloomy, then the rhythm picked up like a speeding train down a dark tunnel. After about a minute the tune sounded like a sweet song of salvation.

THE LIGHT: 27

At the end of every tunnel there's a light. It sounds crazy, but I knew that Candie was my light. No matter what city I visited, I e-mailed her everyday from my hotel room to let her know how the book tour was going. With each e-mail she got a constant reminder of how much I missed and loved her. I told her how much I needed and wanted to share the whole experience of my tour with her. My book signings were well attended. People seemed eager to meet me and they had plenty of questions to ask about my book. They made me feel real special. I read my favorite chapters to hundreds of adoring fans. Each reading and signing was populated mostly with black women. A lot of the women were from book clubs or women's groups. As I spoke the women followed my every word. With each word I captured their hearts and minds taking them deep into my world. Some of the country's finest women were right in front of me ready and willing to spend some private time with me, but each night I went back to my hotel room alone. I stayed in some of the finest hotels throughout the country and ate at the best restaurants.

I sat in my suite e-mailing Candie and telling her about my day. In one e-mail I received from Candie, she reassured me that Troy still didn't know about our relationship. Part of me wished he knew about us, so he would kick Candie out of the house and she wouldn't have any other choice but to join me on tour. Up to this point my tour had already taken me to L.A., Cleveland, Detroit, Chicago and New York. Now, I was in Atlanta. I offered Candie plane tickets to meet me wherever I was, but she declined all of my offers. With each city and each offer she kept turning me down. I closed each of my e-mails telling Candie my location and asking her to surprise me by dropping by my hotel room for a quickie or to spend the rest of her life with me. She knew I was joking about the quickie part, I wanted her for a lifetime.

Just as I closed my e-mail there a knock at my door. I hoped it was Candie coming to surprise me. I kind of feared it was Troy coming to kill me. With my luck, it was going to be some poor lost soul asking for directions.

When I walked up to the door I didn't look through the peephole because I wanted to be surprised regardless of who was on the other side of the door. I opened the door and I couldn't believe my eyes. Stacey was standing in front of me with a beautiful smile on her face and her eyes focused right on me. She wasn't exactly who I wanted to see, but I was happy to see her anyway. I pulled her inside my room and we embraced.

I said, "Oh my God, I can't believe you're here."

"I had some time off and I needed to see you. Are you alone?"

"Lonely is a better word. Candie's not here, if that's what you really wanna know."

"That's good, but I wasn't going to mention her name."

"You're always a sight for sore eyes. How the hell did you find me?"

"I'm a powerful attorney with all types of resources."

"Ooh, you're scaring me."

We laughed.

"I don't want to scare you. I missed you and I still want you. And I hope you want me as much as I want you."

"I'm not sure. You're putting me on the spot. I know you're in love with me, but I can't say that I feel the same way about you."

"I was afraid you'd say something like that, but I understand. After all this time we've been together I shouldn't expect to just sweep you off your feet, right?"

"Listen, I still care for you and I always will. I just need some time to clear my head."

"She's got you messed up pretty bad."

"Who?"

"You know who. I can't believe I came all this way to make a fool of myself."

"You're not making a fool of yourself. It's just that I love her so much."

"Finally, a clue into your secret life."

"I can't lie anymore. Candie's my everything. Thank you for loving me, but she's got my heart."

"So, what about me? I wanted to marry you and now you're in love with a married woman. She belongs to someone else, face the facts. Even if she suddenly comes into your life like you want, who's to say she would be what you really need. She cheated on her husband and she'll damn sure cheat on you. I can give you everything you need, just give me a chance. I can be all yours. Not just a part-time lover."

"Full-time or part-time, it doesn't matter 'cause I've got all her love. She loves me and I know it. You can't possibly understand what she means to me. Candie made me believe in myself again and she believes in us. I can hardly breathe without her. You don't want to see it, but I'm so in love with her that I don't know what to do with myself. You'll always be my first love, but I'm not that little boy anymore."

"I know, but it's so hard to let go."

"Give me time, maybe you won't have to let go."

"What are you waiting for?"

"The light at the end of the tunnel."

Stacey asked, "Candie? Goodbye, Eric."

It hurt, but I had to let Stacey go. It was best that I told her the truth and not run off with her living a lie. The sad thing was that I gave up a good woman to keep holding on to a dream.

The next evening I was at a bookstore in downtown Atlanta. The store was packed to capacity and this was the best turn out of my entire tour. After reading an excerpt from one of my favorite chapters the crowd lined up to get their books signed.

There were so many people in the store that it made me dizzy. I didn't notice anyone behind me, but I heard a voice in my ear say, "Things that hold us down make us lose touch with reality, but that was yesterday. Today is reality and now I'm free."

I couldn't move because this was too good to be true. I think the sun, earth, moon and stars were all in perfect alignment because Candie was right by my side where she belonged. I took her in my arms and we kissed to celebrate her newfound freedom.